"Wh

"It always [...] From this a new direction is birthed; a fork in the road allows two choices that will change all. Loss weeps until the earth is saturated with blood."

"I don't understand what you're trying to say," Reegan said.

Patch let go of her hand and snatched a handful of Reegan's hair. "You listen, girl! Remember my words!"

Reegan's cheeks were tracked with tears, and she glanced at the door hoping her mother would come, wondering if she should call out for help. Then she yelped when her hair was once again yanked. "Patch," she pleaded.

"This is not what I would have wanted, but damn it all to hell, you will listen to what I say!"

Reegan nodded and took her cell phone from her pocket. She found the recorder in her apps and said, "Start from the beginning."

Patch eyed the phone and nibbled her lip. "Once, I can only repeat it once."

"But why?"

"Because that's the promise," Patch whispered. "Envious greed spills out with intent upon an afflicted mind consumed with fear. Fire and condemnation will bring forth the card of death. There is no undoing what is done, but you can trace the path that led to this. Four wanted to be three, and three would never be two—different but ever the same. You must see what was unseen, learn what was unknown, right what was wronged, or suffer the same."

Between Death and Destiny

by

W. L. Brooks

Between Death and Destiny

Cover Art by *RJ Morris*

The Wild Rose Press, Inc.
PO Box 708
Adams Basin, NY 14410-0708
Visit us at www.thewildrosepress.com

Publishing History
First Black Rose Edition, 2016
Print ISBN 978-1-5092-1077-0
Digital ISBN 978-1-5092-1078-7

Published in the United States of America

Dedication

In memory of my dad,
who believed in this crazy idea
that I could write a novel.

REEGAN

Chapter One

Twelve years ago

Reegan McGrath knew the old biddies were whispering about her; she could feel their eyes boring holes into her back as she rode her bike down Main Street, but she didn't turn around. Her stomach rolled; it always did after encountering Willows Bluff's most avid gossips, but she shook it off. Three more days, she reminded herself, and she would be out of this town.

She took solace in the fact that her ticket out of here was zipped up in the pocket of the knapsack she had slung across her back. Reegan smiled to herself. Her knapsack held her future. It concealed not only her bus ticket, but also her camera, which she would use to travel the country and make a name for herself as a photographer. In just three days…

"Ears burning?" Reegan's best friend, Sydney Walters, asked when Reegan came to a halt beside her.

Sydney looked like a J. Crew model with her long blonde hair in a ponytail and her blue eyes shining. Reegan, on the other hand, was just glad she'd taken the time to wash the grit out of her gray eyes and brush her brown hair.

"Always are," Reegan said.

Sydney glared in the direction of the gossips. "One day we'll find out what all the fuss is about," she

1

muttered. "Are you ready for our last adventure?"

"As I'll ever be," she said. "Let me state for the record that the Willows gives me the creeps, and remind you the house is condemned."

"Duly noted," Sydney said, then inclined her head and suggested they get going.

Reegan pedaled behind Sydney as they made their way through town. I'll miss this most, Reegan thought, looking at her best friend. While she traveled the country taking pictures, Sydney would be attending college in the city. It was one of the hardships of growing up, learning to let go.

Her smile returned when they passed Ezra Kelly's gallery; she would miss him second most, Reegan decided. Ezra had invited her to get a sneak peek at tonight's showing, but then Sydney had called and Reegan had to decline his offer. In all honesty, she would prefer seeing the new art collection to walking through a condemned house, but she hadn't been able to say no to her best friend.

"It's magnificent!" Sydney said once they'd reached their destination.

"You would say that," Reegan groused as she wiped the sweat from her forehead. Why, after a five-mile trek uphill, didn't Sydney drip sweat like her? Rather, she glowed. The wisps of her hair curled attractively while Reegan's hair frizzed out like a bad '80s power ballad.

"A little enthusiasm please! Here, take a picture," Sydney said, then maneuvered herself around her bike and posed.

Reegan pulled her camera out of her knapsack, took off the lens cap, lifted the viewfinder, and snapped the photograph. Thinking about each step as if for the first time helped her relax. Reegan lifted the camera again and studied the house through the lens.

They called it the Willows because it was built on the exact spot where a willow tree, the town's namesake, once stood. Constructed toward the end of the nineteenth century by Bertrum Whit, who hadn't wanted his daughters exposed to all the town gossip and sin, the house sat on the tip of the bluffs isolated from everything except the water. Of course, it was a fifty-foot drop before you reached the cold sea, but the purpose still served.

A miniature Tara, the thought sprang into Reegan's mind, from *Gone with the Wind* would be the perfect pictorial comparison if she had to make one, but it was more Stephen King than Margaret Mitchell. What was left of the paint was curling off onto the porch, whose columns were shackled by wild vines. The cobbled walkway was overrun by weeds, and most of the windows were either cracked or broken. Though, as Reegan peered through her view finder, they seemed to be watching her…appraising her.

"Holy—" Reegan screeched when Sydney touched her shoulder.

"Sorry," Sydney said. "You really are scared, aren't you?"

"You don't feel like it's watching us?" She put the camera's strap over her head and continued walking the rest of the way with her bike.

Sydney looked at the house then back to Reegan. "No!" She rubbed her hands together. "Ready?"

"As I'm ever gonna be," Reegan muttered.

Reegan followed her friend up to the porch and

parked her bike. Sydney went to the door, took a deep breath, grasped the knob, and pushed. A drawn-out creak penetrated the silence around them, making Reegan cringe as she crossed the threshold.

"Oh my goodness," Sydney whispered and pulled a red flashlight out of her bag.

The beam of light skittered across spider webs and broken floorboards. Reegan wasn't sure if there could be fog inside the house, but there was definitely a haze. And a mustiness, she thought, rubbing her nose.

The wallpaper that still clung to the wall wasn't like what her father had put up in her grandma's bathroom. No—she reached out to touch it—this was actual fabric. Blood red fabric.

"Okay, we came, we saw, and now we can go," Reegan said turning.

"Are you kidding? It's everything I've dreamed! I won't ask you to stay if you don't want to"—Sydney shrugged—"but this *is* our last adventure together."

Reegan squeezed her eyes shut. "Okay, Syd."

"Here," Sydney said reaching into her bag and pulling out another flashlight. "I brought you one too."

Reegan's brow pinched at the flashlight in her hands. "But, Syd, this is your flashlight."

"I know, I brought Alan's for good luck."

Reegan sucked in a breath.

"Don't worry so much, Reegan. I took the flashlight from his room years ago, and Mother never noticed. I wanted a piece of my big brother with me."

"Aw, Syd, I'm sorry," she said. Sydney shrugged and continued what she was doing.

Reegan wasn't sorry; in fact, she was concerned. Though Alan had died before either of them was born, everyone knew the story of the Walters boy, who at sixteen had lost control of his car and gone off Weatherman's Bridge. The town was never the same after his accident nor, Reegan suspected, was Sydney's mother.

Mrs. Walters kept Alan's bedroom exactly as he'd left it the day he died, and Sydney wasn't allowed to go in there. April Desmond, who was a friend and one of the three maids that cleaned Sydney's house, said it was the only room Mrs. Walters forbade anyone from entering. The idea that Sydney had gone behind her mother's back—

"Hey, you have to see this," Sydney said shining her flashlight on a portrait. "It must be the Whits. They're incredible!"

Reegan stepped closer. The framed photo was of a man and three young ladies.

The man, who had to have been Mr. Whit, stared out of the photo with haunted eyes. His stark white hair stood out against his clean-shaven face. Two of his dark-haired daughters stood directly in front of him, while the third lighter-haired young woman stood in front. She thought their faces were familiar, but before she could say anything, Sydney pulled a pair of tattered drapes apart. A piercing screech rent the air, and a noise came from above her head.

"Did you hear that?" Reegan held the flashlight to her chest and stared at the ceiling.

"Probably rats," Sydney said, wrinkling her nose.

"Are you serious?" She stared at her friend. Opening the drapes had brightened the room a bit, which would have made her feel better if she didn't hear what she knew were footsteps! "Syd?"

Sydney turned, pointing to a staircase that Reegan hadn't even noticed. "Do you want to go investigate?"

"By myself?"

"How are you going to travel the country alone when you can't keep it together now?"

"I'm quite capable of handling things I can freaking *see;* it's what I can't see that freaks me out!"

Sydney huffed. "Fine! *Hello, is anyone here?*"

Reegan glared at Sydney, then jumped when there was movement from upstairs.

"What are you two doing here?"

Reegan wasn't sure if she was relieved or irritated that the voice belonged to Tori Elis. And wait for it, she thought, yep, there was Bernie. It was like a reunion ten years too early.

Bernie, Reegan thought, scrunching up her face, was what everyone called Bernadette Howard when they weren't calling her all the other names they'd made up. She was a little older than they were, and she'd graduated with them despite the time she had spent away from school. Her hair was a tangled mass of raven black and her eyes were...well, Reegan didn't know because she couldn't bring herself to actually look at Bernie.

Reegan was bit ashamed of herself. She'd known Bernie all her life because their grandmas were best friends, but *they'd* never been friends. In fact, she didn't think they'd said more than a few hateful words to each other. Bernie's best friend was Tori Elis, and Tori was Sydney's archnemesis.

Tori was always, as Sydney would say, one unsavory step ahead of everyone. She was the picture of an angel with creamy skin, long golden brown hair, and big brown doe eyes. There was just something not quite right about her, Reegan thought, for the hundredth time.

Tori's family was the wealthiest in town, and Tori was the town darling. Mr. Elis was a partner in a law firm in the city, and Mrs. Elis had been a renowned psychiatrist before they were married. Reegan didn't understand why they let Tori be friends with Bernie; she was one of the poorest kids in school and people were scared of her because…she didn't want to think about that.

"What are *you* doing here?" Sydney asked.

"Browsing," Tori replied, floating down the stairs. "Bernadette and I finally let our curiosity get the better of us." Bernie nodded.

"This is your first time here too?" Reegan asked before she could stop herself.

"Rumor has it they're going to tear it down at the end of summer, so we figured now or never. I'd hoped for more than what's here, but there isn't anything noteworthy."

"So says you," Sydney said and crossed her arms over her chest.

"The house has been deserted for nearly a hundred years, Syd," Reegan reminded her. Almost fifteen years after the Whits had moved in, Mr. Whit died in an accident, and his family went to live with relatives. After decades of abandonment, ownership of the property defaulted to the city, or that's what Reegan had heard.

"The portrait is still here and the drapes," Sydney said.

"No one is telling you not to snoop around, Sydney. Don't upset yourself so. Really, it's not that big a deal," Tori said with a condescending smile.

"Whatever!" Sydney sneered and headed up the rickety staircase.

"I guess that means I'm going upstairs too," Reegan said more to herself than anyone else, so it annoyed her when she heard Bernie's raspy, "Seems so." If Bernie didn't scare her, she would have said something; instead, she took the stairs two at a time.

Chapter Two

They had gone through the house twice, and Tori hadn't lied when she said there wasn't much left. Upstairs were broken pieces of furniture, ripped wallpaper, and trash from partying teenagers. That disturbed Reegan. They lived in a small town. Her graduating class was less than a hundred kids, so she had to know them.

Maybe they were as sheltered as Sydney claimed. Sydney's parents had been teenagers when they had Alan, and in order to keep their daughter from the same fate, they didn't allow her to date, and if Sydney didn't date than neither did Reegan. It wouldn't surprise her if Tori was sheltered too because she had always been sickly. She was fragile as glass. Reegan smiled thinking of a glass angel with horns holding up the halo.

"Why are you smiling? This was such a letdown," Sydney said pouting.

"What happened to 'it's everything I dreamed'?" Reegan took a deep breath, glad to be out in the fresh air again. She stood on tiptoe to see over the bluff and into the rushing water. Pulling off the lens cap, she started taking pictures.

"What happened to 'it gives me the creeps'? Watch your step, Reegan!" Sydney shouted. "You don't want to fall in. You're a horrible swimmer."

"Thanks, I was in the zone," she said stepping

back.

"Off in la-la land you mean." Sydney smirked. "I guess you're glad we came."

Reegan shrugged. "The bluffs are beautiful." She capped the lens and turned to walk back toward their bikes. "Why are you so disappointed?"

"I think Tori ruined it. I know what you're going to say, so don't start. Ow!" Sydney shrieked as she pitched forward and fell facedown on the ground.

"Are you okay?" Reegan moved to the side when Sydney rolled over, then offered her hand to help her to her feet.

"I'm fine. I tripped over something," she said, bending to pick her bag up from where it had fallen.

"Are you sure you're okay?" Reegan inspected Sydney for damage. There wasn't a hair out of place, not even a grass stain on her pristine khaki shorts or white t-shirt. If it had been her, Reegan knew, she'd be spitting out mud or grass or whatever.

"Yeah, I'm just glad Tori wasn't here to see my performance." She winced and glanced around.

"I'm pretty sure they left after we went upstairs."

"Oh, that's good. I can't believe they were here at all!" Sydney said with a stomp of her foot.

Coming around the front of the house, Reegan said, "It's hard to believe that this was their first time here too."

"You think she was lying?"

"I don't know," she said as she moved the kickstand with her foot and they headed down the path. "I mean, what are the chances?"

"You may be onto something, Reegan," Sydney said. "Who's that?" She motioned with her head to the group of guys down the hill.

Reegan lifted her camera and zoomed in. "Looks like Justin, Adam, and Phillip," she said.

"I don't know why Phillip continues to hang out with those two losers, but I'll miss him just the same."

Reegan snorted. "Sydney, you haven't said more than two words to the guy since he hit puberty." Phillip Hastings was the town's golden boy—star quarterback, class president—and his father was the sheriff.

"That's not true!" Sydney said, then giggled. "Okay, it's a little true. But honestly, can you blame me? He went from scrawny to drop-dead gorgeous in one summer."

"Yeah, but he's still the same Phillip," Reegan reminded her. He had sandy blond hair, hazel eyes, and a smile that Sydney said made her knees weak. Reegan didn't worship the guy like Sydney did, but he'd always been nice to her. "I wish you wouldn't call Justin and Adam losers."

"I know you like them, but seriously, Reegan, they have no ambition."

"How can you say that?" Reegan stopped in her tracks. "Justin got a full scholarship to State!" Justin's thick glasses took up most of his freckled face, his dark red hair looked like someone put a bowl on his head and cut, and his hand-me-down clothes were too small for his lengthy frame. But he was smart, funny, and he was doing something with his life.

"You're right, the full ride to State is impressive," she conceded.

"And you don't like Adam because his sister cleans your house!" Reegan's hand flew up to cover her mouth.

"What?" Sydney hissed.

"I'm sorry, Syd, it just came out. I know you've been nothing but nice to April." That was true enough. April had told Reegan the Walterses were more than generous.

"I can't believe you just said that!" Sydney shouted, her face turning red. "It's because you're poor and I'm rich, isn't it?

"Hey!" Her family wasn't poor; maybe they couldn't afford what Sydney's family could, but they did okay. Her mother was a nurse at the elementary school, and her father was a carpenter; money wasn't coming in by the bucketful, but she hadn't wanted for anything.

"You started it! Saying I would treat Adam badly because his sister cleans my house. I don't judge people based on who their family is; I base my opinion on how they treat me," Sydney said, poking herself in the chest for emphasis.

"What's Adam ever done to you?"

"He's a punk, Reegan, and he's scary," Sydney said, then lowered her voice. "Everyone says he's in one of those satanic cults!"

Adam Desmond had his black hair gelled into spikes, he wore shirts held together by safety pins, and his blue eyes were hidden behind black contacts. Reegan knew in Willows Bluff that behavior was a big no-no, but that was beside the point.

"He's just different, Syd. And you know there's no way in hell Justin or Phillip would hang out with a devil worshipper!"

"I don't like the way he looks at me."

"How does he look at you?" Reegan wanted to

know. She *liked* Adam. He was an artist, and he saw things differently from other people. Sometimes she thought he saw things like she did, except he didn't need a camera to actually *see* them.

"Like I'm nothing."

"What?" Reegan asked because Sydney had whispered it as if saying it out loud made it true.

"He looks at me like I'm nothing, okay!" She started walking again, stopping when Reegan put her hand on her arm.

"No one could ever think that about you, Sydney. You're a beautiful, intelligent, and wonderful person!"

"You don't honestly think I look down on April because she cleans my house?"

"No, absolutely not! I didn't mean it. I'm sorry," she said, giving Sydney's arm a quick squeeze before they continued walking.

Sydney sniffed. "Apology accepted. Now, how do I look?"

"Beautiful!" Myself on the other hand…ugh. "Hey," she said, coming up to where the boys were standing. That's when Tori and Bernie came into view; they'd been hidden by a couple of trees.

"See, she's one unsavory step ahead of us!" Sydney said so only Reegan could hear.

"I see that," Reegan whispered back. There Tori was, seeming the angel with her long hair pulled up in a ponytail almost identical to Sydney's. Strange, Reegan thought, she'd never noticed how similar in appearance they were.

"Hey," Phillip said while Justin nodded and Adam acted bored. "Tori said she saw you guys at the Willows."

"Yeah," Sydney said, moving some make-believe out of place hair behind her ear.

"It's pretty creepy if you ask me," Reegan said.

"I can't believe you've never been up there before," Phillip said as he leaned against a tree.

While the boys talked about the Willows, Reegan made the mistake of glancing at Tori, then Bernie; that's when she noticed Bernie staring at Justin. Did Bernie have a crush—that was disturbing. She tried to catch Sydney's eye, but her friend was too busy ogling Phillip, who was staring at Tori.

Sydney had been in love with Phillip since his last growth spurt, and Phillip had been in love with Tori since he could breathe. Everyone knew this; everyone it would seem except Tori and Sydney. Reegan rubbed her forehead, glad when the conversation changed to what everyone was going to do now that they had graduated.

Justin was leaving in a few days for State. Phillip was going to college on a football scholarship. Sydney talked about getting her MBA, so she could run her family's company one day. Adam said he was going to see where the wind took him, but he smiled when Reegan talked about becoming a photographer. She demonstrated by having them pose so she could snap a few shots.

"What about you, Bernie?" Phillip asked while Reegan switched out one roll of film for another.

"I haven't really thought about it," Bernie said shrugging.

"How could you not think about your future?" Phillip asked.

"Kind of hard to think of her future when she's

14

been in juvie for murder."

Silence. Absolute, utter silence for what seemed like an eternity. Reegan couldn't hear herself breathing over the whooshing in her head. Her camera was like lead in her hands as she fumbled to close the film door and put it back in her knapsack. She couldn't believe Adam had said that, and from the rash of red spreading up his neck, he couldn't either.

"How dare you!" Tori hissed.

Bernie put her hand on Tori's shoulder. "It's all right, Tori. Everyone was thinking it."

Reegan knew that was true; those had been the most prominent thoughts in her head. Honestly, seeing Bernie was synonymous with that particular train of thinking. The entire town whispered about it whenever they saw her.

Four years ago, Bernie's father was murdered, and everyone knew she was the one who killed him. People said she blamed him for her mother's abandonment and that gave her motive. The police never found concrete evidence to charge Bernie with murder, so Adam's statement wasn't accurate. When the deputies questioned her, Bernie attacked them; she served two years for assaulting an officer and resisting arrest.

"No, Bernie, it's not!" Tori shouted. "How would you feel if you came home to find your father lying on the ground? You try to shake him awake, but when you pull your hands away, you're covered in his blood. Then the very people who are supposed to help *you*— protect *you*—are the ones who accuse you of murder. I wonder if you would be such a hard ass then, Adam Desmond!" Tori spat out, disgust plain on her face.

"You'd say anything to protect Bernie," Sydney

accused.

Tori stepped forward, and Bernie grabbed her hand. "She's not worth it."

"Excuse me? Oh, that's rich coming from you, Bernie."

"Syd," Reegan pleaded.

"You think you're so superior, Sydney Walters! Well, guess what, you're—"

Phillip covered Tori's mouth with his hand. "Enough! You girls need to leave." He nodded to Sydney and Reegan.

"You're not serious!"

"Come on, Sydney, he's right; the best thing to do is go home," Reegan said gently.

"Fine!" Sydney pointed to Tori as they passed. "You may fool everyone else, but I see who you are."

****

Reegan was at home watching the sun compete with the upcoming storm. This time of year, it didn't get dark until late, but with the storm approaching, the sky wasn't sticking to the rules. Her parents were attending the showing at the gallery; she wanted to see the work, but the events of this afternoon wouldn't leave her.

Sydney had been furious after Phillip had told them to go. Reegan had been upset too, not because of Phillip, but because of what Tori had said. She truly believed Bernie was innocent.

Bernie had always protected Tori, and it wasn't a secret that right after Bernie was sent away Tori became ill. In fact, she'd been homeschooled the entire first year of Bernie's sentence. That spoke volumes about their friendship, didn't it? Reegan thought. Those two stood up for each other no matter what, and that forced Reegan to focus on her own relationship with Sydney.

First, she'd opened her big mouth about April; then there was the scene with Tori and Phillip. Sydney had been horrified. What upset Reegan was that Sydney blamed her for what had happened. She wasn't sure what she could have done differently. She would have been shocked if she could have come up with a coherent word much less an entire sentence.

The cordless phone rang next to her, but she let the answering machine get it. She was brooding, as was her right, after her best friend had called her a traitor.

The ringing began again. "Fine!" she grumbled, then grabbed the phone. "Hello?"

"Reegan, I can't find Alan's flashlight," Sydney whispered on a tear-filled breath. "I searched my bag four times, and it's not there. It has to have fallen out when I fell."

"Oh no, Sydney!"

"I have to find it—"

"We can go first thing in the morning."

"I can't, Mother has us on a tight schedule. It's the only thing of his I have"—there was a small sob—"and I had to steal it."

"I can go in the morning, no problem," Reegan said.

"It isn't dark yet. I think I can make it out there in time to find it."

"Sydney, have you looked out your window? There's a storm's coming."

"Even more reason for me to find it before the rain washes it away."

After what had happened today, Reegan didn't argue. "Okay, I'll meet you in ten minutes."

They didn't speak as they raced up the hill; Reegan pedaled with all her strength against a wind that continued to pick up speed. Sweat slid down her back, and she wished she hadn't put on sweatpants, but she had been chilled.

Reegan's heart jumped to her throat. If she thought the Willows was scary in full sunlight, what lay before her was a picture straight from her worst nightmare. She didn't think the camera in her knapsack could capture the way the house looked now. The curling paint seemed to make it glow. After taking a moment to push down her fear, she parked her bike and headed toward the back of the house.

She caught her breath while Sydney scanned the area. Her legs held firm, though they wobbled a bit when she followed her friend down the walkway leading to the bluffs. She was glad the town was going to tear this place down.

"I think we were about here." Sydney stopped and started searching.

Pushing her knapsack behind her, Reegan got on her hands and knees to get better access; Alan's flashlight was red, and she figured it would stand out against the grass. She felt around in the high grass just in case it had fallen in a divot. She glanced over to see Sydney was doing the same. They had to find it!

The wind continued to gain speed, and it was getting darker by the minute, but she refused to quit. Reegan wasn't sure how long she searched, but nothing was distinguishable. She sat up, noticing that night had fallen around them. "Sydney?"

"Did you find it?" Her question was highlighted by a bolt of lightning, which allowed Reegan to see where she was for two seconds. How did she get over there? Reegan wondered.

"No. Crap," Reegan said. The sky opened up, and rain poured down in torrents around them. She couldn't see but a foot in front of her.

"Reegan?"

"Over here!" Her clothes were already soaked through.

"*Reegan?*"

"*Over here!*" she shouted, realizing that Sydney couldn't hear her over the pounding rain and howling wind.

"*Reeeegaaan!*"

Reegan paused for a split second, then started running. Sydney had screamed, not the pep-rally variety but a shrill that made her blood turn cold.

"*Sydneeey!*" Reegan tried to hear over the rain and run at the same time. Something brushed past her, and she turned toward it, only to have the air knocked out of her lungs as she fell feetfirst into the black abyss below.

The shock of hitting the water stunned her. Reegan was sinking like a pebble dropped in a fish tank. The thought jolted her, and panic set in; she'd never been a strong swimmer.

She tried to swim, but her legs were heavy. The sweatpants are weighing me down! Reegan thought. Once she got the pants off, she pushed upward with all her strength, only to be restrained by her knapsack, which was caught on something.

She tugged on the strap, but it wouldn't budge. Her lungs burned, and knowing she didn't have a choice,

Reegan relinquished the knapsack. She kicked her legs with her waning strength, and though she was making progress, it wasn't enough.

Suddenly, arms were around her, pulling her up. She gasped when they broke the surface; the rain was pounding down around them. She tried to breathe, but they were bobbing up and down and she started to choke.

She couldn't stand when they reached the shore, and her rescuer dragged her by her underarms as she coughed. Reegan didn't care that the earth scraped her thighs and calves; she was on solid ground. Her head lolled to the side when she was laid on the sand. She glanced fleetingly toward the beam of light coming from a flashlight lying beside her; she let her lids close, wanting so badly to sleep.

Water droplets fell on her forehead; she didn't know if they were from the rain or from someone hovering above her. She opened her eyes for a second, and though her vision was blurred, she caught sight of a scar on her rescuer's wrist when the person moved her hair. She couldn't tell if it was a man or woman, but closing her eyes, she decided she didn't care.

"Thank you," Reegan whispered.

"It would do you well to never come back..." the voice began as Reegan passed out...

Chapter Three

Present day

Bolting upright in her bed, Reegan ran her hands over her face and down her arms, automatically taking inventory of herself and her surroundings. She inhaled deeply trying to slow her racing heart. Feeling around her nightstand, she grabbed the alarm clock to see it was five a.m.

Groaning, she got up and found her discarded clothes from the day before on the floor; she put them on over her tank top. Reegan shuffled into the kitchen and hit the button on her coffeemaker before she hit the lights. She had an automatic timer, so the coffee was usually perky before she was; it didn't seem right that she was up before the machine.

She sat down on one of the metal bar stools at her kitchen island, stared out the window at the beginning of another bleak winter's day, and brooded. She hadn't had that dream in a long time. Dream! Reegan snorted and ran her fingers through her long hair; nightmare was more accurate. A memory she couldn't shake after nearly twelve years! She rubbed her eyes trying to scrub the dream from her subconscious.

Reegan still remembered waking up in the hospital with her parents and Sydney by her side. Sydney had run on foot in the middle of the storm to get help that night. It had taken them over an hour to find Reegan where she was passed out. They never found the person who had saved her. They even put a reward in the paper, but no one ever came forward. She'd started to believe, like everyone else, that she had hallucinated the entire rescue, but then the nightmares came. She could still taste the water in her mouth.

She shook her head to ward off the entire scene, then searched for her cell phone under the papers strewn about on the counter. When she located it, she pressed the first number on her favorites list.

"If you're up right now, that can only mean one thing."

"Did I wake you?" Reegan asked while she poured a cup of coffee.

"No, I've been up going over numbers." There was a pause. "Was it the dream again?"

"Yeah"—Reegan sniffed—"same as always."

"I wish I could have it for you."

"Trust me, you don't," Reegan sighed. "Everything is so vivid; it's like every moment of that day plays out from a slide projector in my head. Right down to the highlights in your freaking hair."

"Oh, my hair"—there was a laugh—"if only I currently resembled that young girl."

"You're still gorgeous, Syd!" Reegan smiled, knowing she had made Sydney do the same.

"I wish Martin had agreed."

"Don't start with that jackass!"

"Sorry. I know it's been a year since the divorce was final, but I can't seem to let it go."

"Who the hell expects you to? Screw them and the horse they rode in on, if you ask me."

Sydney chuckled. "Should we make plans for lunch? Meet at that little deli you like so much? Or do you have plans with…what's his name this time?"

Reegan winced. "His name's Paul, but that didn't work out."

"You've got to stop dating these losers," Sydney said, and Reegan could practically hear her eyes roll.

"I'm a sucker for the tortured artist."

"What did this one do again? Painter, sculptor, poet, or was that the last one?"

"Paul is a performance artist," Reegan reminded her.

There was a long pause. "Oh, that's right…the mime."

"Hey, being a mime takes skill!" Reegan argued while Sydney laughed. She couldn't help her own snicker; Paul had been a horrible mime. "I did get some amazing shots."

"If you say so. What about lunch? Say around one?"

"Sounds like a plan!"

"See you then."

Reegan sighed when the picture on her phone faded. They had come a long way from Willows Bluff. She had followed the advice of her rescuer, whether real or imagined, and never gone back. Her bus ticket had been in her knapsack, and when she relinquished the bag, she'd also given up that future for a different one.

After she was released from the hospital, she'd packed a couple of suitcases and had her father drive her to Sydney's house. Reegan could remember it like it was yesterday…

"You're sure this is what you want to do?" her father asked as he pulled his van into Sydney's driveway.

"Dad, a near-death experience can change your point of view," she told him and studied his weathered face. Already his brown hair and sideburns were showing gray, and he had a deep furrow between his brows. "I know this is what I have to do."

Taking a deep breath, she opened her door, and Sydney came out of the house.

"Did you come to see me off?" Sydney asked, then noticed Reegan was unloading her few bags. "Really, Reegan?"

"I'm coming with you," Reegan said, then laughed when Sydney hugged her fiercely.

Once Sydney released her, Reegan said, "Give me a minute to say good-bye."

Sydney nodded and waved at Reegan's father before going back inside.

Reegan went to the driver's side window and waited while her dad rolled it down. "Tell Mom and Grandma I love them, and I'll call when I can. I love you too, Dad." She kissed his cheek through the window. "Think of it like this, I'm not leaving you...I'm finding me."

"If you ever get lost, Reegan," he said, "it's always good to go back and start at the beginning." With that he touched her cheek, then put the van in reverse.

Reegan stared out into space while she remembered. She knew the years had been kind to her. She and Sydney had gone a little mad when they first came to the city. Two small town girls who'd never done anything all of a sudden were free to do everything. That freedom had been heady those first few months, hell, the first few years.

Sydney's parents had a loft apartment that they let them have rent free. Reegan had gotten a job at a coffee house to earn money for her part of the bills; Sydney had told her she didn't have to, but Reegan didn't want to take advantage of the Walterses' generosity.

Unlike Mrs. Walters, who made it perfectly clear she couldn't tolerate either of them, Mr. Walters, or Daddo as he preferred, had been a constant presence in their lives when they lived in the loft. He took them shopping and to shows, treated them to executive dinners, and invited them to extravagant parties. Reegan adored him, and though she didn't see him often, she wouldn't forget all he'd done for her.

Sydney already had a corner office in the mergers and acquisitions department of her family's company. Where business was concerned, Sydney was ruthless, and she had earned every step up that ladder. Reegan couldn't be prouder of her.

Refilling her coffee, Reegan took a seat in front of her computer to peruse her recent photos. She preferred photographing nature to taking portraits, though that had paid the bills many a time. The exception being the men she dated; for some reason, she was obsessed with seeing them through the eye of her lens. But as a general rule, it was places, not faces; things, not beings.

She wasn't a famous artistic photographer with a coffee table book, but her work had been published in a dozen magazines, several greeting card covers, plus a calendar or two, and she had a few prints in a couple of the smaller galleries. She wasn't rich, but she made a decent living doing what she loved most in the world.

There was something about capturing the beauty that people neglected to see while living their everyday lives. She hoped her photos were a reminder that even the most unenchanting place could bewitch in the right light. Anything was capable of being more than what at first was perceived just by changing your point of view.

Reegan was still going through the photos hours later when her phone rang. She smiled when her father's picture appeared on the screen. "Hey, Dad."

"Your grandmother isn't doing so well," he blurted out. "I think you should come home."

Reegan swallowed the lump that had lodged in her throat. "Is she going to die?"

"The prognosis isn't good, and I'm telling you to come so if the worst happens, you won't have any regrets," he said after at least a minute of dead air.

Tears welled up in her eyes. "Of course I'll come."

He sighed. "That's good then."

Reegan hit the end button after getting the details from her father. She couldn't believe this was happening; she had always assumed her grandmother was as resilient as she was nuts. And no one did nuts like Patch McGrath.

Patch was one of those people in small towns that everyone avoided in case the crazy was catching. Reegan was honest enough to admit the whispers about Patch had never been far off base. For instance, the name Patch came from the patchwork bathrobe her grandmother wore into town. And if that wasn't noteworthy enough, she often wore curlers in her hair, cleaning gloves on her hands, and pink bunny slippers on her feet.

Now Reegan's father said Patch had had a heart

attack, and given her recent poor health—which Reegan hadn't been aware of—and her age, the doctors were hesitant to do the surgery. Even if they had been optimistic, Patch refused to have the procedure and demanded to be taken home to her house, with her things and her memories.

Reegan's mother had taken a leave of absence from school to stay with Patch during the day, and they had hired a night nurse to stay with her while she slept. Her parents wanted Patch to stay with them because it would have been easier, but the old lady declined.

"I may be at death's door, but I ain't knocked yet!" Patch declared, according to Reegan's father.

Reegan glanced at the clock on the microwave. It was twelve thirty; she picked up her cell. "I have to go to Willows Bluff," she began once Sydney answered. "Patch is dying…"

Chapter Four

Why did I expect it to be any different? Reegan wondered as she drove down Main Street. She'd called the rental agency, packed a couple of bags, asked her landlord to get her mail, and made the trip back to Willows Bluff. Here she was, back at the beginning.

Sydney had been supportive on the phone, but Reegan could tell her friend was wary. Though Reegan's trauma kept her away, Sydney hadn't returned to Willows Bluff either. Why would she? Reegan thought; this place was never home to Sydney but rather a mausoleum for Alan. Sydney said, many times, going back to Willows Bluff would do more harm than good, and though Reegan agreed wholeheartedly, circumstances had changed.

She glanced again at the clock; it was almost seven, and the weather had taken a nasty turn. But even the snow couldn't supersede Reegan's initial thought; this place was hardly any different than when she'd left. It wasn't until she came to the end of the strip that she noticed a few new places, one being a coffee house whose neon light read that it was open. Deciding it might be nice to have a hot cup of something, she pulled her rented SUV into a parking space.

She made a mad dash for the door and was greeted by the welcoming warmth and the even more delectable aroma of coffee. Despite the fact that she had worked as a barista for five years, she was still addicted to the stuff.

A dark green tapestry blocked a doorway on the sidewall. There was a black sash across it with a sign that read: Bookstore Closed. The flooring was dark, the music was inconspicuous, and the Wi-Fi was free. Reegan couldn't help but smirk at the latter—how times had changed.

"Hello," she called out after a few minutes. "Is anyone here?" She jumped when the stainless steel door behind the counter swung open with enough force to bang against the wall.

"We're closing early," she was told gruffly by the man who came to stand in front of her. "I haven't turned off the sign."

"I understand, trust me, but would it be possible to get a large cup of coffee? Just a blond Joe." The man's lips lifted slightly beneath his trimmed beard; her request was coffee speak—at least where she'd worked—for a cup of coffee with enough cream to make it, well, blond. He seemed to think about it for a moment, then nodded.

Reegan studied him while he prepared her coffee. He was tall, with short dark hair, and she thought his eyes were dark. He wore a tan and burgundy plaid flannel, and his shirtsleeves were rolled up on his forearms, which were dusted with hair. He was thick with what appeared to be muscle and his jeans accentuated the fact that his backside wasn't too bad either.

Then a peculiar thing happened; pictures of the ocean flew through her mind, followed by images of old ships, and then a head bowed over clasped hands. It was as if she were going over photos from her camera's memory card. That's new, Reegan thought, massaging her temples; she needed coffee.

"How much do I owe you?" she asked after the man put the lid on the cup and plunked it down on the counter in front of her.

"Register's closed." He shrugged one big shoulder and came from around the counter. "It's on the house. Just drive home safely," he said, walking her to the front door.

"Wow! Thank you," she said taking her cup and grinning; only in small town USA. She told him to have a good night, then walked briskly back to the rental.

From her seat in the SUV, she could make out his figure as he locked the door and turned off the sign. She buckled her seatbelt and took the first sip, closing her eyes to savor the bitterness lingering on her tongue. He made a flavorful brew, she thought, somewhat delighted. It was only when she went to take her second sip that she noticed there was writing on the cup; she turned on the overhead light and saw *Reegan* scrawled in black marker. Her eyes shot quickly to the coffee shop just as the place went dark.

****

She pulled into her parents' driveway and parked. Shutting off the engine, she sat for a moment; Reegan had forgotten that people in small towns tended to recognize their own even if it had been over a decade. She still couldn't place the man from the coffee shop. Shaking her head, she retrieved her phone from her purse and texted Sydney to let her know she had arrived in one piece.

She opened the door and stepped out into the cold.

The ranch-style house had all the usual mundane amenities, but this was where she grew up; this was home. She waved to her dad when he came down the steps to greet her. Reegan had always thought him handsome, but she was biased. His hair, which was completely salt and pepper now, was still thick and curled around the collar of his jacket. He always had the smokiest eyes, which were now surrounded by deep laugh lines, and a pair of wire-rimmed glasses was perched on his nose.

"Glad you made it," he said as he kissed the top of her head and gave her a hug. "Let me help you with your bags."

She retrieved her purse and camera bag from the front seat, grabbed her coffee, and followed him inside. Her father headed down the hall to put her bags into her old room, and she turned to the right where the den was with a fire roaring in its hearth. Her parents had updated the house and it was nicely done, but it put a pang in her chest for the way things used to be. She walked through the open doorway of the den and into the kitchen, where she found her mother washing dishes.

"Hi, Mom!" Reegan grinned when her mother squeaked and turned around with a dripping pan in her hands. "I like what you've done with the place," she said, setting her things on the counter.

Her mother's brown hair swished as she shook her head and set the pan down. "You're a sight for sore eyes," she said, giving Reegan a hug.

She squeezed her mom one last time before letting go. "It's good to see you too."

Her mother studied Reegan a minute before nodding and going back to the sink. "Did you eat anything?"

"Yeah, earlier." She grabbed her coffee and hopped up on the small breakfast bar near the sink.

"There are two perfectly good stools right there or four sturdy chairs at the table, Reegan," her mother said, humor lighting her brown eyes.

"This is fine." Reegan winked at her father when he came into the room.

"I saved a plate for you. It's in the microwave."

"Thanks, Mom."

"Stop by the coffee shop?" her father asked indicating the cup in her hand.

"Yeah, they were closing because of the snow."

"Oh, Justin was still there?" her mother asked.

"Justin?"

"Justin Blake."

Reegan stared a moment. "I can't believe that was Justin!" Or that he'd recognized her, she thought, her thumb unconsciously running across her name on the paper cup.

"He and his mother, Delores, own the bookstore and the coffee shop," her father said.

"Didn't he get a full ride to State?"

"He finished his degree, then came back to help his mom out. He joined the fire and rescue department, but there was an accident while Justin was on his EMT rotation. He and his partner were caught in an explosion and were pinned down under the burning rubble. His partner died, but the firefighters were able to save Justin," her father said.

"He was in the hospital for months. Delores visited him whenever she could. That poor woman, like she hadn't lost enough," her mother told her.

"What do you mean?" Reegan remembered Mrs. Blake as a sweet, dowdy lady who always smelled like cookies because she worked in the bakery of the local grocery store.

"Well, if you remember, Justin had an older brother named Glen. He…"

"Glen what, Mom?" Reegan asked as she pinched the bridge of her nose. The Blakes had lived on the other side of town in the poorest part of Willows Bluff. The gossip was that Mr. Blake was an abusive drunk who deserted his family after Justin was born.

"Glen was in and out of rehab for years trying to cope with his addictions, but he never could shake them. One night, he drove his motorcycle straight into oncoming traffic," her father explained.

"He died?"

"Instantly."

Reegan's heart ached for Mrs. Blake.

"Justin and his mother have been through hell over the last several years, and I'm happy things have turned around for them," her father said.

"Me too," Reegan said, smiling when her dad nudged her shoulder with his.

Her parents talked about the weather while she ate her reheated dinner. She had always enjoyed watching them together. David and Beth McGrath had been married for over thirty years; Reegan could tell the love was still there.

After she washed her dish and put it away, they talked for a while about Patch's condition and what Reegan should expect before calling it a night. Reegan used the bathroom and got ready for bed. She sighed; it was strange being in her old room when it no longer held any of her things. Shaking off the feeling, she checked her phone to see that Sydney had received her text.

She pulled back the covers and crawled in between the sheets. She inhaled deeply trying to clear her mind so she could sleep. Finally, she closed her eyes and drifted off. Dreams ran across her mind like flipping through an old photo album. The pages turned slowly at first, then the pace increased until the pictures became animated, and soon she was inside them.

"Make haste! We must make haste," the cloaked woman pleaded with her as they ran through the woods.

"Why?" Reegan asked confused. She held the hand of the woman, who wore a deep red cloak.

"Before we are seen; Lord knows what they will do if they find you!"

"Who?" Reegan wanted to know. She felt like she'd been on a bender. *"I ache all over."*

"I am conscious of that, my darling, but we must hurry." The woman paused and turned to face Reegan. *"You are aware of what will become of you if you are found out."*

Reegan was confused. The woman looked familiar, but she couldn't place her. "I don't know what you mean…" she began, but the dream turned, and *suddenly she was on the bluffs in the middle of the storm. The rain poured down around her like the sky was sobbing. Sydney screamed her name, then something brushed past her. She turned toward it, and the air went from her lungs.*

"Reegan? Reegan?"

The water, rain, painful inhalations, skin scraping, and the words "never come back" swirled around her head in a painful array of pictures and paint. She felt shaken; no, she was shaken; no, she was being shaken.

She screeched when she opened her eyes and saw a man standing over her only to realize it was her father. She assured him she was all right as she sat up. He let go of her upper arms and sat on the side of the bed.

"Are you sure?" he asked, while she rubbed her arms, then her face, and finally ran her fingers through her hair.

"I'm fine." That was a doozy, she thought.

"No, Reegan, you were screaming!"

"It was just a bad dream." She patted his hand.

"What was it about?" he asked, then squinted when Reegan's mother entered the room and turned on the overhead light.

"Hey, Mom," she said after her eyes adjusted.

"Answer your father," her mother said from the doorway, tightening her robe.

Reegan looked at her father, who sat beside her in his pajamas with his hair plastered to one side of his head. She tried not to laugh at him while she explained, "It was just a bad dream; it happens."

"Sure, it happens," her father conceded. "But most people don't scream like they're being disemboweled."

"David, really, what an image!"

Reegan snorted. "Yeah, Dad, what have you been watching?"

He glared at her.

"Seriously, it's all blurry."

Her father sighed. "If you don't want to tell us, then that's okay."

"But we're here if you want to talk about it," her mother said.

35

****

Reegan steered the SUV along the snow-covered road as she drove to Patch's house. She felt a bit guilty for not confiding in her parents, but she honestly wasn't sure there was anything to tell. Her mother had left to go to Patch's so she'd had breakfast with her father, who'd eyed her over his morning paper before he left for work. She showered, then texted Sydney to tell her she was going to Patch's today; Sydney wished her luck.

She came around the bend being extra careful in case there was ice and arrived at Patch's home. She couldn't help the emotions that overtook her. In the back of her mind, she saw the house how it once had been, a powder blue Victorian with pink shutters and white lattice across the porch instead of rails. Presently, it was a boring sage green with beige shutters, and *now* there were rails. She knew her father had been making repairs over the years, but she'd loved the house the way it had been, as eccentric as Patch herself.

Parking behind her mother's Jeep, Reegan got out and headed to the porch. She was flooded with sweet memories of this place and the love she felt for Patch. She should have come to see her before this, instead of being scared of something she couldn't change. Ignoring the feelings of self-loathing, Reegan opened the front door and stepped inside.

"What the hell?" she said when she saw the stacks of banking boxes that filled the parlor. Patch had kept that room perfect, and no one was supposed to go in there. It was the one room in the house that had been normal, the one room that made Patch like any other grandma. Currently the place resembled an episode of

Hoarders.

Shaking off the impression of doom, Reegan set her things down in the kitchen and went in search of her mother. The lamp from Patch's bedroom lit a path across the wood floor, and Reegan headed in that direction. She opened the door the rest of the way, and her eyes filled with tears at the sight before her. There in a hospital bed lay her grandma. Reegan studied the pale wrinkled flesh. She had obviously just had a bath because her white hair was damp and combed; her pink nightgown was unwrinkled, and the lace at the cuffs was perfect. At that moment, with all her heart, she wished Patch was in her notorious patchwork robe looking like herself instead of this sickly creature.

A sob slipped past her lips.

"Reegan?" Her mother came out of the bathroom that adjoined Patch's bedroom. "Oh, honey."

Reegan fell into her mother's embrace trying to control the swell of emotions she feared would soon overwhelm her. She hadn't been prepared for this; sure, her parents had warned her, but this—this wasn't Patch. This frail woman was not her grandma who had always been so full of life and nuttier than a fruitcake.

"That my girl?" came the gritty whisper from the slip of a woman on the bed.

Reegan let go of her mother to sit on the bed next to Patch and take her frail hand. "It's me, Patch; it's Reegan," she said as her mother left the room.

One blue eye peeked out from behind short lashes. "Knew you'd come," Patch rasped.

"Of course I came!" Reegan said, bending down when Patch gave a slight tug.

"I had to see you again. Had to tell you myself and

damn the consequences," she whispered peering directly into Reegan's eyes.

"What do you mean, consequences?"

"It always starts with death unplanned! From this a new direction is birthed; a fork in the road allows two choices that will change all. Loss weeps until the earth is saturated with blood."

"I don't understand what you're trying to say," Reegan said.

Patch let go of her hand and snatched a handful of Reegan's hair. "You listen, girl! Remember my words!"

Reegan's cheeks were tracked with tears, and she glanced at the door hoping her mother would come, wondering if she should call out for help. Then she yelped when her hair was once again yanked. "Patch," she pleaded.

"This is not what I would have wanted, but damn it all to hell, you will listen to what I say!"

Reegan nodded and took her cell phone from her pocket. She found the recorder in her apps and said, "Start from the beginning."

Patch eyed the phone and nibbled her lip. "Once, I can only repeat it once."

"But why?"

"Because that's the promise," Patch whispered. "Envious greed spills out with intent upon an afflicted mind consumed with fear. Fire and condemnation will bring forth the card of death. There is no undoing what is done, but you can trace the path that led to this. Four wanted to be three, and three would never be two— different but ever the same. You must see what was unseen, learn what was unknown, right what was wronged, or suffer the same."

"Patch, I don't understand."

Patch peered into Reegan's eyes. "I know you don't and forgive me for that. These are the cards we were dealt before either of us existed. I had hoped—" Her voice broke, but she continued. "*We* had hoped these things wouldn't come to pass, but what goes around always comes back 'round."

"I…" What could she say?

"Promise you'll try!"

"I…I promise."

"Always loved my girl."

"I love you, Patch," Reegan whispered and turned off the recorder.

"Yep, old Patch did well," she wheezed out with a crooked smile. "Broke their hearts when you didn't come back, but I knew what you were about."

Reegan grabbed a tissue from the box on the nightstand and blotted her face. "What do you mean?" The old woman coughed a couple of times, and Reegan helped her sip some water.

Patch huffed. "You ain't been listening to a damn thing I've said. You're supposed to listen!"

"Calm down, Patch," Reegan pleaded. "I *have* been listening, I swear! I just don't understand."

"Annie Mae." Patch started shaking her head. "Annie Mae…"

"Patch, it's me, Reegan!"

"Damn fool woman can't understand plain English. *Annie Mae*!" Patch shouted, then started coughing and wheezing; then she was gasping.

Reegan called for her mother who came rushing in the room. She sat helplessly while Patch tried to catch her breath after her coughing fit. Her mother put the oxygen mask over Patch's nose and mouth amid her grandma's continued cries for her friend. Her mother dialed 9-1-1, speaking hurriedly into the phone as Patch stilled.

Everything seemed to be on mute; Reegan was deaf except to the percussion of her heart beating inside her. She held Patch's gaze as a single tear rolled down her grandma's powdery cheek. In the space between taking a breath and the track of that tear, the old blue eyes that had captivated Reegan all of her life went dark.

Reegan did the only thing that made sense to her…she screamed.

Chapter Five

A storm rolled through Willows Bluff the night Patch McGrath left this world. As Reegan sat in a chair on the deck of her parents' home in the freezing cold, she thought it was only fitting that Patch would go out with the storm; her soul would undoubtedly ride the wind all the way to heaven.

She drank deeply from the crystal glass in her gloved hands, wanting nothing but the fire the amber liquid provided her insides. She'd never been one for hard liquor, but this was what her father had handed her when they walked in the door. She stared at the night sky gratified that even the man in the moon wouldn't show his face to her.

Patch was dead. Her crazy-ass, nuttier than a fruitcake, sweet, loving, and beautiful grandma was gone. This place, Reegan thought for the billionth time, is still trying to kill me. She snorted and took another long sip from her glass.

Her jacket began vibrating. She'd missed four calls from Sydney. She put the glass between her thighs and texted her friend that she didn't feel like talking. She'd left a message on Sydney's voicemail telling her what had happened, and she would call her when she could. At this point, she still couldn't.

Besides, her voice was hoarse from screaming. She knew she would feel foolish for her behavior later, but it was not yet that time. She'd wailed and screamed and sobbed until she could only whimper. Her mother had silently cried while she'd held her.

The blast of winter air would be forever imprinted on her memory as it permeated the room and chilled the tracks of her tears when her father walked in. She could still smell the sawdust that filled her nostrils as he passed her to stand over Patch. He'd knelt at the bed, clasped his mother's hand, brought it to his lips, and held it there while he was racked with his own mourning.

The ambulance came next, and the paramedics documented the time of Patch's death. Two sheriff's deputies Reegan didn't recognize went about their business quickly and quietly following procedure. Mr. Willis from the funeral home arrived after the paramedics and took charge moving Patch with tenderness and respect. They would then take her to the funeral home to prepare her for burial. Patch had made arrangements years ago to be buried next to her husband, so all Reegan's parents had had to do was make the phone calls. The old lady had been more prepared for death than she had for life.

Tears threatened an encore as Reegan wondered if Patch had been waiting for her. Had her grandma waited to die in order to see Reegan one last time? She wasn't sure if she wanted the answer.

Reegan had asked her parents if they had told Annie Mae Howard about Patch. Being that it was the last name to fall from Patch's lips, her one and only friend. Her father said Annie Mae wasn't answering her phone, and he would try again tomorrow.

The doorbell chimed when she came inside. Her

mother patted her father's arm before she got up to answer the door. Reegan stood in the kitchen doorway and spied through the den and into the front hall as the sheriff stepped inside. Only this was not Buck Hastings.

From the side view she couldn't see much because of his thick jacket, but he was well proportioned. Reegan stepped into the den to hear more of the conversation.

"Beth, I'm so sorry for your loss," the sheriff said.

"You're glad to be rid of her!" her father said from his position on the couch.

"David," her mother hissed.

"What? Mom hounded the hell out of the boy, and we all know it. Well, good riddance, right, Sheriff!"

Reegan was pretty sure she and her father had been drinking from the same fountain, which was rare, so this could get interesting.

"Now, David…" The sheriff began, coming fully into the room and making Reegan choke on her drink. "I understand you're upset, but you know damn well that's not true."

"Holy shit!"

"Mouth," her father slurred.

Regan covered her lips with her gloved fingers, and her mother apologized for her father's behavior. The peculiar struck again as pictures sailed across her mind of children on a swing, their bare toes in the sand, a football clutched in a pair of teenage hands while the red jersey behind it was out of focus; and last but exceedingly more disturbing was a black and white photo containing an empty bed whose sheets were a tangled mass; a single shot of color from a dark red rose peeked out from underneath the bed's frame. The last photo was so intriguing because she had never once envisioned having sex with this man. But her blood was ablaze from the feelings the images in her mind provoked.

A smile spread across the sheriff's handsome face, but he sobered quickly. "Heard you were in town," he began. "I'm sorry for your loss, Reegan."

"Thank you, Phillip," she was able to get past her lips. Sydney was going to blow a gasket, Reegan thought, then felt guilty for her lustful inclinations because Sydney had been so in love with Phillip Hastings.

He nodded and turned back toward her mother.

"Thanks for stopping by, Phillip."

"Beth"—he inclined his head—"call if you need anything. Oh, Junebug wanted me to tell you she's sorry you're hurting."

"That's one sweet girl you've got, Phillip," Reegan's mom told him as she opened the front door.

"Most days," he told her, then tipped his hat when he put it back on. "Take care now."

"Is he married?" Reegan couldn't stop herself from asking once the door was closed.

"No."

"But he has a daughter?" she asked getting a quick glare from her father.

"Yes, well, sort of." Her mother rubbed her eyes, and she reclaimed her seat next to Reegan's father. "June is Trish's daughter; that's Phillip's sister. She was probably a year or two ahead of you, and she decided after her husband left her that she couldn't handle raising a toddler on her own."

"That's sad," Reegan said after removing her

jacket and gloves and taking a seat on the other side of her father.

"It's unfortunate, but it happens. June's lucky she had a loving family who wanted her. Buck and Cindy took her in first, but then Buck had his heart attack. Phillip took over not only as sheriff, but also as June's guardian."

"Why are you so interested?" her father asked.

"Curious, I guess." She shrugged, then turned so she was facing her father. "What did you mean that Patch hounded Phillip?"

He shifted in his seat. "When Phillip took over the sheriff's position, Mom wanted to see if he was worth his salt. She called him out to the house every day until she decided she didn't want to pay for a phone. After that, she had Annie Mae call him on her cell phone. Or she would send messages; luckily, she only tried the smoke signal once," he said with a smile, then turned his head away.

"Oh, wow"—Reegan shook her head on a tear-filled giggle—"that's Patch. Smoke signals!"

"It got the tongues wagging for sure," her mother said.

"I bet it did!" Reegan said.

"I asked Mom why she bothered the boy, and it was always the same answer."

"What, Dad?"

"As I said before, 'gotta see if he's worth his salt.' Though it's probably because she had Buck wrapped around her finger," he said sipping from his glass.

Reegan's brow pinched, and she asked him to explain. She couldn't see Buck Hastings ever being wrapped around anyone's finger much less someone as bat-shit crazy as Patch. Buck was, or had been to Reegan at least, the epitome of a sheriff, all law and order with a bullshit tolerance of zero. To think of him being friends with her grandma was absurd.

"Buck's several years older than me, but one day when I was being picked on—no words from the peanut gallery"—he gestured to Reegan's mother, who snorted—"Buck got the bullies off my back and walked me home. Mom was so impressed with him that she invited him in for milk and cookies." He cleared his throat. "Buck came practically every day after that until he went to college, and even then he would come see Mom when he was home on break. When he became sheriff, he would stop by every so often to have coffee with her. After Dad died and Mom changed, he still checked on her. They had a close relationship, so I guess she was just trying to see if Phillip was like his father." With that, he got off the couch and left the room.

"Do you think their relationship hurt Dad's feelings?"

"When he was younger, I'm sure it did, but as he got older, I think he realized there was nothing to be jealous of. After your grandfather died, I think your father was more grateful for the relationship than anything else. Buck made sure Patch was safe and that no one harmed her."

"I never realized that Buck and Dad were friends."

The corners of her mother's mouth lifted. "Neither do they."

Chapter Six

Reegan parked her rental in front of the coffee shop. It had been three days since Patch had passed. Three days she'd spent with her parents going to the funeral home, the lawyer's office, and the bank. Patch had everything in order, which, again, struck Reegan as out of character.

She had spent a couple of hours on the phone with Sydney crying, laughing, and not saying anything at all; knowing her friend was there for her had helped. The viewing was tonight, and the funeral would be in the morning. Reegan was dreading both.

Sighing, she got out of her vehicle and walked into the coffee shop. Two of the booths were full. She winked at the young girl who sat by herself. She had long wheat-colored hair that was pulled back in a ponytail and pretty hazel eyes. Her sweater had a big pink flower, and she was holding a book. The girl winked back, then blushed. Reegan's eyes darted to the floor when she recognized the ladies in the other booth. They were the gossipmongers, the busiest of busy bodies, the hot breath of the whispers that made your ears burn.

She ignored the eyes boring holes into her back while she waited at the counter. She smiled when the metal doors slammed open. "I wish you had told me who you were the other night," Reegan began. "I'm good with faces, but it's been a long time, Justin."

His lips lifted. "I figured you didn't recognize me. I'm sorry about Patch."

His voice had dropped a few decibels, and his words held such sincerity that Reegan's eyes filled. "Thank you," she whispered as she snatched a napkin and dabbed her eyes.

"Don't do that!" he pleaded. "You want the same thing you ordered the other night?"

She nodded and tried to compose herself while he prepared her beverage. "How much?" she asked.

"I'll get hers."

She didn't have to turn around to identify the voice behind her. The black and white photo of a bed that slammed into her brain was enough of a giveaway. Reegan closed her eyes; she could feel his warmth…

"I'll have my usual," Phillip said, his arm brushing Reegan's shoulder while he handed his money to Justin. "And whatever Junebug ordered."

Reegan turned, bringing her so close to him that they were practically embracing. She couldn't look anywhere but into his hazel eyes. There was something…

Justin cleared his throat.

She turned back around, inadvertently lining up her rear with Phillip's front and making her take a sudden breath. She managed to thank Justin, relieved when he smiled and the presence behind her stepped to the side. "Thank you," she told Phillip, intending to make a hasty retreat.

"No problem," Phillip said, taking the cup Justin handed him. "If you're not in a hurry, you're welcome to join us." He motioned to the table with the young girl.

Reegan hesitated, her curiosity outweighing her flight instinct. "Okay."

Phillip grinned and guided her toward the table. "Junebug, this is an old friend of mine, Reegan McGrath. She's going to have coffee with us. Reegan, this is my daughter, June."

Reegan stuck out her hand. "Nice to meet you," she said, and after a brisk shake, June replied in kind. He'd called her his daughter?

Her confusion must have shown because Phillip whispered, "I legally adopted June a few years ago."

"Oh, that's nice." She took a seat across from June and pictures came to mind, but unlike the snapshots she'd been seeing, these were of book covers. Strange, Reegan thought.

"I'm sorry about Patch," June said.

Reegan glanced at Phillip, who sat next to his daughter; he gave her a reassuring smile. "Thank you, June." She sipped her coffee to busy her hands.

Phillip asked June what she had planned for the day since it was a teacher work day and she didn't have school. Reegan partially listened, focusing instead on Phillip; she could see him clearer with the morning light shining in. His hair, which had always been a sandy blond, was longer on top allowing it to curl slightly, and his eyes were a rich hazel surrounded by long dark lashes. His nose had a small bump where it had been broken during a football game their senior year of high school. His lips were equally full on the top as they were on bottom, and when he smiled, the dimple in his left cheek peeked out, which made her insides quicken involuntarily. Down, girl, she advised her body.

"I'll miss Patch something awful," June said bringing Reegan back to the conversation going on around her.

"Me too," Reegan said.

"June often came with me to see Patch, and they got to know each other over the years," Phillip began to explain.

Reegan nodded. "I see."

June opened her mouth to speak, but Phillip beat her to it.

"What time is the viewing?" he asked, sipping his coffee.

"Seven."

He answered his cell phone when it rang giving only one-word answers to the caller. He stood. "I've got to go." Turning to June, he said, "Are you all right here with Justin until your grandma picks you up?"

"Yep," June assured him and waved to where Justin was ringing up a customer.

"I'll walk you out," he said.

"Bye, June, it was nice meeting you," Reegan said as Phillip took her arm and led her to the door. He let her go when they got outside. Reegan stared up at him.

His cell phone rang again, and again he answered it. She couldn't blame him. He was in uniform, obviously on duty. There was something—

"I have to go," Phillip said, once he finished his call. "I'll see you tonight at the viewing, okay?"

"Okay," she replied, though she was confused. Her heart skittered a bit when he caressed her face. "Phillip? What is this?"

He gazed down at her directly. "I haven't a clue."

Some sort of internal struggle played out across his handsome face before she said, "I believe you."

"Good. I have to go, but I'll see you tonight."

"Okay," she told him because he seemed to need an answer in order to leave.

Reegan sipped her coffee and shivered now that her heat source was gone. A thought struck her midsip, and she started walking down the sidewalk. She couldn't help but grin at the plaque when she saw it. Ezra Kelly's Gallery, it read, with a small Open sign under it.

Memories rushed her head like slides in a projector when she walked inside. Her first camera and Ezra's studio; his paints and brushes. Tears sprang to her eyes.

"Can I help you?"

Reegan turned toward the voice, and photos of spikey hair flashed before her eyes, then the images got dark and sped into a blur. Shaking her head to disrupt her mind and sipping her coffee to fight the chill, she stepped forward. "Adam Desmond?" she asked, though it wasn't a question. He was tall, slender, and made for the black suit he was wearing. His black hair was short and styled, his bright blue eyes were no longer hidden behind black contacts, and his smile was still disarming; but it no longer made her weak in the knees.

Reegan didn't squirm under his inspection, though she wanted to. She wondered what he saw. She had left her hair loose today, and she wore her black peacoat over her burgundy skirt and black leggings. Compared to her normal attire, she was dressed up.

"Reegan McGrath," he said with a slow smile as he walked over to her.

His tight hug caught her off guard, but she hugged

him back. "You work here?" she asked after he stepped away.

"No, I'm just helping out." He gestured at the room. "What do you think?"

"It's wonderful," she told him while she studied some of the pieces. "Is Ezra here? I'd love to see him."

"He's out of town on business," Adam explained. "I'm sorry for your loss." He shrugged when she turned toward him. "Small towns; everyone knew that crazy grandmother of yours."

She could call Patch crazy, but she didn't like it when other people did or at least not the way he'd said it. Her stomach rolled a bit, but she said, "Thank you."

"You look good, Reegan," he said. "Age agrees with you."

"Thanks, Adam, you look good too; all grown up."

"Is that Reegan McGrath I hear?"

Reegan looked up as an attractive woman with shoulder-length jet black hair and bright blue eyes came into the room. A picture flashed in her mind of a maid holding a feather duster and pressing her ear to the door. Reegan couldn't help but smile. "April, so nice to see you! Are you helping Ezra out too?"

"No, I just came to discuss a few things with my brother," she said coming closer and giving Reegan a hug.

"Do you still live in town?" Reegan asked.

"Off and on. We have a house here and an apartment in the city."

"You're married, then?" Reegan asked.

"Yes."

"My sister landed herself a rich husband," Adam said with a smirk.

April glared at Adam but then smiled and said, "Instead of working for the richest families in town, I *am* one of the richest families in town."

"Good for you!"

April's cell phone beeped. She checked it and said, "I need to get going. It was nice seeing you again."

"You too, April."

"I always knew you'd come back to Willows Bluff, Reegan," April said, then waved as she left the gallery.

That was strange, Reegan thought, but shrugged it off. She glanced at Adam, who was staring at her. "She sounds happy."

Adam looked out the window to where April was getting into her BMW. "She's done well for herself. But if I've heard correctly, so have you and that camera of yours."

"Yes, I'm happy with my success." She walked toward a painting that caught her eye.

Adam stepped behind her while she assessed an abstract painting done in bold reds, deep yellows, striking oranges, and strokes of sinister black. "What do you see?" he asked.

Reegan looked briefly over her shoulder at him, then back to the painting. She could feel him studying her. There wasn't the same warmth there that she had experienced with the sheriff, but there was something…a nettling in the back of her mind.

"Fire," she began, "is the obvious answer with the boldness and texture of the colors; you can practically feel the heat, hear the crackle. This form, however"— she gestured to the center of the painting, to the streaks of black—"and this darkening of color here gives the impression of something being there…burning." She stepped back taking an uncomfortable breath. "Or someone," she whispered.

Adam's eyebrow rose. "Your perception is indicative of your talents, Reegan. Well done."

She wanted to bask in the praise, but she was conflicted. "Who's the artist?" she asked searching for a signature.

Adam cocked his head to the side. "That would be me."

"Impressive," she said, though she was a bit disturbed as she studied the rest of the canvases. They all seemed to depict some form of pain.

"Thank you. I've had some success too, but more in the private sector than mainstream. When I came to visit my family for Christmas, I ran into Ezra, and when he asked if I would do a show at his gallery, I couldn't say no."

"That was nice of you," she said with a bite of sarcasm due to his implication that she was mainstream. He had meant it as a slight dig to her, and she was annoyed.

"Yes, a certain debt is owed to the place that made you who you are, don't you agree?"

"I'm more inclined to be indebted to the people who encouraged me than the place I lived."

"Touché."

Reegan couldn't discern the impressions Adam presented. Needing a moment to gather her thoughts, she glanced at her watch. "I need to go meet my parents. It was nice seeing you again, Adam. Take care of yourself." She didn't run from the gallery, but her steps were brisk.

****

She stood in the back corner while people found their seats in the chairs provided by the funeral home. The lighting was dim as though lit by candles instead of the fixtures hanging above her head, giving the room a certain ambiance. The atmosphere, though successful in its bleakness, was lovely, and Reegan had to admit the Willises excelled in their field.

TV monitors on the back wall played the digital photo gallery Reegan had created. A moving collage of Patch's life with a beautiful rendition of "Greensleeves" playing in the background; it had been one of Patch's favorite songs.

Patch lay on ivory satin inside an ebony casket with golden rails in a dress she had picked to be buried in. On top of the closed section of the casket was a spray of yellow roses, which were Patch's favorite, with white lilies and baby's breath. The flowers arranged around the room had been sent by the people of Willows Bluff. Reegan thought it fitting, a petal for every cruel word they'd ever said behind Patch's back.

She had stood by the open door with her parents as people walked in telling them how sorry they were for their loss. After she had been hugged, patted, and scrutinized by people she hadn't seen nor thought of in years, she told her parents she needed a minute alone; so here she stood, dressed in black in the back corner of the room studying the mourners.

Her relief was palpable when Sydney walked in the door. Her friend was in the middle of a major business deal, but she told Reegan she wouldn't let her go through this night alone.

"Syd," she called out. She sucked in a breath as photos flew through her brain of two young girls with matching friendship bracelets holding hands, two glasses of champagne with lipstick on the rim next to Sydney's wedding bouquet, and lastly one she'd taken of Sydney posing in front of the Willows.

"What was that look?" Sydney asked after hugging Reegan tightly.

"I've been having these strange flashes of memory"—Reegan shrugged—"like scrolling through the photos on your phone."

"Interesting," Sydney said, releasing Reegan so she could stare at her.

"I think it's stress," she admitted, relieved when Sydney let it go. She glanced down at the long black cashmere coat her friend wore. Reegan couldn't help but smile, inside at least, at the way everyone in the room was gawking. She couldn't blame them really; these people hadn't seen Sydney Walters in years, and Sydney was stunning. She'd cut her blonde hair into a sleek short style, her makeup made it seem as though she'd barely aged, and her blue eyes sparkled.

"Nice to know that Willows Bluff hasn't deviated from its usual course," Sydney said.

Reegan could only shrug at the prying eyes and callous whispers. "What did you expect? You're successful, beautiful, *and* they haven't had a chance to talk about you in years."

"True, let them gossip then," she announced loud enough for people to hear her. "I'm here for you. How are you doing aside from the obvious? You look like shit."

Reegan snorted. "Thanks, Syd. I'm as good as I can be, I guess. This breaks my heart."

"I'm sorry, I wish I could stay here longer—"

"This deal will make your career, Sydney, I know that. I'm proud of your success, and I wouldn't want you to put that in jeopardy in order to dry my tears."

"I think I'm the one who's supposed to make you feel better." Sydney smiled. "But thanks for that. Daddo sends his condolences. He and Mother are in Europe presently; otherwise, he would be here too."

Reegan nodded. "He sent a beautiful arrangement of roses. I guess we should go sit down."

Sydney sat next to her in the front row while the reverend spoke. She let the tears fall when her father stood and talked about Patch. In the moment when her father was finishing up, the door in the back opened, and the room seemed to pulsate.

Reegan's father hurried down the aisle. She and Sydney turned in their seats and stared as her father took the arm of a tiny white-haired woman in a black suit and ushered her to the front. He walked her past the row where Reegan was sitting and right up to where Patch lay. Her father stood beside the woman holding her arm while she said her good-byes.

"Annie Mae," Reegan whispered, and Sydney's eyes widened.

People were murmuring behind her, and it pissed Reegan off. Where do they get off taking this moment away from Annie Mae? How dare they be so disrespectful of someone's right to grieve!

There was a collective gasp when Annie Mae collapsed in Reegan's father's arms. Her mother rose from her seat and went to help. A woman made her way down the aisle, and with every row she passed, the whispers increased.

People were standing, and Phillip radioed for an

ambulance. Reegan was transfixed by the woman. She was wearing a long-sleeved black lace dress over black leggings with black boots. Her dark hair touched her waist; the front strands were held back by a silver barrette that seemed to catch the dim lights and shine right into Reegan's eyes. Then, as if she felt Reegan's stare, the woman glanced up.

Polaroids sliced into Reegan's mind, but the pictures were at the stage where the image was trying to seep through. One after the other, the photos appeared as though someone was dealing cards until the deck ran out. Reegan inhaled sharply when she focused on the mercury-colored eyes that stared back at her. She was more than grateful when the other woman broke the connection by looking away.

"Holy shit," Sydney whispered. "That's Bernadette Howard."

Holy shit, Reegan agreed, standing quickly as Phillip approached them. Her heart leapt into her throat where it pulsated hard enough to choke her. Much to her later embarrassment, Reegan fainted there in the front row directly into Phillip's arms.

Chapter Seven

She sat in the hospital waiting room holding a cup of caffeinated sludge and staring into space. Reegan didn't think the red of embarrassment would ever leave her cheeks. "Fainting," she mumbled to herself. Who the hell does that?

Her father had wanted her to ride in the ambulance with Annie Mae, who had also regained consciousness, but Reegan had refused. They had compromised, of course, by letting her mother and Sydney bring her to the hospital. She'd been cleared by the doctor, but she was waiting for her mother, who was checking on Annie Mae. Sydney was pacing the corridor speaking in clipped tones to her assistant. Reegan knew what was going to happen before Sydney hung up the phone and came to sit next to her.

"Go," Reegan said on a sigh.

"There's a problem in the manifest—"

"Sydney, go."

Sydney rubbed her forehead. "I just"—she shrugged—"I can't lose this deal."

"Sydney, you've worked too damn hard to let this slip through your fingers. I'm fine. Granted, a little mental, but that's nothing unusual."

Sydney smiled. "True. Besides, it looks like you already have someone to catch you." She inclined her head to where Phillip was speaking with one of the doctors.

"Hey!" Reegan said, heat burning her cheeks again.

"There is something there, no?"

"If you had asked me last week, I would have said not in a million years." She waited a beat. "Are you okay with that?"

Sydney's eyebrows drew together. "Honey, that was years ago."

"I understand that, Syd. But would it piss you off if I were to let things happen?"

"Reegan, I'd be pissed if you didn't! This is the first time you've shown an interest in someone who's actually employed," she finished, and Reegan could tell she was trying not to laugh.

"The guys I date have had jobs," she argued.

"You know what I mean." Sydney brushed a strand of hair out of Reegan's face.

"I guess I do. Just to be clear."

"Go for it."

"I will then!" Wholeheartedly!

"Just don't stay too long," Sydney said. "Nothing good has ever come from being in Willows Bluff."

"True."

"Here's your hero now," Sydney said.

"What? Oh," Reegan said, feeling the blood rush to her face when Phillip came to where they sat.

"Ladies. How do you feel?" he asked Reegan.

"Mortified, but otherwise intact. How's Annie Mae?"

"She's resting, and the doctors want her to stay overnight," he said. "Bernie and your mother are in there with her. Annie Mae did want to speak with you, Reegan."

"Bernadette Howard," Sydney said shaking her head. "I never thought I'd hear that name again."

"I know, right?" Reegan scoffed even as the name pinged around her mind. She couldn't be sure if it was her curiosity or a sense of foreboding.

"She probably feels the same about the two of you," Phillip said.

"True."

"I wonder where Tori Elis is?" Sydney said as the same thought floated into Reegan's mind.

Phillip took a quick step back. "I keep forgetting you two haven't been around in the last decade." He shook his head, then took a seat next to Reegan. "Tori's at Shady Pines."

"Bullshit!" Sydney blurted.

Reegan felt the urge to cry. Shady Pines was a sanitarium for the mentally ill about thirty miles outside Willows Bluff. "Why?"

Phillip sighed. "I won't get into particulars, but about seven years ago there was an incident; Tori went to the hospital and was held for psychiatric evaluation. During this time, the psychiatrist and Tori's parents agreed that she needed to be institutionalized."

"Seven years!" Reegan couldn't imagine.

"That's unbelievable," Sydney said.

Reegan glared at her friend before Phillip noticed. Sydney had won her battle with Tori. No matter how Reegan had felt about Tori, she wouldn't have wanted that for her.

Phillip nodded.

Sydney stood up and prompted Reegan to do the same. "If you need me, call."

"You know I will." Reegan smiled and hugged her

friend. After good-byes, Sydney retreated down the hall, and Reegan reclaimed her seat.

"You two are still close."

"Yep." She smiled at Phillip, then caught him up on her life since she left Willows Bluff.

"You sound happy," he said.

"I am. How about you? I thought you were going to marry Tori and become a football star."

Phillip laughed. "Marry Tori, huh?"

"Everyone knew you were in love with her." Reegan felt low for bringing this up, but she had a right to know. Didn't she?

"Back then, I thought Tori needed someone to protect her other than Bernie," he said with a lift of his lips. "When we were in high school, it just made sense, you know, the quarterback and the princess"—he shrugged—"but Tori never felt the same. Once I went away to school, I came to grips with the fact that I wasn't in love with Tori but the idea of her."

Reegan sat back regarding him thoughtfully. "That's a lot to admit to yourself."

"I'm not going to pretend I was over her the minute I passed the city limit sign—that wouldn't be true. It took me about a semester away from here to come to that conclusion. And Anna Baker, a beautiful and talented psych major."

Reegan laughed. "Yeah, that helps. How did you end up back here then?"

"I injured my knee and lost my scholarship. I was able to get a couple of grants and finish school with a degree in criminal justice."

"Still the knight in shining armor," Reegan said.

Phillip thought about it for a second, then said, "I

guess you're right. It runs in the family, you know. I'm the fourth generation of law and order in Willows Bluff."

"Really?"

"Honest. We can trace it back to my great-grandfather William in the early 1930s, then Grandpa in the late '50s, my dad, and now me."

"That's actually kind of awesome," Reegan said with a sheepish grin.

Phillip stood up when Reegan's mother came to the waiting room. "Is she ready for her?" he asked, motioning to Reegan.

"Yes, Annie Mae would like to see you now, Reegan."

"Okay," Reegan said and took a deep breath. She stood, grateful that Phillip walked with her to the door of Annie Mae's room while her mother went to call her father.

"You okay?"

"As good as I'm going to be, I guess."

"You're not going to faint on me again, are you? Though you've established I'm willing to catch you."

Reegan winked. "Maybe later."

She entered the room, and her stomach churned. Annie Mae presented the same image Patch had on the day she died. She sucked in a breath when Bernie appeared in front of her; she'd forgotten that Bernie was a good four inches shorter than herself.

"Don't upset her!" Bernie warned.

Reegan stared into the silver swirls of Bernie's eyes; they were almost unnatural. "Of course not."

Bernie eyed Reegan, then exhaled. "She says she wants to talk to you in private, so I'll be right outside the door."

"Okay."

Reegan took a seat next to the bed after Bernie left the room. She reached out and held Annie Mae's hand. The old lady opened her blue eyes so much like Patch's.

"There, there," Annie Mae whispered and squeezed Reegan's hand. "You appear put out."

"No, ma'am."

She snickered. "Constance and I always agreed you were a bad liar." Annie Mae was the only person Reegan knew who called Patch by her given name.

"I'm not lying."

"Hmm, Bernie scares you."

Reegan glanced over her shoulder and toward the window where she could see Bernie speaking to Phillip. "Concerns me."

"She ain't a killer," she told her.

Reegan cleared her throat. "What was it you wanted to speak with me about?"

Annie Mae studied her. "Constance was my best friend, and I loved her dearly. She left you those boxes in her parlor for a reason. It's your duty to go through each one."

"I plan to. I'm going to rent a storage locker and—"

"No, no, no! You have to go through them here and now."

Reegan withdrew her hand and sat back. "You want me to bring them to the hospital?"

Annie Mae growled. "No, you nincompoop! I'm saying you must go through them before you leave Willows Bluff, and you need to start now."

"I don't see the difference—"

"Makes a damn difference because I'm telling you what Constance expected you to do!"

"Have you seen the boxes in that room? It'll take me over a week to go through all that. I have responsibilities."

"Hush! I don't want to be hearing about your responsibilities! You owe it to your grandmother to abide by her wishes." She was shouting now.

"Calm down, Annie Mae," Reegan said, wincing when the door opened.

"Gran?" Bernie glared at Reegan. "What's going on?"

"She don't wanna listen."

"She doesn't have to do what you tell her," Bernie said.

"She's gotta do what Constance wanted! You girls never listen to what your grandmothers tell you. Never listen to a damn word we say."

"Gran, please don't upset yourself."

Annie Mae pointed an arthritic finger at Reegan. "You do as I say, girl. You stay here, and you go through those damn boxes like Constance expected you to."

"This is ridiculous!" Reegan rubbed her hands over her face. "Fine, fine, I'll do it," she conceded after Annie Mae made a move to snatch her hair. What was it with old ladies and hair?

"Promise."

"Don't make a promise you can't keep," Bernie warned. "She'll never leave you alone if you break your word."

"I'll haunt you from the damn grave," Annie Mae

warned.

"Gran!" Bernie admonished.

"Do you doubt me, girl?"

"No," Reegan said.

"Good! Now, promise and be specific."

Bernie put her head in her hands and said, "Here we go."

Reegan was taken aback by Bernie, or more to the point, she was surprised she felt a kinship with the other woman at that moment. In fact, it disturbed Reegan a great deal. Annie Mae cleared her throat to remind her that she was waiting.

"I promise to stay in Willows Bluff until I have gone through all the boxes."

"There now. See? All's the better," Annie Mae said then pointed to Bernie. "Go get me a Coca-Cola."

"Gran, the doctor said—"

"I don't give a hoot and a half what that little prick says. You go get me a damn Coca-Cola."

Reegan stared as Bernie took a breath and left the room, opening the door enough for Reegan to wave to Phillip before the door closed her in with Annie Mae.

"He's a good man," Annie Mae told her.

"Phillip?"

"Don't play dumb with me, girl! I saw how you two were gazing at each other." She sniffed and straightened her blankets. "Constance would approve."

Reegan snorted. "Thanks."

"Don't sass me!"

How the hell had Bernie lived with this? Reegan wondered. She didn't remember Annie Mae being so aggressive.

"Did you talk to Constance before she passed?"

Reegan swallowed. "Yes."

"Did you listen to what she told you?"

"Do you know what she told me?" Reegan asked as a chill invaded her space.

Annie Mae inclined her head. "I know."

"How?"

"I can't talk about it."

"What do you mean you can't talk about it? You asked me!"

"I had to make sure she kept her promise."

Reegan recalled her conversation with Patch. That's the promise, she'd told her. "Who did she promise?"

"You don't get it. You're Constance's responsibility, and she fulfilled her promise. I have my own promises to keep."

"To Patch?"

"Don't you worry about that, Reegan McGrath. You just heed the warning, and don't tell nobody lessen they see what you see, know what you know, or learn what you learn. Better that way."

"I…" Reegan began, so confused she could pull her own hair.

"Just do what you promised. There's my girl!" she exclaimed when Bernie walked back in the room. "Give me a hug, Reegan, before you go."

I've been dismissed, Reegan thought, as she hugged the fragile bones of her grandma's best friend.

"You'll do fine," Annie Mae whispered in her ear.

Chapter Eight

Reegan sat between her father and a frail Annie Mae as they lowered Patch's casket into the frozen earth beneath their feet. Tears swam in her eyes obscuring the faces of the black-clad mourners, but she didn't need to see them. Reegan knew if she looked through her camera's lens, they would appear to be paying homage to the natural order of things—a murder of crows surrounding the dead. Fitting perhaps, but she found little solace in it.

Later, she stood in the corner of her parents' home while people maneuvered about the house talking about Patch and sharing their grief. Reegan wondered, as they loaded their plates with food and their cups with punch, if they were trying to fill the void that Patch's loss created. She felt empty too, but she didn't think food could help her.

She went to her room to evade formal conversation. She lifted the blinds and stared out at the snow-covered ground. Phillip came in and stood behind her. It didn't take long for her to be enveloped in his arms. She was scared of this thing between them that neither seemed to understand.

She turned in his embrace in order to hold on to something. She rested her hot face against the star, still cold from the winter wind, pinned to his uniform and breathed him in. They stood that way until his cell phone rang, and he had to step away.

Her eyes met his as he spoke to the person on the other end. In that moment, she wanted nothing more than to escape with him. From what and to where she didn't know, but worse, she didn't care. Unnerved, she turned back to the window to lose herself in the monotony of white.

****

Reegan paced the front hallway of Patch's home and stared at the boxes that cluttered the parlor. This was part of the inheritance Patch had left her: thirty-seven boxes that may as well be labeled "Pandora" seemed to stare back, taunting her.

She walked into the room, stopped at the first stack she came to, and took the lid in both hands. Her heart leapt when the doorbell rang, and she hurried to answer it, thankful for another reprieve. The cold air blasted her in the face the minute she opened the door, but what stole her breath was Phillip standing on the other side.

"Hi," Reegan managed to say.

"Good morning." Phillip smiled and shuffled from foot to booted foot. "I thought you might want a hand or"—he held up two travel cups—"at the very least a hot cup of coffee."

She couldn't help but grin. "Found my weakness, huh?" She accepted the cup and stepped aside so he could come in.

"I think it's more that like recognizes like," he said, after she shut the door and came up behind him.

Reegan drank in the sight of him as he stared into the parlor. He was wearing jeans and a green winter coat. "Not on duty today?"

He looked over at her. "No."

"Where's June?"

"In school." Phillip cocked his head to the side with a slight smile. "I figured I would offer you some assistance."

Reegan snorted. "Lancelot."

"Guilty."

Reegan took a breath. She wanted him here or more accurately she didn't want him to leave. "I appreciate the coffee and the offer—"

"But…"

"Ha! No buts, I'm absolutely taking both your coffee and your assistance." Reegan grinned when he laughed.

"Good!"

A few minutes later, they were both staring at the boxes. Well, Reegan was staring at him. He'd discarded his jacket revealing a creamy mechanic-style sweater that fit him perfectly. Phillip's hair was disheveled from the wind and he looked…well, she didn't need her camera to see his allure. Reegan glanced away, startled by her own thoughts.

"You okay?" Phillip asked with his brows pinched.

Reegan sipped from her cup and nodded. "I guess I'm just putting off the inevitable," she said, which was true enough.

Today, she dressed in holey jeans with black leggings underneath, a black t-shirt on top of a white thermal, and her black studded boots. She'd put her hair in a braided bun and taken great care with her makeup. Reegan had known when it had taken her almost two hours to get ready that she was stalling.

"No time like the present," Phillip said, effectively taking her from her thoughts.

"Right," she said and again took the box lid in her hands.

"Wait," Phillip said, and Reegan froze. He took her hand and led her to the other end of the boxes. "This one says 'start here.'"

Reegan stared at him as if he had lost his mind, then glanced at where he pointed, and indeed, it did say *start here* with an arrow going downward. She'd been staring at these boxes for over an hour and hadn't noticed. She looked up at him.

"Don't," Phillip said after Reegan had tilted her head toward him.

Reegan stepped away, embarrassed. "Sorry."

"No." Phillip took her chin between his fingers and lifted her face so she had to look into his eyes. "Do you honestly think one kiss will satiate whatever this is between us? Because I don't!"

Reegan held his gaze a moment, then said, "You're right. Let's just open the boxes."

Phillip nodded. "We should work out a system so you know what you want to keep and what you don't."

Reegan's hand went to her throat. "Patch wanted me to have these things. Wouldn't it be wrong to just get rid of what she expected me to keep?"

"I think these are things she wanted to show you, share with you, and yes, I'm sure she wanted you to keep some of it…but I doubt she expected you to keep everything."

Reegan took inventory and together they worked out a placement system for what she would and wouldn't keep. Now, all she had to do was open the first box.

Taking a breath, she lifted the lid to find stacks of

old journals. Reegan's brow puckered. "Patch didn't keep a journal," she said as she took one out to examine it; Phillip did the same. " 'Property of Edwin Woods' is written on the inside cover."

"Same here," Phillip said and took out the other journals to check inside. "These too."

"Patch's maiden name was Woods," Reegan said.

"Her father perhaps?"

"Makes sense; why else would Patch keep them?" she said.

We work well together, Reegan thought some time later as she took the stack of papers she'd been reading to the hall. They'd gone through a bunch of boxes, most of which contained an array of things one might hoard. Considering the source, Reegan figured they shouldn't have been surprised. There had been two boxes of photos. One held old albums that she'd had seen before, and the other was a mass of loose photographs that would take time to go through.

"More newspapers," Phillip said, bringing Reegan back from her thoughts. "These are pretty old."

Reegan peered around him to get a better look. "Is Phyllis Cox still the librarian?" she asked, thinking she should show them to someone.

Phillip grinned.

"I take that as a yes," Reegan said, shaking her head. Phyllis Cox was the Napoleon of the Willows Bluff public library. Or at least she was if you were late returning your books; otherwise, she was just a prickly old lady with a Dewey Decimal obsession.

Phillip grinned wider.

"Does she still slam down that stupid stamp if you piss her off?"

"Everything is on computer now, so it's the mouse she slams down," he said, and Reegan laughed. "Why?"

"Phyllis might know if there's some significance to these or if it was just Patch being Patch."

"She is good with local history," Phillip agreed and removed the lid of the next box, while Reegan sifted through the box of papers. "Reegan…"

"Oh," Reegan whispered and stared at the patchwork robe Phillip in Philip's hands. She set down the papers and took it from him. She held the robe to her nose and inhaled, letting the tears fall unabashed as she rubbed the robe across her cheek. The second she felt Phillip's arms around her the sob that had been choking her released.

"That's enough for one day," Phillip said once she'd calmed down and stepped away from him.

Reegan sniffled. "Yeah, you're right." With the utmost care, she folded the robe and set it in her keep pile.

Phillip glanced at his watch. "Junebug will be getting home from school shortly, so I need to go."

"Okay," Reegan said, her stomach lurching. "Thanks for helping me."

"No problem," he said as he put his coat back on.

She stared at his back while he walked toward the front door. He turned around abruptly, startling her. The look in his eyes had her insides clenching. "Phillip," she whispered in a voice she barely recognized. His lips were on hers before she could inhale her next breath.

He kissed her with such ferocity, Reegan would later be surprised she wasn't bruised. Her lips parted, and Phillip slipped in his tongue. Her hands fisted in his hair to keep him in place.

Her eyes crossed when she felt his hand slip inside her shirt. Feeling his hands on her skin was disorienting. She tore her mouth from his when he cupped her lace-covered breast. "Please, Phillip."

"I know," he said in a hot whisper across her neck. She reached for the buckle of his belt just as the doorbell rang. They both froze.

"Not now!" Reegan panted.

Phillip stepped back and adjusted his jeans.

Reegan took a deep breath and straightened her shirt. The doorbell rang again, and she opened the door. What the hell?

Bernadette Howard stood there holding a casserole dish looking annoyed. "Sorry to intrude on you, Reegan, but Gran wanted me to bring this to you..." Bernie trailed off, and Reegan felt Phillip come up behind her. Bernie's cheeks went pink as she assessed the situation. "Hi, Phillip, sorry to disturb you."

"I was just heading out," Phillip said.

Reegan opened the door wider, motioning for Bernie to enter. Her position put Phillip directly behind her, which she hoped preserved some of his modesty considering she could still feel his erection pressing into her. She gave Bernie her best smile when the other woman entered.

"Would you mind putting it in the kitchen while I walk Phillip out?"

"All right," Bernie said and headed in that direction.

Reegan exhaled a shaky breath and went out the front door so Phillip could escape. She hugged herself as she stopped at Phillip's Jeep.

They didn't say a word while he unlocked the door

and got in. He buckled his seat belt and she sighed. "You were right," she said.

"About?"

"One kiss isn't enough."

Phillip rubbed his hands over his face. "No, it isn't."

"I'm not going to kiss you good-bye because I don't know if I'd be able to stop myself. Which wouldn't bother me if Bernie wasn't standing in Patch's house no doubt watching us from the window."

The corner of Phillip's lips lifted as he glanced at the windows in question. "I get it, Reegan."

"This is a to-be-continued moment. Better sooner than later," she said, and his eyes flew up to meet hers.

"Lord, Reegan," Phillip groaned.

"I'm serious!"

"I can see that."

"Glad we're on the same page," she said as she shut his door, then headed back into the house. She found Bernie in the kitchen. The woman had started a pot of coffee and gotten plates out.

"Make yourself at home, why don't you?" Reegan said.

"I guess I should apologize for what you obviously assume is rudeness, but I don't intend to," Bernie said, opening a drawer and pulling out silverware.

"It's not assumed," Reegan said under her breath. She took an involuntary step back when Bernie's eyes met hers.

"Yes, it is," Bernie said and took great pains cutting some sort of cake.

Reegan's stomach growled; she hadn't had lunch. Damn. She crossed her arms over her chest and looked over at the sputtering coffee pot.

Bernie poured two cups, put cream in both, and handed one to Reegan. "I stayed with Patch sometimes," Bernie said after sipping her coffee and handing Reegan a plate.

They stood around the island in the kitchen, Reegan on one side, Bernie on the other as it had always been. Looking at their plates, then at each other, neither asked the questions hovering between them.

With more enthusiasm than she wanted to show, Reegan took a bite of the coffee cake and closed her eyes with appreciation. It was delicious.

"Good?"

"Did you make it?" Reegan asked, taking another bite.

Bernie nodded. "I made it for Gran this morning. Of course, she insisted I bring it here to you this afternoon, so she could make sure you were eating."

"Do you still live together?"

Bernie shrugged. "It looked like you made some headway with the boxes," she said.

Reegan eyed the other woman. Bernie was so different from what Reegan remembered. "It's a lot to go through."

"Thirty-seven boxes."

Reegan choked on her coffee. "How did you know that?"

Bernie's brows bunched. "You know I find your tone toward me insulting."

"We've never been friends, Bernie. So this"— Reegan encompassed the island with her arms—"little tea party makes no sense."

Bernie was quiet for a moment, then said, "I don't

want to be here, Reegan."

"You *are* here."

She shook her head. "You really don't get it, do you? I'm here for no other reason than Gran asked me to come check on you. I did what was asked of me, and that's more than enough!"

Reegan didn't know what to say, so she remained silent as Bernie grabbed her coat and left. She sat there sipping her coffee and contemplating the entire scene. Reegan didn't think she'd been unfair given their history.

"Oh, who cares," she said to the empty kitchen. She would go through the rest of the boxes tomorrow and get the hell out of this town before it tried to kill her again.

Chapter Nine

Reegan hit the floor with a thud. She inhaled deeply and willed herself to stop shaking. What the hell kind of dream was that?

"Breathe, damn it," she admonished. She untangled her legs from the vine-like grasp of the sheets and tried to sit up; only then did she feel eyes watching her. She glanced over her shoulder to see her father standing in the doorway, which would have been bad enough if it wasn't for the fact that Phillip was standing behind him.

"Are you fucking serious?" she said.

Her father glared at her. "We *are* going to talk about this," he said.

"It's just a bad dream, Dad. You didn't need to call the cops on me!"

"This isn't funny, Reegan! For the past week, you've screamed us awake, and I'm sick of it. Now get up and shower; then you're going to talk!" He turned around and left.

"Damn," Reegan said, then jumped when a strong hand helped her up. "I'm in my freaking underwear, Phillip."

"I can see that," he said, and she punched his shoulder because he was trying not to laugh at her.

"Just go on," she huffed, then stilled when he caressed her face. If he kissed her now, she would cry. Between her embarrassment and the emotional residue of the dream, she was less than composed.

"I'll be in the kitchen waiting with your father."

Reegan sighed at his retreating back. Wonderful, she thought, as she straightened the sheets and made the bed before she went to get ready.

Reegan was showered, dressed, and putting on her face in good time. Her father was waiting, and she wouldn't make things worse by dawdling. She threw on a burgundy sweater, a pair of jeans, and her boots. She hadn't even bothered washing her hair, still in its bun from yesterday, which suited her just fine. She nodded at herself in the mirror and headed for the firing squad.

Her parents were seated at the table going over the morning paper. Reegan hadn't realized her mother was going to be included in this inquisition; that meant her parents had discussed it. Then there was Phillip standing against the breakfast bar sipping a cup of coffee. He looked sexy with his sandy blond hair tousled from the wind. Why couldn't she dream of him?

"Ready to talk?" her father asked from behind a newspaper page. Reegan sighed when her mother set down her portion of the paper to stare at her. Fantastic!

"Your parents said you've been having nightmares since you've been home," Phillip said, his tone thoughtful, which made her heart do funny things. He made her sappy, which made her straighten her spine.

"That's true," she said as she poured herself a cup of coffee. Her father made a rather loud production of folding his paper, crossing his arms, and staring at her. "I have nightmares sometimes."

"Every night," her father said.

"Reegan," her mother began, "I wish you would tell us what's going on. We're worried about you."

Reegan sighed. "Honestly, I just have nightmares sometimes," she said, and she knew that was the wrong answer when her mother's face pinched.

"How often?" Phillip asked.

"Not this often," she murmured. Reegan glanced around the room and took a sip from her cup. "After the accident, I had nightmares constantly."

"That's understandable; Dad said you were lucky to have survived," Phillip said.

"Yeah, well." She shrugged.

"This is still about the accident?" her father asked. Was it her imagination, Reegan wondered, or did he sound relieved?

"Why didn't you tell us? We could have gotten you help," her mother said.

"Mom, I can handle it, and really, it's been a long time since I've had them. Years...but being here again"—she shook her head—"and Patch's death seems to have opened a can of whoop-ass in my psyche."

"What happens in the dreams?" her father asked.

"I dream of the day of the accident. And I don't mean just the accident, which is bad enough, but it's like I relive the entire day again. Every moment—every breath."

"But..." Phillip said, and her eyes slammed into his.

"*But* since I've been here, they've been different— worse. There's this woman in a red cloak, and she's leading me through the woods by the bluff. She keeps telling me we have to hurry because someone's coming to get us. Then I'm back in the water the night of the accident, drowning. Patch was there last night yelling at me, pulling me under, and then I was at the Willows. It was on fire, and a lady was inside burning." Reegan gripped her coffee cup as the picture of it flared into her conscious mind.

"Did you recognize the woman in the cloak or the woman in the fire?" her father asked in such a way it sent a chill up Reegan's spine.

She glanced at her mother, who was staring at her father; then she looked at Phillip, who was watching her and sipping his coffee totally relaxed. Her father asked her again, and again it gave her the willies.

"The woman in the cloak is familiar, but I can't place her. The woman in the fire, on the other hand, I could see her screaming while she burned...it was my face," she answered, and the second the words left her lips, a look passed between her parents. "What's going on?"

"What do you mean?" her mother asked.

Reegan stared at her parents. "You're hiding something." She turned to Phillip. "You"—she pointed to him—"you know what it is."

"I do?" Phillip asked.

"Yes! And I know you'll tell me the truth," she said, and call it intuition or whatever, she knew with absolute certainty Phillip wouldn't lie to her—he couldn't. And when he ducked his head, she knew she was right.

"Phillip," her father warned.

"What's going on?" she asked the room.

"There's a story you need to hear," Phillip began just as his cell phone rang. He sighed and turned to speak into his phone.

Reegan's thoughts were doing figure eights in her head. What was this story? What did it have to do with her dreams, and why were her parents hiding it from her? They were avoiding eye contact. She straightened when Phillip came back into the room.

"This will have to wait," Phillip said. "Annie Mae's nurse just called the station. She said Annie Mae had fallen asleep about an hour after she got there, and when she went to check on her, she'd already passed on."

"Oh, no," Reegan's mother said, standing.

"Where's Bernie?" Reegan asked around the lump in her throat.

"The nurse tried calling her, but her phone's off," Phillip said.

"She needs to be told," her father said.

"If her phone's off, that can only mean one thing," Phillip said, then took out his cell phone, scrolled the numbers, and made a call. "Good morning, this is Sheriff Hastings over in Willows Bluff. Is Bernadette Howard there? She's probably visiting a patient of yours, Tori Elis. Yes…no, I'm headed your way now. Thank you."

"I'm going with you," Reegan said and grabbed her bag.

****

Shady Pines sanitarium was more eerie than it was beautiful. It was built on an old plantation in the early 1920s as a sanctuary for the rich and disturbed. That still held true today. Shady Pines was a private retreat for those with mental health issues, but it was only available to the ones who could afford it.

Reegan contained her smile as Phillip came around to her side of the sheriff's SUV to open her door. Ever the gentleman, she thought. They hadn't talked the entire forty-five minutes it took to get here. She figured he had enough on his plate, and her questions could wait.

"Thanks," she said after he helped her out.

Reegan followed him up the steps controlling the urge to take pictures with the camera on her phone. This isn't the time or place, she reminded herself while Phillip held the door open. Her eyes widened when they entered the main hall; it looked like the lobby of a posh hotel.

She waited while Phillip spoke with the receptionist. Her eyes followed where the woman pointed, and Reegan's breath caught when photographs cut into her brain. A glass angel with horns holding up a halo; a child on a swing, long hair flowing behind her; and lastly, a concrete bench piled with snow. She exhaled slowly as Phillip came to stand next to her. Her eyes once again traveled across the lobby.

There was a common room behind thick glass, the kind ski resorts boasted, and there in front of the blazing fire stood Bernie with Tori Elis. Reegan had always thought Tori looked like an angel, and that still held true. A long white silk robe covered Tori's frail frame, and her hair hung in golden brown strands down her back.

Bernie caught sight of them before Tori had a chance to turn around. Worry crossed Bernie's features, and she signaled for an attendant. Tori grabbed onto Bernie, and Reegan could hear Tori's sobs through the thick glass begging Bernie for something. Not to leave her here, she guessed.

She peeked at Phillip. Concern etched his features, and pity filled his eyes. He wasn't in love with Tori anymore, that was clear. But there was something there that didn't make sense, an undercurrent of something Reegan couldn't quite understand. "Are you okay?"

Phillip looked down at her. "I don't know why Bernie does this to herself."

"They're best friends. It would be the same for me and Syd," she said as Bernie came up to them.

"Gran?" she asked, her mercury eyes floating between them.

Phillip bowed his head. "I'm sorry, Bernie."

Bernie inhaled and squeezed her eyes closed. How did she do that? Reegan wondered. How did she stay so controlled? She herself had screamed bloody murder when Patch died.

"She went in her sleep," Phillip said and told her what he could. "The paramedics called time of death when my deputies got there. Mr. Willis is already proceeding per Annie Mae's instructions."

"Mr. Willis was always a good friend to Gran," Bernie said, tears making tracks on her cheeks.

"I'm so sorry, Bernie," Reegan whispered, and Bernie glanced at her as if remembering she was there.

"Thank you."

"I didn't want you to find out over the phone," Phillip explained.

Bernie dabbed her eyes with her sleeve. "With Patch gone, I knew she didn't have long."

"Is there anything I can do for you?" Phillip asked once they were outside and in the parking lot.

"No, thank you for the offer," Bernie said and Reegan felt a pang in her chest.

"If you need anything, let us know," Reegan said, and Phillip seconded.

"Thank you," Bernie said, and Reegan stood next to Phillip as Bernie got into her truck and after a few minutes pulled away.

Reegan stared at Phillip while they drove back to Willows Bluff. He was quiet, and his hands hadn't moved from where they gripped the steering wheel. "What is it?" she finally asked.

He glanced her way, then focused back on the road. "I don't think you want to know."

Reegan's brow pinched. "What do you mean?"

"I know you don't like Bernie."

"It's true that we were never friends growing up, and she still makes me uneasy, but I feel for her."

"Did you know Bernie took Annie Mae to see Patch almost every day?"

Reegan sat back against her seat. "No, I didn't. She said something yesterday about staying with Patch sometimes."

Phillip nodded. "Patch would get scared being by herself, and Bernie would stay the night with her."

"Why didn't Patch say anything to my dad?"

"She was probably scared your father would make her move in with him, and she didn't like leaving her things."

"Why would Bernie do it, though?"

"Bernie does whatever Annie Mae asks of her…asked."

"What about her job?" Reegan asked, feeling guilty that Bernie was a better granddaughter to Patch than she was. Or had been. "Phillip?" she asked when he didn't answer right away.

He shifted in his seat. "When Bernie turned twenty-one, she came into a rather large inheritance."

"How?" Bernie had always been one of the poorest kids in school.

"Her mother came from a wealthy family," Phillip explained.

"The mother who abandoned her?"

"Yes. Very few people know about this, Reegan. I'm telling you because I trust you, and I trust you'll keep it to yourself."

Knowing he trusted her felt oddly amazing, and she told him, "I trust you too, Phillip! Don't worry, my lips are sealed."

He smiled at her.

"That doesn't tell me what's wrong with you though."

Phillip made a face. "Bernie's alone out there in that house and out here in the world too." He said the last half so softly she almost couldn't make it out.

"My parents will help her, and I'm sure yours will too."

"They'll try. I'll try but—"

She let out a frustrated breath. "Spit it out, Phillip. Is this more of your gallant knight condition?"

He chuckled. "Maybe, I just...she won't ask for help. Not for herself. With Annie Mae gone, she'll become even more of a recluse, and it pisses me off."

"I can see that," Reegan said. "She's your friend."

Phillip glanced quickly at her. "Is that a problem for you?"

Reegan studied him a moment. "As long as you're not friends with benefits, I don't care."

"No, it's never been like that."

"Well then, we"—she motioned between them—"are good."

Chapter Ten

Phillip dropped her off at her parents' house on his way back to town. The place was empty, and she figured her parents had either gone to work or to check on Bernie. She'd been so caught up in seeing Tori and Bernie that she forgot to get Phillip to tell her the story her father didn't want her to hear. Reegan wasn't concerned; she knew Phillip would give her answers the next time she saw him.

She called her landlord to ask if he'd keep getting her mail for a few more days. She didn't have any plants or pets so she didn't have to worry about that. She'd had a cat, a rescued old man cat named Roger, but he'd gone to the great beyond a few months ago and Reegan was still broken up about it.

Thinking about Roger made her think about Patch, which made her think about Annie Mae, and that made her heart hurt. She'd promised Annie Mae she'd go through those boxes. Grabbing her keys, Reegan decided that's exactly what she would do.

"Right where I left you," Reegan said to the boxes in Patch's parlor. She'd driven straight to Patch's, taken off her coat, brewed a pot of coffee, and here she stood. She sighed. It was so much easier when Phillip was here helping her.

She took a tentative step, then dove in. The next dozen or so boxes were one-hit wonders. Mementos she put into her keep pile. It wasn't until she came across the box with two charred logs that she paused.

Why in the hell would Patch pack this? she wondered. Shaking her head, she stuck the box to the side. Maybe someone else would understand the relevance and explain it to her.

She continued going through the boxes until she came across one that contained a simple jewelry box. Reegan sat on the floor and opened the box. Patch had never worn a lot of jewelry, so Reegan wasn't surprised to find it empty. But if her memory served, a small drawer on the side held the real treasure.

Inside the drawer was a lovely cameo brooch set in black; Reegan took it out and held it in her palm. It had been Patch's favorite. Reegan squeezed her eyes closed holding tightly onto the brooch as a small sob moved up her throat.

Before the tears could come, her mind contorted, and she was somewhere else—someone else. *The room was lit by candles, and the beveled mirror showed her face. And though the eyes were hers, the reflection was not. Her body, fuller than she knew it to be, was naked beneath a dark silk shawl, whose sides where held together by the brooch.*

Air rushed from her lungs the moment a muscled arm wrapped around her nakedness holding her, revealing her, and revering her. Her skin tingled where her neck was kissed by the man she loved more than life. She quivered, she shook, and her eyes flew open...

"Reegan? Are you okay?"

Reegan breathed slowly, taking Phillip's offered hand. The bouquet of roses he held fell to the floor while he helped her to her feet. Worry crossed his face, and then she closed her eyes and kissed him. She clutched the brooch as she wrapped her arms around his head deepening the kiss.

His arms went around her, and her mind flashed to the man in the glass. She sucked in a breath and ripped her lips from Phillip's. She stood back a step, and he panted, staring down at her with questioning eyes. She reached down and lifted her sweater over her head.

"Reegan," Phillip whispered.

She didn't reply, just removed her clothes until she was standing in front of him wearing only her bra and panties. He watched her, and after a moment he mimicked her actions. She felt each breath lift her heavy chest as he bared himself.

Phillip's body was a treasure trove of sinewy muscle dusted with blond hair. She could see his strength without her camera's lens. But her eyes took pictures of this moment, the beauty of his body, the serenity of his face, and the look in his eyes that set a chill on her skin.

She reached out to touch him. The minute her fingers found flesh, her mind shot back to that dim room and the feelings it invoked. Reegan moaned low in her throat and looked up to find Phillip staring at her.

"What is this?" he asked, taking his turn to touch her.

"You see it too?"

He shook his head. "I feel it."

"Go with it," she said.

His hands left her for a moment, and Reegan took the opportunity to undo her hair from its bun. She gasped when Phillip scooped her off her feet and into his arms. He carried her into one of the guest rooms and then set her down so she was standing in front of him.

Reegan stepped closer rubbing her cheek against his bare chest as her hands went behind her to unhook her bra. He inhaled sharply when she stepped back to reveal more of her nakedness. He had brought a rose with him, and he ran the soft petals across her breasts, first one, then the other.

Tossing the flower, he reached out, snatching her around the waist, turning her, and pulling her against him all at once. Her mind fled to some other time when the bodies in the glass mirrored theirs. Her body flooded with heat as his hands devoured her. She moaned when Phillip bit down where her neck met her shoulder.

Reegan wasn't sure if he'd ripped off her panties or if he pulled them off, but suddenly his skin was hot against hers. He bent her forward so she had to catch herself on the dresser. The scene in her head was identical, but that didn't matter the moment she felt him push fully inside her. She could feel him everywhere: in her body, around her body. Inside my soul, Reegan thought, her eyes meeting his in the mirror.

Phillip moved against her in a punishing rhythm. One of his arms went around her from her stomach to her shoulder holding her firmly against him. The other moved downward to the juncture of her thighs, where his fingers played roughly with her sex. Even as warmth spread to her legs and pressure built inside her, Reegan's eyes didn't leave his.

Reegan braced herself against the dresser pushing back against Phillip meeting his brutal pace. She panted and he growled. He expanded inside her, and she moved faster against him, on the cusp of an orgasm.

Her mind went to another mirror in another place, and her blood rushed at the reflection cast. She bit her lip when Phillip's fingers matched her pace, and Reegan stilled as she came with a litany of curses on her tongue. She convulsed around him, and his hands moved to her hips as he pressed deeply into her with slow, sure strokes. Her name fell from his lips when he came.

His breath fluttered against her crown, and she unclenched her hands from the dresser, releasing the brooch she forgot she'd been holding. She set it down a moment before Phillip picked her up and threw her on the bed. Reegan laughed when he hopped up next to her.

"Not that I'm complaining," Phillip said with a satisfied grin. "But what the hell just happened?"

Reegan stared up into his hazel eyes. "It was intense, right?"

He stared at her for a moment. "Yes."

She reached up and brushed the hair from his forehead. "I thought so too," she said and was rewarded with a deep kiss.

"Want to try it again?" Phillip said after they'd kissed and touched for a while.

Reegan grinned. "Oh, hell yeah."

****

They were standing in Patch's kitchen eating the lunch that Phillip had brought. He told her he'd come by to see if she was hungry and found her staring off into space. Reegan didn't want to think about that. No, she was enjoying exchanging silly grins with him.

Technically, Phillip was still on duty, so after he had gotten dressed, he asked Reegan to do the same so he wouldn't be tempted. She'd found the roses when she'd grabbed her clothes from the parlor. He'd actually blushed and said he'd picked them up on a whim. Reegan didn't care; he was the first man, other than her own father and Daddo, to give her flowers.

"You've made progress with the boxes," Phillip said.

Reegan snorted. "Yeah. That's because most of the ones I went through only had one or two things in them."

"Really?"

"Yep, you never know when it comes to Patch."

"That's true enough."

"I'm glad you came," Reegan said, and her face flushed.

Phillip grinned. "Likewise."

Reegan walked him out after they'd finished eating. "I wish you didn't have to go."

"That makes two of us," he said and kissed her forehead.

"Will I see you tomorrow?"

"I think that can be arranged."

"Good," she said, kissing him good-bye properly.

Reegan waited until he was out of sight, then hurried into the house. She shut the door and glanced into the parlor. There were only ten boxes left. That shouldn't take too long, she thought.

Her cell phone was ringing and she hurried to the kitchen to answer it. "Hey, Mom," she said. Her mother was just checking in on her; letting Reegan know they were going to order some pizzas for dinner and take them to Bernie's.

"She shouldn't be alone tonight," her mother said.

"I'll come with you."

"You want to?"

"Yeah." Why did everyone think she was an ass? Reegan wondered. "I agree with you. No one should have to be alone after they lost someone they love."

"We're leaving around six, so make sure you're home by then."

"Got it," Reegan said. After she hung up, she tidied the kitchen. Deciding she didn't want to open any more boxes today, she went to the parlor and set the jewelry box in the keep pile. The brooch, she thought, was still in the guest room. She enjoyed the delicious shiver that reminded her how it got there.

She'd left it on the dresser, she remembered, as she opened the bedroom door and turned on the light. There was no way in hell she would ever part with it now. She grabbed the brooch, hit the light switch, and was about to leave the room when she stopped suddenly.

The sheets were tangled, and one of the roses Phillip had brought was peeking out from under the bed. It was the picture she'd seen in her head when she saw Phillip for the first time all grown up. Reegan did the only thing she could do…slammed the door shut.

Chapter Eleven

What did it mean? Reegan asked herself for the millionth time as she paced the office in her parents' house, wringing her hands and picking her brain, desperate to find some sort of answer.

Those pictures she saw in her mind had started when she came back to Willows Bluff. Who had she seen pictures of? Justin was first and Phillip. She stopped her pacing to run her fingers through her hair; she wouldn't be forgetting that bedroom scene anytime soon.

She hugged herself and glanced at the clock. She had a couple hours before her parents would be home; then they would go see Bernie.

Bernie! Reegan remembered that the pictures in her head of Bernie hadn't developed yet. What did *that* mean? She'd seen pictures of Sydney; oh, and at Ezra's. Not to mention both Adam and April. Then it hadn't happened again until she saw Tori this morning. Why only those people?

She had seen images of June when they first met. But those had been book covers, not photographs. That had to have significance, right? These things had to mean something…other than the fact she was losing her mind.

Reegan pivoted on the woven carpet and went outside to her rental. If she couldn't make sense of the images in her head, at least she could go through the box of loose photos she'd brought from back from Patch's house. She retrieved the box from the trunk, then went back in the house and sat down at the kitchen table.

Reegan studied each picture with a trained eye. The first layer had been in color and from the seventies. She recognized her father in most of them; he would have been in his late teens or early twenties at the time. He was with another guy, and though they were obviously good friends, Reegan didn't recognize him. She set those photos in a stack to the side.

The next layer of photos was black and whites, early fifties; several were portrait postcards. She recognized Patch and her grandfather from the wedding photo that Patch always had in her bedroom. She couldn't help but smile at the happy couple.

The remaining photos were considerably older. One man was in most of them. He was quite handsome with dark hair and light eyes or at least that was her best guess. In some of the photos, he was with a pleasant-looking woman who held a baby; most were portraits taken over the years by a professional and printed on cabinet cards.

His eyes, Reegan thought, as she stared. People used to think photographs held the soul of the subject or stole the soul, depending on who you asked. But that's what you wanted to capture: the very essence of a person or a place, that underlying root that inspires, moves, and connects us. In this case the photographer succeeded; you could feel this man's sorrow.

Shaking her head, Reegan set those photos in their own pile and took out the last one. This photo was of a plain couple holding a toddler. They appeared kind, yet Reegan could see weariness in their eyes.

The front door opened. "I'm in the kitchen," Reegan called out, recognizing her father's heavy footfalls.

"Your mother said you're coming with us tonight," he said when he came into the room.

"That's the plan." His unwavering gaze reminded her of the conversation they'd had that morning. "Phillip didn't get a chance to tell me whatever story it is you're trying to hide from me."

"I don't like your tone—"

"I feel like you're lying to me, Dad."

"No one's lying to you, Reegan," he said and took a seat at the table. He started going through the stacks of photos she'd set out.

Deciding she wasn't getting anywhere, she held up the last picture she'd taken out of the box. "Do you know who this is?"

Her father looked up and squinted. "That's your great-grandfather and your great-great grandparents."

"Edwin Woods?" Reegan looked at the photo, then picked a few from the other stack. "So this is him older with my great-grandmother? And is this Patch?" she asked, pointing to the handsome man and woman with a baby in her lap.

"Yes, that's Mom and her parents."

"You never met them, right?" she asked.

Her father sat back and took the photo from her. "I never met my grandfather. He died in a car accident when Mom was around eight, I think."

"I didn't know that." Reegan sat up straighter in her chair. "What about Patch's mom?

"I don't remember much about her. She died when I was three or four," he said and picked up the stack of photos he'd originally started looking at.

How sad, Reegan thought. The front door opened again, and she smiled when her mom came in the kitchen.

"I'm going to freshen up and then I'll order the pizza; that way we can pick it up on our way," her mother said in a rush.

"Sounds good," her father said.

"Oh, look at those." Her mother took the photos out of her father's hand.

"Who's that in the pictures with you, Dad?" Reegan asked and another look passed between her parents. "Well?"

"That's Ryan Howard," her mother said.

Reegan sucked in a breath, grabbed the photo from her mother, and stared into the eyes of Bernie's father. "Dad, I didn't know you were ever friends."

"Ryan and I grew up together."

"How could I not know that?" Reegan asked, feeling a lump in her throat when her father stood and left the room saying he was going to get ready to go. "Mom?"

"You should probably go and freshen up before we leave," her mother said.

"Mom, will you please tell me what happened?"

Her mother glanced out the door and sighed. "When your mothers spend that much time together, you have no choice but to become close."

"I don't remember Ryan Howard ever being here."

Reegan's mother bit her lip. "They had a falling out. I'd just gone back to work after having you, and

Donna…"

"Who's Donna?"

"Bernie's mother."

"I didn't know you were friends with them," Reegan said. Her mother's eyes filled with tears. "My God, Mom, what happened?"

"Did Phillip tell you that story?"

"What does one thing have to do with the other?" she asked, confused.

"Everything," her mother whispered.

"Then please tell me!"

"It's not my place."

"Mom?"

"Go ahead and freshen up if you're still coming with us," her mother said.

The look on her mother's face told her she wasn't going to get any answers. That being the case, she headed for her room to get ready. Whatever her parents were hiding had them on edge, and though Reegan wasn't sure if uncovering the truth was worth the risk something inside her just wouldn't let go.

****

Annie Mae lived far outside of town in an old cottage in the woods. Even in the dark, Reegan could see it had been updated and well cared for. What she hadn't been expecting was the house that now stood behind the old cottage.

"What's that?" she asked her parents when they pulled up the driveway.

"That's Bernie's house," her mother told her as they got out of the van and headed to the front door of the cottage.

"Oh," she said. The rest of her thoughts

disappeared when the front door opened and Phillip was standing there.

"Phillip," Reegan's dad said in greeting as they walked inside. "We brought dinner."

"So I was told," Phillip said and held Reegan back while the others headed into the kitchen.

"I didn't know you'd be here," Reegan whispered, and he caressed her face.

"Junebug insisted," he said and leaned in to kiss her. His lips were soft, and though the kiss was brief, it was thorough.

Reegan sighed when he kissed her forehead, then herded her into the kitchen where everyone else was. Bernie gave her a look that said she knew exactly what had just happened, but she looked away. Reegan smiled when June came up to her.

"I was hoping I'd see you again," the girl said. Her wheat-colored hair was in a French braid, and Reegan had the overwhelming desire to hug her.

"It's nice to see you again too, June," Reegan said and was rewarded with a shy smile. Reegan felt eyes on her and looked up to see Buck Hastings staring. He was tall like Phillip, but his hair had gone white since she left town; his eyes were still the same whiskey color and just as sharp as she remembered. She'd seen him at the viewing and after the funeral at her parents' house, but she hadn't had a chance to speak with him.

"Hi, Reegan," Phillip's mother, Cindy, said and gave her a hug.

"Hi, Cindy, how are you?" Reegan asked after she let go. Cindy Hastings was tall and slim with attractively styled wheat-blonde hair and soft blue eyes. She'd been the class mom throughout their grade school careers and everyone, including Reegan, had wished she was their mom at one time or another.

They chatted for a few minutes while the rest of the room got pizza and poured drinks. She'd wondered when her parents bought five pizzas who all would be here for Bernie, and now she knew. Her family, Phillip's family, and Justin's mother, Delores, were all here. After Cindy went to talk to her mother, Reegan got herself some pizza and went to snoop around.

Reegan walked into the den checking out Annie Mae's things. Dainty trinkets and worn books were scattered haphazardly on the shelves, tables, and the mantel over the fireplace. Reegan took a closer look at the framed photos on the bookshelf, smiling when she recognized Patch.

She'd just moved toward the mantel when she heard Bernie and Delores in the hall. After a few words, the door opened and closed. She tried to look like she hadn't been eavesdropping when Bernie came into the den.

"They were quite the pair," Bernie said as she came to stand next to her. Reegan couldn't help but smile when Bernie picked up the frame.

"Understatement of the year, I'm sure," Reegan said.

"Friendship," Bernie began, placing the photo back on the shelf, "should be like theirs." She pointed to their grandmothers' smiling faces. "But people are rarely who you see them to be."

"What are you trying to say? What is it you want from me, Bernie?" Reegan asked.

"I think it's more what you want from me."

"That made absolutely no sense." Reegan shook

her head and walked away only to walk right back. "I do want something."

"What?"

"Did you know our dads were friends?"

By the surprise on Bernie's face, she hadn't. "How did you find this out?"

"Patch left me a box of old photos; some were of my dad with a man who I found out later was your dad. When I asked about it, Dad wouldn't tell me. Mom said they had some big falling out, and it had something to do with your mother." Reegan wished she could take that back because Bernie looked like she'd been struck.

"What happened?"

"They wouldn't tell me. Apparently, it has to do with some story that my parents aren't forthcoming about. Phillip knows, and he said he'd tell me."

"What story?" Bernie asked hugging herself.

Reegan cleared her throat. "That's the thing I don't know. Look, you've been through a lot today. You should get some rest."

"No, I want to hear this story," she said and took a step toward the kitchen, but Reegan grabbed her sleeve.

"Whatever this is, my parents don't want to tell me. I think they're hiding something."

"All right, I'll figure out what to do."

Reegan stepped back. "Just like that?"

"Yes," Bernie said and headed into the kitchen.

Chapter Twelve

She handled it, Reegan thought, about an hour later as she waited in the den for Phillip and Bernie to join her. June had gone home with Buck and Cindy, and Phillip would bring Reegan home. She wasn't sure how she'd done it, but Bernie had maneuvered the entire thing to come out in their favor.

Reegan straightened her spine when Bernie came in the room with Phillip behind her. Phillip had two cups of coffee and handed Reegan one.

"Thanks," she said and took a sip.

"You're welcome," he said and surprised her by kissing her temple and taking a seat next to her.

"Phillip, I believe you have a story to tell us?" Bernie said from where she sat across from them on the love seat.

Phillip cleared his throat. "It all started over a hundred years ago when Bertrum Whit built the Willows."

"You're not serious?" Reegan balked.

Phillip blanched. "Yeah, I am."

"Continue," Bernie said, giving Reegan a dirty look.

"Bertrum Whit had two daughters by his first wife, Jessamine. After her death, he moved his family to Willows Bluff. While the Willows was being built, Bertrum stayed at the local inn where he fell in love

102

with the innkeeper's daughter, Clara Marshal. They were wed and had a daughter of their own. When the house was completed, they moved in and for years everything was fine."

"Phillip, everyone knows this story. After Bertrum's death, the Whits abandoned the house, never to be seen again," Reegan said.

"Yes, there was an accident, and Bertrum died, but his family remained in the house. A few years after his death, the oldest daughter, Amelia, was engaged, and her sister Minerva was rumored to be involved with a man who worked for them."

"What about the half-sister?" Bernie asked.

"Fidelia was said to have been lovely, but not much else is known about her. Tragedy struck again for the family when the man Amelia was engaged to died in an accident. At the same time, Minerva had become pregnant out of wedlock."

"What happened to the baby's father?" Reegan asked.

"No one knew. Rumors spread like wildfire about the girls and what went on in the house. Amelia and Minerva's birth mother was rumored to have been a gypsy, and that scared people. The whispers were incessant, and eventually fear overwhelmed the town."

"The Whits were run out of Willows Bluff," Reegan guessed.

"Fear overwhelmed the town," Bernie said.

Reegan stared at Phillip and whispered, "They didn't?"

"A small group of people took matters into their own hands. The Whits only had one live-in maid, so they waited until the rest of the staff had gone for the day to initiate their plan. Amelia and Minerva had somehow gotten wind of what was happening and tried to escape, but they were captured and locked in the barn."

"What about their stepmother and half-sister?" Reegan asked.

"They locked Clara inside so she couldn't help the girls, and Fidelia was hiding somewhere on the property. They had planned to hang the girls, but the barn caught fire, and it burned to the ground with the sisters inside."

Reegan covered her face with her hands. "They burned those girls alive?" This town had burned the witches at the stake. "How do I not know this story? Bernie, did you know?"

Bernie seemed to think about it for a moment. "I heard a different version years ago."

"The story you heard, did you overhear it?" Phillip said, and Reegan wondered why it mattered.

"Let's just say if I hadn't been where I was at the time, I wouldn't have known about it."

Reegan snorted. "That makes perfect sense!"

"Basically, you heard something you weren't supposed to," Phillip suggested.

"Something along those lines," Bernie said.

"You wouldn't have been told; there's a reason this was kept from you."

Reegan stared at him a moment. "When you say 'you,' do you mean her, or do you mean us?" she asked, motioning to Bernie and herself.

"The story goes that when the girls were locked in the barn, they warned that what is done cannot be undone, that the truth couldn't be seen for the lies, and no matter how long it took, the world would right the wrong committed there."

"You're saying they cursed the town?" Bernie said.

"Yes."

Reegan's mind was spinning. "They think I'm one of them! Is that it? They think I'm some reincarnated version of one of the Whit sisters back from the dead to seek vengeance."

"The whispers," Bernie said softly. "All my life there have been whispers, even before my father was murdered."

Reegan had always wanted out of this town because of the whispers. "For as long as I can remember, people looked at me and Syd like we were the devil."

"The same with Tori and me," Bernie said. "They couldn't be sure, could they? We're all about the same age."

"That's why you weren't supposed to hear the story. I didn't even know about it until I became sheriff," Phillip said.

"My parents know," Reegan said sitting up.

"The story's been passed down from generation to generation."

"So is it like a coming-of-age thing?" Reegan asked, disgusted. "Hey, it's time you knew this town burned two girls alive, and one day they may come back to reap what we sowed."

"Twisted, but accurate," Phillip said.

Reegan rubbed her temples trying to process all the peculiar things that happened in the last week. Hell, all the things that had happened to her in Willows Bluff, period. She exhaled a shaky breath and glanced between Phillip and Bernie. "Taking all I know and throwing it together in a mental collage, I'm sure of one thing."

"What's that?" Phillip asked with a frown.

Reegan sat back against the cushions. "I'm one of them."

Chapter Thirteen

"What?" Phillip asked.

"I'm one of the sisters reincarnated or whatever," Reegan said feeling…well, feeling too many things to name one in particular.

"You sound sure," Bernie said as she sipped from her mug.

"Strange things have been happening since I've been back."

"The dreams," Phillip said.

"What dreams?" Bernie asked, and though she was loath to do so, Reegan explained about the nightmares.

"It's too much of a coincidence. I saw the Willows burning, and the girl inside had my face." She stood up and began to pace. "I remember going through the woods, and I was in a lot of pain." She turned and pointed to Phillip. "You said Minerva was pregnant. What happened to the baby?"

"The baby died in childbirth that same morning."

"No wonder it hurt," Reegan said, squeezing her eyes shut at the implications. "That means I was her, right?"

"Minerva," Bernie said.

"I thought you'd think this was nonsense," Phillip admitted as he stood and stopped Reegan's pacing.

"Normally, I would, but it makes too much sense to me not to be true." She touched his face. "Think about what happened between us. Our bodies knew each other…our souls."

Phillip's eyes searched hers. "From the moment I saw you again—"

Bernie cleared her throat. "That would make Phillip the mystery suitor."

"It makes sense," Reegan said. Phillip took her hand and led her back to the couch to sit. Reegan's eyes caught Bernie's. "I fainted after I saw you," she said, and Phillip's body tensed.

"You're suggesting I'm Amelia?"

Reegan studied Bernie for a moment, then looked around the room; her eyes caught on the picture of Patch and Annie Mae. "You know you are," Reegan said and stood again pointing at the picture. "They knew!" Reegan started to pace. Her mind went back to the day Patch died and the things she said; Annie Mae had known what Patch had said. The promise. "What did Annie Mae tell you before she died?"

"I wasn't here when she died," Bernie said with a hitch in her throat reminding Reegan that it had only been this morning. It felt like years.

"But did she tell you anything? Before Patch died she said things to me. Words I thought were ludicrous at the time, but"—she shook her head—"Annie Mae asked me about it. She wanted to make sure Patch had told me."

"What did Patch say?" Phillip asked.

Reegan took her phone out of her pocket, and after a moment of searching, she hit the button. Her eyes prickled when Patch's voice came out of the speaker.

"Envious greed spills out with intent upon an afflicted mind consumed with fear. Fire and condemnation will bring forth the card of death. There is no undoing what is done, but you can trace the path that led to this. Four wanted to be three, and three would never be two—different but ever the same. You must see what was unseen, learn what was unknown, right what was wronged, or suffer the same."

Reegan stopped the recording and looked between Phillip and Bernie. "Annie Mae knew what Patch said to me."

"You said 'start at the beginning' and she wouldn't. Do you remember what she said?" Bernie asked.

"You first," Reegan said.

" 'It always starts with death unplanned. From this a new direction is birthed; a fork in the road allows two choices that will change all. Loss weeps until the earth is saturated with blood,' " Bernie said, looking up with tears in her mercury eyes. "Sound familiar?"

Reegan's hand went to her throat. "That's the beginning of what Patch said. I might not remember it verbatim, but I recognize it when I hear it."

"Those were some of the last words Gran ever spoke to me."

"How do you remember it so clearly?"

"She told me not to forget a word she said, so I wrote it down." Bernie got up from the love seat and left the room.

"Are you okay?" Reegan asked Phillip.

"I was going to ask you the same thing."

Reegan smiled at him. "Oddly, I feel relieved."

"Here," Bernie said, coming into the room and handing Reegan a small notebook. Reegan read the words, and she knew what it meant.

"You have to be Amelia." Reegan took a seat next to Phillip. "Both Patch and Annie Mae spoke of a promise they had made. They promised someone they would tell us, but who?"

"More importantly, what does it all mean?" Phillip asked. "If you two are Minerva and Amelia reincarnated, then we have to figure out—"

" 'You must see what was unseen, learn what was unknown, right what was wronged, or suffer the same,' " Bernie said.

Reegan turned that over in her head. "We have to find out what the hell happened and make it right, or we die too."

"Phillip, in the story, what was it the sisters said before they died?" Bernie asked.

"The truth couldn't be seen for the lies," he said.

"Someone was spreading lies about them."

"I think it's more like they were set up," Bernie suggested. "Someone wanted them dead, and we have to figure out why—"

"And who," Reegan interjected.

Bernie nodded. "Or suffer the same."

****

Reegan closed the door softly and tiptoed into her parents' house. After another half hour of meandering discussion, Phillip had said they needed to go. He hadn't said a word, just held her hand the entire ride home, and when he walked her to the door, he'd kissed her goodnight. Words hung between them, words Reegan wasn't prepared to contemplate, but they had hung there nonetheless.

She knew Bernie was aware of the relationship she had with Phillip, but she hadn't said a word. Reegan didn't understand Bernie—never had—but here they were stuck in this together. They agreed to meet at Patch's in the morning.

She froze when her mother called her name. Taking a breath, she headed toward the kitchen. The light above the sink was on, and her parents sitting at the table waiting for her.

With a sigh, she pulled out a chair and plopped down, setting her purse on the floor. "Waited up for me, huh?"

Her mother's face was worried, but she nodded. "We thought you might need to talk."

Reegan sighed. "Phillip told us the story—"

"Us?"

She glanced at her mother. "As in me and Bernie. There it is again." Reegan snorted. "The look you give each other that says not only do you know something, but you're silently agreeing to keep it to yourselves."

"We're just surprised, that's all," her mother said.

"I don't understand why you wanted to keep this from me."

"We're trying to protect you," her mother said softly.

"You should be trying to help me."

"Help you," her father said, but Reegan knew what he was asking.

"I'm going to say this once because I know how it sounds. Whatever this is, reincarnation, a curse, a Shakespearian 'plague on both your houses,' or whatever the hell else, I know I'm tied to it, or more accurately, I'm tied to Minerva," she said. Her mother gasped, and her father bowed his head.

"How can you be so sure?"

Reegan gave her mother's hand a squeeze. "Oh, there's no doubt in my mind."

"There it is then," her father said as he ran his hands through his hair.

"I'm sorry, Dad. I wouldn't have signed up for this, but I didn't have a choice, did I? And you know, the funny thing is, since I've been back, I've had this overwhelming feeling this place was trying to kill me. Which makes sense now that I know I'm destined to destroy it or whatever."

"Goodness, Reegan!" her mother said.

"I'd like to know what you're not telling me," Reegan said.

Her father sighed. "People thought it was Mom and Annie Mae years ago."

She thought about it a minute. "I can see that."

"That's why Bernie's mother left," her mother said as she fidgeted in her chair. "Donna knew."

"About the curse?" Reegan asked.

"Donna moved here the summer we were sixteen to stay with her uncle. We met and became fast friends. I was already dating your father, and she met Ryan through us."

Reegan looked at her father. "Why didn't you ever mention you were BFFs with Ryan Howard, Dad?"

"Let your mother tell the story," he said with something akin to defeat in his voice. She didn't want to feel sorry for him because he'd been hiding things from her, but she did anyway.

"Donna and Ryan had a rocky relationship, and I honestly didn't think they would end up together. And maybe they wouldn't have if not for the accident—"

"What accident?"

Her mother glanced across the table at her father, who sighed and said, "Alan Walters' accident."

"I'm confused," Reegan said.

"Ryan saw Alan's car go off Weatherman's bridge, and he dove in after him—"

"Off Weatherman's bridge? That's at least a thirty-foot drop into rushing waters."

"Ryan was on the swim team in high school and a trained lifeguard. He was more than capable."

"But he couldn't save Alan?" Reegan said.

"He tried, but he couldn't find the car. Between the current and the storm, there wasn't much he could do. Someone saw Ryan's abandoned truck and got the sheriff. Ryan was hypothermic when Buck found him, and Alan was gone."

"I never knew that," Reegan said. Sydney must not know either; otherwise, Reegan was sure her friend would have said something.

"Ryan always said what he did wasn't important...the boy was what mattered," her father said.

"After that night, Ryan proposed to Donna," her mother told her.

"Near-death experiences have a way of putting things in prospective." Reegan knew that first-hand.

"They were happy when they first married," her mother said. "But after she had Bernie, Donna changed. Ryan tried to get her to see a therapist, but she wouldn't."

"Do you think it could have been postpartum depression?"

"That could have been part of it, I suppose. Not long after you were born, we had everyone over for dinner."

"And?" Reegan asked when her mother stopped talking. She glanced at her father, whose eyes were fixed on the window above the sink.

"Donna went into the nursery with me to get you, and the moment she saw you, she started to scream."

Reegan sat back in her chair. "You always told me I was a pretty baby," she joked, but it didn't work to lighten the mood.

"Everyone ran into the nursery in a panic, and Donna just kept screaming. She said, 'She's not right' over and over. I'll never forget it. Once she calmed down, Ryan said she'd done the same thing with Bernie."

"That's when Mom and Annie Mae told us what happened at the Willows," her father admitted.

"And you didn't believe them? I'm not judging you," she said when they both got defensive. "I wouldn't have either."

"Ryan did," her father said, his fists clenching on the table. "Ryan did, and I didn't."

"David."

"That's why you had a falling out?"

"It's because when Donna fell apart, we didn't get involved."

"What do you mean fell apart?"

"She had a nervous breakdown and was taken to Shady Pines," her mother said as she dashed tears from her cheeks.

"You just said Donna left."

Her mother rubbed her temples. "I did. That's what we've always said so people wouldn't find out the truth, and I guess it's second nature now."

"Does Bernie know?" Considering everyone, including Reegan's parents, had said Bernie's mother walked out on them when she was just a baby, this news was huge.

Her mother nodded. "Ryan took her to visit Donna whenever he could."

Reegan sat up straighter in her chair. "Wait, is she still alive?"

"No, she died not long after Ryan's murder. Annie Mae and Patch made the arrangements, and she was buried next to him."

"Did you ever go to see her?" Reegan wanted to know.

"No," her mother said with her head bowed.

"Ryan kept saying we should find out everything we could about the Willows. I told him I wasn't going to play into some ridiculous ghost story. I refused to discuss it, and because Donna's illness was connected to that, I wouldn't speak to him about her either," her father said and cleared his throat. "Which meant we never spoke again. After Donna was committed, he stopped talking about the curse too, and he forbade Annie Mae and Patch from ever mentioning it again. At least that's what Mom said, and that was the last time she ever brought it up."

"Ryan spent every penny he made to keep Donna at Shady Pines. He and Bernie were practically destitute, but he wouldn't send Donna anywhere else," her mother said.

Reegan couldn't help the tears. She felt horrible for all of them. Her parents, Donna, and Bernie. It was Ryan Howard, however, who her heart broke for. This man who tried and failed to save not one but two people. A man who had everything taken away from him including his life.

"When you didn't become friends with Bernie, I was relieved. That more than anything proved to me they were wrong," her father said bringing Reegan from her thoughts.

"But then I got close to Sydney, and people talked anyway."

"Not everyone knows the truth about what happened at the Willows. There are several different stories."

"I'd never heard about a curse."

"You were never interested in the Willows or its folklore, which again relieved me. Besides, most of my generation thought it was some plot to condemn individuality and inspire conformity. Most not only didn't believe the story, but they resented it," her father said.

Reegan smirked. "That's lucky."

"The older generations are different, and the closer you and Sydney were, the more they talked."

"Then there's Bernadette and Tori to consider," her mother said.

"More like sisters than Syd and I were," Reegan said.

"With Bernadette's reputation and Tori's—I don't know—allure, they were the better choice."

"After Ryan was murdered, there wasn't much doubt among those who believed in the old story. You were in the clear, and then when you had your accident"—her father shrugged his shoulders—"no one questioned that you couldn't be involved."

"Shows what they know." Reegan snorted. "Not

only am I involved in this *Crucible*-esque reproduction, but I'm one of the leads!"

Chapter Fourteen

Reegan sipped her coffee and eyed Bernie over the rim of her cup. She'd retold what she'd learned from her parents last night and waited while Bernie processed the information. They had both shown up at Patch's almost identical in their choice of jeans, sweaters, and boots, which made Reegan uneasy.

"What?" Bernie asked.

"Huh?"

"You're staring at me."

"Oh, sorry," Reegan said with a shrug. "I was just thinking that you aged well." Which, considering Reegan's almost overwhelming need to go get her camera, was putting it mildly.

"Thanks…I think."

"No," Reegan said rolling her eyes. "What I mean is that you're—"

"I get it, Reegan," Bernie said as a blush swept up her cheeks.

"Okay," she said. "There are still about ten boxes to go through." They'd decided finding out what the rest of the boxes contained was the best place to start.

Bernie nodded. "Let's get started."

"I don't understand," Reegan said after they'd gone through all but the last box.

"These are obviously things she wanted you to have."

Reegan shook her head. "Don't get me wrong, I love these old Christmas decorations, but I guess I was just hoping for more."

"There's still one left," Bernie said.

Reegan paused; this was it, the last box.

"What?"

"I promised Annie Mae I would stay until I'd opened all the boxes. This will fulfill that promise." The way Bernie stared at her made her uncomfortable.

"Then you'll be going back to the city?"

"Do I have a choice?" Do I? Reegan wondered.

"I don't know."

"Thanks, that's helpful."

Bernie crossed her arms over her chest. "What would you like me to say?"

"I don't know…your honest opinion."

"I, *honestly,* don't think you want my thoughts on the matter."

"Never mind. I don't even know why I asked." Reegan was about to open the box when Bernie sighed.

"Phillip will never leave Willows Bluff," Bernie said, and Reegan's eyes flew to the other woman's.

"What does that have to do with anything?" Reegan asked, but her heart squeezed in her chest.

"From what I've seen, I think it has to do with everything…You love him."

Reegan snorted.

"Deny it if you want, Reegan. I can see it in your eyes when you look at him, feel it in the room when you're together, and he loves you back."

Reegan inhaled sharply as her mind flew to Phillip and what they'd shared in the brief time they'd been together. Moments that filled a void she hadn't known existed. He meant more to her than anyone…how was that possible? "Do you think what I feel is real?" she asked.

"I thought about that. It's impossible to know for certain, but I believe some souls are meant to be together."

Reegan mulled that over. "You're saying…what exactly are you saying?"

"You're soul mates."

"Soul mates," Reegan parroted.

"You're destined to be with Phillip. His soul and your soul, after being torn apart in another time, have recognized each other again."

"Destiny?"

"You're fated to be together."

"If you believe in those things," Reegan muttered.

Bernie pursed her lips. "You believe you're Minerva reincarnated, but Phillip being your soul mate is a bit of a stretch?"

Reegan couldn't help but smile. "When you put it like that, I guess you have a point." She shook her head trying to remember why they were talking about it in the first place. "Wait, so if Phillip and I are meant to be, and he won't ever leave Willows Bluff…"

"Then if you want to be with him, you won't either. But there's always a choice, Reegan."

Reegan stilled while those thoughts choked her. She couldn't stay here, she thought, and busied herself with opening the box. She tilted forward to stare into the box; then her eyes shot up to Bernie. "What the…"

"What is it?" Bernie asked and came to stand beside her.

Reegan's heart jumped to her throat. "How?" she

wondered aloud as she unconsciously reached over and grabbed Bernie's hand.

Reegan's mind seized. *She was no longer looking at Bernie in Patch's parlor but rather in a dark room. Though the other woman's face was somewhat distorted, Reegan would know Bernie's eyes anywhere, and the woman whose face now boasted them reached out with one hand and cupped her cheek. The touch held such love it was painful, and Reegan closed her eyes.*

"Reegan?"

Reegan's eyes flew open, she sucked in a breath, and let go of Bernie's hand.

"Are you all right?"

Reegan stared at Bernie. "Did you see it?"

"What did *you* see?"

Reegan let out a shaky breath. "When I touched you; I saw you but…but not you."

"You saw Amelia?"

"It must have been. We were in a dark room, and she touched my face," Reegan whispered as tears filled her eyes. "It…it hurt."

"Just breathe," Bernie said and led Reegan to the kitchen. She sat where Bernie steered her and waited until a cup of tea was plunked down in front of her. "Drink it."

Reegan took a sip and let the warmth melt away the chill. "It was so real," she said and tried to explain what she'd seen.

"I believe you," Bernie said. They both jumped when Bernie's phone rang. "I have to take this."

Reegan nodded and listened to Bernie's side of the conversation.

"Good morning…yes, this is she. What? Did you call her parents? No, I'll be there. No, I'm leaving right now. Thank you."

Bernie came back in the kitchen, her face flushed.

"You have to go?"

"It can't be helped," Bernie said, gathering her belongings.

Reegan walked her to the front door. "It's Tori, isn't it?" she asked as they went out to the porch.

Bernie turned at the bottom of the stairs to look at Reegan. "Yes, she's having an episode, and they can't reach her parents."

Reegan nodded.

"Will you be all right?" Bernie asked.

"Yeah," she said, then they both looked up when the sheriff's SUV pulled into the driveway.

Bernie bit her lip after she'd motioned for Phillip not to block her in. "You'll be fine," Bernie said and turned to walk to her vehicle.

Reegan went inside while Phillip and Bernie exchanged a few words. Going back into the parlor, she returned to the last box she'd opened. She took out the bag and studied it.

"Bernie said you had a vision," Phillip said coming into the room.

He was the vision, Reegan thought, in his uniform with wind tossed hair and that want-to-be grin hitching up the corners of his mouth. But she wouldn't tell him that.

"Vision," she said with feigned disdain. "What am I? Clairvoyant?"

"That's what happens, Reegan, whether you admit it or not." He stepped closer to her. Goosebumps rose on her arms when he brushed his lips against hers.

She stared into his hazel eyes after he'd pulled away. They watched one another as those words once again hung there unspoken. Soul mates, Bernie had said, and standing here with him, she knew it was true. That didn't mean she had to like it.

"Are you pouting?"

"What?" Reegan asked, heat sweeping up her face.

Phillip didn't control his laugh. "You are! You're pouting."

"Oh, whatever," she said but couldn't help the silly grin that took over her mouth.

"What happened?" he asked, and Reegan launched into describing what she'd seen when she touched Bernie.

"Interesting."

"That's an understatement. Oh, and you won't believe what my parents told me last night."

"I knew about Ryan Howard trying to save Alan Walters," Phillip said once she'd filled him in. "Dad told me, but I wasn't aware of Bernie's mother."

"It breaks my heart for them." Reegan stared at her hands, only then remembering what was in them. She opened the bag and looked inside. "Phillip!"

"What? What is it?"

"It's my old knapsack," she whispered.

"And Patch kept it? That's nice."

"No, you don't understand. I had this with me when I almost drowned. I had to let it go in order to survive. I lost it at the bottom of the sea."

"Then how did it get here?"

"I don't know," she said, and Phillip followed her into the kitchen. Reegan emptied the contents of the bag onto the island. Her camera was there and three plastic film containers.

"Is it ruined? It should be ruined, right?"

"It should be." Reegan nodded. She studied the camera; it had been an extension of her body when she was growing up. A third eye, she thought, a second sight.

"There's still film in here," Phillip said, and Reegan set down the camera to examine a plastic container.

"The plastic must have protected it." She looked up at him. "But that doesn't make sense." A thought struck her, and she unzipped the inside pocket of the knapsack. Her bus ticket was still there; she held it up to Phillip. "This is barely faded. There's no way it could have been in the water long."

"Which means that someone went back to get it."

"The person who rescued me. I know," she began when he drew back. "No one believed me, but I didn't imagine it. They saved me, went back for the bag, and took it to Patch. This is proof!"

"Why would someone do that?"

Remembering that night was easy. She'd relived the entire day the night before in her dream, so it was fresh in her mind. "They knew."

"Knew what?"

"About the curse."

Phillip stared at her. "You think Patch had someone following you?"

Patch was crazy enough to have done something like that. No question. She looked at Phillip and took a breath. "There's something I never told anyone about that night. My rescuer said something to me."

"You never told anyone?"

"Everyone thought I'd hallucinated it, so what was said to me would be a hallucination too."

"Was it a man or woman?"

Reegan shook her head. "I was disoriented; all I could make out was a scar on their wrist. What is important is that they told me it would do me well to never come back." Those words had altered the course of her life.

"If they knew about the curse, that would explain why they said it."

"I gave myself two options after graduation. I could go to school with Sydney or travel the country taking pictures."

"I remember you saying that's what you were going to do."

"Yes, but then I almost died. All I could think was that by losing this ticket and being told never to come back, the powers that be wanted me to go with Sydney. And that's what I did."

"You never told Sydney this?"

"No, only you." And it felt good confiding in him.

"Have you told Sydney what's happening now?"

Reegan snorted. "Sydney would have *me* committed." She shook her head. "No, telling her isn't a good idea."

"I agree. The fewer people who know the better," Phillip said with a nod.

Something he said struck a chord in Reegan's memory. "When I saw Annie Mae in the hospital, she said I shouldn't tell anyone unless they know what I know, learn what I've learned, or see what I've seen. She said it was better that way."

"I think we need to work under the assumption the people connected to this know, or at the very least are aware, that there's something going on."

"Like the person who rescued me," Reegan said.

"Yes," Phillip said and picked up her old camera. "What I want to know is what was so important about this bag that they went back for it."

"You're right! I mean, it was important to me personally, but that wouldn't explain why someone went back into the water to get it and take it to Patch."

"Exactly! What's on this film?"

Reegan thought about it. "Pictures I took at the Willows the day of the accident."

"That could be handy considering—"

"Considering what?"

"They tore it down," Phillip said.

And even though Reegan remembered the city had planned to do it the same summer as the accident, hearing the news was like a punch in the solar plexus. She hadn't even thought to ask if it was still there. She'd just assumed. "I guess we can't return to the scene of the crime then."

"We can go back, but there isn't much to see."

"I need to get these pictures developed. Usually I do it myself, but since they may be damaged, I need to take them to someone else."

"All we have is the photo shop at the drugstore."

"No, I have a friend who specializes in film restoration. If this is damaged, he's our best chance of saving what we can."

"You're leaving," Phillip said, and though his tone was soft and gentle, his words reached out to choke her.

"Richard has a workspace four blocks from my

apartment. But I'll come back," she said, reaching out to give his arm a reassuring squeeze.

"For how long?" he asked, stepping out of her reach. "We're two consenting adults, and you don't owe me anything, Reegan—"

"But…"

"But I think you know."

"That's kind of the point, Phillip. I don't know!" She spoke a bit louder than she'd intended to, and though it was gone in a second, she'd seen something akin to hurt in his eyes.

"I guess the time away will help you figure it out," Phillip said and headed to the front of the house.

"Phillip," she said.

He turned around before he opened the front door. His eyes seemed to be searching hers. "The circumstances of our relationship are far from ordinary, but I can accept that. I know how I feel when I'm with you, Reegan. How you make me feel."

"It's not that simple."

"Isn't it?"

"I have a life outside this town!"

"But no roots, Reegan. My life *is* rooted here. I have a daughter and people who depend on me."

"I have people too," she argued.

"You mean Sydney? She couldn't even bother to stay for your grandmother's funeral—"

"I told her to go!"

"Wake up, Reegan. You built your life around hers."

"That's ridiculous. You don't know me or Sydney."

Phillip ran his hands through his hair and opened

the door. "You're wrong, I do know you," he said, turning on the steps to stare at her. "I understand you on a level that I can't even wrap my head around. Whatever this is between us, you belong here. I know your soul, Reegan, and if you'd let yourself, you'd know mine."

The veil of tears in her eyes couldn't hide the fact he was walking away from her.

Chapter Fifteen

Reegan swung her legs as Richard Beck prattled on about his latest pictorial endeavor. She'd met Richard at a seminar he'd held when she was taking college classes; they'd been friends ever since. He was in his fifties and attractive with his long gray hair pulled back in a ponytail. He had kind brown eyes, an engaging smile, and was usually quite entertaining, but her thoughts were scattered.

After Phillip had left yesterday, she'd gone straight to her parents' house, packed her things, called her mom, and left. She'd taken the rental back to the dealer, and the salesman had dropped her off at her apartment. Reegan had ordered dinner from her favorite take-out place and talked to Sydney on the phone for over two hours. She hadn't told Sydney anything about the curse or the camera, but she'd told her the truth about her feelings for Phillip.

"It's good you came home, Reegan. You need to clear your head," Sydney had said. And Reegan had to agree with her. She needed to step back and take stock.

"What?" Reegan asked when she realized Richard had been asking her a question.

"I asked where you are today, Reegan? Certainly not here," Richard said with a sympathetic smile.

She sighed. "I'm sorry, Richard. You're right; my mind's somewhere else." More like on someone else.

She couldn't stop thinking about Phillip and the way he'd looked when he walked away from her.

"Ah, relationship trouble." Richard patted her shoulder.

"Yeah," she said and huffed. "Thanks, Richard."

"I've been there myself. Now, you've come to me at the most opportune time!" he said with a clap of his hands. "I don't have anything pressing, so I'll be able to start working on your project right away."

"That's great!" Better than she expected.

"But given what you've told me about the damage these things sustained, this will take some time and delicate handling. My normal rates, of course."

"No problem, Richard. I'm just happy you're able to do it."

He smiled and poured a cup of coffee for each of them. "Now," he began after he handed her a cup, "tell me all about this man who's got you distracted."

"It's complicated."

"Isn't it always?"

Reegan snorted.

"Start at the beginning."

Reegan studied Richard's face for a moment and took a breath. Being careful not to divulge anything about the curse, she told him everything she could about her feelings for Phillip.

"What's the problem then?" he asked once she'd finished.

"He still lives in the town where we grew up. He's rooted there," she said remembering the words Phillip used.

Richard nodded. "And you're here."

"Normally, that would be the end of it for me—"

"But not this time?"

She shook her head. "No, it's different with Phillip." Reegan searched for the words to explain it, and she remembered. "I can see him without looking through my lens. I don't need to capture it on film to see who he is or what he means to me."

Richard stared at her, then gave her a sad smile, and said, "I'll miss you."

****

Reegan sat on her couch replaying what Richard said. She would have asked him to explain himself further, but he'd gotten a phone call and told her he'd get in touch when the work was done. Whether he knew it or not, Richard had just given her what she couldn't give herself...permission to leave.

She rubbed her arms to ward off the chill and admitted to herself that she had run to the safety of her apartment and the secure life she had created far away from Willows Bluff. Reegan had run not only from the curse but also from Phillip. She didn't need her camera to see him, and it scared the shit out of her; she could see his soul and somehow he could see hers.

The banging on the door made Reegan jump. "Coming," she called out. She checked the peephole and opened the door in a rush.

"I need you to come back," Phillip said, and Reegan squeaked when he lifted her into his arms and kicked the door shut.

Reegan clung to him as he kissed her. He didn't break the connection until he had set her on the kitchen table, and she stared into his stormy hazel eyes.

"I'm in love with you, Reegan."

She was torn between the building pleasure in her

body and the pure joy that shot to her heart. "I feel the same," she said.

"Say it," he said, bending to kiss her for a moment. "Say it."

Reegan searched his eyes. She knew he wasn't asking for the words but the promise made by saying them. Knowing there was no going back, that she would be giving up the life she created, and unable to stop herself from wanting anything else, she said, "I love you, Phillip. Heart and soul."

"Forever," Phillip whispered.

Tears filled her eyes. She remembered this moment, they'd been here before...in another life. "For always."

He leaned in, kissing the tears from her cheeks, and then he latched his mouth onto hers. Reegan wrapped her arms around his head while he held her in an almost crushing embrace. Phillip made love to her right there on the kitchen table, seeming desperate in his need to consummate their connection.

She came almost simultaneously with him. Phillip kissed her forehead and held her, skin against skin, as they both tried to catch their breath. Reegan could feel his heart, in tune with hers, beating against his chest.

He was addicting, Reegan thought, then gasped when someone cleared their throat. She peeked around Phillip to see Sydney standing in her kitchen with a bag of take-out hanging off the tips of her fingers.

"I wondered why you didn't answer the door when I knocked," Sydney said.

Phillip tensed, but he smiled down at her and sighed. "If you could give us a couple of minutes, Sydney, I'd appreciate it."

"By all means, don't be shy on my account—"

"Syd, please," Reegan begged.

"I'll wait in the other room."

Reegan shifted, but Phillip stopped her. "You're coming back with me," he said.

She swallowed. When her eyes drifted toward the door, Phillip grasped her chin so she could only look at him.

"You're coming home with me. Coming home *to* me, to our past, and our future."

She searched his eyes and saw the desperation. "I'll come home."

****

"I can't believe this," Sydney said after Reegan explained she was leaving.

"Syd, I told you last night I have a deep connection with Phillip," Reegan said from the couch as Sydney loomed over her.

"More like Phillip has a deep connection *in* you!"

"Sydney!" She was mortified Sydney had seen them making love, but she was going to pretend *that* hadn't happened.

"You've obviously been brainwashed."

Reegan shook her head. "I'm following my heart."

"Your heart? What kind of answer is that?"

"I know how this seems, Syd. I do, trust me. But I *love* Phillip, and if moving back to Willows Bluff is the only way I can be with him, then that's what I'm going to do."

"What the hell is wrong with you?" Sydney asked, stepping up to the couch and bending down to tower over Reegan.

"What's wrong with *you*, Sydney?" She stood up

making Sydney step back. "I'm thirty years old. I can make my own decisions—"

"Clearly you're incapable because this is ludicrous!"

"I love him," Reegan said around the lump in her throat.

"You don't *do* love, Reegan. You foray into emotion in order to capture the carnage on film."

"You're right; that's how I've always been in relationships, watching through my camera's lens instead of living it. That's how I know this is different! I love him, and I'm going back to Willows Bluff."

"You know nothing good can come from being in that damn town!" Sydney took a breath and straightened her suit jacket. "I'm asking you not to do this."

Reegan swallowed. "I've made up my mind."

"I refuse to watch you lose everything you've worked so hard for."

"Sydney—"

"No, if you want to move back to that godforsaken place, that's your decision, but I won't be party to it," Sydney said as she headed toward the door.

"What are you saying?"

"Good-bye, Reegan," she said and closed the door behind her.

Reegan sat back down, held her face in her hands, and did the only thing that seemed right at the time; she wept.

Chapter Sixteen

One day, Reegan sighed, as she looked around her apartment. It had only taken them one day to pack up her things. What did that say about me? she wondered.

She had four months left on her apartment's one-year lease, but her landlord had let her out of the agreement when she'd told him she'd leave most of her furniture behind. Phillip's home was fully furnished, and that's where she'd be living, with Phillip and June.

"What if June doesn't like the idea?" she'd asked Phillip yesterday morning when he told her he wanted her to move in with him.

He'd smiled and led her to the window. Pulling back the curtain, she saw the U-Haul truck parked by the street. "I told Junebug how I feel, and she said not to come back without you."

Reegan smiled, remembering how wonderful it had made her feel knowing June wanted her to be a part of their lives. Phillip told her June said she'd known from the moment she'd met Reegan in the coffee shop that she wanted her to be a part of their family.

So they'd rallied and packed all day yesterday. She made arrangements with the electric, water, cable, and phone companies to put an end date to her services. After speaking with a few colleagues and gallery owners, there wasn't anyone else she needed to get in touch with. Sydney had been her only close friend, and

Sydney wasn't taking her calls.

"Are you ready?" Phillip asked from the doorway. They'd already loaded up the truck; all she had to do was lock the door and go.

"As I'll ever be," she said with a slight smile and moved to stand next to him.

"I know this is hard, Reegan. I appreciate what you're giving up."

"The truth is I can work anywhere, Phillip. Maybe you were right that I built my life around Sydney."

He ducked his head. "I didn't mean to hurt your feelings."

She laughed. "We're going to hurt each other's feelings, Phillip. You will no doubt piss me off, and I'm absolutely positive that I'll piss you off. But I'm not worried about it."

"You're not?" he asked as he brushed a loose strand of hair from her face.

"No, because after we beat the hell out of this curse, everything else will seem trivial," she said, and he laughed.

****

Reegan sat on her bed and stared out the sliding glass doors leading to a private balcony where the snow was falling. She was in her new bedroom or, more accurately, the bedroom she would be sharing with Phillip. It would be their room, he'd said, and their home.

The house was a two-story wet dream. With the help of an architect he'd played ball with in college, Phillip had designed every aspect of the house. It was wood and rock and fluidity, reminding Reegan of the mountains and the bluff, the willows and sea. She'd been enchanted the moment she laid eyes on it.

Buck had been waiting on the porch with June when they pulled up. The girl had run down the driveway and embraced Reegan the second she'd seen her. She'd held her for the longest time, and Reegan didn't think she'd ever felt anything so precious. Any doubts she'd had fell to the wayside in that moment.

They'd unloaded the U-Haul, putting all her boxes in the garage for the night. Phillip said they could unpack tomorrow, but he wanted her to relax this evening and get accustomed to the house. June gave her the grand tour and showed her where everything was, while Phillip talked to his father in the kitchen. She hadn't told her parents yet. That'll be interesting, she thought now as she shifted on the bed.

Phillip had told her to try to take a nap before dinner, but she couldn't sleep. There was too much to think about. With a sigh, she got up and headed into the kitchen where Buck was making iced tea.

"Want some?" he asked, indicating the pitcher.

"Sure," she said and got a glass after he pointed her to the appropriate cabinet. He was wearing a flannel shirt and jeans just like his son, and it made her smile to herself. Never in her life would she have imagined this.

"How do you like the house?" Buck asked after she'd taken a sip of tea.

"It's fantastic. Where are Phillip and June?" she asked when she didn't hear them.

"They went to get dinner and pick up Cindy."

"Oh." Reegan could feel the heat creep up her neck. Bad enough she had to face Buck alone, but Phillip's mother too? Could this get any worse?

"Your parents are on their way," he said, and

Reegan winced. Oh, yeah, that's worse.

"Wonderful," she said.

Buck chuckled. "You'll be fine."

"You think so?"

Buck shrugged. "These are not normal circumstances, Reegan. Allowances are made."

She frowned. "Explain."

"You know what I mean."

"What I *know* is that I don't understand any of this, Buck. I may be an artist, but my feet have been glued to reality for a long time. What I can't get my head around isn't the idea I'm part of this curse, but the fact that I believe it…emphathically."

Reegan held up her finger when Buck moved to speak. "I've been reacquainted with Phillip for not even two weeks, I've given up my life to be with him, and it terrifies me because *that* doesn't scare me—not one bit. He is quite simply the air I breathe. What frightens me is what happens if we don't figure this out," she said lowering her voice and looking up at Buck.

"What happens?" Buck asked.

"I suffocate," she said, holding her throat.

"Then I guess we need to figure this out," said the voice behind her.

Reegan whipped around to see her parents standing there. Isn't this mortifying? she thought and with a curt nod, walked as fast as she could without actually running into her bedroom. She shut the door and leaned against it for a moment before going into the bathroom.

The door opened, but she kept her eyes closed when she turned on the faucet and washed her face. After one more splash of water, a towel was held against her arm. She took it, patted her face dry, and opened her eyes.

Seeing Phillip there watching her with concern and love made her eyes fill again. And then she was safe in his arms, his warmth chasing the chill away.

"You know, I've cried more in the last two weeks than I have in my entire life," she said into his shirt.

Phillip laughed. "Reegan, you don't have to apologize to me. I understand."

"That makes one of us," she said, but she felt better. She sucked in a breath when he lifted her up onto the countertop and kissed her. It was soft, and their lips lingered for a while until he stepped back.

"We have company," he explained, and she couldn't help grinning at him. "Our parents are waiting for us."

She groaned.

One side of his mouth lifted. "Dad filled me in on what upset you. Don't, Reegan," he said when she made a move to get away.

"It's embarrassing." She covered her face with her hands.

"Maybe, but your candor spoke volumes to my dad and your parents."

"That will help when I try to explain what's going on here."

"You don't have to explain anything."

She took his offered hand and got down from the counter. "Of course I do!"

He shook his head. "You've already told them everything they needed to hear."

****

She could barely hear her name being called over the screaming in her head.

"Reegan? God in heaven, Reegan, wake up!"

She continued to sob as she opened her eyes; she reached out, her hands trembling, until she found Phillip's flesh.

"It was a dream," Phillip said trying to soothe her. "It was just a dream."

"You know it's more than that," she cried out, and he captured her in his arms.

"Reegan, please," Phillip said, and the thickness of his voice calmed her down enough to lift her head from his shoulder. The fading moonlight caught the tears that pooled in his eyes. "Please."

"I saw…" She couldn't get the words out. They both jumped at the pounding on the door.

"Our parents," Phillip said. He'd asked everyone to stay over because he hadn't wanted anyone to chance driving on black ice. Both her parents and his had settled into the guest rooms.

"Don't go," she whispered when he would have left her.

The banging continued, and their fathers argued on the other side of the door.

"I have to go talk to them," he said.

She wrapped her arms around herself and squinted when Phillip turned on the lamp. Reegan rocked herself as he went to the door. She'd never had a nightmare like that. Never.

Phillip opened the door, and the other two men barged in. They stopped to stare at her.

"Reegan?" Her father's voice was shaken.

Tears rolled down her cheeks, and she felt depleted. Her eyes circled the men until they landed on Phillip. "I saw them kill you," she whispered.

Chapter Seventeen

Reegan sat at the kitchen table holding her coffee cup in both hands and staring off into space while everyone else around the table stared at her. She'd retold the events of her nightmare knowing she would never get the images out of her head. The man, who was Phillip but not Phillip, dangling from a tree limb.

She wanted to go into the woods, find that tree, and cut it down.

"You said you've never dreamed of this before?" Buck asked.

"No, this is a first for me."

"Other than the man's face—"

"It was Phillip," she told her father. She glanced at Phillip, who appeared calm as he sipped his coffee. How did he do that?

Her father cleared his throat. "Other than Phillip, could you see anyone else?"

"There were three people involved in his hanging, a man and two women, but I couldn't see their faces. And the boy—"

"The one who came up behind you? You're sure he was a boy?" Buck asked.

Reegan nodded. "He was young, and I didn't see his face, but he spoke with an accent. If he hadn't covered my mouth to mask my screaming, they would have found me. He saved me—or her—I guess."

"You said you were pregnant?" Cindy asked.

Reegan held her hand out a good twelve inches from her stomach. "I was out to here," she said. "I felt a horrible cramp and I..." She paused, feeling her face turn pink. "I think I peed."

The men all seemed rather interested in the stain on the kitchen table.

"Your water broke," her mother said.

"If I was in labor, that would explain the pain." Reegan tried to keep herself away from the knowledge that the baby had died that day too.

Phillip reached out to take her hand.

"If the dream is Minerva's memory, then she witnessed her fiancé being hanged, and she went into labor. Which means the same day she saw his murder, her baby dies, and she's burned alive," Reegan said and squeezed Phillip's hand. "We have to find answers. The idea of suffering the same—"

"We will," Phillip said and the rest of the table agreed.

"Patch always said that to solve any problem, you need to start at the beginning."

The entire table turned when June came into the room in her pj's. Her long wheat-colored hair was in a braid, and her feet were in pink bunny slippers. Reegan's heart squeezed at the sight of this child who had opened her home and her heart for her. If anything happened to her...

Reegan's eyes met Buck's. "I think June should stay with you for a while."

"I can help," June said.

"I won't risk your life too," Reegan said, her free hand inadvertently going to her stomach.

142

"Dad?" June said, turning to Phillip.

"She has a point, Junebug. There's so much on the line as it is. I won't put you at risk," Phillip said.

"I think staying with us is a good idea for the time being; at least until you have a better understanding of what's going on," Cindy said.

"What do you think, Buck?" Reegan asked.

"I agree with Cindy. June should stay with us—"

"But Grandpa!"

"The matter's settled," Phillip said.

"Fine," June said sulking.

Reegan stood and took June's hands. "I want you here with us, June, but more than that, I want you safe."

June nodded. "I get it."

"But you don't have to like it," Reegan said and was rewarded with a smile. "And you're right, Patch always said to start at the beginning."

June headed to the fridge. "I think that's where you should start. But you'll need help."

"June," Reegan began, but June shook her head.

"I think I would be great at figuring this out, but I meant Bernie," June said as she poured a glass of orange juice.

"Bernie?"

"Yeah, she's part of this too, right?"

"Maybe we should give Bernie a day or two. She just buried Annie Mae yesterday," Reegan's father said.

Guilt swamped her. She'd been so caught up in her own issues she'd forgotten to pay her last respects to Annie Mae.

"Let's take a break, and I'll start making breakfast," Cindy suggested, and Reegan's mom jumped up to help.

Reegan followed Phillip when he headed toward their bedroom. "I feel horrible for forgetting about Annie Mae," she whispered.

Phillip pulled her into their room and shut the door. "Bernie doesn't hold a grudge, Reegan. And if Annie Mae were alive, she would've read me the riot act if I hadn't gone to get you. I told Bernie when I left that we wouldn't be able to make it to the funeral, and she understood."

"I still feel like an ass," she said and rubbed her arms. A thought struck her. "Do you have to go to work today?" As disgusted with herself as it made her, she didn't think she could handle him leaving, not today.

"No, I took some time off to get you settled, and I can take more if I need to. My deputies are capable when I let them be. Now, I'll call Bernie and see if she wants to join us for breakfast."

"But my dad said we should give her time," Reegan reminded him.

"And normally I'd agree with him, but June's right, Bernie's a part of this, and she should know what's going on. Besides, it will take her mind off Annie Mae."

Reegan sighed and told Phillip to make the call. If she understood anything, it was needing to focus on something other than what if's.

****

Reegan was in the den admiring some of the paintings in Phillip's home. She had to admit he had good taste. Everything flowed. He'd stuck with a traditional vibe and a nature-inspired color palette. The picture she was studying was an oil-based forest scene.

"I like that painting."

Reegan peeked over her shoulder to see Bernie coming up behind her. Phillip had been right about the other woman wanting to get her mind off Annie Mae. She'd arrived in time to eat breakfast with them.

Bernie had been seemingly unaffected when they told her about the latest nightmare, but for a moment, Reegan had seen something in those silver orbs. Something resembling sorrow. She didn't want Bernadette Howard's pity; she wanted her help.

After breakfast, they had openly discussed what they knew. Reegan had rehashed all of the nightmares she'd had since returning to Willows Bluff, and they'd tried to pick them apart. But Reegan needed a break from it.

"I know this is difficult for you," Bernie said, reminding Reegan that she hadn't responded to Bernie's comment.

She rubbed her hands over her face. "I think I've done a damn fine job handling the nightmares…but last night was the most painful thing I've had to experience. Seeing him murdered"—she shook her head—"I can't even begin to explain how that felt."

"You don't have to explain," Bernie said, and Reegan turned around to stare at her. "I understand."

Reegan squeezed her eyes shut. How could she forget Bernie's father had been brutally murdered? "I'm sorry."

Bernie shrugged. "It's easy to forget when the pain isn't your own. I don't blame you for it, Reegan. You're human."

She stared at her. How could she be so blasé about it? Reegan wondered.

"I almost bought that painting, but Phillip outbid

me."

"Really?" she asked as Bernie came to stand beside her.

"Yes, something about the lushness of the leaves on the trees gets me. The brush strokes are intense."

"That's what I was thinking. Where did he get this, anyway?"

"From Ezra Kelly's gallery. Ezra is fond of estate sales, and he had a showing of all the art and antiquities he'd collected over the course of two years. He called it *Art from the Attic*. It was beautifully done. I bought several pieces myself."

Hearing Ezra's name filled her heart. "I'd love to see him."

"He got back in town a few days ago."

"Yeah, I went to the gallery and ran into Adam Desmond," Reegan said.

"What's wrong?"

Reegan glanced at her. "What?"

Bernie cocked her head to the side. "When you said Adam's name, you tensed."

"I did? I guess it's because he kind of gave me the creeps," she admitted. The photos she'd seen of him had been dark, and he'd been an ass.

"Interesting," Bernie said.

"Why?"

"He makes me uncomfortable too."

Reegan nodded. How times have changed, she thought, shaking her head and smiling when her mom came into the room. She turned back to the painting and sucked in a breath. "Oh, my God!"

"What?" her mother and Bernie said at once.

"Adam's painting," she said feeling nauseous.

"Adam was watching the gallery for Ezra, and he had his work displayed. One of the canvases depicted a fire, and I swear it was as if something or someone was burning." Her hand had gone out unconsciously to grab Bernie, and Bernie dodged it.

She stared at Bernie. There was a hitch in the other woman's breathing. She made to reach out again, and again Bernie moved.

"Reegan, what on earth are you doing?" her mother asked, and it distracted Bernie long enough for Reegan to grab her hand.

They simultaneously gasped. Reegan's mind seized…*she was in a room, surrounded by small tin tubes of paint. There was a canvas on an easel. She stood with a paint brush in her hand, while the woman with Bernie's eyes smiled and gave her a half hug.*

"It's lovely, Minni," she whispered. Reegan's heart pitched, and she was once again in the den.

"What was that?" her mother asked.

Reegan turned to glare at Bernie. "You do see it!"

Bernie's face was pale as she put distance between them. "I'd appreciate you not doing that."

"You lied to me," Reegan accused.

"What are you two talking about?" her mother asked again but was ignored.

"I don't make a habit of lying, Reegan. I didn't *see* what you saw last time."

"Then what? You didn't want me to touch you because you knew what might happen, admit it."

"You're right I wanted to avoid it. But not because I saw it last time," Bernie said with a shake of her head. "I could *feel* the pain. And I didn't want to experience it again. It wasn't a physical thing. It was the pain of loss, of sorrow, of love you'll never have again. Knowing you're about to die and that touch would be the last. It was good-bye. That's what I felt at Patch's house."

Reegan crossed her arms over her chest. That was cruelly accurate. She hadn't been able to explain it, but Bernie had. "And today?"

Bernie's stance matched her own. "Today I saw it. I spoke words that weren't mine."

"This painting," Reegan said addressing her mother, "was painted by Minerva Whit."

Her mother's eyes widened. "Oh, my."

"That explains why Phillip and I were so drawn to it," Bernie said.

Reegan sighed. "I'd be interested to know where Ezra got this painting."

Bernie nodded. "I think we should pay him a visit."

"Bernie, your phone's going off," Reegan's dad hollered from the kitchen.

"Coming," Bernie said and left the room.

Her mother moved to stand beside her and rubbed her back. "There's something I want to tell you," she whispered.

Reegan's stomach did a flip. "Okay."

"Remember I told you Donna came to stay with an uncle?"

"Yeah," she said wearily.

"She lived with her father's brother, Mr. Marsh, until he died right after we graduated high school. Donna told me she had another uncle who lived in town. He was her mother's brother, who she'd never met because of some massive falling out they'd had when her mother married her father. Donna didn't think he even knew about her." Her mother leaned in and whispered, "Her mother's maiden name was Kelly."

"As in Ezra Kelly? You're not serious!"

Her mother nodded and glanced at the doorway before she continued. "I don't know if Bernie knows. Donna told me in secret."

"Does Ezra know?" She'd loved and respected Ezra Kelly for as long as she could remember. When she was little, she'd wished he was her grandpa.

"I don't think so."

"I feel like we're in an episode of *The Twilight Zone*," she began, shaking her head. "Willows Bluff is some twisted soap opera, and we're trapped inside it."

Her mother tried not to laugh, and they both turned when Bernie came back in the room with Phillip right behind her.

"You'll have to go to Ezra's without me," Bernie said.

"What? Why?" Reegan asked.

"The alarm company just called—"

"Someone tried to break into Bernie's house," Phillip said.

Reegan looked at her mother. "I rest my case."

Chapter Eighteen

Her fingers drummed the table as she waited for Phillip to come back for her. After much debate, they had decided that he needed to go with Bernie to make sure everything was safe at her house. Reegan couldn't explain it and would never admit it, but she had an almost overwhelming need to make sure Bernie was safe. Then again, she also had a deep-seated feeling that Bernie was hiding something from her; dishonesty was something Reegan had never reacted well toward.

That being the case, she had had Phillip drop her off on Main Street, under the guise of seeing Ezra alone, to get some distance from the other woman. She had bought a cup of coffee first, then gone to Ezra's only to find a sign saying he would be out for the rest of the day. And wasn't that typical.

She had come back to Justin's to get out of the cold and browsed the books in the bookstore before taking a seat in the coffee shop and calling Phillip. He told her it would be awhile before he could come and suggested she call her parents if she didn't want to wait, but Reegan didn't want to disturb them.

So here she sat, waiting. Reegan was thankful she'd at least taken the time to make herself presentable. She had taken a shower, braided her hair, done her makeup, and put on a nice sweater. She may feel like a train wreck, but she didn't look like one.

Now she worried she should have bought a book, so she wouldn't be stuck thinking about things that would more than likely cause her to cry.

It was almost one now, so she knew it would be another hour or so before Justin got his afternoon rush. She tried not to eavesdrop as he spoke with his mother, who was cleaning the glass pastry case. She smiled when he looked over at her and wondered what Phillip had told him.

I guess I'm about to find out, she thought, when Justin took the seat across from her in the booth.

"I heard a rumor," Justin said, crossing his arms and sitting back against the cushion.

She leaned in. "Why doesn't that surprise me!"

He grinned.

"What's this rumor?" she asked.

"That you're shacked up with my good buddy Phillip."

It was her turn to grin.

"It's true then?"

"Guilty as charged. I'm actually waiting for Phillip to pick me up."

"Is he on duty?"

"No, he went up to Bernadette Howard's house," she said, and Justin tried to cover up his flinch. Was that good or bad, she wondered.

"Why?"

"Someone tried to break into her house." She sipped her coffee as a multitude of emotions flashed across Justin's face, none of which she could outright. They were both spared when his mother came over.

"Did I hear you say someone broke into

Bernadette's house?" Delores asked while she fiddled with her necklace.

"Phillip's there now. I'm waiting for him to come and get me," Reegan explained.

"Nonsense," Delores said and nudged Justin's shoulder. "Justin can take you up to Bernadette's right now."

"Mom, I'm not leaving you by yourself," Justin argued, but he stood up.

"I'll be fine for a bit. You two go on," she said, and Reegan found it interesting how quickly Justin did his mother's bidding.

"Ready?" he asked, after grabbing his keys and leather jacket from a hook behind the counter.

"Sure," Reegan said and hopped out of the booth because they were both staring at her like she needed to hurry the hell up.

****

Reegan was relieved when they pulled into Bernie's driveway. She felt a pang in her chest when they passed Annie Mae's cottage. She rubbed her face with her hands when she thought about how Bernie must feel.

She peeked at Justin out of the corner of her eye when they parked. He hadn't said a word to her the entire drive. Not one. He'd just stared straight ahead while his hands flexed on the steering wheel. She hadn't said anything either, not even when they'd passed a deputy's vehicle.

He was out of the SUV before she could unbuckle her seatbelt. He at least had the decency to wait for her, she thought, as she got out and shut the door. Again, he didn't say anything, just pivoted on his booted foot and headed to the front porch.

Phillip answered the door before Justin could knock. Thank God, she thought.

"What are you doing up here?" Phillip asked with a concerned expression.

"I called you, but you didn't answer," she said and was placated when he reached in his pocket to look at his phone.

"Sorry, I didn't hear it," he said and stepped back.

"Is everything okay?" Justin asked, and Phillip nodded when they entered.

She didn't listen to what they were saying because she was trying to pick her jaw up from off the floor. Bernie's house was amazing. The ceilings were high, the furniture plush, but it was the décor that held Reegan captive. Beautiful things were displayed in the two front rooms, from paintings and busts to antique candelabras. Reegan took a few moments to study the paintings before rejoining the group.

She found the boys in what she assumed was the den. A large TV adorned the wall, and books, movies, and records filled old-fashioned bookcases. The overstuffed sectional and matching love seat invited lounging, and through the French doors, she saw an indoor pool.

"It's good exercise."

Reegan looked at Bernie after the other woman spoke. "I can see that," she said. No wonder Bernie was so fit, Reegan thought.

"Do you want to see the rest of the house? It's safe," Bernie said, not acknowledging Justin.

Reegan glanced at Justin, who seemed annoyed; then her eyes landed on Phillip who, bless him, appeared to be as confused as she was. "Sure," she said.

The house wasn't nearly the size Reegan had assumed. There were three bedrooms, one of which was Bernie's office, two and a half bathrooms, and a state of the art kitchen. It reminded her of Phillip's house. When she mentioned it to Bernie, the other woman said she'd hired Phillip's friend too.

They walked into the kitchen where Phillip and Justin had taken up residence. Someone had made coffee, and Reegan eyed it long enough for Phillip to pour her a cup and hand it to her. She grinned at him.

"Bernie, maybe you should come stay at our house for a few days," Phillip said, and Reegan's heart did funny things; he'd called it their house, as in his and hers.

"The alarm worked," Bernie said with a shrug of her shoulders.

"I've said it once, I've said it a thousand times, I don't like you up here by yourself."

"Phillip, though I appreciate your concern, I have the alarm, and I can take care of myself."

Justin stood so fast that Reegan jumped. "Just let her stay here, Phillip," he said.

"You really should stay with us, Bernie," Reegan said and was rewarded with a wink from Phillip.

"I appreciate the offer, but I'd prefer to stay here."

"Whatever." Justin glowered, moving past Reegan.

He reached for a coffee mug and something caught Reegan's eye. "Justin?" she said.

"Yeah?"

Reegan pointed to his wrist. "What's that?"

He looked down. "What's what?"

Her heart thudded. "That," she said, pointing.

"What are you seeing?" Phillip asked.

Reegan grabbed Justin's wrist and pointed to the nasty-looking scar. "This," she said as her throat tried to close up.

"Don't worry about it," Justin said and pulled his arm out of her grasp.

"Reegan, what's wrong?" Phillip asked.

"What is it?"

"My business," Justin growled.

"Answer me!" she shouted, once she'd gathered her nerve. She glanced at Bernie, who'd lost every ounce of color she possessed.

"It's my business," Justin said through gritted teeth.

"I've seen it before. Twelve years ago," she said, her eyes searching his.

"That's impossible," Justin said.

"No, I saw it." She turned to Phillip. "I know I'm right."

"Justin?" Phillip asked.

"It's not possible," Justin said again. "I didn't have it then."

"Then why not just tell me what happened?" she asked.

"It's personal," Justin shouted. He ran a hand over his beard and took a deep breath. "I had a hard time dealing with what happened the night of the explosion."

"You're talking about the accident when you were an EMT? The one that killed your partner?" Reegan asked. She remembered her father telling her Justin had been in the hospital for months after.

Justin nodded. "It haunts me sometimes, and this particular night was worse. I locked myself in my house, and I started taking shots—"

"I've never seen you have more than two beers in my life," Phillip said.

"That's because my old man was a drunk. Mom says it's a sickness that runs in our family. I drink in moderation if I drink at all. But that night I was worked up, and I kept drinking. I punched my fists through the sliding glass door. Afterward, I went out on my back porch, sat down in a lawn chair, and had another drink. I knew I'd nicked arteries in both wrists—I was bleeding all over the place—but I didn't care."

Reegan gaped at him. "You survived."

"Yeah, someone found me, called an ambulance, and made sure I didn't die waiting. I was in the hospital for a while after that. Sorting shit out and putting my head back on straight."

"You should have told me," Phillip said.

"Mom's the only one who knows. Mom and the person who found me," Justin said, and Reegan glanced to where his eyes were fixed.

Phillip noticed too because he said, "Bernie?"

"Course," Justin whispered. "She's got a pair of her own."

Reegan's eyes went wide, and she grabbed Bernie's wrist before the other woman could get away. Her mind cramped, and she was in the water.

Arms reached her and pulled her to shore as she choked and coughed. She could feel the sand on her bare thighs. She opened her eyes when her rescuer moved her hair. There was something wrong with her wrist. She knew that voice, she thought, didn't she? Yes, it was...it was...why in the hell was Bernadette Howard saving her life?

BERNADETTE

Chapter Nineteen

Bernie pulled her wrist free and tried to breathe. She glanced over at Reegan, who was doing the same. She swallowed as a plethora of questions flitted across Reegan's face.

"Ask," Bernie said.

Reegan's gray eyes were stormy as she covered her mouth with one hand. "How...why?"

Bernie mentally counted to five to keep her emotions in check. She could be and would be calm about this. "Ever since I was a teenager, I get these inexplicable moments of clarity when I know I need to be at a certain place, and that night it directed me to the bluffs. I was walking along the shore when it started to storm, and I almost turned around, but someone screamed and fell from the bluff into the water. I knew that was why I was there."

"How did you know you'd reach me?" Reegan whispered.

"My father was strong swimmer, and he made sure I was too."

"Why didn't you come forward?" Phillip asked.

She smiled on the inside. Phillip had been and continued to be one of the few people who didn't treat her like she was a leper. "No one would have believed me."

"Why didn't you tell me?" Reegan asked, her gaze

searching…accusing.

"Reegan, be honest, you wouldn't have believed me either."

"Why did you tell me not to come back?" Reegan pointed a finger at her. "You knew something then!"

Bernie sighed. "I knew some things."

"Wait, what the hell is going on here?" Justin demanded.

Phillip cleared his throat. "Justin, this might be a good time for you to go."

Justin crossed his arms over his chest. "Not until I get some answers."

"I'm sorry to be a bitch right now, especially after what you shared with us," Reegan said to Justin. "But I've waited twelve years for my answers, so get in line."

"Fine," Justin growled.

"Let's get back to this 'I knew some things,'" Reegan said.

Bernie had known the day would arrive when she'd have to come clean to Reegan, but she hadn't realized there would be an audience. "Remember when I told you I'd heard the story before? Or overheard it?"

"What story?" Justin asked, and Phillip gave him the short version. "That would mean—"

"Not now, Justin," Reegan pleaded, then pointed to Bernie. "You were saying."

Bernie held up her wrists. She'd covered the scars with tattoos. One said *Death* and the other said *Destiny*. "When they sent me away—" She cleared her throat as the memory tried to choke her. "When they sent me away—" she began again and was relieved when Phillip spoke up.

"The paperwork and the transcripts were doctored, and instead of sending her to juvenile detention, they sent her to the state psychiatric ward."

"Oh, my God," Reegan said.

Bernie wouldn't meet their eyes; she didn't want their pity, but she figured she should share this truth. "They put me in a padded room alone for days at a time." She shook her head. "I don't remember much. They said I was combative, and most of the time, I was heavily sedated. It took Gran a month of cutting through the red tape to find me. But by then, I was undergoing their treatments, and the doctors convinced her I needed to be there. I was trapped until they moved me to my own room with a metal-framed bed. It didn't take me long to find a jagged edge on the corner long enough and sharp enough to do the job."

She could still see it in her mind's eye, lifting up the mattress in a fit of desperation and seeing that sharp corner. Bernie had thought about it for days, stared at that sliver of hard steel until she finally impaled first one wrist, then the other, stabbing deep enough to pierce the artery. She'd sat on the floor with her legs crossed, her hands lying limply in her lap, and waited as her white gown soaked up the blood that poured from her. She could still feel the cool tiles beneath her thighs.

"Jesus," Justin said.

"They found me before I bled out. There were no doctors on staff that night, so the nurse called the paramedics, and they took me to the hospital. Gran was there when I came to."

She'd never forget the fear on Gran's face or the anger. Annie Mae Howard had been furious, carried on about how Bernie was letting them win by giving up.

Just breathing bests them. Make them dirty their hands; don't do it for them, she'd said.

Bernie shook the memories aside. "She told me I couldn't leave this world because I had to right a wrong. I thought she was talking about my father, until one night I overheard Gran and Patch whispering in my room at the hospital. They were discussing the Whits and curses. Tori had been obsessed with the Willows for years, so I was well acquainted with the folklore, but I'd never heard the things Patch and Gran spoke of. I pieced together what I could, and even though I wasn't aware of what my part was, it gave me something to hold onto." Someone to fight for.

"Did you ever tell Tori?" Reegan asked.

"No," Bernie said standing straighter. "Tori had her own demons." Her own curses, Bernie thought.

"You may as well let that cat out too, Bernie," Phillip suggested, and though she appreciated his honesty, Bernie wished he would keep some things to himself.

"What?" Reegan's gaze went from hers to Phillip's.

"I told you there was an incident several years ago, and Tori was committed," Phillip said.

"Yeah."

"Tori tried to kill Bernie," Phillip whispered.

He may as well have screamed it, Bernie thought.

"Damn it, Bernadette," Justin shouted.

"It was an accident," Bernie explained. "She didn't know what she was doing." Tori hadn't been Tori that night, nor since.

Reegan gasped and pointed to Phillip. "That's why you were acting so strange when we saw Bernie with

Tori at Shady Pines!"

"What do you mean?" Bernie asked glancing at Phillip, who appeared to be hiding something.

Reegan's cheeks turned pink, and she whispered an apology to Phillip. "He mentioned that he didn't know why you did that to yourself," Reegan said. "And he had this look that I couldn't name, but now I understand—and I'll keep it to myself."

Bernie lifted a brow. "Yes, well, Tori's troubled, but her heart, at its core, is still good."

Phillip sighed. "Bernie."

"You won't change my mind on the subject." If Gran couldn't do it, no one could. And the old lady had tried countless times.

"Back to the part where you saved my life," Reegan began. "None of this explains why you said not to come back."

Bernie decided she needed a cup of coffee and poured herself one, aware that they were staring at her. She needed a moment to choose her words. "That's what I had to say."

"Why?" Reegan asked.

"It just was." Bernie wouldn't meet Reegan's eyes.

"You're lying," Reegan said.

"Reegan," Phillip warned.

"No, she's right," Justin said, and Bernie's gaze flew to his.

"I am?" Reegan stood straighter. "I am! Tell the truth. I mean, after everything we've found out, why lie?"

"You're protecting her," Phillip said.

Bernie bit the inside of her cheek and counted to five. "I—"

"Why?" Reegan asked, disbelief plain on her face.

"You're not ready," Bernie said, which was true. If she revealed everything about that night, Reegan wouldn't believe her.

"You're not serious?" Reegan scoffed.

"You're not," Bernie said again, and Reegan started to pace. Bernie caught Justin staring at her, and she sighed. Let them be suspicious; she was used to people feeling that way toward her.

"Have you known this whole time who I was and who you were in this?" Reegan asked as she crossed her arms over her chest.

"No," she said, but doubt clouded their eyes. "Until the other night when Phillip told us his version, I only had what I'd overheard to go on. I was aware that I had some part to play, and that night when I saved you, I assumed you did too. Did I know the details? No, and I still don't. The links will reveal themselves, but *we* have to make the connections."

"Bernie," Phillip admonished.

"Reegan has to see things for herself, or she won't trust it; won't believe it," Bernie explained.

"The nightmares? That's how I'm supposed to see?" Reegan asked.

"What nightmares?" Justin asked.

"I've been having nightmares since I came back," Reegan said.

"What were they about?"

Bernie didn't think Justin was asking out of curiosity. Before she could say anything, Reegan sucked in a breath, pointed to him, and said, "You've been having them too!"

"Justin?" Phillip said.

"They're usually about the explosion," he admitted. "But the last few weeks have been different. I'm on a ship, and I've uncovered something vital; it's imperative that I inform someone. When I try to leave, I'm jumped from behind; we struggle, I end up going overboard, I can't reach the surface, and before I drown I wake up."

Before anyone else could say a word, Reegan grabbed Bernie's sleeve and pulled her toward the door. "I have to speak with Bernie in private," she shouted.

Chapter Twenty

Bernie snatched her sleeve out of Reegan's grasp once they were alone in her bedroom.

"Justin's him, isn't he?" Reegan asked, pure satisfaction written on her face.

Bernie stared at the other woman as a million thoughts flooded her brain. A thousand images she'd secreted away flashed through her mind. She knew what Reegan was asking, but she wasn't sure how to answer.

"Oh, just admit it," Reegan said.

"No," she whispered, not wanting to put it out there for the fates to hear her.

Reegan eyed her. "No, you won't admit it or no, he isn't the guy?"

Bernie stared at the floor and counted to five.

"My God, Bernie, how long have you known?"

Her gaze flew up to meet Reegan's; her tone held sympathy…understanding. How could she possibly understand?

"You've known since we were teenagers, haven't you?"

How could she know that? She'd never even told Gran. Reegan hopped up on Bernie's bed and sat Indian-style. She gave Bernie a sad smile.

"I've relived the day of my accident countless times. And that day when we were gathered around the trees talking, I caught you staring at Justin. Back then, I thought you had a crush on him, but right now I'm seeing things differently."

Bernie blinked trying to remember. Tori hadn't even known, never even suspected it. But Reegan had seen it in her eyes way back then.

"I'm right, aren't I?"

She turned to look out the window. "Yes and no," Bernie admitted. "Yes, I pictured myself in love with Justin all those years ago, but no, I couldn't have imagined the connection. I convinced myself it was just a crush, and when he left for school, I was relieved. I let him go and lived my life." She'd done all she could to forget Justin Blake.

"But you did figure out you were connected to him specifically, didn't you?" Reegan asked.

"Yes, the night I found him." Bernie bit the inside of her cheek.

"After he'd"—Reegan cleared her throat—"you know."

Bernie turned back to Reegan. "Yes, I was headed home that night, when out of nowhere, I got this overwhelming feeling to check on Justin."

"Like you did the night you saved me?"

"Yes, it's hard to explain, but I had learned not to ignore the visions. I got to his house. Delores had mentioned where he kept the spare key, so I unlocked the door and found him. I called the paramedics and wrapped towels around his wrists to control the bleeding. His blood was literally on my hands, and all I could think was *not again*."

"Because he'd been killed in our other lives?"

"No, I didn't know about our past lives then. It was

167

because of my father," she said, meeting Reegan's eyes. "His blood was everywhere too."

"Oh, God."

"As I sat there with Justin thinking that I could *not* do this again, he stared up at me and said he was sorry he had to leave me again. He said 'again' as though I'd lost him before. He kissed my hand, and I realized I was meant to be with him in some way."

"You never told him?"

Bernie sighed. "You have to find out for yourself. That's how it's supposed to be. He didn't remember any of it, and we never spoke of what happened that night."

"Then how'd he know about your scars?"

"I showed him when he was in the hospital. I told him I understood what he'd been going through, I knew he hadn't done it on purpose. But after"—she shrugged—"he wouldn't look at me. Not that we were anything but acquaintances before, but even that was more than he could stand." That had eaten away at her, but she had to be thankful he was alive; she could go to the bookstore and spy on him through the curtain. She'd learned to live off those moments and resigned herself to living without him.

"You saw him at his weakest."

Bernie nodded. "He didn't intentionally try to kill himself, like I did…but once it was done, he made no effort to save himself, and that's where his guilt lies. Until today, I've been one of the only people who knew that. He needed to move past it, and I wouldn't get in his way. We've said more to each other today than we have in years." Seeing him in her space even if he was upset with her—

"I don't understand you, Bernie."

Bernie bit her lip, so she wouldn't smile. She'd learned to enjoy not being understood. "You don't have to."

"I think I do. We're all connected to this…"

"What?" Bernie asked. She stepped closer to Reegan as the other woman jumped off the bed.

"Come on," Reegan said and again took hold of Bernie's shirt sleeve.

"What now?" Bernie asked while Reegan led her into the kitchen. The men stopped talking and looked up when they entered.

"I want to try something," Reegan said, and Bernie knew she wasn't going to like this.

"What?" Phillip asked.

"When I touch Bernie, sometimes we see things. I want to see what happens if we all hold hands," Reegan said even as her cheeks turned pink.

"I don't want to do that," Bernie said.

"Just do it!" Justin snapped and grabbed Bernie's hand. His warm fingers gripped hers, and her entire body went hot.

Justin took Phillip's hand, and Phillip took Reegan's. Bernie flinched when Reegan would have taken her hand.

"Come on, Bernie." Reegan sighed, and with some reluctance, Bernie held out her hand.

A moment after their palms touched, Bernie's stomach dropped. *They were in a parlor, all four of them, laughing and talking. Their faces were different, but there was no doubt who they were, and just as quickly, it was gone. In its place was a beat-up house with a rotting fence. Bernie's heart hammered when she heard her own voice.*

"Dad...Daddy? Where are you?" Bernie called out with a laugh.

She walked through the fence and into the backyard. He was lying on the ground. "Dad, it's too early to look at the stars, you weirdo...Dad?"

Her father was in dingy work jeans and a dark blue polo shirt. His black hair was disheveled, and he lay on his side. Bernie knelt down and shook him with a giggle. "Dad, I'm too old to fall for you playing possum." She shook him again, pulling on his shoulder until his back was flat against the earth.

She put her hands on his chest to shake him, jerking away at the soaked fabric. Bernie stared down at her crimson fingers. She shook her head and once again shook her father, this time harder. "Dad? Daddy, please," she cried, and then she heard a noise and glanced up somewhere beyond the fence and into the woods; someone was watching...

Bernie ripped her hands away, breaking the connection. She grabbed onto the counter to catch her breath. She tried to steady herself as a ball of torment tore into her chest. She'd felt it again. Every second of that hell. What was worse was that they'd felt it too or at least Reegan had; that Bernie knew.

"I'm so sorry, Bernie," Reegan said, her voice thick with emotion. "I didn't know that would happen."

Bernie wanted to speak, but she was trembling too hard. Suddenly, Justin grabbed her arm and dragged her into her bedroom. He slammed the door shut, maneuvering them so she now stood against it, caged in.

Justin was almost a foot taller than her, and Bernie

was captivated by the rise and fall of his chest. She hadn't been this close to him in years, not close enough to feel the heat from his skin. Bernie drank him in. His beard was trimmed short, his red hair was dark enough to be mistaken for brown, and his freckles had faded a bit. He'd had laser surgery on his eyes, so he hadn't worn glasses for years.

"Why didn't you ever tell me?" he whispered.

"Tell you what?" she asked and flinched when his hand hit the wall next to them.

"Stop playing games with me."

"I'm not," she choked. "I don't know what you mean."

"Why didn't you ever tell me who I was!" he said with one hand on his chest.

"I didn't know who you were, only that we were connected. But that doesn't matter because you have to see it yourself; that's the way it is."

"Says who?"

"It's just the way it's supposed to be. I can't tell you. You have to find out for yourself. You have to be ready for the truth, or you won't believe it!"

Justin stared at her, and her pulse quickened. "I never thought you killed your father," he said.

Bernie stopped breathing for a moment. Her eyes searched his.

"I want us to be clear on that."

She scrutinized him, not knowing how to react.

"Whatever connection you and Reegan are able to sense"—he shook his head—"I felt it too."

"I'm sorry." She wouldn't wish those feelings on anyone.

"Don't be sorry for something you couldn't

control." His eyes hardened. "I don't like being played, Bernadette."

"I don't know what you mean."

"You've known this for years. Known who I am to you and who you are to me, and you didn't say a damn word. Not one. And don't feed me that bullshit about having to find out on your own because it is bullshit!"

"No, it's not," she argued. "That's how it has to be. You have to see it yourself, or you might not accept it. And as I've said, I didn't know *how* we were connected."

"Is that why you've been saving my ass all these years? And please don't patronize me by denying it. Mom came clean to me this morning." He folded his arms, his fists clenched. "No comment?"

Bernie masked her face and steadied her voice so her emotions wouldn't show. "What do you want me to say?"

"The truth!" he shouted at her. "The truth, for once."

"I haven't lied to you," she told him. Not outright, anyway.

"No? Who owns the coffee shop? Who owns the bookstore?"

"Your mother—"

"Lie! The bank wouldn't give Mom the loan, so you paid for the space and you provided the start-up capital!"

"Delores needed help, and I gave it to her. She makes payments to me just like she would a bank, only I don't charge interest. I don't see why you're upset."

"Bullshit! You know why!"

"Because we didn't tell you," she said, rubbing her

forehead.

"You went behind my back."

"We didn't mean for it to seem that way." They'd never meant for him to find out.

"You know what my mom said when I figured it out?" he asked.

Bernie shook her head.

"She said, 'We did it because we love you,' not 'I did this because I love you.' We—we, as in you and her. And then I thought about all the times you've shown up to save my ass. To save my damn life!"

Bernie pursed her lips. "Should I apologize?"

Justin's blue eyes searched hers for what seemed to Bernie like forever. "Was she right? Do you love me? Is this the curse, or are we fated to feel this way?"

"We?" she choked.

"Answer the questions."

"The curse is about righting a terrible wrong, not about who you love. Do I believe in fate? Yes. Destiny? It's really the same, isn't it? So yes. If you're fated to be with someone, then you will be. Curse or no curse. But more importantly, I believe in having the right to walk away. Curse or no curse. Your life is your own, and your destiny is what you make it." She sighed when his phone rang. He spoke with his mother, then put his phone back in his pocket.

"I have to go," he said, and she moved away from the door so he could open it. He stopped before he left the room. "You know, I fell in love with you the night you saved my life. The connection was so intense, I knew it wasn't normal. I thought it was some kind of psychological misplacement of feelings so I kept it to myself." His phone beeped. "Mom needs me."

Chapter Twenty-One

Bernie stared into the empty room. Justin had told her again that he'd needed to go, and she'd been unable to reply. She could have said a multitude of things, but her mouth failed to process the flurry of her thoughts; he'd left without a word from her.

She was stunned by his revelation and needed time to think it over. He'd said he'd fallen in love with her the night she saved his life. He'd thought his feelings were misplaced. For years she'd watched him from afar, hoping he would at least look at her, talk to her, but his words had been courteous at best. She had taken great pains to forget what he hadn't wanted to remember.

It turned out he'd been aware of the truth but just hadn't known what to make of it. She understood the difficulty of accepting what seemed irrational, but he could've talked to her about it, asked her. Instead she'd suffered—

"Bernie?"

Bernie focused on Reegan when she came into the room. The other woman's eyes searched her own. "I don't understand."

Reegan huffed out a breath. "Welcome to the club."

"He knew there was a connection between us. It may not have made sense to him, but he's known since the night of the incident."

"And you're hurt because he never said anything?"

Bernie hesitated. "I know it's not fair, but I feel…I—"

"You're pissed," Reegan supplied. "You have every right to be pissed, Bernie. Not just about Justin either."

Bernie stared at her trying to come to grips with what she'd learned.

"You need to stop being a martyr," Reegan said, and Bernie stepped back.

"I'm not trying to be." Am I?

Reegan rubbed her forehead. "That, actually, makes it worse."

"My mother was sick, and it tore my father apart," Bernie began abruptly. "There was a constant sadness in his smile and pain in his eyes. I didn't want to feel that. I didn't want anyone to be able to hurt me that way."

Reegan leaned against the doorjamb. "That's why you fought first, so no one would hurt you," she said.

"I got them before they could see that they could hurt me. People don't pick on you when they're scared of you. I protected myself that way and protected Tori too, though she took it too far sometimes."

"I noticed that," Reegan said.

"After I tried to kill myself, they were going to send me back to the state facility, but Gran found a way around it, and they sent me to Shady Pines instead."

"How'd she do that?"

"Buck got a judge to sign off on it while Gran sold the house I lived in with my father. The house wasn't worth much, but the land was. With the money and the judge's signature, I was able to go to Shady Pines. My mother had died there the year before, so—"

"Wait, your mother died not long after your father's murder. That means you were in the state institution for a year?" Reegan asked, her tone horrified.

"I was so heavily sedated time had no relevance. Days felt like weeks. Weeks felt like hours. I spent the last year of my original sentencing at Shady Pines. There I learned how to contain my feelings instead of using anger to protect myself. After going through what I had, I didn't want to be the cause of anyone else's pain. I protected Tori and perfected my technique. I try not to let my emotions overtake me."

"You do a pretty good job, I'll admit, but not wanting to hurt someone is different from defending yourself when they've hurt you. You have every right to be angry. I'd be royally pissed."

Bernie's lips twitched. "I can see that."

Reegan sighed loudly. "There is something I have to say, and you can be upset with me."

Bernie's brow puckered. "All right."

"Up until I realized who we were before and how we're connected now, I thought you'd killed your father."

The vision must be compelling everyone to confess these things, Bernie thought. She cocked her head to the side. "I was aware of that."

"See, these are the times when you can be openly pissed."

"Why? Because you believed what ninety-eight percent of this town *still* believes? You took the information in front of you at face value. I can't blame you for that."

"Why not?"

"Because we see what we need to see when we need to see it. No matter if the timing is bad or even too late. That's how things are."

"Is this more of the being 'ready' crap that you keep going on about?"

"Yes, exactly! Time has its purpose and its casualties."

"I guess I can see that, and for what it's worth I *am* sorry."

"I know." That was plain to see in her eyes.

"Even sorrier about what happened in the kitchen. You were right, by the way."

"About what?"

Reegan straightened from the doorway. "Every horrible feeling you had when you found your father is like what I experienced in the dream when I saw them murder Phillip. I'm thirty years old," she said, her voice wavering. "You were fourteen. I don't know how the hell you survived it."

Bernie stared at her for a moment, then held up her tattooed wrists. "I nearly didn't."

Reegan nodded. "We have to figure out what happened to the Whits."

"I agree."

"Listen, I feel like the visions have a meaning. They're telling us something. Today we saw your father and…"

"You think it's connected," Bernie finished because she could see Reegan was reluctant to.

"First, I figured it was a cosmic fuck-you."

Bernie snorted.

"But then I thought about what Patch said. 'It always starts with death unplanned.' "

Bernie thought about it. "His death is part of the curse."

"It has to be, right? I mean, why else would we have seen it?"

"All right," Bernie said and pointed Reegan out of the room and into the kitchen where Phillip was sitting.

"Everything okay?" he asked as he stood.

"Yes," Reegan said, then told him what they'd figured out.

"That makes sense," Phillip said. "Bernie, why don't you pack a bag and head to the house with us?"

"I'm more than capable of staying by myself," Bernie said.

"I think we should all stay together, if only for access," Reegan said.

"What? Why?" Bernie asked. She needed to process everything that happened today and contain it as best she could. That took both time and privacy.

"We need to figure this out together; which means we need to *be* together if one of us has an epiphany," Reegan said.

Bernie sighed, and Phillip grinned.

****

Bernie sat at Phillip's kitchen table with her arms crossed. She'd packed a small bag and, per request, met them here. Reegan had insisted on getting dinner, which somehow turned into Phillip going to pick up pizza. Bernie had to admit they were amusing to watch.

She was glad Phillip had found love. He was a good man, and he deserved nothing but happiness. She tried not to think about Justin. Bernie knew they were connected, but that didn't necessarily mean they would end up together.

"Are you brooding or pouting?" Reegan asked coming into the kitchen.

Bernie crinkled her nose; she didn't think she'd ever been accused of either. "Neither, just thinking."

Reegan snorted. "If you say so."

Bernie uncrossed her arms and picked up her legal pad. She'd been jotting down some notes. "On the drive over here, I was thinking about what you said about my father's murder being connected."

"And?"

"It says death unplanned, not murder."

"You don't think it's connected?"

"I didn't say I disagreed with you, just that maybe it's not the starting point."

"Because it was murder?"

"Yes," Bernie said and looked up as Phillip came in with two pizza boxes.

"Did you ladies think of anything else while I was away?"

"No, I put fresh sheets on the guest beds while Bernie made notes," Reegan told him.

Bernie followed Reegan to the fridge to get some water and a plate. She hadn't realized she was hungry. She grabbed a slice of pizza and sat back down with her notes. It was nice to eat with people her own age, but she missed Gran…

"I dropped a pizza off with Dad, so I could check on Junebug," Phillip said.

"How's she doing?" Reegan asked. Bernie could see the genuine concern in her eyes.

"She's fine. Actually, it worked out that she's

staying with Dad because she's doing a family tree as a project for her history class."

Reegan turned toward her. "Did you know Phillip is the fourth generation of law and order in Willows Bluff?"

"Really?" Bernie smiled.

"Yep, we can trace it back to my great-grandfather."

"That's interesting," Bernie said, then took a bite of pizza. Reegan and Phillip were talking about the boxes in the garage when a thought occurred to her. "Hold on," she said.

"What is it, Bernie?"

"You said you can trace it back"—she waved her hand in the air—"your family tree. You said trace."

"Yeah," Phillip said.

Bernie looked at Reegan. "Gran and Patch said, 'There is no undoing what was done, but you can trace the path that led to this.' "

Reegan gasped and grabbed Phillip's forearm. "They meant literally trace it back."

"What are you saying?" Phillip asked.

"It's their family tree."

"Yes," Bernie said.

"Where do we start?" Phillip asked.

"At the beginning," Bernie and Reegan said in unison.

Bernie flipped the paper on the legal pad to a clean page. "Bertrum Whit's first wife was Jessamine. They had Amelia and Minerva. After Jessamine died from fever—"

"Death unplanned," Reegan said.

"You're right!" She tore another sheet from the

pad. "If what we thought earlier is correct, that it's connected, then what if it's not just past lives reoccurring?" She stopped when Justin walked in.

"I told Justin to meet us here," Phillip explained. "We all have a part in this."

Bernie met Justin's gaze, then looked back down at her notes. Reegan came to stand next to her as if she too were studying the page.

"Breathe," Reegan said so only Bernie could hear, then she spoke up. "Don't break Bernie's concentration. We're in the middle of an epiphany."

Bernie tried to focus, but the words blurred in front of her and she lost her place.

"You were saying something about it not just being past lives," Reegan said nudging Bernie with her elbow.

She cleared her throat. "Right," she began. "If it's connected, then maybe it's not only our lives that are repeating but events as well."

Reegan sucked in a breath. "And we can trace it!"

Their eyes met, and Bernie smiled because Reegan understood. "Yes, and if we can trace it—"

"Then we can stop it!" Reegan grinned.

"Exactly!" Bernie wrote down Jessamine's death on one page and under it she wrote death unplanned. "After Jessamine's death, Bertrum Whit moved to Willows Bluff, and he met and married Clara Marshal."

"That's two choices," Reegan said, and Bernie knew she was referring to what Patch and Gran said.

"Yes. 'From this a new direction is birthed; a fork in the road allows two choices that will change all.' "

"Moving to Willows Bluff and marrying Clara, right?" Reegan asked.

"You said it's in their family tree," Phillip reminded them, then brought Justin up to speed.

"If that's true, then it's the daughter," Justin said.

"Two choices that changed everything. Moving to Willows Bluff introduced Bertrum to Clara. By marrying Clara, they had Fidelia," Bernie said.

"They were betrayed by their own sister," Phillip said.

"Do you think Fidelia could be the cloaked woman from your dream?" Justin asked Reegan.

Reegan shook her head. "She was trying to help me escape."

"The Whits had one maid who stayed with them. She could have heard what the villagers were planning and tried to save you," Phillip suggested.

"That makes sense," Reegan said.

"Let's go back to the correlation for a moment," Bernie suggested. "Here, read this." She set a piece of paper between the men where she'd written down what Gran and Patch had told them.

Reegan peeked at it. "You memorized it?"

Bernie shrugged. "I've read it a hundred times, and I guess it stuck."

"The death unplanned had to provoke a choice that made all this possible," Justin said.

"All the pieces had to align for this to work," Bernie said. She sat back down while Reegan paced and the men hovered over the table studying her notes.

"We're the pieces," Reegan said.

"It's plausible. Didn't your dad say people thought it was Annie Mae and Patch back when they were kids?" Phillip asked Reegan.

"Yeah."

"There was a generation between what happened to the Whits and your grandmothers. Not to mention our parents," Justin said.

"We have to assume all the pieces weren't available until now," Phillip said. "And with all the pieces in place—"

"It's a chain reaction," Justin finished.

"What we need to do is figure out what set it off," Bernie said.

"We know that, before, the choice led to Fidelia being born; perhaps this one does too," Phillip suggested.

"Oh, my God," Reegan said and stopped pacing.

Bernie didn't like the way she was looking at her. "What is it, Reegan?"

"Remember what I told you my mom said about how your parents ended up getting married?"

"Oh, God," Bernie whispered. "Alan Walters is the death unplanned."

"How?" Justin asked.

"My dad tried to save Alan Walters and couldn't."

Reegan explained. "Not being able to save Alan made Bernie's dad see how short life was, and he married Bernie's mom and they had Bernie. Without Bernie, none of this would be possible."

"It fits," Bernie said. "Even if I don't like it, it fits."

"But what's the other choice?" Phillip asked. "If this is repeating, then there should be a second choice, right?"

"The marriage is one choice, and the baby would be the other. Or it could be that they chose to stay in Willows Bluff," Reegan suggested.

Bernie shifted in her chair. "Could be."

"You said you thought Bernie's dad's murder was part of it. A reenactment of events," Justin said.

"Yeah," Reegan said.

"What if it's this?" He pointed to the paper. " 'Loss weeps until the earth is saturated with blood.' "

Bernie stared into space for a moment, then cleared her throat. "That makes more sense," she said. Her father's blood had soaked into the ground beneath him.

"Amelia and Minerva's father died too. An accident—"

"What kind?" Reegan asked.

"He fell from one of the balconies, if I remember correctly," Phillip said.

"What if he didn't fall?" Bernie said glancing around the table. "What if he was pushed?"

"You're saying you think he was murdered like your father?"

"It makes sense; he was murdered, and my dad suffered the same."

Reegan sat down next to Bernie. " 'Different but ever the same,' " she whispered.

"So it would appear," Bernie said.

Chapter Twenty-Two

The screaming woke her. Bernie leapt out of bed, grabbed her robe, and left her room. She stopped short when Justin came into the hall in the midst of putting on his shirt. She caught a glimpse of marred flesh before he pulled the fabric down; she averted her eyes and continued toward the other end of the house.

The four of them had gone over various possibilities last night until she'd had a headache. She'd been grateful when Phillip had called a halt to all discussion and suggested they get some rest. Justin had wanted to speak with her, but at that point she didn't think she could handle any more emotional turmoil, and she'd rushed to her appointed room. She passed him now without a word.

The screaming had quieted to a dull sob, but that didn't stop her from knocking on Phillip and Reegan's bedroom door. She glanced over her shoulder when Justin stepped behind her. He crossed his arms over his chest and scowled. She sighed and knocked again.

"Does this happen every night?" she asked after Phillip opened the door in his pajama bottoms and said they were okay.

"Pretty much," he said and Bernie pushed past him to find Reegan shaking amongst the sheets.

"Do you want to talk about it?" she asked, standing next to the bed. She glanced over her shoulder for a

185

moment to see the men colluding.

Reegan shook her head and sniffled.

Bernie retrieved some tissue from the bathroom and handed it to Reegan, but instead of taking it, the other woman grabbed her wrist. Images assailed Bernie instantly.

Once again, she was saving Reegan from the depths of the sea; then two young girls drew in the sand and made a promise to one another to share a secret. Suddenly, she was in the woods watching in horror as a man was hung.

She sucked in a breath and stared into Reegan's weepy eyes once she was released from her grasp. Bernie sat on the bed before her legs gave out. "Is that what you dreamt?" she asked once her pulse was steady.

"That's the Cliff Notes version."

"I'm sorry you have to go through that."

Reegan blew her nose in the tissue that had dropped on the sheets. "Me too," she said around a sniff.

"How did you know I'd see what you saw?"

"Honestly, I didn't even realize I was going to grab you until it was done. Sorry."

"It's all right." Bernie took Reegan's hand, gave it a squeeze, then let go. "I guess it doesn't work every time."

Reegan fidgeted. "What do you think that means?"

"If I had to guess, I would say that we see what we need to when we're supposed to. Which suggests we can't force the visions, but we have to let them happen. Was there anything different about this dream?"

"It's the first time I've dreamt of Patch and Annie

Mae when they were little."

"They already knew about the curse, but who would have told them?"

Reegan's brow bunched. "Dad said Patch's dad died in a car accident when she was around that age."

"That's one pattern that seems to be repeating," Bernie said and rubbed her temples.

"Fathers keep dying," Reegan said, and Bernie nodded.

"I think I'll start some coffee," Phillip said from the doorway. Bernie had forgotten about them.

"Wonderful idea," Reegan said.

"I need to go open the shop," Justin said.

"He wanted to talk to you," Reegan said once they were alone.

Bernie glanced at the empty doorway. "I don't want to talk right now."

"Why?"

Bernie got off the bed and crossed her arms. "What good would come of it?"

"Seriously?" Reegan shook her head. "Bernie, now is not the time to get cold feet. We need all the help we can get—all the connections."

"I thought you said I have a right to be upset." And for the first time in a long time, she was letting herself be upset.

"Absolutely!" Reegan said. "But there's a difference between being pissed and being scared. I can say from experience that it's going to happen even if you run away, like I did. Why fight it?"

"I'm not fighting it," Bernie said, but she knew Reegan was right. She was scared. It was common knowledge that things could only hurt you when you gave them power to, and love was not the exception.

"Liar." Reegan smiled. "Let it happen, Bernie."

"I'll let the cards fall as they may."

"What should we do today?" Reegan asked a moment later, and Bernie was glad for the change of subject.

"I have to go up to Shady Pines."

"Today?"

"Well, I…" She had to go, especially after Tori'd had an episode the other day.

"Why don't I go with you? I'll stay out of the way."

Bernie studied Reegan for a minute. "All right."

****

She stood next to the fireplace waiting for the nurse to bring Tori. Bernie hadn't wanted Reegan's presence to upset her old friend, so she'd asked her to stay out of sight. Reegan had then received permission from the powers that be to take photographs of the Shady Pines architecture; she was presently outside with her camera.

Bernie caught a glimpse of herself in the glass on the picture above the mantel, then looked away; she wasn't much on her own reflection. Though she'd been given many compliments as she aged, sometimes she still felt like the ugly duckling. Growing up, most people had stared at her with fear, loathing, or pity in their eyes, and some people still did, but when she looked at herself, all she saw were the shadows of things she couldn't change.

Bernie sighed while the fire crackled in the hearth. If Shady Pines was anything, it was a sanctuary. She felt protected here; first when she visited her mother, then during her own stay, and now with Tori. It was almost as though the walls themselves were safeguarded.

"Bernadette," Tori said softly as she walked into the room. "Should we sit?"

"Of course," Bernie said and sank down into the cushions next to her old friend.

Tori's skin was pale, and her lips had lost their color. The medications had stolen the luster from her long golden hair and dulled the look of mischief that had once lit her brown eyes. But her beauty hadn't left her. She'd always reminded Bernie of the ballerina that danced inside Gran's favorite snow globe. So precious and delicate that she needed to be protected.

"How are you today?" Tori asked, clasping her hands.

"I'm well, Tori, how about you? Were you able to read yesterday?" Shady Pines provided their patients with a multitude of activities, but reading was Tori's favorite. She'd loved to read when they were children. Her love of books and studying was how she'd been top of their class in school. Bernie had always admired Tori's mind...at least until that mind turned against her.

"Yes," Tori said. "I wish they'd get some new books."

"I'll bring you something next time I come."

"That would be wonderful," Tori said and went into a long story about what she suspected the nurses were up to when everyone was asleep. After about twenty minutes, she stared at Bernie and whispered, "I'm sorry I tried to kill you."

Bernie sighed. "I know."

Tori nodded and squeezed her hand. "I just didn't want you to leave me."

"I won't leave you." This is what they did each time, and it always meant that it was time to go. Bernie stood and helped Tori to her feet.

"You're leaving now, though."

Bernie inclined her head to signal the nurse that it was time. "I'll be up to see you again soon," she promised.

Tori nodded, then threw her frail arms around Bernie hugging her with all her strength. "Bring me a present next time," she whispered, then pulled back and giggled.

"I'll bring you something special," Bernie said, and she waved back as the nurse led Tori out of the room. She counted to five and turned to leave. That's when she noticed Reegan was in the lobby, and she was speaking to Tori's mother. She quickened her footsteps.

Mrs. Elis had changed over the years. She'd once worn her pedigree like a tiara, every move a calculated dance meant to impress. Now, though she was still lovely, most of the polish had worn off. Her once-blonde hair was almost completely white, and Bernie hadn't seen her smile in years.

"...I'm sure you'll get back into the swing of things, Reegan," Tori's mother was saying as Bernie approached the two women. "Oh, Bernadette, there you are. How is she this morning?"

"Today's a good day," Bernie said and glanced at Reegan, who seemed uncomfortable. "I didn't realize you were coming." They tried to space out their visits so Tori wouldn't feel alone.

"My husband has a case in the city and he needs my assistance, so I'll be gone for several days."

"You're a psychiatrist, right?" Reegan asked.

"Yes," Mrs. Elis said. "My aunt was never quite right when I was a child. She suffered from delusions most of her life, and it broke my father's heart. I took up psychiatry to get a better understanding of her affliction for both my father's sake and my own."

"It runs in the family then," Reegan said, and Bernie winced. "Sorry."

Mrs. Elis straightened her spine. "Don't be sorry, Reegan. You're correct; mental illness has been linked to genetics. They appear to be waiting for me," she said and pointed to where the doctor was standing by the door.

"Nice seeing you again, Mrs. Elis."

"Good luck to you, Reegan. Bernadette." She inclined her head, then walked away.

"That was intense," Reegan said after they'd been driving for a few minutes.

Bernie agreed.

"Is it always that way?"

"Usually." Reegan turned in her seat, and Bernie's cheeks heated at her unwavering stare. "What?"

"You can talk to me, Bernie."

She glanced at her. "What do you mean?"

"You know, talk to me or get it off your chest or unload or whatever."

"Why?" She never talked about her problems.

"Because that's what friends do."

Bernie kept her eyes on the road. "Is that what we are?"

Reegan swiveled even farther around in her seat. "I think we have to be."

"There's always a choice," Bernie said. She felt like she was a child again, and someone was being a friend to her because Gran had bribed them to be.

Reegan threw up her arms. "I don't get you, Bernie, I swear! We're thrown in this crazy situation together, so we may as well be friends."

Bernie didn't know what to say. She had a couple people she considered friends, but no one she opened up to. She didn't want to burden anyone. But Reegan was right about their situation. "All right," she said.

"Finally! Now, as your friend, I think you need to start being honest."

"I don't lie, Reegan," Bernie said, and took their exit.

"You omit. And you omit a whole hell of a lot."

Bernie bit the inside of her cheek. "What do you want to know?"

"Seriously?"

"Yes, I'll answer what I can."

"Why did you tell me not to come back?"

"I honestly don't know; I can tell you it wasn't at all what I was thinking at the time," Bernie said. "Remember I told you I get these moments of clarity sometimes and just know I need to be somewhere? In this case, I opened my mouth, and that's what came out." The voice had been hers but not the words. In fact she—

"There is something about that night you're choosing not to tell me."

"I'm not choosing—you are. Think about it, Reegan. If you were supposed to know, you would have seen it when you saw the night of the accident or you would have dreamt it."

Reegan took a moment before she said, "True."

"Do you want to see if Ezra's at the gallery?" She

wanted to get a peek at the paintings Reegan had mentioned.

"Yes! Maybe we should get a cup of coffee first."

Bernie eyed her. "Do you want coffee, or are you trying to set me up?"

"I'm a coffee junkie, Bernie. The fact that Justin owns the shop is a perk," she said with a wink.

"I wanted to go to the bookstore anyway."

"For Tori, right?"

"Yes, she mentioned it. On good days, Tori's mentally a teenager, Reegan, she's innocent."

"Other than the trying-to-kill-you thing, of course."

Bernie wouldn't acknowledge that.

"I never understood how you two were friends," Reegan said after ten minutes of silence.

"Phyllis Cox read books aloud at the library a few times a week, and Dad would take me when he had time. I met Tori there; I guess we were around four years old. Mrs. Elis told Dad I was the only child Tori had ever shown an interest in. She asked if he would bring me over to play. We were friends from that day on."

"Syd and I met in preschool," Reegan said, and Bernie glanced over to see Reegan staring out the window.

"Why does that make you sad?" Not that she wanted to hear about Sydney Walters, but she thought Reegan wanted to talk about it.

"I didn't tell Syd about the curse, but I did tell her how I feel about Phillip. I explained to her I was moving back home to start a life with him."

"And?" Bernie asked after more than a minute of unclaimed air.

"She said she couldn't be party to it." Reegan shrugged.

"I'm sorry." And she was for Reegan's sake.

"Me too," Reegan said.

Bernie sighed as she pulled onto Main Street and into an empty parking space right in front of the bookstore.

"Before we go in, will you tell me what the deal is with you and Tori's mom?"

"Mrs. Elis needs me because Tori doesn't do well if she doesn't see me on a regular basis."

"Bernie, she tried to kill you."

"Because she thought I was going to move away and leave her."

"Were you?" Reegan asked, unbuckling her seatbelt and turning to face Bernie.

Bernie stared straight head into the store window. "No, I couldn't leave."

"Why?"

"I couldn't leave Gran, not after everything she'd done for me. The idea that I was leaving—and I don't know where she got such an idea—sent Tori into a tailspin that she's yet to come out of. She's not well, and if I don't see her regularly, she'll refuse to eat or worse. I won't have that on my conscience, so I go."

"But you don't want to."

"I love Tori, and I would do anything to help her or protect her."

"That's not an answer."

"She's in there because she couldn't let me go, even if my going was imagined. Do I like seeing her wither into a corpse? No! Do I want to be there? No, Reegan, I don't." She jumped when Reegan took her hand and gave it a squeeze.

"But you go anyway."

"Yes, because I know she'll die in there."

"God, Bernie, you're blaming yourself!"

She snatched her hand out of Reegan's and wiped away a tear that had escaped.

"You might not want to hear it, but I'm going to tell you what I saw when I watched you and Tori's mom. She wouldn't meet your eyes for more than a second."

"What's your point?" Bernie was embarrassed by her tears and by Reegan's relentless insistence on sticking up for her. She wasn't used to people being sincere.

"The reason she can't look at you isn't because she thinks this is your fault," Reegan said and Bernie met her eyes. "It's because she *knows* it's not."

"What?" Bernie whispered.

"What Tori's mom is asking you to do is wrong and unfair—to you. And she damn well knows it. She won't look at you because she doesn't want you to see her shame."

Bernie sat back against the seat and stared at Reegan.

"That's the truth, Bernie. I know you believe things will unveil themselves when the time's right, but sometimes a person deserves the truth even if they're not ready." Reegan opened the door on her side of the truck. "Now, since I'm fairly certain I just blew your mind, I'll buy you a cup of coffee!"

Bernie swallowed. She'd need some time to process all Reegan had said. But for now she said, "I'll take a latte…a big one."

Chapter Twenty-Three

Bernie perused the bookshelves until she found what she was searching for. She pulled out a copy of Lewis Carroll's *Alice's Adventures in Wonderland* and smiled as she flipped through the pages. This was the book Phyllis Cox was reading the first time Bernie met Tori. She wasn't sure if Tori would remember it, but it was worth a try.

She mulled over what Reegan had said about Mrs. Elis; she had to admire Reegan's tenacity. Bernie remembered her being a somewhat timid girl, but perhaps that was because she'd been hidden by Sydney's shadow. Though Gran spoke highly of Reegan, Bernie's own feelings for her had been ambivalent at best. Fate, it would seem, had other ideas.

She may not say it outright, but Bernie liked that Reegan was loud and somewhat outlandish. There was something comforting about being around her. Perhaps it was because Bernie missed Patch, and Reegan was similar in many ways. Then again, she could chalk it up to their previous life connection.

Bernie paused a moment. What mattered was Reegan was trying; maybe she herself should try harder. The problem was she'd spent so many years containing her feelings she didn't know if she could open the box without unleashing all of its contents; that prospect made Bernie shudder.

"There you are," Delores whispered, and Bernie sighed, familiar with the worry on Delores's face.

"Hello, Delores. Everything's fine."

"Is it?"

Delores was only a few inches taller than Bernie, and her frame was built for the hugs she loved to give. Her brown hair was graying attractively, and her deep blue eyes mirrored her son's. She'd been through more than her fair share of heartache, yet she remained one of the kindest people Bernie had ever met.

"Yes, now don't worry yourself, Delores. I'll take this one," Bernie said, holding up the book and walking toward the counter.

"Justin said he told you he found out about our deal."

"Yes."

Delores took the book and rang it up. "I'm thankful I don't have to hide it from him anymore. Secrets weigh down a person's soul," she said. She took Bernie's money, then gently clasped her hand. "I noticed you came straight into the bookstore; I'm guessing that was to avoid my son. What would it hurt just to talk to him?"

Bernie stared at her. What wouldn't it hurt?

"Hey, I got your latte with an extra shot," Reegan said, coming into the store, all smiles.

"Thanks," Bernie said.

Delores let go of her hand, so she could take the cup.

"Where are you girls off to?" Delores asked as she walked with them to the front of the store.

"I want to stop by the gallery and say hello to Ezra," Reegan said.

"And I want to take a look at a painting Reegan was telling me about," Bernie said; then her heart lurched when Justin appeared in the doorway between the bookstore and the coffee shop.

"Bernadette, can I get a minute?" Justin asked.

Reegan stepped on her foot, and Bernie glared at her. "I'll wait for you," Reegan whispered. As Bernie began walking toward Justin, Reegan shouted, "Don't take forever. I want to go to Ezra's before he gets away again."

"All right," she said when she stood in front of Justin. "Talk."

He narrowed his dark blue eyes, took her free hand, and led her through the empty coffee shop into the stock room. "You're avoiding me," he said.

Bernie was relieved no one had seen them. She had enough to worry about, like the fact that looking at him made her heart ache.

"Bernadette?"

"Probably."

He crossed his arms. "Why?"

"Simple. I don't want to have this conversation."

"Why?" He reached out and touched her face.

Bernie froze while his eyes searched hers. When he moved closer, she stepped away. "Reegan's waiting for me," she reminded him.

"Why the hell won't you just talk to me?"

Bernie spun around from the door to face him. "You have some nerve, Justin Blake! For years, *years*, I've waited for you to say more than two courteous words to me. Then I find out that you've had feelings for me this entire time and said nothing, *did* nothing. Do you have any idea how that makes me feel?"

He stood there staring at her.

She blinked back tears. "I've done all I could think of to make sure you were all right, and you couldn't even speak to me."

"Why? Why go to all the trouble?" he asked.

"Why do you think?" She shifted her bag. "Reegan's waiting."

"Bernadette," he said, and she paused. "The last thing in the world I ever wanted to do was hurt you."

She nodded and went through the swinging door, feeling Delores's eyes on her as she walked out. Reegan was outside talking on her phone.

Bernie sipped her latte to give herself a moment while Reegan left yet another voicemail for Sydney. If memory served, this was message number fifteen. She wouldn't mention it because it wasn't her business. Reegan ended the call, and her gray eyes turned to Bernie.

"I'm guessing that didn't go well."

"It didn't go anywhere. Let's head to Ezra's," Bernie said and started down the sidewalk.

"You can talk to me, Bernie," Reegan said, then held up her cup in surrender. "When you're ready, of course."

They obviously weren't going to talk about Reegan's relationship issues with Sydney, so Bernie gave in a bit. "I don't know why I'm so upset. I understand why he kept his thoughts and feelings to himself. I get it, but—"

"It still hurts," Reegan said.

"Yes," she said, opening the door to Ezra's. "Ready?"

"Yeah." Reegan grinned and followed Bernie

inside.

Reegan squealed and ran into Ezra Kelly's welcoming arms the moment they entered the building. Bernie hid her smile and stepped to the side, not wanting to intrude. She watched out of the corner of her eye as they played catch-up.

Ezra looked like the older version of Bilbo Baggins with his white hair going this way and that. He wore jeans that had more swatches of color than Crayola and a white long-sleeved shirt covered by an old suit vest; under the vest were bright red suspenders. Bernie had always loved the suspenders.

Her eyes left them to peruse the gallery. Ezra had beautiful things, and she was a sucker for beautiful things. She came to a wall that held several pieces, and her heart lurched. In front of her had to be the painting Reegan had mentioned. Bold strokes of flame-inspired color consumed the canvas. In the center was a darkness; she unconsciously reached out to touch it.

"That's the one I was telling you about," Reegan said.

Bernie shook herself and dropped her hand. "I guessed it was."

"You can practically feel the heat, can't you?"

She turned toward Reegan. "I feel like it may singe my fingers if I touch it."

Reegan's eyes searched hers. "Exactly!"

"Hello, Bernadette, I didn't see you sneak in," Ezra said as he came to stand next to them. "Ah, I see you've found Adam's work."

Bernie had to turn to see if his face matched his disapproving tone.

"You don't like it?" Reegan asked.

Ezra was quiet for a moment before he said, "It's a remarkable canvas."

"But?" Reegan said, motioning with her hand for him to continue.

Ezra sighed. "But I find his work a bit…dark."

"Like Adam," Reegan said, then glanced around the gallery.

Ezra snickered and patted Reegan's hand. "He's gone back to the city, dear. No need to fret."

"Did he tell you I stopped by to see you?" Reegan asked.

"I don't remember him mentioning it, but then my memory isn't what it used to be."

"April was here too; I hadn't seen her in years either."

"She's back and forth between here and the city," Bernie said.

"I didn't realize you were friends with April," Reegan said.

"More like acquaintances," Bernie explained. "She worked at Tori's house on the weekends." Unlike her brother, April Desmond had always been courteous and friendly to Bernie.

"She worked at Syd's too," Reegan said.

"Both Adam and April have come a long way, though I—"

"Ezra," Bernie began, wanting to get back to the subject at hand. "Reegan and I were discussing a painting Phillip purchased. You remember the one from your attic sale that Phillip outbid me for?"

Ezra pursed his lips. "Ah, yes, the forest scene. A lovely piece."

"We were wondering if there were any other

paintings like that one," Bernie said because Reegan had apparently lost the ability to question Ezra.

"No, I believe that was the only painting I purchased from that particular estate sale."

"Were there other paintings at the sale?"

"None that I thought were worth what that one was."

"You wouldn't happen to remember whose estate it was from, would you?"

"Not off the top of my head. Why the interest?"

"I was curious, Ezra," Reegan said, and Bernie was glad she was adding something to the conversation.

"I see."

"Do you know who the artist was? I didn't see a signature, and I would like to know if there are other paintings out there."

"No, I asked the same question and was told the painter was an unknown. Perhaps someone in the family painted it once upon a time."

"Thanks, Ezra," Reegan said.

"You're welcome. Now that you're moving back to Willows Bluff, perhaps you might consider an offer to run this place."

Reegan's face lit up, and she threw her arms around him for a quick hug. Stepping back, she said, "Seriously, Ezra? You want me to take over?"

"I've always known you were meant for the art world. You're an established photographer now with marketable connections, and I can see you still love this old place as much as I do. It would be a wonderful opportunity for you, Reegan, and it would give me a chance to relax. I don't know if you've noticed, my dear, but I've gotten old."

Reegan struggled with her words. Bernie caught a glance from her as though she were trying to gauge her reaction. Strange, Bernie thought.

"I need time to get settled in, Ezra, but yes, I'd love to take over the gallery!"

"You take all the time you need. When you're ready, we'll sit down and hammer out the details."

"Thank you, so much! Wow."

Bernie smiled. She knew this meant a lot to Reegan, and she was happy for her.

"I wish I had champagne," Ezra said with tears in his eyes.

"We'll celebrate later," Reegan said and pulled out her cell. "I've got to call Phillip and tell him the news."

Ezra led Reegan to his office so she could make her phone call in private. He stood next to Bernie when he came back in the gallery. Hooking his thumbs in the pockets of his vest, he said, "I was sorry to hear about Annie Mae."

"She'll be missed," Bernie said.

"Yes, she will."

Not liking this discussion, she said, "I meant to ask you who managed the estate sale?"

"I'll give you the company's card," Ezra said, then he reached into his pocket and pulled out a stack of business cards held together by a rubber band. He shuffled through the deck and handed a card to Bernie.

"Thank you."

Ezra nodded. "They should have the information you're looking for."

They both turned toward Reegan when she entered the main gallery. "Phillip's ecstatic!"

"Of course he is!" Ezra said.

"I wish we could stay and talk, Ezra, but we need to get going. I'll call you when I know more," Reegan said as she took hold of Bernie's sleeve and headed for the door.

"You take your time and get settled, dear. I'm not going anywhere," Ezra said and waved them out.

Chapter Twenty-Four

"Where to next?" Bernie asked as she pulled out of the parking lot.

"I want to go to Patch's and bring the boxes to Phillip's."

"To your house, you mean." Bernie smirked.

"Yes," Reegan said smiling. "It takes some getting used to. Anyway, I thought it would be easier to go through that stuff at Phillip's, um, at home."

"That sounds reasonable. Oh, what was in the last box? You never said."

"Oh, my God! I completely forgot," Reegan shouted. "You have some explaining to do, Bernadette Howard!"

"About what?"

"I've been so caught up in everything that's been going on, I forgot about the last box. There was a bag inside, a knapsack to be specific; you should remember it because you had to be the one to go back into the water to get it."

Bernie tried to concentrate on the road as she headed to Patch's house.

"Pull over."

"What?" She glanced at Reegan, who had crossed her arms tightly over her chest.

"Pull over, Bernie."

"There's too much snow piled up on the side."

"Pull over…please."

Bernie waited until she found a safe spot and pulled over. She held onto the wheel and stared out the window while Reegan glared at her. She sucked in a breath when Reegan put her hand on top of hers.

They were at the shore the night of the accident. Bernie was checking Reegan's pulse after she'd passed out. She needed to get help, but she was afraid they'd think she pushed Reegan off the bluff like they thought she'd killed her father. Panic filled her at the thought, but she contained it.

She rubbed her bare arms, then pinched the bridge of her nose when an image filled her mind. A knapsack caught on a fallen log deep in the water. Then she saw Gran's best friend, Patch. Opening her eyes, Bernie looked down at Reegan, whose breathing was steady, then out to the sea. She knew what the images meant. She had to get the knapsack and take it to Patch. Standing up she walked into the water, then dove; she knew exactly where it was…

"What the hell?" Reegan said after she'd broken the connection.

Bernie glanced at her as she tried to get her bearings. "I hate when you do that."

"I wouldn't have to if you would be honest with me!"

Bernie squeezed her eyes shut for a moment. Taking a breath, she put the truck in drive and got back on the road. She was pretty sure she heard Reegan growl.

"I *hate* it when you go in robot mode."

"What are you talking about?" Robot mode?

Reegan waved her hand in the air. "You're all

controlled as though it doesn't affect you, and I'm over here freaking the fuck out."

"All right."

"Stop it," Reegan said. "Stop pretending everything's fine when we both know it's not. You put up that wall, and you don't have to do that with me!"

"I—"

"And don't say you don't know what I mean because I know you do."

"What do you want me to say?" Bernie asked, though she was afraid of the answer.

"Whatever it is you're not saying. Whatever it is you're hiding from me. We can't do this and have secrets…"

Bernie glanced at her as she pulled onto Patch's street. Reegan had gone quiet, and that couldn't be good.

"I guess I can't say that when I know something you don't," Reegan said.

"All right." Bernie pulled into the driveway.

"Aren't you curious?"

"You'll tell me when you're ready," Bernie said and got out of the truck. She waited for Reegan because she had the key to Patch's house. She raised an eyebrow when Reegan slammed the truck door.

"Ezra is your great-uncle!" Reegan said as she stomped toward her. "Judging by your reaction, you already knew that."

Bernie's gaze followed Reegan while the other woman passed her with a glare. Sighing, she shoved her hands in the pockets of her coat and headed up the porch stairs. Closing the door, she could hear Reegan mumbling. She walked around the pile of boxes in the hall toward the kitchen were Reegan was taking off her coat.

"My mom told me about Ezra," Bernie said, and Reegan's head whipped up. "She told me never to mention it to anyone, not even Dad or Gran." That had been hard, keeping a secret from the people she loved most.

"You didn't tell them?"

"No. You have to understand my mom didn't say much when we would visit; Dad did most of the talking. One time Mom was having a good day, and Dad went to the front desk to see about getting her some flowers. My mom told me Ezra had delivered a painting earlier that day, and then she told me how they were related. She said Ezra didn't know, and she wanted to keep it that way; she made me promise not to tell anyone. And I didn't. Ezra still doesn't know."

"Why not tell him now?"

"There's a certain stigma that comes from being friends with me, Reegan, let alone being related. I wouldn't do that to him." Though she'd been tempted, she'd kept her promise. "How did you know?"

"Your mom told my mom." Reegan shrugged. "They were close. Is that why you stay up at your house all alone? Because of the stigma?"

Bernie took a seat on one of the stools after Reegan had hopped up on the island. "I've had Gran and Patch to take care of and talk to all these years."

"You never asked about the curse?" Reegan asked.

"Once I alluded to something about it to Gran. She told me to drop it, and I did. The morning she died, she called me into her bedroom and relinquished the promise to me before I left for Shady Pines." Tears prickled Bernie's eyes. Her Gran had been so wound up that morning, she'd almost stayed home with her.

"Do you think she knew she was going to die? That's why she told you?"

"I've thought about that, and I have to assume she did. She probably sensed it as I sense things."

"That sense is what I saw in the truck, right?"

"Yes," Bernie said.

"Does that happen often?"

There was something off about her tone. "What is it, Reegan?"

"It's not only the nightmares I've been having. Since I returned, I've had these strange images in my mind, photographs or snapshots, when I've seen certain people…"

Reegan explained her experiences. She'd had visions when she first came into contact with certain people and places. Bernie's eyes widened when Reegan told her about the bedroom scene and how that picture had come to pass.

"Your gift of sight seems to be escalating," Bernie said, and Reegan jumped down and started pacing. "First the nightmares, then the snapshots, and now the visions."

"Don't tell me this is going to get worse!"

"I'm not sure, but it would seem your gift is getting stronger."

"But I only get the visions when I touch you."

"When you touched the brooch," she said, and Reegan's face turned an interesting shade of pink.

"What about you? Have you had any moments of clarity recently?"

"No, I haven't." She wasn't sure whether she

should be relieved or worried.

"How did you know to follow them anyway?" Reegan asked when she stopped pacing.

"Haven't you had enough coffee?" Bernie asked when Reegan moved to start a pot.

"It helps me think," she said and poured water into the carafe. "Tell me how you figured out that you had to follow your visions."

"I was fourteen when I had the first one. I was waiting for Tori to meet me at the library, and all of a sudden I saw my house and my dad with such clarity that it scared me. I shook it off. It happened again, and I ignored it again because I wanted to hang out with Tori. Phyllis Cox came to me and said I had a phone call. Tori had popped a tire on her bike and had to go back home, so she wasn't coming. When I hung up, I got the image a third time, only everything was distorted. I went home right then, and you know what I found."

"God, Bernie." Reegan shook her head.

"I had a lot of time to think about it when I was away. If I had gone when I first had the vision, I could have saved him," Bernie said and wiped a tear away.

"You don't know that for sure, Bernie. Stop torturing yourself." Reegan gave her hand a quick squeeze. "Wait. If you were at the library and Phyllis Cox saw you, then you had an alibi for your father's murder."

"They said I had time to do it," she said not wanting to remember.

"How could Buck think that?"

"Buck wasn't there."

"What?" Reegan stopped pouring her coffee.

"Buck was testifying in city court when Dad was

murdered. He didn't get back until after my arraignment."

"That's convenient! How does everyone not know this? If Buck thought you were innocent, then—"

"I assaulted Deputy Carter," Bernie explained. "I broke his nose, so I wasn't innocent of what they charged me with." Part of her wasn't sorry either. She'd more than paid for it.

"How the hell did you break the nose of a grown man?"

"Dad taught me to defend myself, and I was angry." She fisted her hands. "It was bad enough my father was murdered and they thought I'd done it; but Carter said maybe Dad deserved it and maybe that's why my mom left him. He called my dad a monster, and then he said it didn't make a difference because we were trash."

"I would have killed him," Reegan said.

Bernie could still remember the hate she'd seen in Carter's eyes. He'd enjoyed saying those things about her father, taunting her. She let the anger take over; he never saw it coming. She'd reached across the small table and punched him in his face, not once but twice. He'd screamed, blood pouring from his nose, until the other deputies came in, and she'd fought them until they tackled her.

"I'm lucky they stopped me," Bernie admitted.

"Do you think he's the one who doctored the paperwork so you went to the state facility?"

"All I know for certain is that the deputies involved either transferred or quit when Buck came back."

"Why don't people know all this?" Reegan asked, and Bernie was again touched by the indignation in her tone.

"People believe what they want to. They need me to be guilty, and Buck was never able to produce a viable suspect, even though he tried."

"I'm so sorry, Bernie."

"Our experiences make us who we are. Good and bad. I've done things I'm not proud of, and I've been through my own personal hell. Most days I'm grateful for the person I've become because of and in spite of those things—"

"But?"

"But sometimes I wish things were different, that I was different."

Reegan toasted with her mug. "You're human after all."

Chapter Twenty-Five

It was early evening, and they were back at Reegan's house sitting at the kitchen table. They had repacked all of the boxes Reegan wanted to take and loaded them in Bernie's truck. She suspected Reegan didn't want to have a reason to go back to Patch's empty house. She could relate; seeing Gran's cottage every time she pulled into the driveway was like twisting a knife in her heart.

"So what do you do with your free time?" Reegan asked.

"I've always had Gran to take care of." There was something about the way Reegan said it that had her looking to where Phillip was talking on the phone in the other room. "Phillip told you about my inheritance, didn't he?" Bernie guessed.

"Do you want to tell me about it?"

Bernie sat back in her chair surprised that she did.

"It's actually not my business so—"

"My mother's uncle had amassed quite a fortune," Bernie began. "He left everything to her. After my parents married, Mom bought their house and put the rest of her inheritance in a trust for me when I turned twenty-one. Mom didn't tell anyone about it. Not even my dad. He'd thought her uncle had left them the house, and he sold that to pay for Shady Pines."

"And you moved into—"

"The shack," Bernie said so Reegan wouldn't have to. "Dad said we didn't need stuff when we had each other."

"That's horrible and wonderful at the same time."

Bernie glanced up to find compassion on Reegan's face. Would she ever get used to that? "Dad worked two jobs to keep Mom at Shady Pines, and Gran went through hell trying to make ends meet. I tried to find a job—"

"But no one in town would hire you."

She shook her head. "Phyllis Cox believed I was innocent, and she let me catalog books at night after the library had closed. We couldn't afford school, and I didn't qualify for a scholarship or a loan, so I worked as much as I could."

"You never thought about leaving? Going where no one knew you?"

"Like I said, I couldn't leave Gran, and she wouldn't leave Patch. I don't begrudge them, Reegan," she said when Reegan frowned. "It was hard, but we did the best we could."

"Then you got the money."

"Yes, Gran and I had never seen so many zeros." Bernie grinned. "She never had to worry about not having enough again." She looked up to see Reegan swiping tears from her cheeks, and Bernie blushed.

"I'm happy for you."

"Then why do you look so sad?" Bernie asked.

"It makes me think about Patch."

Bernie nodded.

"She knew you saved me, but she never said anything."

"Gran begged her not to."

"Because people might think you tried to kill me," Reegan guessed. "What did they say about your visions?"

"They said they couldn't give answers; I would find them for myself when and if I was ready. That's how it works, they said. You can't always be shown; sometimes you have to look to see."

"That's where you get that nonsense from," Reegan huffed.

"My dad used to say Gran and Patch were the canniest broads he'd ever met. I hoped they'd left us clues."

"The boxes?"

"Gran helped Patch pack them."

"Maybe that's why Annie Mae insisted I open them right away. She wanted to ensure I'd be here to make the connections," Reegan said. "Like the knapsack led me to you. And the pictures led me to the relationship between our parents that again led to you."

"I'd like to see those pictures," Bernie said.

"Phillip picked them up from my parents' house. I'll go get the box."

****

Bernie unconsciously caressed a photo of her father. He was so young then, and she'd never seen him so happy. They'd gone through most of the box, but she kept coming back to this picture of her father with his arm around Reegan's father's shoulders.

"What are you two looking for?" Phillip asked as he came into the room.

"Who have you been talking to?" Reegan asked.

Bernie looked down at the table to keep from laughing. She peeked up to see Phillip glance between herself and Reegan. He sighed and joined them at the table.

"I was talking to my deputies. June said she overheard some kids talking about going up to your house yesterday, Bernie. I had my people check into it, and it turns out they went up there on a dare."

"Does that happen often?" Reegan asked.

"Not as much as it used to," Bernie said. She didn't let it hurt her feelings anymore or tried not to. "I'm a kind of morbid attraction; come see the murderess."

"Punks," Reegan said.

"I'm all right to go home then?" Bernie asked, and Phillip squirmed in his chair.

"I think you should stay here with us until we figure this thing out," Reegan said.

"We're not holding you prisoner, Bernie, but you should be aware that another bad batch of weather will be rolling through here in the next hour or so," Phillip said, and Reegan scowled.

"Good to know," she said, then Reegan began telling Phillip that they were trying to figure out the clues, if any, that Patch left.

They stopped talking when Justin came in. Reegan kicked Bernie's shin and mouthed, "It'll be okay." Bernie nodded, even though she didn't agree.

"Mom wanted to contribute, so she bought dinner," Justin said as he began taking containers out of a bag. "She says they always get Chinese takeout on TV when they're trying to solve something."

"Did you tell her what's happening?" Phillip asked while he got plates.

"Forewarned is forearmed, as they say," Justin said.

Once they had filled their plates and were sitting around the table, Phillip brought Justin up to speed. Justin's eyes were on her every few minutes, but Bernie kept her head down while Phillip spoke. She smiled when Reegan changed the subject to taking over the gallery for Ezra and the information they'd found about the painting Phillip had purchased.

"Did Ezra know who handled the estate?" Phillip asked.

Bernie looked up when she realized he was asking her. "He gave me the company's card."

Phillip took the card Bernie fished out of her pocket and nodded. "I'll give them a call and see what they know. They might say more speaking with the sheriff."

"Excellent idea," Reegan said.

Bernie smiled at the sheepish grin that took over Phillip's face. She made the mistake of glancing over at Justin. He was staring at her. She looked away and sipped her water. When she set the glass back down, a photograph caught her eye from the stacks they'd moved to the end of the table.

Reaching out, she used her finger to turn the photo and drag it closer. It was an older picture of a handsome man with dark hair and light eyes. A lump form in her throat as she studied his face; she recognized pain when she saw it.

"The photographer captured a true moment there," Reegan said.

"His face is so familiar," Bernie said.

"That's my great-grandfather, Edwin Woods," Reegan said, grabbing a stack of pictures to show Bernie the rest of her family.

Bernie went back the image of Edwin Woods. "I've seen him before, but I can't place it."

"Maybe you saw the photo at Patch's? Maybe she and Annie Mae were going through them together?" Reegan suggested.

Bernie jumped up from the table. "I have to go home," she said and took her plate into the kitchen.

"Wait, why?" Reegan said following her.

"I have to check something," Bernie said, nervous with the thoughts running around her head.

"I'll go with you," Reegan said as she cleared off her own plate.

"No one is going anywhere with this storm passing through," Phillip said.

"I thought I wasn't a prisoner," Bernie countered, and Reegan agreed.

"There's no way in hell I'm letting you go anywhere in this weather." Phillip was speaking to Reegan, then turned and pointed to Bernie. "You either."

"It can't wait." She had to know.

"What is it, Bernie?" Reegan asked.

"I don't want to say until I see for myself that I'm right," she said as she pulled her boots on.

"I'll take you."

She looked at Justin, who'd said the words so softly, Bernie wasn't sure how she'd heard him. Her stomach did a flip, and she swallowed.

"I'm blocking you in, so you go with me or you don't go," he said and crossed his arms over his chest.

She didn't have a choice, did she? "Fine."

"And we'll be right behind you," Reegan insisted, and Phillip, though reluctant, agreed.

****

Bernie watched Justin out of the corner of her eye as he maneuvered the snow-covered streets. His hands flexed on the steering wheel every few minutes. She sighed and looked out the window. Reegan and Phillip were following them, but she hadn't seen their headlights in a while.

"Would you mind telling me what's so important that we're risking our necks to get it?" he asked after several minutes of silence.

"I have to check something out."

"That's it?" His hands flexed again.

"You didn't have to bring me," she reminded him. "In fact, I believe I wanted to come alone!"

"Fine," he growled.

"Fine," she countered feeling childish.

"You know this would go smoother if you would talk to me."

"*That's* convenient?"

"Don't make me stop this vehicle, Bernadette," he warned.

She snorted. "And what would you do? Reprimand me?" She didn't know why she was goading him, but she couldn't seem to help herself.

"I didn't mean to hurt you; I've said so. I apologized, and I'd appreciate it if you would stop throwing it in my face!" he shouted. "Did it ever cross your mind I was waiting for you to give me a signal? That I was waiting to see if you felt the same? But all I ever got from you was pity."

"I've never pitied you, Justin. I, of all people, understand what you went through. You acted like you couldn't bear to look at me." She could handle that

219

from strangers but not from him. It had crushed her.

"Because you wouldn't meet my eyes—like I was too damaged."

She turned in her seat. "You are not damaged! You've fought your entire life to be better than your circumstances. Yes, you've gone through things no one should, and yes, you lost your way, but when the dust settled, you didn't quit when you could have. No, *you* stood back up and kept fighting. That's who you are!"

Bernie straightened in her seat, steadying her breath as his hands gripped the steering wheel. She blinked back tears. His silence was unnerving. She didn't know what he was thinking and she wouldn't ask; they didn't speak the rest of the way.

"Stop here," she said after they'd pulled into the driveway and were about to pass Gran's cottage. She dug in her purse for her keys and hopped out of the SUV before Justin had turned off the engine. The snow was falling harder, and the wind blew her hair in her face.

Bernie unlocked the door and shivered. Her chest tightened when she caught a whiff of Gran's perfume that still clung to the air. She bit the inside of her cheek and hit the light switch just as Justin's boots thudded up the porch stairs behind her.

She glanced around him to see if Phillip and Reegan were behind them.

"They'll be here soon," Justin said and shook out of his coat.

She nodded and flicked on the light for the front porch, so they'd know where they were. She rubbed her ungloved hands together and turned, running into Justin's torso. His hands grabbed her arms to steady her. She glanced up and met his gaze.

"You do love me, don't you, Bernadette?" he asked and his eyes searched hers.

She tried to look away, tried to pull away, but he held firm. The truth choked her, exposed her, and Bernie didn't think she could let it go.

"Bernadette?" Justin's fingers squeezed gently into her biceps.

She could only stare into his deep blue eyes.

"What you said earlier"—he shook his head—"no one has ever made me feel the way you do." He wrapped his arms around her then, hugging her to him, holding her.

Bernie closed her eyes and let herself embrace him. He shifted and bent down until his lips were against hers. She froze for a second, then fell into him.

His beard was soft against her skin, while his lips were demanding. She opened her mouth to his, and his tongue played with hers. He pulled her closer to him, cradling her head in his arms and hers tightened around his back. Justin kissed her as though quenching a thirst; Bernie understood the need because she felt the same.

With care, he slowed and released her. Bernie's hand trembled when she reached up to touch her swollen lips. She couldn't discern his expression, but the sound of doors shutting had her sucking in a breath.

She moved to turn, but Justin caught her arm and said, "What you feel…I feel it too."

He let her go, and Bernie fled into the kitchen busying herself with making coffee. She tried to get her breathing under control and covered her lips to contain the joy that threatened to overwhelm her.

"You read my mind!" Reegan said coming into the

kitchen.

"Coffee," Bernie said, proud she could say anything at all.

"Exactly! I was just telling Phillip I would ask you if we could make some to ward off the chill. Hey, are you okay?" Reegan asked.

Bernie wished herself invisible when Reegan took her by the shoulders to give her the once-over.

"Oh, my God!" she squeaked, then whispered, "You were making out with Justin!"

Bernie's entire face went hot.

Reegan grinned. "How was it?"

Bernie covered her mouth with her hand feeling giddy. She didn't think she'd ever felt giddy in her entire life. "He kissed me…I…it just happened."

"Do you want to talk about it?…I didn't think so." Reegan sighed and took over the coffee preparation while Bernie stood motionless.

I do want to talk about it, Bernie thought. She wanted to share, but she wasn't sure how. If Gran were here—Gran! She shook herself and said, "I'll be right back."

She passed the men, ignoring the blush that swept her cheeks. Bernie went into Gran's room and turned on the lamp beside the bed. She swallowed as the emptiness tried to choke her.

She went into the closet and surveyed the contents. She glanced over her shoulder when Justin came into the room.

"Need help?" he asked.

"I'm looking for…there it is!" High on the top shelf, crammed against the ceiling, was a vintage hat box. "Can you reach that?" she asked, pointing to it.

He glanced at the shelf. "Yeah," he said. He had to strain but was able to get it down.

"Let's take that into the kitchen," she said, and he nodded.

"Coffee's ready," Reegan said as she sipped from her mug. "Is that why we came here?"

Bernie asked Justin to put the hat box on the table, and she opened it. "It's what's in the box." She pointed to the old photographs inside. "Gran was born out of wedlock and raised by a single mother. She said there were circumstances that kept her parents apart." She began removing photos.

"How does it pertain to our situation?" Phillip asked.

Bernie didn't answer him right away. She'd found what she was looking for—a faded old photo. She held it against her chest. "Gran had one picture of her father—just one," she said and handed the picture to Reegan.

Reegan choked on her coffee and looked up to stare at Bernie. "Patch and Annie Mae weren't just best friends."

"No," Bernie said. "They were sisters."

Chapter Twenty-Six

"You're sure?" Phillip asked after he'd inspected the photo.

"Positive," Bernie said. "When I was little, Gran kept that picture in her Bible. I asked her once who it was, and she told me it was her father. That's Edwin Woods."

"She's right, that's Patch's dad," Reegan said. "I'd know that face anywhere."

Bernie nodded. "I knew I recognized him, but I couldn't be sure it was the same man."

"That's why you insisted we come here," Justin said from where he leaned against the kitchen sink.

"I knew what it would mean if I was right."

"That Patch and Annie Mae were sisters or half-sisters," Reegan said.

Bernie glanced around the room, and a thought occurred to her. "Edwin had to tell them about the curse. He was their father, the link that connected them."

"They made their promise to him. Which means he's connected to all of this," Reegan said, encompassing the room with her hand.

"Didn't you say Patch left you her father's journals?" Bernie asked Reegan.

Reegan sucked in a breath. "Yes!"

"I guess this means we're headed back into the

storm," Phillip said, resigned.

Justin's lips twitched when Reegan said, "Damn straight."

"If we go, we're not coming back here tonight," Phillip said. "Bernie, I suggest you get anything else you need to stay at our house."

Bernie sighed. "All right."

After she'd grabbed a couple more things from her house, they tidied up the cottage, locked everything up, and headed to their vehicles.

"You know what else this means?" Justin asked.

"What?" Reegan asked.

"You two are cousins," Justin said with a sly grin.

Bernie stopped. Cousins? She glanced at Reegan, who was staring at her.

"It makes sense," Phillip said when he opened the door for Reegan.

Reegan's eyes left hers to ask Phillip what he meant.

"There's a resemblance," Justin said, taking hold of Bernie's hand and guiding her to his SUV.

"Yeah," Phillip agreed as he helped Reegan into her seat.

"I'll be damned," Reegan said before Phillip shut the door.

"Come on, Bernadette," Justin said, and Bernie sucked in a breath when he lifted her up and put her in the SUV. He shut the door before she could say anything.

She looked at Justin when he started the engine.

"You okay?" he asked as he eyed the rearview mirror.

She glanced behind her to see Phillip pull out of

the driveway. Her thoughts spun in her head. Circumstances had changed, and no doubt they would again before this was over. In her entire life, she'd been absolutely certain of one thing. "I do," Bernie said with a nod and straightened in her seat.

Justin sat back and gave her an odd look. "You do what?"

"Love you," she said. "I've loved you for as long as I can remember. That's why I—"

His lips found hers before she could finish her sentence. She cupped his cheek loving the feel of his beard under her fingers. His breath fanned against her lips after he'd pulled away.

"You don't know how long I've waited to hear you say that," he whispered. She swallowed the lump in her throat at the sincerity of his words, and her eyes filled with tears when he said, "I love you, Bernadette." Justin kissed her forehead and straightened in his seat.

Bernie was too afraid of what might come out if she spoke, so she nodded.

****

Bernie stifled a yawn and sipped her coffee while Reegan stared off into space. She knew Reegan had dreamt the same nightmare as the previous night because she'd seen it when she'd taken the other woman's hand again this morning. It was six a.m., and they'd been up until after one reading Edwin's journals.

They'd gone through half the box before they'd found a link between Patch and Gran. Edwin had written about meeting Bernie's great-grandmother. He'd talked about falling in love with her and feeling desperate because he'd committed adultery so soon after Patch's birth. He had wanted to leave his wife, but she threatened to take Patch away. He couldn't lose his daughter, but he wouldn't lose the love of his life either, and they'd continued the affair in secret.

"What are you thinking?" Reegan asked now.

"I'm running through what we found last night in my head," Bernie told her, looking up when Justin came into the kitchen.

"I've got to go open the shop," he said as he put his coat on and filled a travel cup with coffee. He'd brought his duffel bag last night, so he wouldn't have to go home to get ready for work. They hadn't had time to talk privately, and Bernie was relieved because she wasn't sure what she'd say.

"You need to hire a manager," Reegan said, and Bernie hid her smile.

"He won't," Phillip said. He came into the kitchen fresh from his shower, wearing jeans and a nice sweater.

"Maybe someday." Justin's eyes met Bernie's, and she looked down at the table. "I'll talk to you guys later."

Bernie's eyes shot up to Reegan's after she kicked her in the shin. "She should go talk to him, shouldn't she, Phillip?" Reegan said.

Phillip put his hands up in the air. "I'm not getting involved."

"Bernie, he wants to talk to you," Reegan said.

"All right." She wasn't afraid to speak with Justin. She was afraid of the things he made her feel. She wasn't sure how to contain those emotions. With a sigh, she pulled her robe tighter, thankful she at least had on slippers.

She went out the side door, into the open garage,

and shivered as the winter wind cut through her clothes. Justin had already started the SUV and was scraping snow off the windows. He looked up when she got closer.

"Bernadette, it's freezing out here," he said, coming over to her.

She wrapped her arms around herself as her eyes searched his. Bernie was a bit embarrassed and thought about blaming it on Reegan. Instead she said, "I wanted to say…"

Justin saved her from herself and enveloped her in the warmth of his jacket. Her arms went around his back, and she rested her cheek against him. "I love you and I always have," he whispered against the top of her head, and her heart filled.

"I love you too," she mumbled into his flannel shirt.

"There are a lot of things we need to discuss," Justin said, then kissed her brow and he stepped away. "Unfortunately, they'll have to wait." She nodded, and he studied her. "You realize in order for this to work you're going to have to let me in—full disclosure."

"I'll do the best I can."

"That's a start. Now go inside before you freeze," he said, and after a quick kiss, he pointed her back toward the house.

"Reegan went to take a shower," Phillip said when she walked in. "We've invited our parents for dinner tonight."

"That's good. They can be brought up to date, and I can finally go home."

"I think you should be here too."

"Why did I know you'd say that?" She rubbed her

face. Part of her wanted to stay so she didn't have to face Gran's empty cottage, but the other part of her resented that weakness. Regardless of either of those things, she did want some time to herself to process all that had happened.

"I know this is hard for you, Bernie, trust me I do; but there's too much at stake for us to cater to any one person's feelings. It's important for us to stick together."

Phillip had been a friend to her when not many had, and he'd never wanted anything in return. She was being stubborn when all he wanted to do was help. "You're right, of course."

He seemed surprised, and it took a moment, but he smiled. "Good, I'm glad we're on the same page…Now, I have to go into the office for a few hours. Reegan said she wanted to finish going through your great-grandfather's journals, if that's okay with you."

Hearing the family connection caught her off guard, but she was able to say, "Yes, that's fine."

Bernie waited until Phillip left before she went and took a shower. She put on jeans, a dark gray sweater over a white t-shirt, and a pair of black boots. She dried her hair, then pinned it up off her face before she put on her minimal amount of makeup.

She found Reegan in the den with a cup of coffee. She'd also put on a pair of jeans and a sweater, though hers was burgundy. Her brown hair was up in a bun, and her gray eyes were staring holes into Bernie.

"What is it, Reegan?"

"I know we didn't get a chance to talk about it last night, but you do see it, don't you?"

Bernie sat down on the couch. "See what?"

"The resemblance?"

She sat back and studied Reegan's face. "I can see it." She didn't know if she was allowed to be happy about it or not, so she didn't comment further.

"Me too. I'm not sure I would have noticed if it hadn't been pointed out. This I did notice," she said and picked up two photographs from the coffee table. She handed them to Bernie.

Bernie studied the two photos: one of her father and the other of Edwin Woods. "They have the same eyes," she said, and Reegan nodded.

"I wonder why Patch and Annie Mae never told anyone."

Bernie set the pictures down. "People thought Gran and Patch were the ones who would bring about the curse, and that was only because they were friends; imagine if people knew they were sisters. They probably kept it secret for so long that it became second nature to them. Besides, knowing them, it's safe to say they relished outsmarting everyone."

Reegan smiled. "You're probably right on that last part, but it makes me wonder why not them? I mean they *were* sisters."

"That thought occurred to me too. It would make more sense, right? Then I remembered how we said all the pieces needed to be in place—all the players. That hasn't changed just because we found out that Gran and Patch were sisters."

"You're right," Reegan said, though she didn't sound happy about it. "I guess we should finish going through these journals."

"May as well." Bernie took the one of the

remaining books from the table.

They read in silence most of the morning stopping when either found something interesting. Like when Gran and Patch were first introduced, and it was love at first sight. Then there was the entry about Edwin's father dying of consumption and another about his mother finding out about Gran and loving her despite the circumstances. This was their history, hers and Reegan's; blood connected them.

"Holy shit!" Reegan shouted, startling Bernie.

"What? What is it?"

"Listen to this," Reegan began. " 'I'm not who I thought I was.' "

Bernie stared at Reegan who had stopped to read ahead. "Reegan?"

"Sorry. 'I'm not who I thought I was. Today my mother, or the woman I've always known to be my mother, died, but before she met our Lord in the hereafter, she made a confession. She told me that, though she loved me as her own child, I had not come from her loins—' "

"What?"

"Look," Reegan said and pointed in the journal so Bernie could follow along as she read. " 'I was given to her by her mistress, who begged my mother to keep me safe. I was given to her on the morning of my birth along with a few trinkets and two years' wages. I asked who had given birth to me, and my mother said she'd sworn an oath that she'd never say the name. What my mother didn't realize was that she'd given herself away. The only time she'd served a mistress was at the Willows.' "

Bernie sat down, and Reegan sat next to her. "Does

this mean what I think this means?" she asked and turned to look at Reegan, who appeared dazed.

"He didn't die," Reegan choked out, her hand going to her abdomen.

Tears filled Bernie's eyes when Reegan began to cry. "Edwin Woods was Minerva's son. Which means—"

"We're the descendants of Minerva Whit."

Chapter Twenty-Seven

Bernie sat back as shock played across the faces around the table. Reegan's father was the most disturbed by what they'd uncovered. She could relate; it was a lot to take in.

She and Reegan had sat in silence until Phillip came home, and they went through the motions again. She suspected Reegan felt things deeper than she did because her soul had once resided in Minerva's body. Bernie was relieved not to have to feel that kind of agony.

Phillip had called Justin and told him what they'd found, so he was composed in the seat next to her. Cindy and Reegan's mother, Beth, were both teary-eyed while they took turns reading form the journal. Every now and again, she'd catch a glimpse of a shadow in the doorway, and she knew June was eavesdropping. Bernie glanced at Reegan to bring her attention to June, but the other woman used her eyes to direct Bernie's attention to Buck. He was unmoved.

"How much did you know, Buck?" Reegan asked.

Bernie hid her smile. Being that she'd been on the receiving end of Reegan's questioning, Bernie was familiar with the tone; somewhere between an accusation and a delicate F-you. Buck, of course, barely blinked.

"I knew they were sisters," Buck said shocking

everyone.

"Mom told you?" Reegan's dad asked.

"No, David, she didn't. I suspected and acted on those suspicions by testing their DNA."

"Buck," Cindy admonished.

"I told them I was doing it, and they didn't care as long as I kept it to myself. Which I have, thank you. As for the other thing, no, I didn't know. But I'm not surprised."

"Dad, if there's anything else you'd like to share, now's the time," Phillip said, sitting back and crossing his arms over his chest.

"No, son, I'm good," Buck said and sipped his coffee. Father and son stared each other down for a few minutes until Reegan's mom asked a question.

"What I want to know is how Edwin found out about the curse when his mother wouldn't even give him a name? And his mother says 'her mistress,' which would mean the stepmother, right?"

"You're on to something, Beth," Cindy said. "The lady of the house would have been Clara, not either of the girls. She had to be the one who gave Edwin to the Woodses."

"Which means Clara was trying to protect the baby," Reegan added.

"That and making sure no one could use the child against Minerva. Do you think Gran and Patch knew all of this?"

"They had to have, right? I mean, they had the journals," Reegan said.

"I don't understand why they didn't tell us this in the first place," Reegan's dad said and pushed away from the table.

"I don't like it either, Dad, trust me, but they had their reasons."

"I agree," Bernie said. "But Beth's right. If Edwin's adopted mother wouldn't tell him the name of his birthmother, then how'd he find out about the curse? We read all the journals, and none of them mention it."

"That's what you girls have to find out. You have to learn what was unknown and make it right," Buck said as he too got up from the table.

Later, Bernie stayed seated while Reegan and Phillip walked their parents and June out. Justin stared at her, and her cheeks heated. "What?"

"You're taking this well."

"On the outside I am," she said, startled when he took one of her hands between his.

"You can talk to me," he whispered.

"Reegan says that all the time too," she said and pulled her hand from his grasp. "What you two don't seem to understand is that I don't know how." She looked up to see Reegan and Phillip standing there. How humiliating, she thought. "I wanted to take a look at the things in the other boxes."

"Sure," Reegan said, and Bernie was relieved that no one made any other comments.

"Oh, this one makes no sense," Reegan said after she lifted the lid of the first box she'd come to. "It's old firewood."

Bernie peeked in the box. "That's strange even for Patch." She lifted out a log. It was heavier than she thought, and Reegan grabbed the other end when she lost her grip. Her eyes slammed shut, and her mind seized.

"Hear me now," Bernie shouted, though it was not

her voice she heard. "She has deceived us all! You must see beyond her lies." She looked beside her to where the woman, who Bernie knew was Reegan, panted. They were tethered at the waist to two neighboring posts, their shoulders close enough to touch.

"How could I not have seen it? How could I not have known?" her sister whispered.

Tears fell from Bernie's eyes. "You cannot undo this once it is done. Do not damn yourselves," she shouted.

She blinked, and the room had darkened as though some time had elapsed. A hiss, like the serpent from Eden himself was beckoning, penetrated the silence before the side of the building was engulfed in flame.

"No matter how long it takes, the world will make this right!" she screamed, hoping her words would reach someone. No one came, and soon the fire surrounded them; embers scorched their skirts. She reached out her one free hand touching her sister's cheek as the inferno fell upon them, consumed them...

The flames licked at Bernie's skin, and she tried to shake off the embers. Gasping, she pulled off her sweater leaving her in only her undershirt. Bernie stomped on the fabric, then turned and tripped on a branch, falling facefirst onto the cold ground. She could smell her flesh burning.

Arms were around her, and she screamed.

"Bernadette, stop! Calm down, you have to calm down. Breathe!"

She twisted in the man's grip trying to break free. She was on fire.

"Bernadette, it was a vision. You're safe now. I swear to God, I'll keep you safe."

Bernie choked on a sob and stilled in Justin's arms. It took a moment to get her bearings and realize the vision had ended. She looked around and wasn't sure how she got outside.

She took a shuddering breath. She wasn't burning alive. Knowing the truth couldn't stop the tears, she began to tremble. She shook in Justin's arms, sucking in a breath after he took off his coat and put it around her. His warmth seeped into her flesh. She tried to stand and failed. Justin swept her up in his arms and carried her back to the house.

He walked them through the house and into the guest bathroom, where he set Bernie on the vanity. He turned the shower on, then took the coat from around her shoulders and rubbed her bare arms with his hands.

"You need to get warm. Bernadette, do you understand?" he asked when she didn't respond.

What could she say? Bernie wondered. She didn't want to speak, afraid of what she might reveal. She didn't want to think, afraid of what she might remember. All she wanted to do was feel. With that in mind, she reached up and started unbuttoning Justin's shirt.

His hands stopped hers, and his eyes asked questions she didn't know how to answer. She could show him. She reached up and brought his lips to hers. She poured the words she couldn't speak into the kiss, and when she began undoing buttons, he didn't stop her.

Her lips left his so he could set her on her feet. She undid her hair, undressed without a word, and entered the shower, where steam billowed above the stall. The spray was hot, seeming to pierce her flesh. She closed her eyes while the door opened and shut behind her. Justin's frame took up most of the stall, and she moved so he could get under the spray.

"You need to get warm," he whispered, and Bernie turned to face him because there had been a tremor to his voice.

He cupped her cheek and kissed her softly as he reached up and adjusted the showerhead so the spray was fully on her. He released her lips and wrapped her in his arms. Justin held her while both his heat and the water warmed her.

His erection pressed into her, but Justin made no attempt to act on it. Bernie rubbed her cheek against him and moved her hands up around his back, feeling the marred flesh. She opened her eyes and pulled back to examine him. He stilled beneath her palm when her fingers traced the scars; she glanced up to gauge his reaction.

"It's not pretty," he said.

"You're beautiful to me, Justin," she said reaching up to caress his bearded cheek. "You nearly died in that explosion, were trapped under burning rubble for goodness knows how long, and you survived. These scars are a tribute to your courage. That's what I see when I look at you, at these—"

He kissed her then. His tongue conveyed the things *he* couldn't say. She wrapped her arms around his neck as he leaned down for better access.

Without preamble, he lifted her up against the wall of the shower; her legs went instinctively around him. The tiles were cool on her back, while his mouth was hot on hers. Her arms tightened, and somehow he deepened the kiss.

His hands gripped her backside, and the head of his erection was at her entrance. She dug her heels into his back hoping to encourage him, and after a moment, he pushed upward.

Bernie gasped as he stretched her. Justin released her lips, and she opened her eyes to find him staring at her. He adjusted their position, and her eyes closed when he went deeper.

"Relax," he whispered.

Bernie let out a shaky breath, then bit her lip when he began to move. Slow deep strokes allowed the pleasure to build while his mouth made love to hers. His hands shifted to her thighs, and he picked up the pace.

Justin's fingers bore into her flesh to control the rhythm. The pressure built as her orgasm began to coil inside her. Her nails dug into his back, and he groaned while his hips slammed against her.

Bernie pulled her lips away from his; her entire body clenched, and she convulsed around him. Swearing, Justin set about an impossible pace. He stopped abruptly and pulled her tight against him as he too climaxed.

He let her down after a few moments, her legs sliding along his while he kissed her brow. Bernie stepped under the shower's spray on shaky legs. Justin caught her elbow to steady her, and she glanced up at him, amused at his concern.

They showered together, Justin giving her sly glances and she giving him shy smiles. He wrapped a towel around her after he turned off the water. He knotted the towel at his waist, then lifted her chin so she would meet his eyes.

"You're not regretting this, are you?" he asked.

She shook her head, and he nodded. Once he turned around, she covered her mouth with her hand to try to keep the joy in. Justin opened the bathroom door and peered outside.

"We're clear," he said, then scooped her up in his arms and carried her to her room.

She stood in the middle of the room while he went to get his duffel bag. Bernie caught her reflection in the mirror and had to do a double take. She could practically see the happiness radiating from her. She straightened and covered her mouth with both her hands trying to gather her wits.

She looked up when Justin came back into the room. His eyes held hers as he shut the door.

"You need to get dressed so you can stay warm," he told her, setting his duffel down. He took some clothes out of his bag and dropped his towel.

Bernie couldn't help gaping at him while he dressed. She hadn't had time before to appreciate the view. She knew Justin took care that his body would hold up to his firehouse standard, and he'd succeeded. The scars from the explosion ran from his left side and covered his back. The shrapnel scars on his arms and legs didn't detract from the powerful image he presented.

Of course she'd loved him when he was gangly and awkward. It hadn't mattered that his shirts were too small or his pants too short. She'd been able to see the rugged beauty beneath.

If she were honest, his looks had been a second thought to her; his mind had been the first. They'd had many discussions as children on the playground. He hadn't been afraid of the bully she projected, and she hadn't cared that he was the poorest kid in school. They'd been friends until—

"Bernadette, please get dressed," he said once he'd finished.

She nodded and went to the drawer. She let her towel fall turning her back to him while she put on her underwear.

"What's that?" Justin asked coming up behind her.

Bernie ignored him and put her bra on. She turned to grab her jeans, and he stopped her. She stilled while he moved her hair off her back. She been so caught up in him that she'd forgotten herself. "You're not the only one with scars," she said with a tightlipped smile. She put on her jeans and pulled a sweatshirt over her head while he stared at her. She sat on the bed to put on some socks.

"I know stab wounds when I see them," he said.

Bernie stared at him.

"Full disclosure."

Bernie bit the inside of her cheek. "It was an accident," she said and tried to pass him, but he blocked her escape. "I want to go check on Reegan."

"Phillip's taking care of her," he said, then pointed at her. "I want the truth! One scar is an accident; several is not."

"Phillip told you Tori tried to kill me," she said, though she didn't know how the words passed her lips. She didn't discuss it. Ever.

"Tried and nearly succeeded are not the same thing, and you damn well know it."

"I don't want to talk about it." She sat back on the edge of the bed.

"That's not an option; you're going to tell me."

Bernie closed her eyes for a moment. "All right," she began, and Justin stood legs apart and arms crossed as if bracing himself for what she was about to say. Bernie sat straighter and told him what happened as though she was presenting a case rather than reliving a memory. It was the only way she could keep the emotions contained.

"Jesus," Justin said when she finished.

"Gran found us and called 911."

"And you didn't press charges?"

Bernie shrugged. "Tori will never be fit for trial."

"That doesn't answer my question. *You* didn't press charges?"

"Tori wasn't Tori that night, and I wouldn't condemn her to what I went through."

"She tried to kill you!" Justin shouted, walking over to her and taking hold of her shoulders.

"You don't understand. They wouldn't have sent her to prison. They would have sent her to the state facility. I couldn't do that to anyone, much less Tori."

Justin dropped his hands and stepped back. "You're right, I don't understand."

"Gran didn't either," she admitted. "So I'll tell you what I used to tell Gran. Tori's mind is gone, and unless they find a way to get it back, she'll die there; they don't plan on ever releasing her."

"That's something, at least. Don't look at me like I'm the bad guy. I love you, and I'll do whatever it takes to protect you from the curse, from Tori, even from yourself."

She regarded him for a moment, then sighed. "I'll do the best I can to accept that."

"Good," Justin said. "Now tell me what the hell happened in that vision."

Chapter Twenty-Eight

It wasn't Reegan's screaming that woke her the next morning; it was Justin leaping out of bed from where he'd been sleeping next to her. Bernie sat up and turned on the bedside lamp to see him jerking as though trying to shake off the devil.

"Justin," she said calmly, then repeatedly with more aggression, until he stopped and looked at her. "What's wrong?"

He shook his head. "That damn dream!"

"The one you told us about where you drowned?"

"Yeah," he said taking a shaky breath. "This time was different."

"How?"

"I caught a glimpse of the guy who pushed me."

"Did you recognize him?"

Justin ran a hand over his beard. "That's the thing; I don't know who it was, but he did. Does that make sense?"

"Unfortunately, that means whoever you were before recognized the person who pushed him overboard."

"You're thinking it's another betrayal?"

"Yes, it's all connected. You uncovered something, and they wanted to silence you."

"*They* succeeded," Justin said.

Bernie stared down at the tattoos on her wrists. She

didn't want to think about the implications; what if death was their destiny? This curse would kill them if they didn't uncover the truth.

"Bernadette?"

"Sorry." She sighed, and he leaned in to kiss her forehead. "I have a million thoughts running around in my head."

"I'd prefer you didn't filter your thoughts with me."

"Full disclosure."

He half-smiled. "Yeah."

"I just—we have to figure this out."

He took her hand and squeezed it. "We will." He moved to the dresser to turn off the alarm when it started buzzing. "I'm going to grab a quick shower," he said and left the room.

After making the bed, Bernie put on her robe and slippers and headed to the kitchen to make coffee. She was surprised to find Reegan sitting at the table holding a mug in both hands. She watched her out of the corner of her eye as she poured herself a cup. "Are you all right?" she asked sitting across from Reegan.

Reegan took a sip from her mug. "I dreamt of the day of my accident last night; I never thought I'd be happy to have that dream, but I can honestly say I'm relieved."

"After everything you've seen, that's understandable," Bernie said. "About the vision last night—"

"I don't want to talk about it…ever."

"Agreed."

"I did notice Justin's room was empty this morning."

Heat crept up Bernie's neck, and she cleared her throat. "Yes, he slept in my room."

"So"—Reegan sipped her coffee, grinning—"how was it?"

Bernie stared a moment.

"Not saying anything lets me draw my own conclusions."

"It was intense."

"That's more like it," Reegan said and toasted Bernie with her mug.

Bernie's blush deepened, and she changed the subject by telling Reegan about Justin's dream.

"I thought you weren't going in today," Reegan said to Phillip when he came in the room wearing in his uniform.

"I just have to finish up a couple of things from yesterday, then I'll be back."

"Okay."

"Phillip, did you get a chance to call the company that handled the estate sale?" Bernie asked as Justin came in the room saying good morning.

"Yes, I did. With all the revelations you two made yesterday, I didn't want to add to the chaos."

"What do you mean?" Reegan asked.

Phillip squirmed.

"What did they say?" Bernie asked.

"The estate belonged to Tori's great aunt," Phillip said.

Before Bernie could think, Reegan started shouting at her. "Did you know? Bernie, you tell me the truth right now!"

"How could I have possibly known?"

"*Maybe* you didn't want to admit that Tori could be

part of this," Reegan accused.

"What do you want me to say, Reegan?" Bernie asked standing. "Do I want Tori to be involved? No, but that doesn't even matter. She's never getting out of Shady Pines, so she's not a threat to us. You may have forgotten this, Reegan, but I'm in this with you. I have as much to lose as you do!"

"I'm just saying your view is pretty skewed when it comes to Tori."

"How many voicemails have you left for Syd—"

"Don't you dare—"

"That's enough! How about we check all the facts before we go jumping to conclusions?" Phillip interjected.

Reegan said, "Oh, whatever."

"Fine," Bernie said. She'd keep her opinions to herself. But she wasn't the only one who was blinded when it came to childhood best friends. At least she could admit it, if only to herself.

"Phillip's right," Justin said. "Remember Annie Mae and Patch told you 'You can trace the path that led to this'? We know that meant tracing genealogy, so maybe it's not only yours that needs to be traced."

"Good point," Phillip said. "You'll need to go check records; our online services only go back to 1920."

Reegan frowned. "Where do we go for that?"

"They've moved the records to the library while they renovate town hall," Phillip said.

Bernie stood up. "We need to go see Phyllis Cox."

Chapter Twenty-Nine

Phyllis Cox was in her late seventies with steel gray hair that she wore in a short bob. Her style hadn't changed from the sleek suits she'd worn in the eighties, except now she wore orthopedic shoes with her pantyhose instead of heels. Her glasses were trendy and perched on her nose, enlarging her light blue eyes.

Bernie had called Phyllis to see if she would mind letting them in early, and the librarian had agreed. She'd said she'd meet them at the back door at seven. She was doing them a favor, and though Bernie was grateful, she wasn't sure why Phyllis would go to the trouble.

"Come on in, girls," Phyllis said, her voice hurried and her eyes darting around.

"Are you all right, Phyllis?" Bernie asked.

"Are you?" Phyllis whispered as she shut and locked the door.

Bernie studied the woman a moment. There was something off about her, but before she could comment, Reegan shifted the box she carried to her side. "We need to look through some of the older records that aren't online," Reegan said.

Phyllis looked Reegan up and down. "That's what Bernadette said when we spoke on the phone. The records are in the basement, and you two are welcome to them."

"Thank you for helping us, Phyllis," Bernie said while they made their way down the tiled hall.

"You're welcome. I'm sorry about Annie Mae," Phyllis said, pushing the down button on the elevator. She glanced at Reegan. "I'm sorry about Patch too, dear."

Reegan was taken aback by Phyllis's comment, but she shook it off. Bernie took a deep breath. They'd both lost so much and stood to lose more if…

"What's in the box?" Phyllis asked Reegan.

"These are some old newspaper clippings Patch left me."

"We wanted to see if you thought they were worth keeping," Bernie said as they boarded the elevator.

Phyllis nodded. "I'll take a quick look. We have a couple hours before I need to open up."

Once they got to the bottom floor, Phyllis walked them down another hall, passing a small bathroom and stopping at a room whose door read Study Hall. She unlocked the door and hit the lights. The rows of fluorescent ceiling fixtures popped on in an eerie procession.

Bernie was startled when Reegan put her lips to her ear and whispered, "That's not ominous or anything."

Bernie snorted. The lights did little to brighten the windowless room. There were four rows of old bookshelves, each shelf packed with bankers' boxes, on one side of the room. Two dark oak tables and chairs were on the opposite side. At least they'd have plenty of space to spread out, Bernie thought.

"All the records predating 1920 are in those rows there," Phyllis said, pointing to the two rows farthest from the door.

"Thank you," Bernie said. She shrugged out of her jacket as Reegan set the box she carried on one of the tables, and Phyllis went to the corner of the room and hit another light. There was a small table with a coffee pot; she glanced at Reegan, who grinned.

"It gets cold down here, so you may want to fix some coffee to warm yourselves up," Phyllis suggested, then pointed to the box on the table. "Let me have a look at those."

Bernie and Reegan set up their workspace while Phyllis went through the box. They'd commandeered legal pads and pens from Phillip's office, so they could take notes. Reegan set up her laptop and hooked it up to the Wi-Fi once Phyllis gave her the password. Bernie unpacked and reread the notes she'd already made.

"I'm going to get water so we can make some coffee," Reegan said.

"The bathroom is up the hall on your right," Phyllis said.

Bernie went back to her notes. After a moment, she looked up to find Phyllis staring at her. "Did you find something?"

Before Phyllis could answer, Reegan came back in the room.

"Phyllis, where are the coffee filters?" Reegan asked, and Phyllis got up from her seat to show her.

Bernie shook her head and made a few notations on one of the legal pads. The other women talked as they prepared the coffee. After a loud bang and a soft thud, her head whipped up.

"Are you okay?" Reegan asked.

Bernie was quick to rise when she saw Phyllis had fallen. She stood next to Reegan, both of them hovering over her. "Are you all right?" Bernie asked.

"Indeed," Phyllis said from her position on the floor. "I tripped on the trashcan, of all things!" Bernie and Reegan helped her to her feet. "There now, no worse for wear," Phyllis said.

They hadn't yet let go of Phyllis's hands when Reegan whispered, "Bernie."

Bernie knew what Reegan was asking. Though reluctant, she took Reegan's hand. It only took a moment for the world to shift beneath her.

The young girl pressed her ear against the door so she could hear what her mother and aunt were saying...

"What if it's true? What if my daughter and that friend of hers, Annie Mae, are the ones who will bring about the Willows curse," her aunt said.

"Do you believe that? Truly?" her mother asked.

"He went to see her at Shady Pines the day he died."

"You said he was doing research for a novel."

"That's what he told me, but what if he wasn't? I've always felt there was something off about my little girl—"

"You can't possibly believe that!"

The child waited until her aunt had left to go into the kitchen. Her mother was staring out the window. "Mamma," the girl said.

"Yes, darling?" The woman squatted down to look her daughter in the eye.

"What's a curse?"

Her mother stood, took the child's hand, and led her to the study. "I do believe it's time you learned a few things, my darling"—she closed the door—"and Phyllis?"

"Yes, Mamma?"

"This must be our secret…"

"What was that?" Phyllis asked after the connection was broken.

Bernie took a step back. "You saw it?"

Phyllis nodded.

"It was a vision," Reegan explained.

Bernie thought Phyllis might either faint or run; she did neither. No, Phyllis Cox, proclaimed Napoleon of the Willows Bluff public library, started to giggle until she could barely contain herself.

"I wasn't expecting that reaction, were you?" Reegan asked Bernie.

"It's always the quiet ones," Bernie said, biting her lip.

"I knew this day would come," Phyllis said. She straightened her suit and clasped her hands. "And I knew it would be you two."

"How?" Bernie and Reegan asked at once.

"My aunt was your great-grandmother," she said pointing to Reegan as she took a seat at the closest table. "Patch's mother."

"You and Patch were cousins? No one ever told me," Reegan said.

"That's because your great-grandmother became quite paranoid and cut ties with most people not long after that day. She'd always been a bit of a recluse, or so Mother said."

"Patch knew you were cousins though, right?" Reegan asked.

Phyllis laughed. "Of course she did!"

"Dad never mentioned it."

"David doesn't know," Phyllis said with a shrug.

"Why the hell not? What is it with everyone keeping these family connections a secret? What's the big deal?" Reegan asked.

"The big deal, young lady, is that it's difficult to make assumptions about one's true purpose if the links are not there to connect them to one another."

"Huh?" Reegan said.

Having worked with Phyllis for several years, Bernie was familiar with the older woman's thought process. "What I think Phyllis is trying to say is that they didn't want anyone to realize the family connection; then they'd have the upper hand in whatever clandestine operation they had going on here."

Phyllis nodded. "Exactly!"

"Wait, so you're saying you're a spy or something?" Reegan asked.

Phyllis pursed her lips, then a moment later, a smile spread across her face. "Yes."

"I need that coffee now," Reegan said and went to pour herself a cup.

Bernie turned to Phyllis. "All these years you've been a sleeper agent for Patch and Gran?" she asked feeling absurd. That had to be why Phyllis had seemed so nervous when they'd arrived.

"Not exactly," Phyllis said when Reegan handed her a cup of coffee.

Bernie took the mug Reegan offered and took a sip while Reegan took the seat across from her.

"I'm here for you," Phyllis said as though that explained it all.

"For us?" Reegan asked.

"You said you knew this day would come and you

knew it would be us," Bernie said.

"Yes, and thank you for not trying to deny the truth," Phyllis said with a smirk. "As you saw, my mother told me a secret that day, one that would change my life forever."

"Explain," Reegan said.

Phyllis cleared her throat. "Well, my mother's mother, my grandmother, was a cook—"

"Let me guess, she worked for the Whits," Reegan said.

"Yes," Phyllis said. "She was at the Willows a month or so after the fire, after rumors of the curse were polluting the streets, and long after Clara's father, Mr. Marshal, had taken his daughter and granddaughter out of town to safety."

"I thought they were safe because they were born here," Reegan said.

"Mr. Marshal knew what he was about, or so my grandmother said."

"Reegan," Bernie said, waiting for the other woman to look at her. "Think of everything Clara did to try to protect Amelia and Minerva."

"You think her father knew the truth about what she'd done?"

"If people found out, they may have tried to capture her too. She needed help; I would have gone to my father," Bernie whispered and jumped when Phyllis patted her hand.

"That's how I knew you were one of them," Phyllis told Bernie.

"What do you mean?" Bernie asked.

"I knew you were here the day your father was murdered and that deputy tried to cover it up. He didn't fool me. Even then, the odds were against you. And when Reegan had her accident, I knew she was the other."

"My dad said people believed that excluded me," Reegan said.

"You survived the obstacles thrown at you just as Bernadette did."

"Let's get back to your grandmother," Bernie suggested.

Phyllis nodded. "When my grandmother went back to the Willows that day, she wasn't the only one who'd come to pay their respects. Clara was also there, and they cried together. They spoke of the girls and then of the curse. Clara told my grandmother she hoped it was true—"

"Wait," Reegan said. "Hoped what was true?"

Phyllis gave Reegan a pained look. "She told my grandmother she hoped the girls' souls would find their way back and make those responsible pay for what they'd done. That's when my grandmother gave her word to Clara she'd keep the truth accounted for; if and when the girls came back they would have someone to turn to for help. My grandmother promised Clara, my mother promised my grandmother, and I promised my mother the records would be kept and kept safe."

Bernie sat back in her seat eyeing Phyllis, who sipped her coffee as though she hadn't said what she'd said. "Did Gran know?"

"She and Patch may have suspected, but we never spoke of it."

"Why not?" Reegan asked.

"Because it wasn't theirs to know."

Reegan snorted. "Oh, that makes perfect sense!"

"Reegan, they had their secrets too," Bernie reminded her.

"True," Reegan said. "So, Phyllis, where's this account of the truth?"

"It's here. I brought it with me after I spoke with Bernadette this morning." She got up, moved to the last row, and picked up a box. "This is everything we've compiled over the years," she said setting the box on the table between them.

Phyllis pulled out a stack of papers and two old leather-bound ledgers. Bernie covered her laugh with a cough after Reegan sang a few bars from *The Twilight Zone*.

"Grandmother took her promise to heart. She made a list of everyone who worked at the Willows or was involved with the Whits in any capacity. Mother made it her business to keep tabs on anyone who stayed in Willows Bluff."

"Did she know about Edwin Woods?" Reegan asked.

"Of course," Phyllis said without looking up from her notes.

"So you knew he was Minerva's son—"

Phyllis gasped. "A direct descendant? We thought he was connected because he was born the same day the girls died."

"Same day they were murdered," Reegan murmured.

"Did you know about Edwin's affair?" Bernie asked.

"Did you know Patch and Annie Mae were half-sisters?" Reegan asked at the same time.

"Yes, of course."

"Did you know Gran and Patch kept a promise to themselves as well?"

Phyllis took a seat. "I'm listening."

Bernie went to her notes. "Before Patch died, she told Reegan something, a promise she'd kept."

"And before Annie Mae died, she told Bernie the same thing," Reegan added.

"Our guess is the promise stemmed from their father, but we don't know for sure," Bernie said, handing Phyllis a copy of what Gran had told her. Phyllis read and reread the words; Bernie then explained the correlation between then and now.

Phyllis looked up with tears in her eyes. "Do you girls understand what this means?"

"That history's putting on a killer reproduction, and lucky us, we're the headliners," Reegan said with a toast of her coffee cup.

"It means we were wrong!" Phyllis stood and began to fidget.

"Phyllis, please explain," Bernie said.

"We've been preparing for the wrong occurrence. Oh, Lord, what should we do?"

Reegan stood and said, "We're not following you here, Phyllis."

"Don't you see? It was a red herring," Phyllis muttered. "A way to insure this!" She waved Bernie's notes in the air.

"Phyllis, you're talking in circles," Bernie said.

"The story goes that Amelia and Minerva would come back seeking retribution and would destroy the town that sent them to the grave. But that was a fabrication."

"All right," Bernie said, though she didn't

257

understand and from the confusion on Reegan's face she didn't either.

"The town doesn't need protection from the curse. It was about them—always them! How could we have lost sight of that?"

"Wait, so we're not going to destroy Willows Bluff?" Reegan asked.

"Don't you see? The town was never cursed," Phyllis said and stopped pacing.

Reegan threw her hands up in the air. "And you've lost me!"

Bernie could only nod.

"The girls didn't put a curse on Willows Bluff. No, it's the two of you alone who are meant to suffer." Phyllis pointed between Bernie and Reegan. "The town's not cursed...you are."

Chapter Thirty

Bernie tapped her pen against the legal pad in a repeated tattoo as her mind tried to compute. She didn't have to look at Reegan to know she was pacing up and down the rows of records, and Phyllis fidgeted in the seat next to her. She was at a loss for words and, it would seem, thoughts.

After another ten minutes of silence, Phyllis said, "Doesn't anyone have anything to say?"

"I'm beyond words," Reegan shouted from within one of the rows.

"Bernadette?"

Bernie glanced to where she thought Reegan was, then looked at Phyllis and sighed. "Understand, Phyllis, Reegan and I are aware that *we* are cursed, and trust me, it's already cost us. That being said, I think we accepted the curse on the town from the story we were told was one and the same as what Gran and Patch revealed."

"That's understandable," Phyllis said.

"But what you're implying is the curse on the town was fabricated, so when the souls of the sisters were reborn the town would again destroy them out of fear."

"It's quite devious, if you think about it," Phyllis said.

Reegan came out from the rows to pace in front of them. "The thing is someone knew the sisters would

259

come back," Reegan said.

"Or they were preparing in case they did," Phyllis offered.

"Because of the stories, the town is predestined to be against us," Bernie said.

"Like I said, quite devious."

"Okay, everyone's been manipulated and it sucks, but what does it change?" Reegan said. "Nothing, right? I mean, we've been going about this knowing the good people of Willows Bluff are lying in wait with their torches and pitchforks."

"You're right," Bernie said, then looked at Phyllis. "What does this change for you?"

"My grandmother promised Clara, when and if the girls' souls returned, they would have a true record of the Willows and the people connected to it. We planned to help you in any way we could, no matter the cost," Phyllis declared, getting choked up at the end.

"Thank you, Phyllis," Bernie said.

"Yeah, Phyllis, thank you; it's nice to have someone else we can count on," Reegan said.

"Where does that leave us?" Phyllis asked.

"Back to learning what was unknown," Reegan said.

Bernie rubbed her hands over her face. "All right, in the vision you overheard your aunt say that *he'd* gone to see *her* the day he died. I'm guessing the 'he' is Edwin Woods, but who is the 'her' referring to?"

Phyllis pushed her glasses up and sighed. "Yes, she was talking about Uncle Edwin. My mother had it on good authority that Edwin ran his car into a tree on purpose."

"Suicide?"

"Yes, Bernadette."

"If I didn't already know it, this would be the time I would say our family is cursed or doomed or whatever," Reegan said.

Bernie snorted, then turned to Phyllis. "But who was it he went to see at Shady Pines?"

"The stepsister, Fidelia."

Bernie couldn't have been more stunned if she'd smacked her. She glanced at Reegan, whose face had lost all color. "Fidelia was at Shady Pines?" she asked.

"Yes, she was committed sometime in the twenties. We never did find out what happened to her; she just disappeared. The only reason we know she was at Shady Pines at all was because Uncle Edwin mentioned it."

"Why would he go see her?" Reegan asked.

"Knowing his true parentage, he may have gone looking for her. Uncle Edwin did keep a journal religiously, so perhaps he wrote the answers there."

Bernie shook her head. "Patch left Reegan his journals, and we've been through all of them. He doesn't mention Fidelia."

"That's how we knew he was Minerva's son," Reegan explained.

"Gives us something to consider, doesn't it?" Phyllis said.

"That's one of the reasons we came here today. Gran and Patch said that we could trace the path, and we figured out they meant tracing our lineage," Bernie said.

"You've come to the right place." Phyllis pointed to the two leather-bound ledgers. "Those contain all the names my grandmother acquired, the relations my mother added, and the ones I updated as well. Anyone involved with the Whits will be listed." Phyllis glanced at her watch. "I need to open the library. You're welcome to stay here, but those ledgers and notes are yours to take."

"I don't know how we can thank you, Phyllis," Bernie said and Phyllis stood to leave.

"Don't fail," Phyllis said and closed the door behind her.

****

They pored over the ledger written by Phyllis's grandmother until the names and places bled together. The woman was nothing if not thorough; there were dozens of entries.

"Do you think this means anything?" Reegan asked at one point. She pointed to the name Hazel Collins, with a tiny "A" next to it. The sentence underneath had been smudged out; the only legible word looked like "child."

"Probably a mistake," Bernie said. "We'll have to ask Phyllis."

That was one of several odd notations. The name Lucian Matthews was crossed out with a skull and crossbones next to it. The name Duncan Clacher had a circle around it with a tail that linked to the initials W. H. and the word "stables." Then there were names that were easily marked as housekeeper, groundsman, businessman, and so on.

"That poor girl," Reegan had said when they learned the live-in maid was a fifteen-year-old local girl named Hattie Bailey. "She has to be the one from my dream."

"Write the name on the list," Bernie had told

Reegan. They'd compiled a list of names whose lineage they would research further.

Around two, Phyllis came back down and suggested they head home before the high school kids started showing up to work on their school projects.

"Before we go, we had a couple of questions," Bernie said and picked up Phyllis's grandmother's ledger. "We wanted to know if you knew what this said." She pointed to the name Hazel Collins.

"Hazel Collins was the governess for the girls when they first arrived in Willows Bluff. My guess is that it said 'she taught the children.' "

"That also explains the teachers 'A,' " Reegan said.

"Yes, well, Ms. Collins left her post to tend to a sick family member, and she didn't return to Willows Bluff for some time," Phyllis said, pausing a moment. "If I remember correctly, she moved back married to a wealthy man and they had a few children, but that's neither here nor there."

"And what about this one?" Bernie asked, pointing to the skull and crossbones.

"Death of a sailor," Phyllis said and looked straight at Bernie. "You're connected to Amelia, correct?"

Bernie nodded.

"He was the naval officer she was engaged to."

Bernie looked down to the page where the name Lucian Matthews was written. Her finger traced it. This was where Justin fit.

"Duncan Clacher," Reegan whispered.

Bernie straightened from the ledger and turned the page to where they'd seen the name.

"It's not a circle with a tail…it's a noose," Reegan said, then turned away from the table.

"We get visions sometimes, like the one this morning, but Reegan suffers from nightmares—memories," Bernie explained while Phyllis hurried to the stacks of paper and sifted through them as though possessed.

"Here," Phyllis shouted and held up a loose page. "Reegan, come here, dear."

Reegan went to Phyllis, and Bernie knew she was trying to ward off the memory of the things her nightmares had shown her. With that in mind, she moved to stand next to Reegan to remind her that she was here if she needed her. Just like Reegan had done for her.

"Grandmother made special note of Duncan," Phyllis began. "He was a Scotsman staying with his cousin and working with the horses at the Willows."

"It was a secret affair," Reegan said.

"Yes, but before they could elope, one of the girls' society friends—Grandmother didn't know which—told Clara about the affair. Duncan was a foreigner with nothing to offer. Clara could do nothing but denounce the union."

"But Minerva got pregnant," Reegan said.

"Yes, and Clara had to let them get married."

"But they didn't," Bernie said.

"The day before the wedding, he disappeared. People thought he'd returned to Scotland. He'd been gone a week, but the day of the fire—"

"He was found strung up in a tree," Reegan said, her voice thick with tears.

"Yes," Phyllis said as she gave Reegan's arm a squeeze.

Chapter Thirty-One

Phyllis had snuck them out of the basement with all of her family's notes. Bernie had promised they wouldn't leave her in the dark, not after all she'd done. They'd ridden home in silence. She'd never seen Reegan so quiet, and Bernie was starting to worry.

She carried in the banker's box and set it on the kitchen table, which had become their workspace. Reegan poured a glass of water and walked down the hall to her room. Bernie texted both Justin and Phillip to let them know where they were and that they had a lot to tell them. Phillip had texted back that he would be there in a couple hours, and Justin said he would close after the evening rush.

Bernie put the notes they'd compiled into two stacks. The first were the ones they'd taken themselves, and the second were what Phyllis had provided. Bernie grabbed one of her legal pads, opened Reegan's laptop for a quick reference, and began trying to make sense of what was in front of her.

Over an hour later, she looked up from her notes. She stared down at the page. She'd been working on the connections they'd made so far, starting with the unplanned death of Amelia and Minerva's mother, Jessamine; so many lives were changed by this one event. If Jessamine hadn't died, then none of this would have happened; it was quite possible none of them would have been born. How could one life—one death—cause such a ripple effect? Bernie wondered as she circled the name repeatedly.

Then there were all the names they'd learned today, names that finally connected the past to the present. Lucian was Justin, Duncan was Phillip, and they suspected Hattie Bailey was the cloaked woman from Reegan's dreams. The pieces were coming together, and the connections were being made, but there was something not setting right with Bernie. She wondered if they'd missed something; was there some piece of the puzzle that they just weren't seeing?

Bernie sighed and decided she wanted to freshen up. She went down the hall, checked to make sure Reegan was still in her room, and then headed for the bathroom. She was in her room after her shower in her underwear with her hair up in a towel when her door burst open.

"Good Lord, Reegan," she said, startled. Her arms involuntarily moved to protect her modesty.

Reegan closed the door and said, "I'm not into girls if that's what you're freaking out about."

"I don't care who you're into, Reegan. I care about my privacy," Bernie said feeling awkward.

"You should let me shoot you," Reegan said, then laughed when Bernie glared at her. "I meant take your picture. I'm not big on portraits, but I think you'd photograph well."

Bernie stared at her. "Did you hit your head and not tell me?" she asked then turned to get her robe.

"Holy shit, Bernie!"

Bernie squeezed her eyes shut. That was twice in twenty-four hours she'd forgotten to watch her back.

Reegan was behind her before she could say a word, and before Bernie could stop it, Reegan's fingertips touched the scars on her back. Her stomach dropped.

"Tori, I'm not leaving," Bernie said. "You know I'd never leave Gran after everything she's done for me."

"What about me? What about what I've done for you!" Tori shouted.

"I wouldn't leave you either, Tori. You're my best friend, and I love you. Besides, if I were leaving, you'd be the first person I'd discuss it with."

"You're lying. You want to get away from me!" Tori accused.

"Why would I want to get away from you? I think you need to go home and calm down," Bernie said heading for the front door. "Call me later when you're not so upset."

Her hand reached out for the knob when she felt the first sharp piercing of her flesh, then another and another until she was on all fours. Her blood roared in her ears along with Tori's hysterical screams. She didn't know how much time passed, but her body was both heavy and numb as she lay facedown in the hall.

It took a moment to realize that Tori was half-lying on top of her. She could feel Tori's breath against her cheek before she gently brushed her hair. Bernie opened her eyes enough to see Tori staring at her.

"There, there, Bernadette, you can never leave me. We'll be together forever," Tori said with childlike whimsy.

Bernie sucked in air when the connection was broken. Tears filled her eyes, pain filled her heart, and she clutched her stomach. "Get out," she said.

"God, Bernie, I'm—"

"Get out!" she screamed, tormented by what she felt. Bernie turned away from Reegan, but she knew the other woman left the room because the door shut. She couldn't catch her breath.

She sat on the floor, took the towel off of her head, held it to her mouth, and screamed. She screamed until her screams became sobs and her sobs became gut-wrenching cries as all the feelings she'd kept tightly contained rushed to the surface.

She sat there while the misery that was her past overwhelmed her. Her mother's illness, her father's murder, the state facility, Tori's betrayal, and the torment she'd seen in Gran's eyes countless times on her behalf. Blood, so much blood, she thought, breaking out into a sweat. One after another, waves of pain and grief crashed upon her until she was drowning in the unrelenting sea of memories.

Bernie lay curled in a ball until she was numb enough to let the anger take over. It gave her the strength to breathe, to move, and she stood up on shaky legs. She threw on some clothes and shoved her feet into her boots. Her hair was damp against her neck as she opened the door and headed into the kitchen.

"There's something else I wanted to tell you," Phillip was saying to Reegan when she entered the room and began searching for her keys. Phillip didn't finish what he was saying, and their eyes bored holes on her back.

"I'm sorry—"

"Shut up, Reegan!" She found her keys, but Phillip had put himself between her and the door. She stared at his badge and said, "Get out of my way."

"Bernie, talk to me. Reegan said she touched you, and you shared a vision. She didn't know it was going to happen."

Her eyes flew to his. "Didn't know it was going to happen?" she scoffed.

"It doesn't always work, Bernie," Reegan said from where she sat on the kitchen counter. "You've said so yourself."

Bernie stepped away from Phillip, gripped her bag, and pointed at Reegan. "Don't play innocent with me, Reegan McGrath! You knew what could happen," Bernie accused. "I'm sick and tired of you picking at my memories—my wounds—like I can't feel it. Not expressing my feelings doesn't mean I'm immune to them. I'm *not* a robot!"

"You forget, Bernie," Reegan said, sneering. "I can feel everything you feel. And trust me, I'm no masochist."

"Sadist maybe," Bernie retorted.

"You know, if you have a problem with me, you should just say so!" Reegan jumped off of the counter and walked toward her.

"You'd like that, wouldn't you? Something to justify your incessant need for me to be the villain."

"You weren't kidding when you said it was urgent," Justin said when he walked in the room.

Phillip opened his mouth to speak but just shrugged.

"You're the only one here who thinks you're the villain, Bernie. Everyone else knows damn well it's Tori! How could you even look at her after what she did to you?" Reegan shouted.

"You don't know what you're talking about,"

Bernie said with a clenched jaw.

"Don't know what I'm talking about? I was just there reliving the entire fucked-up scene with you," Reegan said and pointed to Justin. "Did she tell you what happened? What Tori did to her?"

"Leave him out of this," Bernie shouted.

"He's in it, Bernie!"

"She told me," Justin said.

Bernie couldn't meet his eyes. She knew she would lose what little strength she had left if she looked at him.

"That's something at least," Reegan said. "How could Annie Mae sit there and let you go see that psycho!"

"You don't understand!" Bernie said.

"No, Bernie, I see it a lot clearer than you do."

The hurt started to bleed through the anger leaving Bernie raw. "She loved me too much, and it destroyed her." Destroyed them.

"That wasn't love, Bernie," Reegan said. "That was something else—something evil."

"It wasn't her," Bernie whispered.

"I saw her," Reegan said and swallowed. "My God, I can still feel her."

Bernie shook her head, not wanting to hear any more. Justin reached out to hold her, but she moved. She needed to get control—to contain the feelings.

"Bernadette, talk to me, talk to us," Justin said.

Her gaze darted across the floor, desperate to rebuild, if not her wall, then her anger—something to protect her from the pain. And then she sucked in a breath, her eyelids slamming shut, as Shady Pines came into her mind with the utmost clarity: the grand staircase leading to the entrance, the main hall glowing in the old lamplight, and the fire dying in its hearth.

"What's happening?" Reegan asked.

Bernie opened her eyes with a slow exhalation of breath. "I have to go to Shady Pines."

"You had a vision?" Phillip asked.

"I have to go now," Bernie said.

"I'll take you," Justin said, and Bernie nodded.

"We're all going," Reegan said.

"And that's not up for debate," Phillip added when Bernie started to protest.

Chapter Thirty-Two

They had ridden together in silence. Four people whose lives were irrevocably intertwined. Four souls replaying a past that had led their predecessors to their deaths. Bernie had to wonder if what they'd accomplished thus far was in their favor or leading them closer to ruin.

It had been years since Bernie had been to Shady Pines at night. The only building for miles, it glowed like an ember against the dark winter sky, a beacon of safety in a world of chaos. But tonight, with each step toward the entrance, she felt dread.

Justin reached for the door, but it was locked. That's odd, Bernie thought. They don't lock the door until eight o'clock, and it's only six. She knocked on the door and kept knocking.

"Good Lord, Ms. Bernadette, how did you hear?" the receptionist asked as she opened the door and let them in.

"What's happened?" Phillip asked.

"What is it, Deborah?" Bernie asked.

The middle-aged, dark-haired receptionist glanced around and whispered, "We've had an incident, and we're on lockdown."

"It's Tori, isn't it?" Bernie asked though she knew it was, had known since having the vision.

Deborah leaned in close to Bernie and said, "She's

gone."

Bernie closed her eyes as emotions bombarded her. Justin was by her side instantly.

"Dead?" Reegan asked.

"No," Deborah said. Bernie's heart jumped and her stomach rolled. "She's escaped."

Bernie grabbed Justin's arm.

"How long has she been missing?" Phillip asked Deborah.

"A couple hours. The orderlies and doctors are combing the grounds."

"This isn't my jurisdiction, but maybe I can be of assistance," Phillip said. "Who's in charge?"

"That would be Dr. Michele."

"Dr. Michele's been the director of Shady Pines for thirty years," Bernadette explained. "He's good man."

"I'll see what I can find out," Phillip said and asked Deborah to take him to Dr. Michele's office.

"Are you okay?" Justin asked.

Bernie didn't know how she was, in shock perhaps. One thought kept circling her mind. "Tori's never mentioned leaving Shady Pines before; not once."

"You're wondering why now?" Justin asked.

"Yes, something had to prompt her."

"Did anything out of the ordinary happen today?" Justin asked Deborah when she came back in. "Workman, visitors you've never seen before, deliveries—"

"A painting! We hung it in the library!" Deborah said. "They delivered it today. An anonymous donation."

"Who delivered it?" Bernie asked.

"Can we see the painting?" Reegan asked at the

same time.

Deborah motioned for them to follow her down the hall. "It was our usual courier," she explained. "We get donations once in a while." They followed Deborah into the library. She turned on the lights and pointed. "There, see for yourselves. I have to go back to my post, so turn off the lights when you're done."

Bernie stared at the painting that hung in the center of the room between two bookcases. She turned to Reegan, who was an interesting shade of both white and green. "I have no words."

"Fuck," Reegan whispered, "is the most appropriate word."

"Yes, in this case I'll have to agree." Bernie approached the flame-colored canvas painted by Adam Desmond.

"You've seen it before?" Justin said.

"In Ezra's gallery," Bernie said, then explained.

"Adam," he said, seemingly more to himself than to them. He stepped closer to where the painting hung.

"What is it, Justin?" Bernie asked.

"The face from my dream," Justin said.

"The man that drowned Lucian," Reegan said.

"Lucian?" Justin said, turning away from the painting and toward them.

"We found it today," Bernie explained. "Phillip was Duncan Clacher, and your name was Lucian Matthews."

"Mom's maiden name is Matthews," Justin said.

Reegan scoffed. "Of course it is!"

Bernie took his hand in hers. "The man from your dream," she prompted.

Justin gave her hand a squeeze, then turned back to

the painting. "I didn't see it before but"—he shook his head—"it's in the eyes."

"It was Adam?" Bernie guessed.

"Oh, God," Reegan whispered.

Justin thought about it for another minute. "Yes, it was Adam."

"The painting is a memory," Reegan said. "His memory."

"No wonder it affected us the way it did," Bernie said.

Reegan nodded. "You think Tori saw this?"

"She comes to the library every day."

"We need to find Phillip and tell him what's going on," Justin suggested.

Bernie turned off the lights, and they started down the hall. They'd just turned the corner when Reegan grabbed hold of her sweatshirt. "What?"

"Look," Reegan said as she pointed to an old picture. "That woman looks familiar somehow."

The walls were lined with photos taken through the years. The one Reegan pointed to had a marker which read *Founders on opening day, June 1921*. Before Bernie could comment, Phillip came around the corner with Dr. Michele.

"There you are," Phillip said.

"Ah, Bernadette, how are you holding up?" Dr. Michele asked. He was in his late fifties with caramel skin, compassionate brown eyes, and a charming disposition. But Bernie could see the worry behind his horn-rimmed glasses.

"As best I can."

He studied her a moment as though gauging her sincerity. "Sometimes that's all we can do."

"Do you know who these people are, Dr. Michele?" Reegan asked pointing to the photograph.

He squinted at the photo. "As it says, these are the founders of Shady Pines," he said. "This man here, with the top hat, was the financial backer for this institution; he was one of the wealthiest industrialists in the area at the time. His wife began suffering from horrible delusions not long after the birth of their only child. He built Shady Pines and filled it with the best and brightest doctors in hopes that someone could help his wife."

"Were they able to help her?" Reegan asked.

Dr. Michele's lips pinched. "No, I'm sorry to say, they couldn't. Today, perhaps we could have helped her, but back then they just weren't equipped. She died here in 1945, I believe."

"You wouldn't happen to remember her name, would you, Doctor?" Phillip asked.

"Well, if you look here"—Dr. Michele moved down the wall and pointed to a photograph—"this is a better picture."

Both Bernie and Reegan moved so they could read the small plaque. "It's her," Bernie said. "It's Fidelia."

"Yes, Fidelia. Odd that you should ask about this photo," Dr. Michele said.

"What do you mean, Doctor?" Justin asked.

Dr. Michele took a step back. "Because of what's happening."

"You mean with Tori?" Bernie asked.

"Well, yes. This woman is Tori's great-great grandmother." There was a long pause when no one spoke, then the doctor said, "I always thought you knew."

"No," Bernie said, staring at the photo. "No, I didn't." She'd surely passed these photos dozens of times, but she hadn't paid much attention. She'd been too wrapped up in the safety provided by Shady Pines to wonder who had provided it. She couldn't even remember being curious. All these years, she'd found comfort in the arms of—

"Did Tori know?" Reegan asked, breaking Bernie's train of thought.

"Her mother's family has always been on the board of directors here in one capacity or another. Tori is well aware of her family's connection to Shady Pines. It's of no consequence, really," Dr. Michele said.

Bernie wanted to laugh at the inaccuracy of that statement. Instead she said, "Doctor, where do you think Tori went?"

He cleared his throat. "To find you, of course."

****

She was uncomfortable in her own skin, as though it wasn't fitting quite right over her bones. Her thoughts collided making it impossible to find answers. But the truth, Bernie knew, was she had no answers or at least none she could accept.

The surveillance video showed Tori walking right out of the front door of Shady Pines. To their credit she hadn't looked like a patient. She'd gotten a hold of a pair of scrubs, some sneakers, and had braided her hair into a bun. Bernie hadn't seen Tori in anything other than white silk in years; she could understand how others were fooled.

During the drive back, Phillip asked Bernie where she thought Tori would go. She'd guessed either Tori's parents' house or Gran's cottage.

"What about your old house?" Justin had asked.

"Gran sold the property years ago," Bernie said. "The people who bought it tore down the house and planned to build, but they ended up putting the property up for sale again."

"I can check public records to see who owns it," Phillip offered.

"No need, Phillip, I bought it back a few years ago."

"Why?"

Gran had asked her the same thing after she'd signed the papers. She didn't know why, but she couldn't let it go, not without answers; that's what she tried to explain.

"I think I understand," Phillip had said, and Bernie hid her smile.

Justin suggested they add that to the list. "You keep saying Tori's mind is like a teenager's, and that's where you lived when you were teenagers."

"I'd agree with you, only Tori never came to that house," Bernie said. "If we didn't go to her house or the library, we went to Gran's cottage. Dad worked two jobs and Tori's mother wouldn't let her come over if there wasn't an adult present."

Reegan had sat ramrod straight in the front seat with the visor down and stared at Bernie in the mirror. Bernie wasn't sure what Reegan was thinking, but the questions showed plainly enough on her face to guess.

Here they were again sitting at the kitchen table surrounded by their notes and staring at each other. She had the information now to connect Tori directly to Fidelia, the Whits, and the curse. She pushed the pad away, not wanting to think about the connection.

Phillip was on the phone coordinating with his deputies. They would have people checking the locations Bernie had given them in case Tori showed up.

"You'll be safe here with us," Phillip said, for what Bernie believed to be the hundredth time. She thanked him.

"How could you not have known?" Reegan said after hours of silence.

Bernie closed her eyes and counted to five.

"Reegan," Phillip warned.

"What? It's a valid question, Phillip. She's been going to Shady Pines since—"

"Enough!" Justin said banging his fist on the table.

"No, that psycho is out there, and it's not just Bernie's life that's at stake," Reegan said.

"I understand the situation, Reegan, but unlike you I don't think Bernadette's at fault!"

"I never said it was her fault, Justin!"

"It was the painting," Bernie said. "The painting must have set her off."

"What painting?" Phillip asked.

"You know the one that was donated anonymously to Shady Pines. The one I told you I saw in Ezra's gallery"—Reegan waved her hand in the air—"you know, the one Adam painted."

"We saw it before the photo of Fidelia; I guess between that and finding out the details of Tori's escape, we forgot to mention it," Justin said.

"What is it, Phillip?" Bernie asked because he'd grown pale.

"You think the painting is the reason Tori left?" Phillip asked and Reegan explained to him how they believed it was connected. Phillip looked at Justin. "You're sure it was Adam in your dream?"

"It's the eyes. I didn't make the connection at first, but my gut says it was him."

"This changes things," Phillip said.

"How?" Bernie asked.

Phillip took Reegan's hand. "Remember when I told you I had something else to tell you? Before you and Bernie got in your argument."

"Vaguely," Reegan said.

"I got a call from a homicide detective in the city. Adam died late last night when his studio caught fire," Phillip said.

Bernie stared at him. "That can't be a coincidence."

"No way in hell!" Justin said.

"Hold on a second," Bernie said standing. She went through a stack of papers and started going through her notes. She found where she'd written down what Gran had told her. "Here it is! 'Envious greed spills out with intent upon an afflicted mind consumed with fear. Fire and condemnation will bring forth the card of death.' Tori's the 'afflicted mind' and she's consumed with the fear that I'm leaving her." Bernie shook her head, then pointed to the stack of papers. "Adam died in a fire."

"Card of death," Justin said and rubbed a hand over his beard.

"That makes sense, but what about the envious greed?"

"You said he made a comment about your work," Phillip reminded Reegan.

Reegan shook her head. "That was more arrogance

than envy."

"He's connected to this, no question. He's dead, and Tori's on the loose," Justin said.

"Maybe you're right," Bernie said. "When we first figured things out, I assumed the fire and condemnation was referring to Amelia and Minerva being condemned, burned, and murdered."

"You're saying Adam was a casualty of the curse; the afflicted mind is the cause, and the card of death is the effect," Justin said.

"Yes." Bernie didn't like it, and she felt some guilt for being so callous about Adam's death, but the facts were irrefutable. "Tori's free, which means—"

"She's going to hand out the card of death—kill us," Reegan said.

Bernie nodded. "I believe she's going to try."

W. L. Brooks

Bernie's Notes

Death Unplanned
Jessamine—Alan Walters
Two Choices
Fidelia is born—I'm born
Loss Weeps
Bertrum is killed—Dad is killed
Envious Greed
?—Adam?
Afflicted Mind
Fidelia—Tori
~*~
Amelia Whit—Me
Lucian Mathews—Justin
Fidelia Whit—Tori
Minerva Whit—Reegan
Duncan Clacher—Phillip
Hattie Bailey—Cloaked woman from Reegan's dream?
What are we missing?

Chapter Thirty-Three

Justin slept next to her, but Bernie's thoughts kept
her awake. They'd learned quite a bit today, but what
they'd found did little to ease her mind. Reegan, on the
other hand, had found information that put some things
into perspective. After figuring out Adam's connection,
they'd worked on the lineage of the names she and
Reegan had written down. As it turned out, Sydney's
mother was the great-granddaughter of Hattie Bailey,
the fifteen-year-old maid who'd lived with the Whits.

"The cloaked woman trying to save me in my
dream was Sydney," Reegan had said, obviously
gratified.

Bernie kept her comments to herself. Even with the
new information at hand, she didn't care for Sydney.
Though if she were honest with herself, Bernie would
have to admit one of the reasons she didn't like
Reegan's incessant need to see the good in Sydney was
because it mirrored her own situation. Of course, unlike
Reegan, Bernie knew Tori's guilt.

Justin shifted in his sleep, cutting off Bernie's
thoughts and bringing her attention to the small box that
sat next to her on the nightstand. They'd come into the
bedroom after calling it a night and made love. Slowly
at first, thoroughly, as if to replace the bad moments of
the day with the meeting of their bodies; then their
movements had become greedy, desperate for the

connection that bound them together by nature and by fate.

He'd spoken of his love for her, saying all the words Bernie had only dreamt would fall from his lips. Then he'd pulled the small box from beneath his pillow.

"I don't plan on ever letting you go," he'd said, bringing tears to her eyes. He lifted the lid revealing an intricate band of diamonds and white gold. "Say you'll marry me."

Every hope of love she had ever dreamed of was wrapped in those words. There were a dozen reasons she should say no, but this time she wouldn't deny herself. Not of this happiness, not of the man she had loved all her life. Just this once, she would be selfish and she had said yes.

He had kissed her then, a thousand promises unspoken. For the first time in a long time, the happiness she felt reached the innermost parts of her. Her heart hurt, not from pain, but from joy, and her tears were ones of hope. They'd held each other until Justin had fallen asleep.

Here she sat watching the man she loved, the man she would marry, while he slept. For a moment, there was a bright light in the cursed storm, and then her eyes slammed shut. With the utmost clarity, she saw the place where an old shack had once stood and a crooked fence had swung open.

Bernie sucked in a breath when her vision returned, her eyes darting to Justin, who stirred but didn't wake. She tried to slow her slamming heart as she carefully got out of the bed. Grabbing some clothes, she took one last look at Justin and went into the bathroom and dressed. She put her hair in a ponytail and stared into the mirror. The reflection dashed tears away from her cheeks; there was no doubt what the vision meant.

****

The artic wind bit at her exposed skin as she walked up the snow-covered drive. The people who had purchased the property from Gran had cleared the lot of all debris, but by the time Bernie bought it back, it had been overrun with weeds. She had taken back the land the house had sat on and planted a beautiful garden filled with flowers. And in the center was a stone bench with a plaque that held her father's name, so he would know she hadn't forgotten him.

Bernie gripped the flashlight she'd found in Justin's SUV, but the full moon reflecting off the snow gave enough light to navigate. Technically, she had stolen his vehicle, but she didn't think he would mind. She had wanted to get here before anyone was the wiser, before they could talk her out of coming or insist on coming with her. She had left a sticky note on the coffee pot, so they'd at least know where to look.

Bernie pulled up the collar of her coat and turned when she heard what sounded like a car door shutting behind her. Then she heard footsteps in front of her, and she shined the flashlight in that direction. "Tori?"

There was a giggle. "You came!"

"Of course, I did. I had to make sure you were all right," she said, startled when Tori jumped in front of her. Looking up at the taller woman, Bernie didn't know if she should be relieved or frightened.

"Yes! Yes! I'm wonderful," Tori said spinning around in a circle.

"It's freezing out here, Tori," Bernie said. Tori had on a thick winter coat, a hat, and gloves, leading Bernie to believe she'd stopped somewhere else first. Her parents hadn't yet returned to town, so Bernie guessed that's where she had gone.

"Don't be a stick in the mud, Bernadette!" Tori pouted.

"Why did you leave Shady Pines? Did someone upset you?" Bernie asked as Tori danced around in the snow. She hadn't seen her old friend this coherent or energized in years. In fact, Bernie swallowed, Tori was manic.

"I had to stop you," Tori said, her tone sorrowful.

"Stop me?"

"From leaving me."

Not this again. "I'm not leaving you, Tori. We've been over this."

"Yes, you are!" Tori hissed, coming closer. "They told me all about it, so don't lie. You're leaving me to be friends with her!"

"Wait, Tori. Who told you?" And who is her? Reegan?

Tori waved her hand in the air. "Them! The voices. I hear them"—she put her finger to her eye—"I see them."

"You see them?" Bernie asked as Tori began twirling around. How was that even possible? Was she having delusions?

"The voices—the signs! I see them."

Bernie stared at Tori, wondering if these were the effects of a psychotic break. "Tori, we need to go where it's warmer."

Tori came to stand in front of her. "But you like it here. He's here."

"Who's here?" Bernie asked and used the flashlight

to look around.

Tori put her lips to Bernie's ear and whispered, "Your father's here."

Bernie recoiled. Tori grabbed her upper arms, and Bernie dropped the flashlight in the snow. "Don't say things like that!" she said and tried to move, but Tori held firm.

Tori's wild eyes searched hers. "It's true! Can't you feel it?" she asked. "He's right where we left him."

Tori's words sank in, and Bernie squeezed her eyes tight. For years she'd suspected, but there had been no proof, and until this moment she hadn't let herself believe it. "It was you, wasn't it?" She pulled free of Tori's grasp and rubbed her hands over her face. She was going to be sick.

"He wasn't going to let us be friends anymore!" she screamed. "He came to my house and told Mother it would do us some good to spend time apart—*make new friends*!"

"You killed my father!" Bernie bent down and put her head between her knees trying to get control. She had turned a blind eye to the truth, and now there was no escape.

"He wouldn't listen!" Tori shouted. "I came here to talk to him, and he wouldn't listen. He said he didn't want me seeing you anymore, that there was something wrong with me! And that's when I heard them."

Bernie bent down and grabbed the flashlight as Tori began to pace with agitated steps. "What did the voices say?"

"That he couldn't take you away if he wasn't here! I couldn't live without my best friend." She shook her head. "I did what I had to do to keep us together. He never saw it coming. I was merciful."

"You were merciful," Bernie choked out.

Tori moved to stand in front of her again. "Yes, he didn't suffer! But do you know what? You left anyway! They took you away from me," Tori screamed. "I told Mother we couldn't let them take you away, that you did nothing wrong. But she did nothing! Nothing to help me, nothing to stop them from taking you; then she sent me away too."

"Your mother knew you killed my father?" Bernie asked, feeling once again that she was going to be sick.

Tori stared. "Of course she knew, Bernadette. I came home covered in blood. Who do you think washed my clothes?"

Bernie gagged. All these years she'd felt indebted to Tori's mother, and that woman had known the truth all along. Reegan was right about seeing the guilt in Mrs. Elis's eyes but wrong about what put it there. She felt violated.

Tori tsked her. "Don't make yourself ill, Bernadette. It's not Mother's fault…it's theirs."

"Theirs?" Bernie asked. "Did *they* tell you to kill me too?"

Tori cocked her head to the side. "He was going to take you away from me; they told me you'd forget about me."

"Who? Who would take me away?" Bernie asked confused. She stepped back when Tori's angry eyes bored into hers.

"Don't play dumb!" Tori hissed. "Him, that boy you were always mooning over."

"Justin?" Bernie asked. He'd moved back to town around that same time, but she hadn't thought Tori ever noticed her feelings for Justin.

"Yes, yes, him," Tori sneered. "You belong with me. Just the two of us, not three!"

"I don't understand," Bernie said more to herself than to Tori.

Tori sighed. "And now *she's* trying to take you from me. I can't let that happen. Not her! You can't be friends."

Bernie needed to calm her down. "No one could ever take me away from you, Tori."

"How can you not see? You don't belong with her!"

"I only belong with you, Tori; just the two of us as it's always been."

Tori smiled wistfully. "Don't worry, Bernadette, it will be," she said and pulled a knife out of her pocket.

Bernie swallowed, and her head whipped around when someone cleared their throat behind her.

"Bet you're glad I'm nosy, aren't you, Bernie?" Reegan asked, coming out from where she'd been hiding.

"Noooooo!" Tori screamed and lunged for Reegan.

Bernie dropped the flashlight as she grabbed Tori's shoulders and wrestled her to the ground. There was a flash of pain, once, then twice, and they rolled into the concrete bench. She was able to get the upper hand and moved swiftly to knock the knife out of Tori's grasp. Bernie sat on top of Tori punching her in the face and knocking her unconscious.

Bernie took a few deep breaths, glanced at Reegan, and crawled a couple feet away from Tori. She knelt in the snow and, using her teeth, took off her gloves to unzip her coat.

"I called Phillip the minute I saw Tori. He was pissed, but he and the cavalry should be arriving soon," Reegan said, standing next to her. "You dropped this."

Bernie glanced up to see her flashlight. "You hold onto it a minute," she said. She reached inside her coat and felt the wetness. Not taking her hand out of her coat, she sat down. She glanced at Tori lying in the snow and let out a breath. "You heard everything she said, didn't you?"

Reegan seemed to think about it, then took a seat next to her in the snow. "I did…you knew, didn't you? That Tori killed your father."

Bernie stared at Reegan a moment, then nodded. "I didn't have proof, but that day, the day of your accident—"

"I remember it well."

Bernie's lips twitched. "Tori talked about my father's murder using details she couldn't have known unless she'd been there." She shook her head. "We have to find out the truth for ourselves or we won't believe it, and I guess I couldn't bring myself to accept what I'd found."

"I just don't understand why, after everything she's done and all that you suspected her of doing, you continued to be her friend."

Tears filled Bernie's eyes and again she glanced at Tori. Why, why had she done it? "I can't even give myself an answer to that question. Not one to justify my actions or rectify hers. I can tell you she loved me when no one, other than my Gran, would. And I loved her, Reegan; I'd spent most of my life trying to protect her. Don't you get it? I couldn't see the truth for the lies—I wouldn't. I accused you of not being ready, when in reality I wasn't, and now it's too late," Bernie said around the lump in her throat. She pulled her hand out of her coat and held it up. Her fingers were crimson.

"Oh, my God, Bernie," Reegan cried. "Why didn't you say anything? Just hold on; Phillip will be here any minute."

Bernie smiled sadly, her body going hot and cold. "It's all right, Reegan. Tell Justin I'll love him until the end of time, but there's always a price—"

"Shut up!" Reegan choked out.

Bernie lay back on the snow and breathed. "You need to see," she said and held up her bloodstained hand. Reegan took her hand, and Bernie's eyes closed as her stomach dropped.

The wind swept up the shore with a resonating howl. Bernie didn't know why the vision had sent her here in the middle of a storm, but she wasn't going to leave just yet. Then she heard it above the wind...screaming.

She turned in time to see a body drop into the water, and instantly she knew why she was there and what she had to do. Throwing her flashlight to the side, Bernie ran toward the shore. She looked up as lightning struck the bluff. She saw her then, her long hair blowing in the wind, and then she was gone back into the blackness. Bernie shook herself. It couldn't be, she thought, it just couldn't be...

The connection with Reegan was lost, but there was another presence with her, calling her name.

"Bernadette?" She knew that voice!

"Daddy?" Bernie said, once again a young girl running toward the sound of her father's voice. The sun hit her face after she went through a small door. It was

summer, and the roses were in full bloom. Her father stood on the cottage porch waving to her. "Dad!"

"Bernadette, come home," he called smiling.

She ran as fast as her legs could take her. She saw Gran on the porch drinking a Coca-Cola and smiling. "Gran!"

"There's my girl."

Bernie raced up the driveway until she reached her father. He scooped her up in his arms and hugged her tight.

"I've missed you," he said, kissing her forehead.

"I've missed you too," Bernie said and tightened her arms. She was home. She was safe.

FULL CIRCLE

Chapter Thirty-Four

Reegan gasped as the connection with Bernie ended. She looked down to find Bernie hadn't woken up. "Bernie?"

No response.

"Bernie? Wake up!" she shouted and shook her. She took off one of her gloves and felt for a pulse. "No," she cried. "Oh, God, don't do this to me."

Reegan straightened, and her gaze landed on the bench covered with snow, exactly like the picture she'd seen in her mind when she saw Tori for the first time at Shady Pines. She sat back on her haunches and panicked. Tori wasn't there. She felt around the snow for—

"Leave her alone!" Tori shouted from above her.

Reagan tried to dodge, but the flashlight hit her in the side of the head. Tori pulled back to swing again, and a gunshot rang out just before everything went black.

****

Reegan opened her eyes and found herself staring at a tiled ceiling. I'm in a hospital, she guessed. She groaned and reached up to stop the pain in her head, only to realize her hand was being grasped. Her heart leapt when she saw Sydney's head. Tears sprang to her eyes, and she squeezed Sydney's hand.

Her friend lifted her head, and her blue eyes went

wide. "Thank God," Sydney whispered.

"What are you doing here?"

"I can't be pissed at you if you get yourself killed, Reegan," Sydney said with a small smile. "I'm sorry for being so selfish. If I had lost you"—she shook her head—"I never would have forgiven myself."

Reegan squeezed Sydney's hand again. "Nothing like a near-death experience to change your point of view."

"Don't joke," she said, then laughed after Reegan made a face. "Do you forgive me?"

Reegan sighed. After almost thirty years of friendship, twenty desperate phone calls, and two long-distance talks with Daddo, there wasn't a doubt in her mind. "Of course, I do." She looked up when the door opened and Phillip stepped in. Her heart lurched; he looked like he hadn't slept in days.

"You look like shit," Sydney told Phillip as she stood. "I'll give you two some privacy."

"Thanks, Syd," Reegan said and waited until the door was closed to ask Phillip about Bernie.

Phillip sat on the edge of her bed and took her hand. "She was lucky. Tori missed her major organs, but she's in a coma."

His teary eyes matched hers. "Will she make it?" she asked.

"They don't know. We were able to resuscitate her at the scene, but she hasn't regained consciousness. What the hell were you two thinking going there alone?" he shouted, letting go of her hand to hover over her.

She shook her head. "We weren't. Or I wasn't."

"Explain?"

"For once my dreams didn't wake you, so I got dressed and went into the kitchen just as Bernie was sneaking out the door. She left a note saying where she was going."

"Why didn't you come and get me?"

"I should have—I wish to God I had—but there wasn't time if I was going to follow her. I had to go right that second." She rubbed her forehead wincing at the IV in her arm. "How long have I been here?"

"You've been unconscious for about twenty-four hours." He sat on the bed again and took her hand. "You scared me to death, Reegan. I can't lose you. If you hadn't called me when you did, I don't know what would have happened."

Her eyes searched his. "I can't lose you either." Or Bernie, who'd saved her from Tori. "What happened to Tori?"

Phillip pulled back a bit. "She's dead." Emotions played across his face.

"Oh, God! The gunshot I heard…it was you?"

He nodded.

"I'm so sorry!" she said. Phillip had been in love with Tori most of their lives. He'd done what he could to protect her, but because of Reegan he'd had to take her life. It didn't matter that she saw contempt in his eyes when he'd seen Tori at Shady Pines.

"It was you or her," he said after a moment. "I didn't even flinch."

"I didn't want that for you."

"It's over now," he said.

"It doesn't feel like we won, does it?"

"No," he said softly.

"She killed Bernie's father," Reegan said.

"What?" Phillip turned on the corner of the mattress to stare at her.

Reegan nodded. "Tori murdered Ryan Howard. I heard her tell Bernie."

"Good Lord."

"And deep down Bernie knew or at least suspected." Reegan thought for a moment and added, "Tori's mom knew, Phillip. She even washed Tori's bloody clothes!"

Phillip stood and ran his hands over his face and through his hair. "That's not only obstruction of justice, but she could be considered an accessory after the fact. What they put Bernie through!"

"Bernie showed me something else," she said. "We had a vision of the night of my accident. Tori was there on the bluff, Phillip. Bernie saw her."

"She pushed you?" He sat down again on the edge of the mattress to take her hand.

Reegan nodded. "That's my guess."

"But why?"

Reegan thought for a moment and sucked in a breath. "It wasn't me she was after that night. It had to have been Sydney. They'd always hated each other, and they had that big argument that day. Maybe that's why Bernie said to never come back. I needed to protect not only myself but also Sydney."

Phillip shifted. "Are you going to tell Sydney about all of this?"

"No, she'd never believe it. Besides, it's over now. Did you call her?"

Phillip shook his head. "Her parents did. They got back a couple of days ago, and the news of what happened has spread like wildfire."

Reegan tried to sit up straighter, smiling when Phillip helped her. "What are they saying?"

"That Tori escaped from Shady Pines and tried to murder Bernie, not knowing you and I were there waiting to capture her. We're also getting married."

Reegan's heart stopped beating for a split second. "We are?"

Phillip gave her a crooked grin and shrugged. "If you believe the gossip, then yeah."

"Interesting," she said not knowing what else to say.

"Course, being I started that particular rumor—"

She swatted at him. "Shut up! You didn't."

He snatched her hand and brought it to his chest. "I did. I love you, Reegan. I realize these are unusual circumstances, but we plan on spending our lives together anyway," he said and kissed her hand. He reached into the breast pocket of his uniform and pulled out a gold band with a single emerald-cut diamond. "Will you marry me, Reegan? Make it official?"

"What does June think about this?" she asked because it mattered. It mattered a great deal.

A smile spread across Phillip's face. "Who do you think helped me pick out the ring? I got your parents' blessing too."

Reegan's eyes prickled. That meant a lot to her parents. She held out her hand. "In that case, you bet your ass I'll marry you!" she said, and he put the ring on her finger.

****

Reegan kept her eyes on Phillip's boots as she followed him down the hall. The doctors had released her, and she was ready to leave except for one last

299

thing…she had to see Bernie.

She ran into Phillip when he stopped abruptly, and he tensed. She peeked around him. "Syd? What are you doing here?" she asked, coming from behind Phillip to stand next to Sydney, who was looking through the glass into Bernie's room.

"I wanted to see for myself," Sydney said and put one arm around Reegan. "This is the woman who saved your life. I feel as though I owe her."

The sincerity in Sydney's eyes was apparent. "You can thank her when she wakes up," Reegan said.

"I'll have to," Sydney said.

"I'm going to go in and sit with Bernie for a bit; then I'm going home to rest. Are you staying with your parents?"

"Yes, Mother is overjoyed!" Sydney smirked. "I'll head there for the evening; call me if you want company."

"Thanks, Syd," she said after a quick hug.

Once she and Phillip were alone, Reegan took a deep breath and went into Bernie's room. The monitors beeped, but Bernie appeared peaceful, beautiful in her stillness. Someone must have brushed her hair, Reegan thought; the long black strands were shining. Justin was sitting in a chair, his head bowed. He was holding Bernie's hand. Reegan squeezed her eyes shut for a moment; it was the picture she'd seen when she first saw Justin at the coffee shop.

She swallowed. "How is she?"

"She isn't dead yet, if that's what you mean," Justin said.

"Justin," Phillip warned as he came to stand behind her.

Tears filled Reegan's eyes. "You can blame me if you need to, Justin, but don't you dare pretend like I don't care what happens to her."

"Sorry," Justin mumbled.

Reegan nodded, then sighed when Phillip's cell phone rang.

"I have to take this," he said and left the room.

She took a tentative step toward the end of the bed. "She told me to tell you she would love you until the end of time," Reegan said.

He wiped a tear away. "We're going to get married," he whispered.

Reegan's nose burned with unshed tears. "You got her to agree to that?"

Justin huffed out a breath, then half-smiled. "Yeah, I did."

She wasn't sure if she should say congratulations or not, so she just watched the rise and fall of Bernie's chest. She glanced up when Phillip knocked on the glass and mouthed that they had to go. She nodded. "I'll come back tomorrow."

She turned to leave, stopping when Justin said her name.

He stared at the hand he held. "Why is it Bernadette could save our lives, but when she needed it most, we couldn't save her?" he asked.

Reegan choked on the lump in her throat. "I don't understand it either, Justin, and if I could change it I would. We can't give up hope; if I've learned anything about Bernie, it's that she's a fighter, and I know she'll fight to come back to you."

Justin cleared his throat and rubbed his cheek with his shoulder. "Thanks."

She shuffled her feet, one in front of the other, but she wanted to run away. From the pain she hadn't expected, from Bernie's sleeping beauty, from the anguish she'd felt in Justin's words. Why did she feel so defeated when they'd won?

Chapter Thirty-Five

Reegan leapt from the bed and landed on the floor on all fours. She bowed her head, then peeked to see that Phillip was still asleep. She figured he was either exhausted or his body was getting used to her freaking out in the middle of the night.

She showered and dressed in record time. She opened the door and stuck her head out listening for Phillip's even breathing. Feeling a bit victorious at her stealth, Reegan crept out of the bedroom and headed to the kitchen.

After hitting the on button on the coffee maker and getting down a mug, her eyes caught on the banker's boxes and stacks of notes on the kitchen table. It was done. Bernie had gotten Tori before Tori could get to them. She saved us all, Reegan thought.

She sifted through the legal pads. They'd learned so much about themselves this past week. Her hand stilled above the pages. She'd only been back from the city for eight days. Was that even possible? Patch hadn't been gone three weeks, and Reegan's life was irrevocably changed.

The coffee pot sputtered out the last of its brew, and she sighed as she walked toward it. She glanced up after taking her first sip and smiled at the sound of shuffling feet.

"You're up early," June said around a yawn. Her

wheat-colored hair was plastered to one side of her head, while the other side looked like she stuck her finger in a wall socket.

"Why are you up?" Reegan asked. She felt silly wanting nothing more than to give June a hug and hold her for a moment. They'd picked her up from Buck and Cindy's on the way home last night. With the curse behind them, it was time to start living as a family.

"I like to take my time getting ready before the bus gets here," June said, smiling while she poured a glass of juice.

Reegan laughed. "I was a sleep-in kind of kid when I was your age. I'd still be asleep if it weren't for the nightmares," she said.

"I thought those would stop," June said.

Reegan glanced up at the child, who saw too much, and shrugged. "It's just the dream from the day of my accident. I've had that one on and off for years, so don't worry. Do you want some breakfast?" she asked going to the fridge.

"You cook?"

Reegan snorted. "If by cook you mean put the milk in the cereal, then yes, I cook."

June laughed so hard juice came out of her nose, which made Reegan giggle.

"What'd I miss?" Phillip asked, coming in the kitchen with a grin.

"Nothing, Dad, Reegan's just glad we have milk," June said. She winked at Reegan and went off to get ready for school.

"What was that about?" Phillip asked after he kissed Reegan's forehead.

"I was informing June that my culinary prowess is

less than stellar."

Phillip grinned. "I realized that when I saw all the take-out menus in your apartment."

Reegan stuck her tongue out at him, then looked away.

"What?" he asked.

"It feels wrong to be so happy when Bernie's lying in a coma." Dying, she thought.

Phillip put down his coffee to take her in his arms. She rested her head against his t-shirt, feeling his heartbeat against her cheek, and closed her eyes. "I have to believe she'll wake up," Phillip said.

"She has to," Reegan said swallowing at the pain she heard in his words. "Did Justin tell you he proposed?"

"He got her to say yes?"

Reegan controlled her smile behind her lips. "That's what I said." She stepped back to see his face. "Bernie said yes. She has only the good stuff to look forward to now. I want her to have the life she deserves."

"I want that too. For her and for us," Phillip said and kissed her.

Reegan fell into the kiss, into him, and would have continued if the phone hadn't rung. She jumped making Phillip chuckle as he went to answer it.

"Reegan," Phillip said after a moment of listening to the other end. "How rusty are your barista skills?"

Reegan snorted. "Cooking no, but coffee I can do."

"Justin wants to know if you would mind opening the coffee shop with his mom."

"Tell him I'll meet her there," she said and went to change her clothes and put on makeup. There was no doubt in her mind that the good people of Willows Bluff would come out in hordes to get a glimpse of the girl who survived.

****

It was around one when Reegan and Delores finally got a break. She had been correct; there had been a line waiting outside by the time Phillip dropped her at the coffee shop. Rumors were running rampant around town. The curse, which the oldest of gossips had only spoken of behind closed doors, was out in the open. Even more titillating than the curse was the news that, after fifteen years, Ryan Howard's murder had been solved, and Mrs. Elis was being questioned about her involvement.

The people of Willows Bluff had come in droves to see if there was more dirt to be dug. Reegan knew if not for the cups of coffee, they would have all left empty-handed because neither she nor Delores were talking. The best they got was when they asked if she was going to marry Phillip; to that inquiry she stuck up her ring finger and let the diamond speak for itself.

She'd just taken a seat in one of the booths when the door opened again. She looked up and said, "Thank God it's you, Syd, I don't think I could take one more prying eye." She smiled when an "Amen" came from the vicinity of the bookstore where Delores was hiding.

Sydney was wearing what Reegan knew was her favorite business suit. It was a black Armani pant suit. She wore it with a stark-white camisole, topped with a beautiful floor-length black coat. She looked like she was going to a funeral, which technically she was because she was about to bury someone's company.

"Rough day?" Sydney asked as she slid into the

booth.

"Tedious," Reegan said and went to grab her friend a cup of coffee.

"Thanks," Sydney said after she sipped. "This reminds me of college."

Reegan grinned. "It does, doesn't it?"

Sydney leaned in. "What's all this talk of a curse?"

Reegan forced a laugh, then made a production of rolling her eyes. "I heard something about that too. It's bullshit, Syd."

"I heard Tori and Bernadette were—"

Reegan held up a hand. "Not you too! I swear people are passing out the Kool-Aid with all this crap."

"Just as I suspected. This damn town," Sydney said with a shake of her head.

"I'm guessing by the suit that you're headed back to the city."

She nodded. "Yes, if everything goes well we should be signing the papers late tonight or in the morning."

"Congratulations! You've worked hard for this."

"It's Martin's company, Reegan," Sydney whispered, speaking of her ex-husband.

"Oh, Sydney."

"I guess that's why I was so horrid to you."

"Because of Martin?"

"I've worked so hard to tear him down economically the way he tore me down emotionally. The divorce—"

Reegan reached across the table and took Sydney's hand. "It's okay."

She cleared her throat. "When you said you were moving back here, all I heard was that you were giving up everything for a new life that wouldn't include me."

"How could you think that?"

Sydney squeezed Reegan's hand. "I was too busy being selfish to think, and for that I'm sorry."

"Me too, Syd," Reegan said.

"I'll come back soon; we have a wedding to plan!" Sydney said.

Reegan stood up, and after a hug and a quick wave, her friend was gone.

She sat back down and rubbed her temples. What a day, Reegan thought. The bad news from Justin was that Bernie's condition hadn't improved; the good news was it hadn't worsened.

She looked up when the door opened again. She couldn't help but smile. "Phyllis, do you want some coffee?"

"No, thank you, I'm going to the hospital with Delores."

Reegan frowned. "Now?"

"In a few minutes."

This was news to her. She glanced behind her when Delores came out of hiding.

"I'm going to close early, Reegan," Delores said wringing her hands. "Justin needs to get some rest."

"I was planning on going to sit with Bernie later," Reegan said.

"It's just as well."

What did that mean? Reegan wondered. "Does Justin not want me there?" she asked around the lump lodged deep in her throat.

"Oh, Reegan, it's not that at all," Delores said and Phyllis shook her head.

"Then what is it, exactly?" Reegan asked, crossing

her arms over her chest.

"Justin won't listen to you if you tell him to go get some rest, but he'll listen to me…hopefully," Delores said.

"And Phyllis?"

"I would like to see her," Phyllis murmured.

Reegan hadn't realized Phyllis genuinely cared for Bernie, but she could see it now. "Okay," she said.

"I'm going to make a sign, and then we can go," Delores said before disappearing back into the bookstore.

"Oh, wait, I don't have a ride," Reegan said.

"We can drop you off at the sheriff's station if you want. I'm proud of you girls," Phyllis said surprising Reegan.

"You helped us shed light on a lot of things," Reegan said.

Phyllis preened a bit. "Glad to be of service."

"I was curious about something," Reegan said.

"What's that?"

"What you and your family accumulated was passed down from generation to generation, but you're an only child with no children of your own. Who were you planning on passing it down to or did it end with you?" That question had been lingering in the back of her mind.

Phyllis looked her up and down. "Your June was already under my tutelage."

Reegan's heart did a jig at hearing "your June," but then the words sank in. "June?" Copies of book covers flashed in her brain. The books! She'd seen images of books the first time she'd seen June. Books, the library, all leading to Phyllis.

"Yes, it's fitting considering Buck would have passed his part on to Phillip and I would have passed mine on to June."

"Buck's part?"

Phyllis pursed her lips. "Didn't mention it, did he? I'm not surprised."

"What didn't he mention?" She'd known that man was hiding something.

"My grandmother wasn't the only one Clara talked to at the Willows that day. The stable boy, William, was there too."

The word "stables" from the ledger flew to the forefront of Reegan's mind. It had been next to the initials W. H. and linked by a noose to Duncan Clacher. Duncan, who, according to Phyllis's grandmother, was working with his cousin at the Willows. "William," Reegan said.

"Yes, William Hastings. He was just a boy then."

A boy? Reegan covered her mouth with her hand just as the young boy had done in her dream. He'd saved Minerva that morning. Buck had even asked about him!

"Are you all right, dear? You look like you've seen a…did you have a vision?" Phyllis asked and guided Reegan to a seat.

Reegan shook her head. "No, a dream—a memory fell into place."

"Because of something *I* said?"

Reegan wanted to laugh. "Yes, Phyllis, because of you. So, William made a promise to Clara too. Do you know what it was?"

"That he would make sure they were protected from anything or anyone that might try to hurt them.

That's why William became sheriff when he was of age. Then his son, then Buck, and now Phillip."

"They covered up Edwin's suicide, to protect Patch and Annie Mae," Reegan guessed.

"You should ask Buck for the details; that stubborn old goat is playing his cards close to the vest."

Reegan stood. "Well, we'll just see about that! In fact, I think Buck would love the opportunity to take his future daughter-in-law home," she said as she pulled out her cell phone.

Phyllis cackled. "There's no denying you've got spunk!"

Chapter Thirty-Six

She was scared, no nervous, Reegan admitted to herself as she peeked at Buck out of the corner of her eye. Her bravado had faded when he'd picked her up from the coffee shop. He'd hugged her, turning her resolve to dust.

They were getting close to the house, and Reegan didn't want to lose her opportunity. "For the record, and to satisfy my personal curiosity, do you make it a habit of lying or is it just me in particular you enjoy deceiving?"

His lips twitched. "What are you referring to?"

"We asked you if you knew anything else, and you said no."

"I believe Phillip asked if there was anything else I'd like to share, and there wasn't," Buck said.

"Semantics."

"Wording is important," Buck said, then sighed. "Just ask, Reegan."

"I know about William Hastings, who he was and what he did to help Minerva when he was a boy. I also know he promised Clara Marshal Whit to protect the girls when and if they returned. But William knew things Phyllis's grandmother didn't, right?"

"What else do you think you know?" Buck asked as he pulled into the driveway.

Reegan thought it through. "William was there the

morning they murdered his cousin, and my guess is he knew the baby survived. So when he became sheriff, he watched Edwin and protected him when he could. That's why no one ever found out that Edwin was having an affair or that Annie Mae was his daughter."

"I have to say I'm impressed. There's my son," he said, pointing to where Phillip was approaching them.

"You should come inside, so we can finish this discussion." Reegan unbuckled her seatbelt and reached for the handle. The ignition turned off after she shut the door.

"Hey, I was going to come get you, but Delores said my dad picked you up; I decided to meet you here instead," Phillip said and kissed her. "Is he coming in?"

"Yes. He's finally going to give us some straight answers, right, Buck?"

Buck opened the trunk and pulled out a briefcase. "Looks that way."

Phillip looked down at Reegan. "What's going on?"

By the time they were sitting around the table, Phillip was up to speed. And though he was outwardly calm Reegan knew he was upset that his father was still keeping secrets. Reegan eyed the briefcase wondering what on earth it could contain.

"Tell me, Reegan, what other theories do you have regarding my grandfather?"

"Edwin died in the forties, which means William was still sheriff. We suspect that Edwin committed suicide, and William covered it up to protect Patch and Annie Mae. He may have suspected they were Amelia and Minerva returned. That's why you protected Patch all those years."

"I met Patch when I was a kid," Buck said with a twist of his lips. "She baked cookies and didn't find the idle chitchat of a boy bothersome. My father supported the friendship and told me I should always look out for her and hers. I didn't realize the true meaning of his words until after he died."

"And you couldn't tell us any of this when we asked?" Phillip demanded.

"He left me a key to a safe deposit box," he said, ignoring Philip and opening his briefcase. "In it was a letter. I burned it after I read it as he'd requested. In the letter, he told me about the curse and what the town had done. When Phillip took over the sheriff's position, I relayed that information to him."

"But you left something out," Phillip said.

"The letter spoke of my grandfather promising Edwin's grandmother that our family would always look out for hers. That I was honor bound to keep the word of my grandfather, as were my children and their children, et cetera."

"Wait," Reegan said. "You didn't know that Minerva was Edwin's birth mother? Or that Clara was the woman your grandfather gave his word to?"

Buck shook his head. "I've been putting it together with the information you've found."

"That's all your grandfather said?"

"My father wasn't prone to innuendo; he gave facts, not theories. Maybe my grandfather didn't confide everything to protect their true identity, or maybe Father didn't believe him. One thing my father knew for certain was that *his* father believed in this promise so much he covered up a suicide to protect Edwin's family and reputation."

"Edwin did kill himself?" Reegan asked.

"My grandfather thought so." Buck reached into the briefcase and pulled out a journal. "This was in the wreckage."

Taking the journal, Reegan looked to see that the inside cover said Property of Edwin Woods, but the pages were blank. There was something odd about the inside spine. "Did William tear out the pages?"

"No, he found it like that. Turn to the last page," Buck said.

Phillip gave her an encouraging nod. She read aloud, "It says, 'She said until the key is given to the rightful owners, a sacrifice must be made by those who pass it down. I will be that sacrifice. Forgive me, my darlings, but I will not let you pay my debt.' "

"It's his suicide note," Phillip said.

"Why did William keep this?"

"I learned from Patch that, around the time of her father's death, both she and Annie Mae were stricken with fever. He thought it was connected to this key. He believed that if he sacrificed himself, they wouldn't die and they didn't."

"Did you tell Patch and Annie Mae?" Reegan asked.

"No, I thought it best not to."

Reegan nodded. She couldn't blame him for that. She reread Edwin's writing. "What key?"

"I'm home!" June said, coming into the room with her book bag on her shoulder. "Hey, Grandpa! Dad, what's going on?"

"How was school?" Phillip asked.

"The usual," June said putting her bag down.

Reegan smiled as June looked back and forth

between Phillip and Buck.

"Is Grandpa in trouble again?" June asked.

Reegan snorted. "Happens a lot, huh?"

Buck shrugged, and June snickered.

Phillip opened his mouth to comment when the doorbell rang.

"I'll get it," June called out and ran to the front door.

"Saved by the bell," Reegan said.

"Reegan, you need to sign for the package."

"I wonder what it is?" she said after she signed the electronic key pad and closed the door.

"Reegan got a letter," June said when they returned to the kitchen.

Reegan smiled at Phillip after reading the return address on the envelope. "It's from Richard!"

"Who's Richard?" Buck asked.

"He's a photographer friend of mine who specializes in film restoration. I hired him for a project," she explained, frowning. "That's odd, he's never sent his work before he got paid."

"He called while you were in the hospital," Phillip said.

"You didn't mention it," she said as she began opening the seal.

"I wanted it to be a surprise."

Reegan looked up from what she was doing. "You paid Richard?"

It was obvious he was trying not to laugh at her. "Is there a problem?"

Everyone was staring at her, and her face flooded with heat. "I don't expect you to pay for me."

"It was important to you, and that makes it

important to me."

"To us," June added.

Reegan looked between the two of them. "Thank you."

"You're welcome," Phillip said and kissed her forehead.

She felt ridiculous as she opened the envelope. She read Richard's note. "He says he likes my young man and he wishes us well. The film was damaged, but he was able to get some decent prints. He hopes I find what I was looking for." She shuffled through the photos.

"Unbelievable," Phillip said from behind her. "I haven't seen the Willows in years."

They were looking at a picture of Sydney posing with her bike in front of the Willows. She'd dreamt of taking this photo last night. She kept going through the photos, and her stomach rolled. "That house gave me the creeps even then. Oh, wow! Look, Phillip." She held up the group photo she'd taken.

"It's hard to see this now, knowing what we do," Phillip said.

"Some people believe photographs steal the soul of the subject. I never believed that, but looking at these"—she shook her head—"it's like I captured the curse on film."

"Let's put them away for now," Phillip suggested.

Reegan agreed and shoved them back in the envelope. Taking a breath, she raised her head and noticed an unfamiliar box on the counter next to where Buck was standing. "Is that yours too?"

Buck looked to where she was pointing. "No."

"Dr. Michele had it brought to me, and I was

saving it for Bernie," Phillip said.

"What is it?" Reegan asked.

"They're Tori's things from Shady Pines; she wanted Bernie to have them in the event of her death."

"Do you think Bernie would want them?" June asked.

"Maybe it's time you started on your homework," Phillip suggested.

June sighed.

"I'll give you a hand," Buck said and followed June into the other room.

"She's right, Phillip. I don't want Bernie to see this," Reegan said.

"Do you think I do?" he asked.

Reegan went to stand in front of him. "Of course not! You're the kindest man I've ever met, and I know you well enough to know you're keeping this to give Bernie the choice. What I'm saying is that I know Bernie too. She'll go through that damn box, and it will bring her nothing but heartache."

Phillip nodded. "What do you suggest?"

"Why don't we go through it and then decide?"

"Sounds good," Phillip said, taking the box lid in his hands. "Ready?"

"Let's get this over with."

There were two framed photos: one of Bernie and Tori as children, another taken on the day of graduation. "Do you think these belong to the library?" she asked, holding up a couple of books.

"*The Scarlet Letter*. Why would Tori be reading that?"

Reegan shrugged. "Bernie was always saying Tori's mind was that of a child or teenager, right?

Maybe she was thinking she was in high school again."

"Makes sense."

"I was expecting more than this or maybe hoping—"

"For an answer?"

"For closure."

"You don't feel like you have closure?"

"Yes and no. I feel like something's missing."

"Bernie is," Phillip said, and she knew he was right.

****

"You just missed Mom and Phyllis; they went to get something to eat," Justin said when Reegan and Phillip came in the room.

"Did the doctors have anything new to say?" Reegan asked.

"No," Justin said as he stood to stretch. "You can sit here, Reegan."

"Thank you," she said and took a seat next to Bernie, who appeared peaceful in her slumber. "June wanted to come with us, but we thought it best she stay with Buck."

"She's a sweet kid," he said to Reegan, then turned to Phillip. "I'd like one of your deputies to be stationed here if you don't mind."

"Did something happen?" Phillip asked.

"Willows Bluff and its insatiable curiosity happened. I've caught several people passing by to sneak a peek."

"You want protection?"

"I can protect Bernadette from them," Justin said. "But you might want to protect those assholes from me."

"Damn straight!" Reegan cheered, then apologized when Phillip gave her a look.

"The last thing we need is for you to end up with assault charges. I'll see what I can do about a guard," Phillip said and left them.

Justin pulled out a chair on the other side of Bernie and sat down. "Thanks for helping Mom today, Reegan. She said you were amazing."

Reegan blushed. "Being a barista for five years is nothing to laugh at, and you're welcome."

Justin nodded.

"We found out some things today if you want to hear about it."

"I'm sure she would," Justin said motioning to Bernie.

Reegan swallowed. "Bernie, you're not going to believe this," she began and filled Justin in on what she'd learned.

"Did you bring the pictures with you?" Justin asked.

She shook her head, then reached in her knapsack and pulled out the journal. "I did bring this," she said, standing up to give it to Justin. She reached across Bernie, taking her friend's hand as she did, and the air went out of her lungs.

"They think it's them who's cursed, but it's not them! No, they had no power. They weren't born with it as was said; no. No, they weren't. But it was sought. Found where no one else would venture," the woman with light hair and wild brown eyes said.

"You're saying someone had a curse put on them?" the man asked, his silver eyes darting around the room.

"Yes," the woman said. "And if history does repeat, the next are also cursed to fall."

"The next?"

"My sister's last words proclaimed that the world would right the wrong. Last words such as those hold power. To defend against this, a curse was placed on those who would follow. You must break the curse, and only the truth can do that."

"Then I beg you to tell me!"

The woman giggled. "I cannot tell you what you must find for yourself. You must see what was unseen, learn what was unknown, or suffer the same."

"How? How am I to do this?"

"The fates will choose their moment, the pieces will align, and it shall begin again."

"Then how do I stop it?"

"You cannot stop it! But perhaps it can be changed; I will give you the key. What I tell you, you may repeat only once. Promise!"

His hands fidgeted but he said, "I promise to tell my daughters."

"They too will keep this promise, and before their light extinguishes, they will be relieved of their burden. Listen well, nephew, it always starts with death unplanned..."

Reegan sucked in air, dropped Bernie's hand, and stared at Justin, who had taken the book out of her hand and broken the connection.

"What the hell just happened?" Justin asked.

Chapter Thirty-Seven

"What happened?" Justin asked again.

"It was a vision," Reegan said, looking up as Phillip came into the room. "The missing pages in Edwin's journal."

"What did you see?" Phillip asked.

"Edwin went to see Fidelia when she was at Shady Pines. I recognized them from their photographs. She's the one who told him what to tell Patch and Annie Mae. She said it was the key. The promise *is* the key. I think we missed something."

"So it's true," a man's voice said behind Reegan. She turned around.

"Ezra, what are you doing here?" Reegan asked. His white hair was wild, and his cheeks were pink from the wind.

Holding up a bouquet of roses, he said, "I brought these for Bernadette."

Reegan stared at him as he watched Bernie from the doorway. "How long have you known?"

"Known what?" Justin asked.

"That Bernie's his grandniece," Reegan said, and both men stared at Ezra.

"She knows?" Ezra asked.

"Yes," Reegan whispered and gave Ezra's arm a squeeze.

Tears glazed his eyes. "She didn't let on."

"Her mother told her never to tell anyone," Reegan said. "She was protecting you from the stigma, as she called it, of being related to her."

Ezra bowed his head. "I never dreamed she knew the truth."

"Why was it a secret?" Phillip asked.

"My sister and I had a falling out when she got married." Ezra stepped farther into the room and lowered his voice. "The women in her husband's family had a history of turning sick-minded."

"They were insane?"

"Not all of them, no."

"What does this have to do with Bernadette?" Justin asked.

"Years after the events at the Willows, one of Clara Marshal Whit's brothers moved back to Willows Bluff under a different name. My family was the only one to recognize him, and we kept it to ourselves, but we knew what blood ran in his veins. I warned my sister to stay away."

"What are trying to say, Ezra?" Reegan asked, though she knew the truth.

"Bernadette is the great-grandniece of Clara Marshal Whit," he said and took a breath. "It would seem she's being punished for her heritage."

"What do you know about the curse?" Phillip asked.

Ezra shifted his feet. "Just that the souls of the Whits would one day return seeking vengeance. I heard you say you'd missed something."

"It's more complicated than people know," Reegan said.

Ezra nodded. "I know where becoming obsessed

with such things leads. Look at Adam Desmond."

"Adam?" Justin said.

"He became obsessed with the curse. He *and* his sister, April." Ezra cleared his throat. "And it killed him."

"He died when his studio caught fire," Phillip said.

"No doubt using fire as a medium to produce his art. The curse was his muse, and it consumed him."

Reegan shivered when the image crossed her mind. "Wait, you said April was obsessed with the curse too?"

"Oh, yes. She said the Whits built themselves a pedestal there on the bluff and then fell from grace. She thumbed her nose at the Whits and the families she waited on, but she envied them. Then she came into money and...well"—Ezra shook his head—"such a waste."

"What?" Reegan asked.

"Such a beautiful girl stained by her greed."

Reegan grabbed Phillip's forearm. "Envious greed," she whispered.

Phillip stared at her a moment. "Ezra, do you know if April's in town?"

"She's helping her mother settle Adam's affairs," Ezra said. "They should be back tomorrow or the day after."

"Thanks, Ezra," Reegan said.

"Do you think I could sit with her a minute?" he asked.

"We'll give you some privacy," Justin said and motioned everyone else toward the door.

Reegan kissed Ezra's cheek and left him to sit with Bernie alone. She hoped Bernie could feel how much people loved her. How much they needed her. She looked at Phillip. "We need to find April."

The group turned as Phyllis and Delores approached them. Phyllis nudged Delores's shoulder and said, "I told you we were missing something."

"So you did," Delores said and handed Justin a takeout box.

"How do you feel about coming home with me and Phillip?" Reegan asked Phyllis. "Ezra gave us some information that will be of interest to you, and I need your help finding a link."

Phyllis gave a curt nod. "You can count me in."

****

Reegan was sitting at the kitchen table again with her parents, Phillip's parents, and Phyllis trying to make sense of what they now knew. Phyllis had nearly had a heart attack when they'd told her about Clara's brother changing his name. But Reegan assured her that she didn't think anyone but Ezra's family had figured it out. Unfortunately, the news had impelled the woman to pore over all of her mother's notes, which meant she was hogging the ledger that Reegan wanted to see.

She went to the counter and started a pot of decaf. Her father stood and came over to her.

"How are you holding up?" he asked.

"I don't think Annie Mae knew about Bernie's connection to Clara Marshal," she blurted out.

"Why?"

Reegan shook her head. "We've been assuming Patch and Annie Mae had the answers, but I don't think they did. First off, I'm pretty sure they didn't know it was Fidelia who gave their father the key or promise, or whatever. For one, they didn't have that journal, and two, I don't think he would have told them."

"Why not?"

"Because he was terrified of her; I could feel his fear and so could she. She enjoyed it."

"Was Tori like that?" her father asked without meeting her eyes. She knew her parents were worried about her, and the least she could do was give them the truth.

"Don't get me wrong, I was scared, but *she* wasn't scary. Creepy? Yeah, but this wasn't about power for Tori. It was always about Bernie; everything she did was because she didn't want to lose her. I think Tori planned to kill herself that night too."

"Murder suicide," Buck said coming into the room.

She regarded him a moment. "Yes."

"What makes you think that?" her dad asked.

"She was…giddy, like a child finally getting what she wanted most." Something occurred to her. "Tori couldn't have gotten out of Shady Pines by herself."

"You think she had help?" Buck asked.

Yes, Reegan thought, but who? It would have to be someone familiar with the sanitarium. Someone who'd been there more than once, a familiar face. "Shady Pines gets donations from some of the wealthiest families in the area. How much do you want to bet that April's family is one of them?"

"I'll have Phillip make a call," Buck said and went to find his son. Reegan knew he was making sure June was actually in bed and not listening through the door.

"April was a maid for both Syd's parents and Tori's. Tori would trust her."

"I found it!" Phyllis called from the table.

"What?" Reegan asked, coming around to hover over the old librarian.

"Remember I told you that governess moved away and got married?"

"Hazel Collins, right? She's the one who came back married to a wealthy man," Reegan said.

"Yes, her married name was Desmond!" Phyllis pointed at the page. "One of her daughters, Hester, was friends with the girls." She sat back, closing the ledger.

"There's the link you were looking for," Reegan's mother said.

Reegan grabbed one of the legal pads and quickly wrote down the names of the past that linked to the names of the present. "All the names are accounted for now," she said, looking up.

"What?" Phillip asked when he came into the room.

"Take a look," Reegan said, handing the legal pad to Phillip.

As Phillip looked over Reegan's notes, Phyllis explained what she'd found about Hazel and Hester Desmond.

W. L. Brooks

Reegan's Notes

Then—Now
Minerva Whit—Me (Reegan)
Amelia Whit—Bernie
Fidelia Whit—Tori
Duncan Clacher—Phillip
Lucian Matthews—Justin
Hattie Bailey—Sydney
Hazel Collins Desmond and daughter Hester
Desmond—April and Adam
****

"The parallels are uncanny," Phillip said.

"What do you mean?" Reegan's dad asked.

"Hester's mother was a governess, by no means wealthy, and working for the Whits. Then she married a wealthy man, and her children could break bread with the same people she once served."

"Just like April was a maid, and now she's wealthy," Reegan said.

"Were you able to speak to anyone at Shady Pines?" Buck asked Phillip.

Phillip straightened. "That's what I came to tell you. Not only does April's husband give money every quarter, but April often brings flowers for the patients."

"Including Tori," Reegan guessed.

"Especially Tori," Phillip said. "A dozen long-stemmed roses every month. Dr. Michele is meeting me in the morning to go over the surveillance footage."

"We got her," Reegan said.

****

The dreams went through Reegan's mind in an unnatural flurry…*The day of her accident, making love with Phillip, the fire, the photos, and the death. The pain came next forcing its way through the blood in her veins, catching in her heart, and there in the darkness stood a figure watching her, waiting for her to die.*

It was June's sobs that penetrated the horror, and Reegan was able to open her eyes. June hovered over her holding her hand, and Reegan involuntarily flinched away. Phillip stood on the other side of her, and only after her lips closed did she realize that she'd been screaming.

"Sorry," Reegan said.

June nodded, her face flushed.

"You've never screamed like that before," Phillip whispered.

"I'm sorry," she said, again sitting up and rubbing her face with her shaking hands. Her cheeks were wet. She took June's hand again. "I didn't mean to upset you, sweetheart."

"It's okay," June said around a shuddering breath.

"June, could you give us a minute please?" Phillip said.

"I'll make you some coffee, Reegan," June said before leaving the room.

"That'd be great," Reegan said with as much enthusiasm as she could muster.

Phillip sat on the bed and took her hands in his. "What happened?"

He gave her hand a squeeze, and she began to tell

him what she'd seen. "And then, right before I woke up, there was a figure on the bluff watching me, waiting for me."

"You think it was a warning?"

Reegan nodded. "When I ran into April at Ezra's, she said she always knew I'd come back; I thought it was strange but now—"

"I'll do everything in my power to keep you safe!" he said, wrapping his arms around her.

She laughed and held him tighter. "That's the one thing I *am* sure of."

Chapter Thirty-Eight

It was noon by the time Reegan was feeling normal. Phillip had gone to meet Dr. Michele and go through the security footage. So when the school called saying they were closing early due to the severe storm expected to hit, she called Phillip to ask him what she should do.

"Don't worry, Reegan, my dad will pick her up."

"Okay." She felt silly. "Have you found April on the tapes yet?"

"We're going through them now; I'll let you know when we find something."

"Good. Are you coming home soon? They're saying on the news it's going to get nasty."

"After I finish here, I have to go to the station and check on our emergency protocol. It's my department's responsibility to make sure everyone is safe. I can ask Dad to stay if it would make you feel better."

What would make her feel better was if *he* was home. "That would be good," she said.

"Reegan, what is it? You agreed much too quickly."

"I guess I'm still freaked out from the dream."

There was a long pause, then, "I'll tell him to stay."

Half an hour later, Buck showed up with June in tow, and Phyllis was with them. The library had also closed early, and when Phyllis ran into Buck and June, she asked to tag along.

"I wanted to go over what we found one more time," Phyllis said.

"Of course, help yourself," Reegan said as they went into the kitchen.

"How about I fix us some lunch?" Buck suggested.

"I'm starving," June said.

"June told us about your dream," Phyllis said, taking a seat at the table.

Reegan glanced at June, then to Buck, who pretended not to be listening. "It was disturbing."

"I didn't know it was a secret," June said, staring at her shoes.

"It's not," Reegan assured her and filled in the blanks for Phyllis, who had an exponential number of questions.

"Would you mind if I took a look at these?" Buck asked after they'd finished lunch. He held up the envelope Richard had sent.

"Be my guest," she said, though she didn't think she'd ever want to see them again.

"What's this book about, Miss Phyllis?" June asked, and Reegan looked up in time to see June going through Tori's box.

"June, please don't go through that," Reegan said. She didn't want June exposed to Tori in any way.

June blushed. "Sorry."

"It's okay," she said with a guilty smile. She glanced at Phyllis and sighed. "Go ahead."

"*The Scarlet Letter*," Phyllis began, giving June an in-depth description until Reegan interrupted her.

"Hester Prynne was the main character."

Phyllis glared at her. "Yes, Hester—"

"Wait!" Reegan hurried to the table. "What year was it published?"

"I believe it was 1850. It was Hawthorne's greatest work in my opinion. Why is that relevant?"

"If I'm right, it means your grandmother was being trying to be subtle!" Reegan said, taking the ledgers away from Phyllis. She combed through the pages until she found what she was looking for. She pointed to the page. "The 'A' we thought was because she was a teacher!"

"Who?" Phyllis asked leaning closer.

"Hazel Collins, the governess! Your grandmother smudged out what she'd written under her name about children or a child and replaced it with a single 'A,' which she would know stood for adultery," Reegan said in a rush. "Hazel came back with a *child* who befriended the Whits, a daughter named Hester Desmond; Hester, for God's sake!"

Phyllis gasped. "She was his child; Bertrum Whit's illegitimate daughter!"

Reegan reached across Buck and grabbed Bernie's notes. She flipped through the pages in a frenzy. "Here, it says: 'Four wanted to be three, and three could never be two—different but ever the same.' Four daughters! Hester was probably jealous of the three legitimate daughters, and Fidelia was jealous of Amelia and Minerva because she was only a half-sibling. Different—"

"But the same because of Bertrum," Buck said.

"Yes!" Reegan covered her mouth with her shaking hand.

"You did it, Reegan," Buck said, and he stood so he could look over the ledgers alongside Phyllis.

"I guess it was a good thing I went through that box after all," June said with an impish smirk.

Reegan laughed. "Yes, it was."

"Hester's line isn't listed in any of the ledgers," Phyllis said, pointing to the pages. "She must have moved away from Willows Bluff not long after the girls were killed."

"She probably wanted to wait until the smoke cleared," Buck said, then winced. "So to speak."

"You're probably right," Reegan said, rolling her eyes when she noticed Buck had set his water bottle on top of one of the photos. "Buck, I'm sure you know better than this!"

Buck looked up, all innocence.

She went to move it when something caught her eye. The water had magnified something that shouldn't be there. She lifted the photo and tried getting a better angle but couldn't. She hurried into her bedroom and dug through her camera case until she found her magnifying lens. She checked and rechecked. "It can't be," she whispered.

"Reegan, what's wrong?" June asked when Reegan came back in the kitchen.

She put on her coat and pulled on her boots. "I need to take care of something. Can I borrow your car?" she asked Buck with her hand out.

Buck stared at her open palm for more than a minute, then relented and handed her his keys. "Want to tell me where you're going?"

She stared at the keys a moment, swallowed, and before the door shut behind her, she said, "The beginning."

****

She trudged up the hill with labored breaths. The sky was smoky gray, announcing more snow was imminent. The wind picked up, and Reegan pulled her hat lower on her ears. She reached the top and shivered. The Willows had long since been torn down, but she could still feel its pulse.

A figure moved toward the edge of the bluff, and she closed her eyes over the sting of tears. Without hesitation, she walked closer to the edge.

"I've been waiting for you."

"How did you know I'd be here?" Reegan asked.

"Call it intuition. I like it here. It's the first place I felt completely in control."

"You mean when you pushed me off the bluff?"

"How did you figure that out?"

Reegan pulled the photo from her pocket. "You know I was rescued that night. Bernadette Howard saved me and then saved my camera. Which included the photos I'd taken that day. You can imagine my surprise when I noticed this." She pointed to a spot on the group photo.

"What is it?"

"It's Alan's flashlight, Sydney, that's what." Reegan didn't know if she whispered it or screamed it. When she'd seen that little red object in Sydney's bag, she died a thousand deaths. If Sydney had her brother's flashlight when the photo was taken, it meant that she'd lured Reegan up to the bluff.

Bernie hadn't shown her Tori that night; she'd shown her Sydney. That's why Bernie hadn't wanted to tell her the truth; she'd been protecting Reegan as she'd protected everyone else.

"Aren't you going to ask me why?" Sydney asked,

her tone bored.

When Reegan didn't answer, Sydney turned and grabbed her hand, asking again if she wanted to know why. The connection had Reegan's eyes slamming shut.

"Make haste! We must make haste," the cloaked woman who Reegan knew to be Sydney said as they ran toward the barn. *"In here."*

Reegan's breath came out in pants; she was in so much pain. She stood back while her friend opened the door to the barn and pushed her into the vast darkness. Hands grabbed her arms, and she screamed.

"Shut it, witch," the man said with hate in his eyes. *Adam's eyes.*

She opened her mouth to speak, but the man hit her. The next thing she knew she was tied up. Her friend stood over her. "You betrayed me!"

Reegan's eyes opened, and she sucked in a breath; Sydney was clutching her stomach.

"What the hell was that?"

"A vision," Reegan said, stepping back as snow began to fall heavily around them. She didn't understand why Hattie Bailey had turned on them. Hester must have manipulated her the way she'd manipulated Fidelia. "How long have you known about the curse?"

Sydney glared at her. "You mean the curse you told me was bullshit? That curse?"

Reegan snorted. "That's the one."

"I'd been warned about the two for as long as I can remember, but I never imagined you were one of them. Until Tori was lashing out at me, and you did nothing!" she spat.

"So you push me off the fucking bluff?"

"I'd only planned to scare you, but then I thought, why not? If you died, then I killed either one of the two I'd been warned about or a traitor. When you survived, I knew I'd have to finish the job, but you didn't remember anything and you changed your life to stay with me. That's when I thought you were the third, the one who could be swayed to do my bidding. Then you said you were seeing pictures in your head, and I knew we'd been mistaken. Needless to say, Tori being the third was *quite* unexpected. Here Daddo and I had been grooming you for—"

"Bullshit!" Reegan choked.

"Really? I've had the pieces in place for years…waiting."

"You've been manipulating everything this entire time?"

The ruthless grin that lit Syd's face made Reegan's skin crawl. "But how did you get to Tori? She hated you," she said, then remembered the image of a maid listening outside the door. "April gave you information, didn't she?"

"April's pathetic! I introduced her to a world of wealth, and in exchange, she divulged secrets. She's been my pawn for years."

"And Adam?"

She snickered. "You tried to hide your crush on him, Reegan, but whenever he came into a room, you unconsciously squeezed your thighs together!"

Reegan stared, horrified.

"You were too scared to do anything about it, but don't worry, I fucked him for you. He was quite talented both in and out of the bedroom. Such a shame he didn't know when to stop."

"You killed him?"

Sydney shrugged a shoulder. "You know what they say about playing with fire."

"Who the hell do you think you are? These are people's lives you—"

"Stop sniveling, Reegan." She pulled a gun from her pocket and pointed it at Reegan.

"You're really going to kill me?"

"Yes," Sydney said without hesitating.

Reegan stared at the barrel unmoving. She couldn't outrun a bullet. She looked to her right, toward the edge of the bluff; she could at least go down trying.

"Are you thinking about jumping?" Sydney laughed. "Please do. You're still a horrible swimmer, and Bernadette isn't here to save you this time."

Bernie! "You said you owed her one for saving me."

"Don't worry; I always repay my debts."

"You're going to kill her?" Reegan asked. She couldn't let that happen. She moved to her left; she'd need a running start.

"The two of you must die, Reegan. That's how this goes. Pay attention!"

"Why?"

"It's the prophecy," she said. "Through death, there will be life, and through life, there will be a return. Two with unnatural gifts will set out to reclaim the past, but they will turn easily against one another. A companion, of fragile mind, will present herself from an unexpected place. Mold her to do your bidding, and through her, blood will spill. To protect all that is yours you must succeed. Do not be fooled, for the price of victory is always three."

"Three?"

"Yes, three, obviously! Do I have to draw you a picture?" Sydney lifted her arm, so the gun was trained on Reegan.

"Phillip will never stop hunting you."

"Well"—she cocked the gun—"we'll just see about that." She pulled the trigger.

Reegan dodged to her right in time to feel a burning poker cross her jaw. She fell to her knees, turning when Sydney approached. The water was rushing behind her, but she knew it was too late. She sat on her haunches staring into Sydney's blue eyes while her ex-best friend stood above her.

"You don't have to do this," Reegan said.

Sydney's smile was rueful. "Try as we might, we can't escape our fate."

A shot rang out, and Reegan flinched, then Sydney stumbled forward. Reegan maneuvered to her knees while blood spread across Sydney's pale sweater. Sydney's eyes met Reegan's, and she fell to all fours.

Reegan ignored the urge to go to Sydney's aid and got to her feet to search the area. She was looking for Phillip, but that wasn't who she found. When her eyes met the steel blue gaze of the woman walking toward her, Reegan's knees gave out.

She didn't know how she should feel when the woman stood above where Sydney had collapsed. Sirens sounded in the distance, but she knew the paramedics would never make it up here in time. She didn't know if she herself was safe.

As if sensing her thoughts, the woman said, "Don't be frightened, my dear. You're safe from me."

Reegan swallowed. "There's still time," she said.

"You can give me the gun, and I'll say I shot her."

The woman smiled, a sight Reegan had never seen, and said, "Thank you, dear, but I know what I'm doing."

"But, Mrs. Walters, you just shot your daughter," Reegan whispered.

"Oh, she's dead," Mrs. Walters breathed. "Finally, I can get some peace."

Chapter Thirty-Nine

Reegan paced the narrow hall in the sheriff's station, glancing out the window now and then at the snow piling on the sidewalk. She didn't care if they got snowed in here as long as she got some answers.

"Reegan, you need to sit down," her father suggested for the millionth time. He'd been with Phillip and Buck when they came over the hill with the deputies and paramedics. Of course, if Buck hadn't had a GPS tracking device on his car, they wouldn't have known where to look.

The bullet Sydney fired had grazed her jaw. The EMTs had bandaged the wound and said she might have a scar; otherwise, she was in good shape. "I'm still hyped up on adrenaline," she said, jumping when the door to the conference room opened.

"You can talk to her now," Phillip said.

Reegan hurried through the door. Phillip had taken the time to deputize her, so all their bases were covered. He'd told her he doubted this would go to trial but better safe than sorry. Mrs. Walters had shot Sydney in defense of another, a justifiable homicide. Phillip said the DA would settle if they pressed charges at all. But he wanted Reegan to speak with her while she had the chance.

Buck sat to the right of Sydney's mother, who sat at the end of the medium-sized conference table.

Reegan sat to her left, and Phillip sat next to her. Her father waited in the hall, but the door was open, so she knew he could hear.

Reegan studied Mrs. Walters. She still wore her own clothes, a gray sweater and black slacks. Her skin was fair, with hints of wrinkles in all the usual places. Her hair was a stunning shade of silver which she wore in a short style, and her eyes were steel blue and unwavering. This was the most relaxed Reegan had ever seen her.

"How?" Reegan asked at last. "Why?"

Mrs. Walters studied her for a moment. "After my son Alan's death, my husband's family was adamant we have another child right away. We gave in to the pressure, and ultimately we gave his parents the heir they so desperately wanted. And it was a girl. I didn't know what that meant at the time."

"They wanted you to have a girl?" Reegan asked.

"Where Alan would have inherited from us and a small trust from his grandparents, a female heir would inherit the entirety of the Walters' estate. The houses, the money, the business—everything. There hadn't been a female born into the Walters family in generations."

"I don't understand," Reegan said. "What does this have to do with—"

"With your curse?" she asked, and Reegan wasn't the only one surprised.

"You didn't mention that before," Phillip said shifting in his seat.

She turned toward Reegan. "My official statement is accurate. I wasn't aware of what Sydney had planned when she left the house, but I had a bad feeling so I followed her. When I saw you, that feeling intensified so I grabbed my gun—I have a concealed weapons permit; you never know these days, dear—and went up the hill behind you. I saw her try to kill you, and I knew I had to stop her." She paused, motioning to the carafe of coffee and stack of mugs in the middle of the table. "May I?"

"Allow me," Phillip said, rising from his seat. He poured a cup for each of them, taking one out to Reegan's father, who was still listening from the hall, before returning to his chair.

Mrs. Walters took a couple of dainty sips from her mug, then said, "What I didn't mention and what I'm sure everyone will agree should be off the record is that I knew what was going on."

"How?"

"When I was little, my great-grandmother would tell me fairy tales about two beautiful princesses, a wicked stepsister, and an evil witch."

"Your great-grandmother was Hattie Bailey?" Reegan asked, confused. It had been Hattie who tricked Minerva, hadn't it?

"Yes. After Sydney was born, Great-grandmother told me the truth about what happened at the Willows. Hester Desmond started a friendship with Minerva. She learned that Fidelia had accidently shoved her father off a balcony during an argument, killing him. Armed with this knowledge, she was ultimately able to use Fidelia against them. Now, Amelia was protective of Fidelia and she didn't trust Hester, so she had her fiancé look into the Desmonds; he died not long after that."

"He must have found something worth killing for because Lucian Mathews, Amelia's fiancé, was murdered by one of the Desmonds," Phillip said.

"Do you know what he found?" Reegan asked Mrs. Walters.

She shook her head. "No, I don't know anything about his death. I do know during that same time, Hester learned Minerva was having a secret relationship with a man who Hester herself wanted, so she went to Clara Whit and told her of the affair."

"Duncan Clacher," Reegan said softly, remembering the hanging from her dream.

"They murdered him too," Phillip said and squeezed Reegan's hand.

"Maybe it wouldn't have happened if the sisters had been united, but Hester saw to that too. After telling Clara about the affair, Hester told Minerva that it was Fidelia who had revealed her secret. Amelia begged Minerva to stay away from Hester, and Minerva told Amelia that it was their own half-sister they shouldn't trust."

"Divide and conquer," Buck said while topping off his coffee.

Reegan nodded. Sydney had said something to that effect earlier, something about them turning on each other.

"Yes. They locked my great-grandmother in the cellar with Clara that evening. By the time they escaped, the barn was burning, and there was nothing they could do. They found Fidelia hiding under her bed screaming that they were damned."

If that was true, then how had Hattie Bailey led her to the barn? Reegan wondered.

"If Hattie knew this, why didn't she tell anyone? Why didn't Clara?" Phillip asked.

"Clara didn't know who was behind it. My great-grandmother didn't uncover the truth until years later."

"Why didn't she tell someone at that point?" Buck asked.

"She did…I didn't believe her," Mrs. Walters said.

"What?" Reegan asked, ignoring the loud creak that came from the conference room door; her father had never been the stealthiest eavesdropper.

"She came to stay with us after Alan died, and she was shocked when my husband's family started pressing for an heir. Then when I had Sydney and found out about the inheritance, my great-grandmother started digging. And then she told me."

"Started digging?"

"Yes, into my husband's family. Their fortune came from what his great-grandmother had amassed."

"Wait! Are you saying that Sydney's great-great-grandmother—"

"Was Hester Desmond, yes," Mrs. Walters said and sighed. "Let me guess, you found out Sydney was related to Hattie Bailey and stopped there."

"Yes. And I stopped at the name Desmond," Reegan admitted, red-faced. The cloaked woman who took Minerva through the woods and trapped her had been Hester Desmond. Sydney was a direct descendant of the fourth.

"Seeing what you want to see is something we're all guilty of, Reegan. We rally for the deception because, more than anything, that's what we want to be true. I'm guilty of the same. I couldn't believe my husband or his family were capable of such things."

"What made you change your mind?"

"Great-grandmother said history would repeat

when all four were born again. She said I should take care that my daughter didn't hurt anyone. I wouldn't allow myself to believe such nonsense."

"When did you start believing?" Phillip asked.

"A mother knows things about her children, and I recognized a darkness in Sydney. Then, of course, there was her relationship with you, Reegan, and the way my husband encouraged it. The night you had your accident, they were in his study whispering. I began to wonder if it *was* an accident."

"She pushed me," Reegan said, and Phillip tensed. She explained about the photograph and what she'd found. "I went up there to try to find the flashlight. I'd convinced myself it was a mistake, that if I looked hard enough, even after all these years, I'd find it. She was there waiting."

"She had a way of sensing things," Mrs. Walters said, and a look of fear crossed her face.

"You were scared of her," Reegan said.

"When Sydney was young, I began to see exactly what she was capable of. At first, I chalked it up to her being spoiled; then I thought maybe she could tell I'd loved Alan more than I'd ever loved her. As a mother, I felt guilty and ashamed. How could I not love my child? She was devious but brilliant in her manipulations, and my husband encouraged it."

"He knew," Reegan said.

Mrs. Walters, though reluctant, nodded. "He groomed her for it."

The chair scraped against the floor when Reegan pushed away from the table. She crossed her arms over her chest and began to pace. "All these years they—"

"Reegan, don't do that to yourself," Phillip said.

"They thought you were the third, the one who would do their dirty work; they needed you. After my husband called Sydney and told her about what happened with Tori Elis and Bernadette Howard, I put the pieces together and knew what was coming. You and Bernadette had to be the two, which meant—"

"She would have to kill us," Reegan said and returned to her seat, exhausted. She squeezed her eyes shut as photographs of Sydney flashed behind her closed lids—a lifetime of memories.

Mrs. Walters waited for Reegan to meet her eyes. "It was truly a matter of time. If it hadn't been for the merger, she would have tried sooner."

"Why?" Reegan asked.

"When you died, she would have had to mourn appropriately to keep up the facade, and she needed to close her deal. Perhaps fate stepped in for you."

"I think you stepped in."

"Great-grandmother wasn't able to help, but I could."

"Did you know Hester Desmond was the illegitimate daughter of Bertrum Whit? Did your great-grandmother know that Minerva's son didn't die and he had not one but two daughters?"

It was Mrs. Walters' turn to sit back in her chair as Reegan told her the secrets they'd uncovered and the truth they had found.

"Full circle," she said. "Great-grandmother always said it would come back full circle."

Chapter Forty

Reegan called out to Justin as she walked toward Bernie's room. He stopped and waited for her. She'd made Phillip bring her straight to the hospital after Mrs. Walters was released. She needed to see Bernie.

"What the hell happened to you?" Justin asked when she came closer.

"He'll get you up to speed," she said, pointing to Phillip who was walking toward them. She sighed and looked into Bernie's room. "Who's that with Bernie?"

"Huh? There's no one there," Justin said.

"Yes, there is. Right there." Reegan pointed to the woman with long blonde hair holding Bernie's hand. She looked at Justin and Phillip. "You can't see her?"

"No," they said in unison.

Reegan nodded, took a breath, and went in the room. "So who are you?" she asked the woman, who turned to her.

When the woman smiled, it lit up her beautiful face. "My name is Clara Marshal Whit. You may call me Clara," she said.

"Why are you here?"

"They say a soul may not rest when things are left undone." She reached down to take Bernie's hand again. "I've been here all along, for both of you."

"But I'm not even related to you."

"Do you not love young June as though she were

your own flesh and blood?" Clara asked, standing taller.

"Yes, I…from the moment I saw her, there was a connection."

"That is how I felt when I first met Amelia and Minerva. One glimpse and I was in love with them. And Bertrum…was quite simply the air I breathed. You understand those feelings."

Reegan glanced out of the window at Phillip and Justin. She'd said those exact words about Phillip. "Yes."

Clara nodded. "The day before my daughters' deaths, my father sent word that the rumors had reached fever pitch. He believed we were in grave danger. I asked Hattie to get our bags ready but to keep it a secret. We were supposed to leave the next morning."

"But you told Fidelia," Reegan guessed.

Clara cleared her throat. "Yes."

"And she told her, Hester."

"In life, I never had that knowledge." She shook her head. "That morning when we found Duncan hanging, I knew we were in danger."

"Minerva went into labor, and you gave the baby to Mrs. Woods."

"I told her when we got away, I would tell Minerva the truth, and we would send for the baby. Otherwise, Mrs. Woods was to raise Edwin as her own."

"You couldn't risk anyone knowing. Not even Minerva."

"I had to protect them. I tried, but they locked us in the cellar. By the time we got out, I…I could hear them screaming," Clara whispered and tried to control her tears.

"Oh, God." Reegan squeezed her eyes shut. If

someone had done that to June…she couldn't think of it.

"I found Fidelia hiding under her bed. She confessed her part but never gave a name. The next morning Father came and took us away."

"Edwin went to see Fidelia, and she told him about the curse and gave him a key," Reegan said. "A riddle to help us figure out what happened then and what is happening now."

"When you die, you are shown certain things, but in life, Fidelia already saw death."

Reegan frowned. "What do you mean?"

"She could see things that were not of this world. She had visions, and they twisted her mind. Did you know when they started to build the Willows, they didn't destroy the old willow tree the town was named for?"

"I heard they cut it down," Reegan said.

"To protect its legacy—and its secrets. They replanted it deep in the woods where not many would venture."

Reegan rubbed her temples. "When Edwin visited Fidelia at Shady Pines, she said something about *it* being found where no one else would go; she was talking about the tree?"

"The willow sat overlooking the bluff, and the first settlers would gather there."

"For what?" Reegan asked while satanic rituals came into her mind.

"To hang the witches."

A chill raced down her spine. "You're serious?"

"They would hang them, and if their necks didn't break, they would throw them over the bluff to see if they would drown. That tree was used to murder and condemn countless women. Its very roots were strengthened by the blood of the innocent, seeded in hate as the branches wept."

"Hester knew about the tree?" Reegan asked. The machines beeped, and she wondered if Bernie could hear their conversation.

"Her mother's family were among the original settlers," Clara explained.

"I never heard that Willows—"

"They didn't name the town until the early 1800s, at least a hundred years after the hangings. Something that holds that much death and hate also holds power."

"The tree gave Hester whatever she needed to destroy the witches, or showed her how to do it," Reegan said. She knew she should balk at such a ridiculous idea, but in her heart, she understood Clara was right. She'd experienced firsthand the kind of power an object can hold; the brooch had held desire and love, while the log had held fear and death.

"Yes."

"And Fidelia saw this too?"

"Sometimes Fidelia could see the dead."

Again, Reegan looked through the window to where Phillip and Justin were staring at her. "Me too, apparently."

"Your gifts have always been subtle. You needed a camera to believe what you were able to see all along, the underlying beauty of the world. Bertrum's family had the gift of second sight, but in my family, only every other generation of women had it."

"So the women weren't insane?" Reegan said.

"They were unable to control or understand their

gifts, and that drove them mad. Fidelia's gifts overwhelmed her, and Hester took advantage. We were able to find a physician who created a tonic that quelled whatever it was that Fidelia could not. She was stable enough to be married, but when she was pregnant, she wouldn't take the tonic, and then—"

"Her husband built Shady Pines."

"I died before it was built. I'd never been well after what happened."

"Your soul stayed."

"Yes, I hadn't helped the first time, but—"

"How did Fidelia know?" Reegan asked abruptly.

"When she was lucid, she spoke of a woman who'd offered her forgiveness and told Fidelia she could help make it right but it would cost her."

"This woman was a ghost or spirit or whatever?"

"Fidelia didn't confide in me completely," Clara said, "but she said she had the key to making it right."

"Why not just tell Edwin the truth?"

"That is not the way this works." Clara bent down and kissed Bernie's forehead.

"Is she going to live?" Reegan asked, a lump in her throat.

"There is more than one way of life," Clara said.

"That's not an answer."

Clara held out her hand.

Reegan stared a moment, then reached out and put her hand in Clara's. She was startled by the warmth, by the peace, but mostly by the love she felt. She looked up into Clara's blue eyes.

"I think the time has come for you to help her," Clara whispered.

Reegan leaned forward when Clara gave a gentle

tug. Clara kissed her forehead, then vanished. Reegan turned toward the window to find her audience had grown to include her parents and Buck.

Reegan sat on the edge of the mattress next to Bernie. She held Bernie's hands in hers, rested her forehead between the words *death* and *destiny* tattooed on Bernie's wrists, and took a deep breath. Knowing pictures had never failed her, Reegan closed her eyes and pulled her memories to the forefront of her consciousness; she might not be able to tell Bernie why she needed to come home, but she could show her.

Her tears fell unabashed while the retrospective of memories danced across her mind. The Polaroids she'd seen when she saw Bernie at Patch's funeral were now fully developed, and they depicted the moments of love Reegan had witnessed on Bernie's behalf. She shared those images with Bernie, silently daring Bernie to see what she was showing her, and to feel it as well.

Reegan sat like that for what seemed like hours pushing her thoughts into Bernie's subconscious; suddenly, her hand was squeezed. She looked up to see Bernie's mercury eyes staring back at her.

"It's about damn time!" Reegan said.

Chapter Forty-One

Reegan wasn't alone with Bernie until early the next morning. All hell had broken loose when Bernie woke. Justin had picked Reegan up and set her out of his way, so he could talk to Bernie. She kept getting shuffled closer and closer to the door as more people moved into the room. She hadn't minded; in fact, her face hurt from smiling.

The storm outside had stopped, and Phillip had gone to check on his deputies. Bernie convinced Justin to get some sleep, and with the help of a sedative, he was snoring softly in a cot they'd brought in for him. Reegan sat in the chair next to Bernie's bed.

"I was with my dad and Gran," Bernie explained. "He's been waiting for me, and she's waiting for him. I was going to stay with them; then your pictures started playing in the sky like we were at a drive-in movie. Dad said he couldn't be selfish, and he told me to go."

"Did Annie Mae say anything about the curse?"

The corner of Bernie's mouth lifted. "She said it took a good swift kick to get us started, but she was proud of us and she knew that Patch was proud too."

Reegan couldn't help but laugh. After a moment, the words began to pour from her as she described to Bernie what they'd uncovered—the connections, the lineage, April, Hester, Sydney, Mrs. Walters, and Clara. She sat back taking a breath while Bernie processed it all.

"When the key said 'a new direction is birthed,' it literally meant births," Bernie said.

Reegan nodded. "After Amelia and Minerva's mother Jessamine died, the choices Bertrum made led to both Hester and Fidelia's births."

"And Sydney and I were born as a direct result of Alan Walters' death."

"His death, your birth, the murder of your father, and the Desmonds."

"Envious greed."

"Hester Desmond used her half-brother and sister to destroy the Whits and anyone else who got in their way, while Sydney used April and Adam to manipulate Tori's fragile mind. April had been taking flowers to Tori for years, setting the stage for the main event. Adam arranged to have the painting delivered before he died to fan the flames, so to speak, and April provided the items necessary for escape."

"Phillip arrested April, right?" Bernie asked.

"The minute she passed the city limit sign," Reegan said. "There's not enough evidence for any charges to stick, but he said holding April overnight will take away what she loves the most."

"What's that?"

"Her reputation."

"That's something," Bernie said as she adjusted the blanket. "I thought I'd feel more relieved than this. It's like—"

"A nettling in the back of your mind," Reegan said, feeling the same.

"You know what I think we need?"

"A vacation!" Reegan said.

Bernie bit her lip. "I was thinking we need to find that tree. Why would Clara even mention it if it wasn't important?"

Reegan sighed. "That thought crossed my mind too. Wait, what? You mean right now?" she asked when Bernie pulled back the covers. "You just came out of a coma!"

She stood back while Bernie got up. "I'll just be slower than usual. Did anyone bring me some clothes?"

"Yeah," Reegan said and pointed to the small bathroom. "Now what are you doing?" she asked when Bernie opened Justin's shirt and moved the small pads that monitored her heart beat from her chest to Justin's.

"This way the doctors won't know I'm gone," Bernie said and placed a kiss on Justin's forehead before she headed into the bathroom to change.

How the hell would they even find the tree in the woods after a good ten inches of snow had fallen? Reegan wondered. Oh and, "Bernie, we don't have a ride."

"Buck's still here, isn't he?" Bernie asked through the door.

"Yes!" If anyone was up for anything, it was Buck Hastings. Reegan turned to start looking for him, but there he stood against the doorjamb, one eyebrow raised.

"We're going somewhere?"

Reegan rocked back on her heels. "Yep."

Buck's lips pursed as he eyed Justin sleeping. "My guess is that if I don't take you, you two will find a way on your own."

"We're going, and we're going now," Bernie said, coming out of the bathroom dressed in warm clothes. "I can steal Justin's keys again."

Reegan looked between Bernie and Buck grinning. She liked Bernie like this, all piss and vinegar. She hadn't seen her this feisty since before Annie Mae died.

****

Reegan would never have guessed she would come anywhere near the bluff again, but here she was not fifty feet from where the Willows once stood. Buck had driven them, and they'd hiked up in the snow. Both she and Buck had to help Bernie, who was weak from her ordeal. They reached the bluff as the sun came up.

"Are you all right?" Bernie asked. "I know it's hard to be here after what happened with Sydney."

Reegan exhaled. "It would be if Phillip hadn't brought something to my attention." She'd been in the hospital cafeteria waiting for her turn to talk to Bernie, when Phillip came in and gave her something to think about.

Bernie shifted on her feet. "What?"

"Sydney kept telling me no good ever came to anyone in Willows Bluff. She told me not to stay too long when I came to see Patch, and when I told her I was moving in with Phillip, she asked me not to."

"She was giving you a choice," Bernie said.

Reegan nodded. "It went against everything she was groomed to do—against the prophecy. Phillip told me to hold on to that; he said it proved Sydney did love me…in her own way."

Buck cleared his throat. "My son has a knack for finding the good in people."

"Your son is a throwback to the days of Camelot, and I'm thankful for it," Reegan said, turning to stare out over the bluff. "Maybe we should hold hands,

Bernie; that usually inspires something."

"If you can see what I'm seeing, I don't think we'll have to," Bernie said.

"Oh, wow," Reegan whispered when she turned and saw who Bernie was referring to.

"What do you see?" Buck asked.

Reegan looked at Bernie, and Bernie nodded. Reegan walked to Buck and took his left hand while Bernie took his right.

"Do you see her now?" Bernie asked.

Reegan glanced up at Buck's face and saw the wonder in his eyes. Oh, he sees her, Reegan thought, this bewitching creature standing before them with long black hair curling loosely down the back of her purple cloak. Her wide gray eyes sparkled against her dusky skin.

"Who is she?" Buck whispered.

"Jessamine Whit," Bernie said.

"Amelia and Minerva's mother," Reegan added.

"It was her death that set all of this in motion," Bernie explained.

"Full circle," Reegan said remembering what Hattie Bailey had told Mrs. Walters. "It started with Jessamine."

Bernie nodded. "And it ends with her."

"This is incredible," Buck whispered.

"This is the way," Jessamine said, inclining her head and motioning toward the trees.

They followed Jessamine as she walked deep into the woods. The air seemed to thicken the farther they went, and Reegan focused on her breathing.

"We are not far," Jessamine said.

Something occurred to Reegan. "You're the one

Fidelia spoke to; she could see the dead and she saw you."

"Yes, she wanted to hurt my daughters the way a child would seek petty revenge. She was unable to understand the gravity of what Hester had orchestrated."

"You saw Hester come to the tree?" Bernie asked.

"You knew what she was going to do, and you tried to help by going to Fidelia; she was the only one who could see you," Reegan added.

"I was unaware Hester had already poisoned the child's mind, that my presence sent her farther into her darkness. Only years later was Fidelia able to understand why I was there. I told her the truth of how Hester received her power—"

"You gave her the key," Reegan said.

"Yes. Spirits are not supposed to give answers that could alter one's destiny, but we can help you find your own. Your journey was cursed before you existed; your deaths guaranteed. There is a cost to help alter such a fate."

"You gave Fidelia the key, or rather the words that would lead us to the truth."

"You had to find the answers for yourselves; that is the way of it. No one could interfere."

Reegan sighed. "Go ahead and say 'I told you so,' Bernie. I deserve it."

"I wasn't going to," Bernie said, but amusement lit her voice.

"Why didn't they die when they repeated the key?" Buck asked Jessamine.

Damn good question, Reegan thought.

"Because it belonged to them," Jessamine

explained.

"Why didn't Fidelia die? I mean, Edwin died. Patch and Annie Mae died, but Fidelia lived at least a few years after his death."

"Her body lived," Jessamine said.

"That's why the doctors couldn't help her," Reegan said. She shouldn't feel sorry for Fidelia; she didn't want to, but a teeny, tiny bit of her did.

A moment or two later, they stood hand in hand around a weeping willow. Snow and ice blanketed the tree causing its branches to brush the ground. It was breathtaking, ghostly in its form. Reegan wished she had her camera.

"Girls, I think she wants you to do something," Buck said, using their clasped hands to motion to Jessamine.

Reegan looked around Buck to meet Bernie's eyes. "We have to let go, Buck," Reegan said.

Buck stepped away. "I'm here if you need me."

They both nodded and stepped forward toward Jessamine. Reegan didn't know about Bernie, but she was shaking from the inside out and not from the cold. She could feel the malevolence from where she stood. "Ah, fuck, we have to touch the tree, don't we?"

"Reegan," Bernie admonished.

Reegan glanced to where Jessamine stood staring at her. "Sorry."

"You two are quite strange," Jessamine said.

"Because hanging out with our dead relative is *so* normal," Reegan said.

Jessamine smiled.

"Reegan's right. You do want us to touch the tree," Bernie said.

"It is about need, not want."

Reegan turned to Bernie. "We may as well get this over with."

Bernie nodded, but she hesitated. Reegan remembered the last time they'd touched a piece of wood and the horrors they'd endured.

"Together," Bernie said and held out her hand.

Reegan nodded. She took Bernie's hand, and they touched the willow. *The tree didn't spare a moment of the torment it had witnessed or been party to. Reegan saw every life taken, heard each and every plea, felt the fear and pain. The roots let her feel all that the tree had absorbed: the blood that fell, the hate, the depravity, and the sinister enjoyment of the crowd. The tree showed her how it was dug out, uplifted, and moved to new earth, thus reawakening the cursed souls.*

Reegan saw Hester come to the tree in a red cloak with a dagger in her hand, spilling her blood and demanding justice. The trapped spirits showed Hester how she could obtain what she desired, and she promised to destroy the people who had moved them from their resting place.

When Hester returned, she was carrying a bucket of ash. She spread it around the tree packing it in around any exposed roots, and she asked that anyone who tried to ruin her be stopped. Again, the spirits gave her what she asked for and helped her curse the souls that would come.

Rain fell later that night pushing the ash into the ground, and Reegan could taste what the roots drank in. The spirits absorbed the memories from the ash and screamed in horror finding that they had been deceived. They had brought death to the innocent as death had been brought to them.

The curse couldn't be rescinded, but it could be broken. The spirits cried out to any who would listen until Jessamine arrived, and they whispered to her the words—a key to help break the curse. In return, Jessamine had to promise that if the two succeeded, she would lead them back here.

Stepping away from the tree, Reegan sucked in a breath. She looked at Bernie, whose hand she still held, then over her shoulder where Buck was staring at them. "Are you girls all right?" he asked.

Reegan nodded. "Do you have a pocket knife?"

Buck's brows drew together, but he reached in his pocket and handed it to Reegan. She let go of Bernie's hand to open the knife, took a breath, and drew the blade across her own palm. As blood pooled in her hand, she gave the knife to Bernie, who mirrored her actions. Bernie wiped the knife on the leg of her jeans and handed it back to Buck, who had turned a couple of shades whiter than normal.

"Are you ready?" Bernie asked her.

Reegan nodded. Together, they put their hands, their blood, upon the bark and began to speak the words the spirits had given to them. "Blood incurred the curse we bore, and with our blood it is no more," they chanted until the bark grew warm beneath their hands.

Reegan opened her eyes. The tree was a glittering orange ember, though it did not burn them. She swallowed and glanced at Bernie, who was staring at the tree as well.

"Reegan, I think we should say—"

"Gotcha," Reegan said, and Bernie smiled.

Reegan directed her gaze back to the tree and

together she and Bernie said, "We forgive you." A moment later, the tree turned red, then back to orange, then red again, until it burst into glittery particles that floated down to the snow at their feet.

"It is done," Jessamine said with tears in her eyes. "Thank you." She kissed both Reegan and Bernie on the forehead. A smile spread across her face, and she disappeared.

"We did it," Reegan whispered.

"We made right what was wrong," Bernie said, swaying a bit.

"It's time we get you back to the hospital, Bernie," Buck said. "And on the way, you girls can fill me in on what you saw."

Reegan nudged Bernie with her shoulder. "Come on, Bernie. Let's get out of here before someone yells for an encore!"

Epilogue

Bernie closed the curtain to the bookstore and smiled, aware of Justin staring at her back. They'd been married for over a year, but she could still remember the first day he'd brought her to work at the bookstore. She'd been scared her presence would destroy his business, but people had come and continued coming to quell their curiosity.

Their lives had changed so much in the past year, and it all started with a full-page spread in the paper. Though the article never mentioned the curse, it told how she and Reegan, with the help of unnamed individuals, had uncovered the truth about Willows Bluff. The truth about the legendary tree, the Willows, and the links connecting the most prominent members of the community to murder. The gossips had feasted on the fodder they'd been served.

Though the writer of the article was anonymous, both she and Reegan knew the culprit could be found at the Willows Bluff public library.

"I'm headed to bingo with Phyllis," Delores said, speaking of the person in Bernie's thoughts.

Bernie laughed. Phyllis would be running the game before the night was over, Bernie thought.

"Bye, Mom," Justin said from where he was wiping down the counters.

Bernie peeked at him and then waved to Delores.

She wondered if there would ever come a time when he didn't do funny things to her heart.

"Phillip asked if we could close early and have dinner with them," Justin said now.

"That sounds nice." She liked spending time with the Hastingses.

Reegan had taken over the gallery soon after she'd returned from honeymooning with Phillip. She and Ezra had expanded, and now they offered art classes for children and adults. Bernie was sure that Reegan had surprised everyone, including herself, by the success. All the classes had filled within a week.

Bernie was still a bit shy around Ezra, but he didn't seem to mind. In fact, every time he saw her, he hugged her. Reegan said since neither of them had grandfathers, they should share Ezra, and the old hobbit had agreed.

They parked in Reegan's driveway, and by the number of cars, it looked like both Phillip's and Reegan's parents were here. June was the first one to greet them when they walked in.

"Hey!" Justin ruffled June's hair, then headed for the kitchen.

Bernie returned June's hug, and they walked hand in hand to the kitchen. Reegan had adopted June, who now called her Mom. Reegan had told Bernie that made her cry the first time.

"June, do you want to help set the table?" Phillip asked.

"Sure," June said.

Bernie smiled as she listened to Buck and Reegan's dad discussing the renovations on Patch's house. David and Beth were giving June the house after she graduated college, and the grandpas had turned it into a joint project. Sometimes the debates would get a little heated, and the grandmas would leave the room together.

Given the glares she could see the women in question giving the men, Bernie guessed that would be happening soon.

"Psst," Reegan said.

"What?" Bernie asked, and Reegan motioned toward the next room. Bernie sighed, knowing Reegan was bringing her into something that would no doubt land them in trouble.

"Have you felt any vibrations lately?" Reegan whispered when they were alone.

Bernie's brows bunched. Since the dissolving of the tree, they hadn't had any joint visions. Reegan's nightmares had stopped, and other than the occasional glimmer of memory, things were pretty normal. But Reegan was right; lately, Bernie had experienced a peculiar sensation and she said so.

"Yeah, me too," Reegan said and gave Bernie an odd look, one Bernie was familiar with.

"I'm not posing for you," she said, rolling her eyes.

Reegan smirked. "One day you will, Bernie, but that's not what's going on in my head. This is going to sound strange, but I need to touch you."

"What? Reegan, what's going on?" Bernie said, uncomfortable.

"Just remember I asked first." Reegan stuck her hand under Bernie's sweater onto her stomach. Bernie covered Reegan's hand with both of hers and closed her eyes.

There was something there—*a presence, not one but two, both filled with hope and love. She saw a pair of extended stomachs and waddling forms. Then she and Reegan were side by side in the hospital each holding a bundle with a little blue bonnet. And as though they were flipping through a photo album, they saw these boys grow together—always together—until the pictures faded.*

Bernie sucked in a breath when the connection was gone.

"Holy shi—"

Bernie covered Reegan's mouth with her hand, and she tried to breathe. Her mind spun, her heart raced, and her smile glowed as her gaze once again met Reegan's. She removed her hand, and for what Bernie realized was the first time, they embraced. They held onto each other for dear life laughing and crying together.

"Um, Reegan, Bernie, what's happening?" Phillip asked.

Letting go, she opened her eyes to find they were surrounded by sparkling blue lights. Bernie and Reegan both laughed as the lights disappeared, and they turned to take in the crowd.

"You boys better hold onto your hats," Reegan said, then nudged Bernie's shoulder.

Bernie cleared her throat. "We're pregnant," she said, and after a moment of complete silence, the room burst with conversation.

"Phyllis, for once you've landed us in the right place at the right time," came a whisper from the back of the room.

Bernie turned with everyone else to see Phyllis and Delores standing there with matching sequined ball caps that said *Bingo*.

Phyllis kept nodding. "I'm glad those bingo

bureaucrats kicked us out!"

Bernie covered her mouth as she giggled. This, Bernie knew, while the entire room shook with laughter, was the life she never dreamed she could have. This was the love worth living for.

A word about the author...

W. L. Brooks likes to write what she reads, with a bit of mystery, romance, suspense, and, to keep it interesting, a dash of the paranormal. Living in Western North Carolina, she is currently working on her next novel. W. L. Brooks loves to hear from readers at w.l.brooks80@gmail.com

Thank you for purchasing
this publication of The Wild Rose Press, Inc.

If you enjoyed the story, we would appreciate your
letting others know by leaving a review.

For other wonderful stories,
please visit our on-line bookstore at
www.thewildrosepress.com.

For questions or more information
contact us at
info@thewildrosepress.com.

The Wild Rose Press, Inc.
www.thewildrosepress.com

Stay current with The Wild Rose Press, Inc.

Like us on Facebook

https://www.facebook.com/TheWildRosePress

And Follow us on Twitter
https://twitter.com/WildRosePress